TO:- Amy

PROM:- JACKIE

LOTS OF LOVE

HADASSAH

HADASSAH

J. Francis Hudson

A LION BOOK

With sincere gratitude, as always, to Keith, Mandy, Mum and John, for contributing so much time, support and encouragement; to Lois for her enduring enthusiasm and incisive editing; and special thanks to Nick (for medical advice on the making of eunuchs), to Daniel (for topographical and climatic information on Iran/Iraq), and to Catherine (for the astonishing photograph which inspired my creation of Hegai).

Copyright © 1996 J. Francis Hudson

The author asserts the moral right
to be identified as the author of this work

Published by
Lion Publishing plc
Sandy Lane West, Oxford, England
ISBN 0 7459 3037 9
Albatross Books Pty Ltd
PO Box 320, Sutherland, NSW 2232, Australia
ISBN 0 7324 1263 3

First edition 1996
10 9 8 7 6 5 4 3 2 1 0

A catalogue record for this book is available
from the British Library

Printed and bound in Great Britain by
Biddles Ltd, Guildford and King's Lynn

IN MEMORY OF ESTHER;
of the many thousands for whom she was
ultimately prepared to die; and of the
six million who half a century ago did
not escape their enemies

And this was the dream of Mardochaios: babel and tumult, clashes of thunder and a shaking of the ground, everywhere chaos upon the earth. There appeared two dragons, poised to struggle with one another, and the noise which they made was awesome. Every nation was roused by it to prepare for war, to fight against the righteous people. It was a day of darkness, of distress and anguish, of oppression and world-wide turmoil. And all of the righteous ones were in torment, dreading the evils in store for them; and they readied themselves to face death.

The Rest of the Chapters of the Book of Esther, from the
Greek version of the book as found in the Apocrypha, 11:5–9

Ahura Mazda is the Great God who gave us this earth and sky, who made Kshayarsha the King reign over multitudes as Sole Sovereign. I am Kshayarsha the Great King, the King of Kings, the Emperor of all nations and speakers of all tongues, the Ruler of this entire earth; the son of Darayavaush of the House of Hakhamanish,
a Persian, son of a Persian,
an Aryan of Aryan seed.

From the text of a foundation tablet
discovered at Parsa (Persepolis), Iran

ALEPH

*'I have seen how my people
have suffered.'*

ZECHARIAH 9:8

I

My eighth birthday party was the first of its kind ever held in Jerusalem—or so they tell me. I do know that it was the last for many, many years; and little wonder. Even today, some twenty years on, I can scarcely bring myself to recall it; for so long I have suppressed all thought of it whenever it has surfaced in my mind. Now I have no choice but to dwell upon it, if I am to tell my story from the beginning and not leave my cousin's version of events to stand alone.

The day began well enough. No; that doesn't do the occasion justice. It began perfectly, and continued perfectly, right up until the hour when the last glimmer of sunset was gone from the sky, and the last guests who weren't staying the night had said their goodbyes. They could linger no later; no one walked the streets of David's City after dusk if it could be avoided.

It was the thirteenth day of the month of Adar in early spring, at the close of the thirty-fourth year of the reign of Great King Darayavaush of Persia. My mother had got me up at the crack of dawn to set about the task of making me ready to receive my visitors. She'd washed and combed out my hair and curled it with rags, then rubbed scented oil all over my body, and for the first time in my life painted my eyes and reddened my cheeks and lips.

I was in my element. From earliest infancy I'd always taken delight in being pampered, and it was so rare in those tough pioneering days for us to have the time or the money to spend on such luxury. Shameless luxury, my older sister Rachael called it, as she busied herself with cooking and cleaning and clearing things away obtrusively around us; I would wind up looking and smelling like a little Jezebel.

But I just laughed; I was the pretty one, Mother's favourite. I knew it, I'd always known it, and I revelled in it.

The finishing touches were still being applied to my make-up when my brother burst in upon us. Like Rachael, Pithon was older than I, but only by a year. She could give me six.

9

'Hadassah, Hadassah, come quickly!' he was shouting. 'People are here already.'

Mother upbraided him for his interruption, but half indulgently. Privacy was as rare a luxury for us as perfume, since our house was smaller than a Persian peasant's—at least, the part of it which my parents had so far rendered habitable. It must have been much larger in the days before the Exile, before most of it tumbled into the valley below along with the city wall to which it clung. And we *were* no more than peasants, if truth be told, squatting among ruins which seemed to crumble faster than we could repair them, scratching a living from a land over which we fought against a host of thorns and thistles. But we thought of ourselves as the army of God.

Mother dusted surplus powder from my nose, and passed me a mirror. I admired myself briefly in its bright bronze face: delicate features frequently extolled ever since I'd been a baby; long-lashed eyes, now larger still with the kohl; a mass of curled hair, black tinged with red, the redness enhanced by the bronze that reflected it. The bronze lent my skin a false ruddiness also—in fact I have always been pale for a Jewess, and my father had once remarked that I might be taken for a Persian. This meant nothing much to me, having known no other home than Jerusalem. But my parents had once lived there, in Shushan the Persian capital; I was a true-born daughter of Zion.

I put the mirror down, and Mother's expression asked if I was satisfied. I nodded, and ran out into the yard with Pithon. A wave of heat hit us; it was the first truly hot day that year.

The early arrivals were Uriah and his family. Uriah was a builder who worked with my father, as did his wife and daughters whenever they were able. In Persia it was apparently quite normal to see women and children working on building-sites alongside the men; and like so many Persian customs the Pioneers had brought it back with them despite their professed desire to cast off all things pagan. Now the members of this industrious family were dressed in fine linen and soft sandals, which had no doubt lain in storage chests since they'd fetched them from Shushan. You could still see some of the crease-marks where the clothes had been folded, and their wearers stood awkwardly, blinking in the sunlight, looking uncomfortable as though the finery didn't really belong to them.

But I ran up and kissed them, each in turn, and especially Deborah, their eldest, who was my age and my closest friend.

The pair of us ran inside, arm in arm and giggling, to catch up on girlish gossip and then rehearse the dance which we were to lead later on when everyone was gathered. Our gossip revolved around the names of the boys we hoped would be present; I already took more than a passing interest in Pithon's friends, and though Deborah failed to understand what I saw in them, she pretended that she did. Mother never objected to such discussions of ours. She'd chosen my father for his looks, she said, and I saw nothing unusual in that. Self-confident as she was, and revered by everyone, she seemed to get a choice in most things, unlike nearly all the women I've encountered elsewhere. At the time I took it for granted.

As for our dance, it went to an ancient tune reputedly composed by Aphiah, the founder of our clan, which belonged to the tribe of Benjamin. While Deborah and I practised our steps and laughed at our mistakes, we could hear more guests being welcomed by my parents. Anyone who was anyone had been invited, even Jehoazar the Governor, and the High Priest Joiakim. Their titles were grand, but their flock small enough for them to show their faces at its gatherings.

Soon the yard was humming with chatter, and other girls came in to join us one by one. Musicians arrived and struck up with a chorus: some labourers' refrain which spoke of conquest and comradeship and the joy of rebuilding our nation. It was hardly suitable for a child's birthday, but I don't suppose they knew many others.

And so things got under way. There was feasting and drinking, and folk got very drunk very fast in the heat, and because they hadn't had wine in such quantities for years—or ever before, in the case of the Zion-born. The music was loud, and the singing turned to chanting, in which the young men railed against the Canaanites, the Amalekites, the Samaritans . . . anyone and everyone who could be said to have opposed the vision of the Remnant. The Remnant was one of the names we called ourselves: the faithful ones, the godly ones, the ones from the tribes of Judah and Benjamin who had left everything, in order to effect the Restoration.

Deborah and I led our dancers to rapturous applause and acclamation. The men and boys whistled and the women hooted, flicking their tongues against their teeth and the roofs of their mouths. All were past caring whether we danced well or not—they would have cheered us regardless. As it happens, we did, and better than we ever had. My friend and I headed a column of girls each; we marched them and

II

matched them like captains with their troops, mirroring one another's movements, advancing and retreating, joining hands then dropping them, weaving first one way then the other, and all to perfection. The success went to our heads and we went on dancing for ourselves long after the public performance was over.

Never before had I been so happy. I hadn't yet heard the saying which the Greeks have: the sweetest pleasure comes before the sharpest pain. It was just so exciting to see so many people, so many Jews, all together in one place. The city still felt so empty whenever you went about. Its once burgeoning population had been decimated. War had claimed so many young lives: first against the Assyrians, then the Babylonians. Entire clans had fled as refugees to Egypt and beyond, even more had been taken into exile. And many were still there, although King Darayavaush and his predecessor Kambujet, and before them both Kurash, who had made Persia mighty, had each given permission for all Jews to return to their Promised Land.

It had been a great day for our people when Kurash of Persia, divinely-favoured son of the House of Hakhamanish, had taken possession of Babylon's empire. Our prophets had hailed him as the servant of Adonai our God, and he'd been happy to use the title himself. Not that he cared a jot for Adonai—or so most of us assumed—but he was a clever diplomat. So we had nothing but contempt for those of our kinsfolk who so loved Persia that they chose to remain there.

Still, I don't suppose so much would have been made of my birthday if my parents hadn't once lived in Shushan. The Children of Abraham have never set much store by the anniversaries of things as mundane as being born, since we have so many more important events in our history to celebrate. But in Shushan a full-grown horse might be slaughtered and roasted whole in the oven on a wealthy man's birthday. I remember being awestruck when I first heard that, and wondering what kind of ovens they must have in the capital of the Empire.

I wondered what kind of wealth they had, too. For I'd been told that *all* the native Persians were rich, because they weren't made to pay taxes like the subject peoples. My father managed to pay his dues—just. Not everyone could. Fields had been mortgaged, and children sold.

Eventually I was dragged away from the dancing, since the time had come for me to receive my presents. The heat was going out of the sun; the tables had been cleared away from the courtyard, and a makeshift tribunal set up from the stones and rubble which lay all too readily to hand. A chair was brought for me, and I sat there like a queen while the guests filed past me, and hugged me, and brought me their gifts. Each person had a kind word to say to me. Some praised my dancing and others my beauty, saying I had Saul's looks already and no mistake. That made me smile. Hardly a day went past without Mother reminding me that the first king of Israel had been among our ancestors. He'd been famous for his face as well as for his valour; and for his height. I was tall for my age, and I'd never tried to hide it.

When the rest of the gifts had been presented, my family brought theirs. Pithon came first, blushing to have so many pairs of eyes trained upon him. He gave me a wooden doll which he'd carved himself. Little skill had gone into it, but a great deal of time, and I loved it, because I loved him. It was Rachael's turn next; her gift was a ring, considerably more valuable, but in my eyes all but valueless as a token because I was sure she didn't like it. She'd been given it by a suitor for whom she cared nothing; with so much work to do, she had no time for thoughts of marriage. She lived for the Restoration, she ate, drank and breathed it, and whatever might distract her from it was there only to be despised.

Thirdly came my father Abihail. He was urged to make a speech, but graciously declined. He was a man of few words but much wisdom, it was often said, and also much talent. He was an architect, and had served his time as an apprentice under a Phoenician master in Persia. There he had worked on imperial building programmes both at Shushan and at Parsa, where the Great King went to worship his god. The work had been highly paid, but Father had given it all up some ten years before, to return to Israel. Thus he was one of the most highly respected men in our community.

With a gentle smile and a barely perceptible wink, he bestowed on me a silver charm in the shape of a small trowel.

'It's to show that you're now grown-up enough to use one,' he announced, but so softly that only I heard him. He spoke as though he were giving me a sword. 'I shall expect to see you working with the women from tomorrow.' But he never did, and these were the last words he ever said to me.

Thus it fell to Mother to make the speech which was called for in my honour. No one was surprised. Although it might be deemed unusual for a woman to speak in public, and even unseemly, it came quite naturally to her. She was like Aaron, who spoke long ago on behalf of Moses, that great leader of our nation in the days when it was young. Moses was the prophet, he had the vision, but Aaron had the voice. And there were those who looked upon my father as a prophet too, in his quiet way. It was so long since a prophet of power had arisen among us, he was all we had.

Even as she started to speak, Mother was making her own presentation of gifts to me. They comprised pieces of jewellery which had been in the family for generations, and which I was now presumably considered old enough to wear and look after. The first was a pair of heavy gold earrings—I'd known I was getting some because I'd had to have my ears pierced specially a month or so earlier. The pain had been intense, but I knew that beauty exacted its price so I hadn't cried.

The most important item however was a neck-chain, one of a set of three, of which Mother herself and my sister owned the other two. She hung mine in place, fastening it carefully behind my bowed head, saying, 'After this you must never bow your head again, my little birthday queen. You must hold it high wherever you go, because you are a special person and you belong to a race of special people. You are descended from Saul's great-uncle on your father's side—and Saul himself on mine, if your grandmother's tales were to be trusted, and if we had the records to prove it. You, Hadassah, and your brother and sister, are the only ones left who can pass on the blood of Saul and his kin. May you have a long life and many children, my daughter, and many birthdays as happy and happier than this one. May your descendants grow up in a Jerusalem fully restored to its former glory; and may they once again have their own king—a king as brave and blessed as Saul was.'

In his younger days, perhaps, I thought, for I'd learnt my history as diligently as any member of a race with a pride in its past. Like all my friends I knew that Saul had died in disgrace upon the blade of his own sword, having rebelled against the God who had chosen him.

But no one was minded to recall this just at that moment; they were all cheering and clapping and chanting again like the victorious army which they felt themselves to be. I concluded that I ought to stand up, in acknowledgment of all their good wishes. However, I must have taken too long about it, because Mother launched afresh into her eulogy; except that now she was eulogizing our community as a whole.

'We must *all* look forward to a prosperous future!' she exhorted us. 'For the time being we may have no king, yet what does it matter when we are *all* anointed by our God? We are the Remnant, the ones who have passed through the purging waters of exile and emerged spotless, pure, acceptable to Adonai! We have witnessed the fulfilment of the Restoration prophecies! We shall go on from strength to strength, from glory to glory.'

You might have been forgiven for hoping that *she* wouldn't go on for too much longer, but this wasn't the hope of most of her hearers. They savoured her every word, devouring it as starved men devour even the stodgiest gruel. For hope was in short supply among us, along with most things. We had weathered many setbacks and faced massive opposition. When the first exiles had returned, full of their own importance and imagining themselves repopulating a deserted waste-land, they had in fact found other folk already living in the cities and the towns and the countryside through which they passed. Some of these folk were descendants of Canaanites who had been there from time immemorial, and whom our distant forebears under Joshua's command had never quite succeeded in wiping out. Some were foreigners who had been deported there from their own lands by the Assyrians in a more recent century. Some were nomads. Others were fellow Jews whose families had never been displaced by the Babylonians. But we ourselves would never have debased the word 'Jew' by applying it to them.

All these folk had regarded the homecoming exiles as arrogant invaders with no right to be there, and had therefore harassed us in any way they could, sometimes openly, sometimes by stealth. If we journeyed through their territories they would jeer at us or throw stones. My father had taught me to ignore their taunts. If life throws stones at you, he said, use those stones to build your city walls. But lately atrocities had been taking place more frequently. There had even been murders.

Whatever they called themselves, we in turn saw all our persecutors as godless heathen whom Adonai had not deemed worthy of purging or even of destroying. The prophet Jeremiah had called those who hadn't been exiled bad figs, too bad to be eaten; *we* were the good figs. We referred to our opponents collectively as People of the Soil, an insulting name coined on purpose to echo that of the Earth Folk, Canaanite vermin whom our ancestors had been instructed to drive from the Promised Land. And these People of the Soil had evinced their godlessness by obstructing the rebuilding of the Temple, in company with the people of Samaria, the northern Israelites, who had initially offered to share in our enterprise but been turned away. As if we could pollute ourselves by sharing a yoke with renegades from the apostate northern kingdom! As if their tainted hands could touch stones destined for the House of God, the God whose very name is too holy to be spoken and who is thus known only as Adonai—the Lord—the God of Israel and King of the Universe. These northerners were no more worthy of the name Israelite than their neighbours the Soil People were of the name Jew.

So *my* people had built alone, and won back what land they could with bribes or by the sword. But the very earth seemed to have lost hope since the Babylonian depredations. Precious soils had been washed away where ancient trees had been felled. Crops didn't flourish the way they once had, and the land of milk and honey existed only as a wistful memory.

I was fifty years too young to have been among those first Pioneers, but we were all brought up to believe that we had somehow been a part of their experience, just as we had also been present at the exodus from Egypt with Moses, getting on for a thousand years earlier. He and his followers had themselves been maliciously attacked, by the Amalekites, a nomadic people whom God had ordered to be eradicated as a result. Saul had almost but not quite achieved it.

I think my mother probably made mention of all this in her address, but my mind was wandering. I myself was in no mood for rhetoric. I could see Deborah pulling faces at me as she wormed her way forward through the assembled throng, and mouthing at me that it was time for more dancing—couldn't I get my mother to stop talking?

When I was starting to fear that I'd been forgotten, and that everyone had lost sight of the very pretext for our gathering, Mother turned her attention back to me. She announced that all present must now pray for my welfare, and to that end she invited various friends and colleagues, and any present who were priests, to come up and share the platform with us. I closed my eyes as they formed up around me and placed their hands on my head and shoulders.

It was only as the priests began to intone their invocations that I fully realized the extent of the hopes that were pinned on me. It wasn't so much what they prayed for, as the way in which they prayed it. They asked for all the usual things on my behalf: that I might continue to know the indwelling of God, that I might recognize myself to be a Shining One after the pattern of Moses and Joshua, Saul and David, and all those in our history who had been marked out by the radiance which comes of having met with Adonai. In olden times this had been the privilege of a favoured few; nowadays the Pioneers considered it to be the right of everyone whose forbears had passed through the purging. We were the heirs to God's promises made through the prophet Joel: Adonai would pour out his spirit upon all of us, our sons and daughters would prophesy, our old men would dream dreams and our young men see visions. And I believed it; we all did, for it never occurred to us not to do so. When we saw the bitter fire of determination burning in one another's eyes, what could it be but the radiance of God? And when we listened to brave words of exhortation such as those my mother had spoken just now, what could be prompting her other than the spirit of the Divine?

No, there was nothing new in this for me, as I basked in the warmth of their ministrations, safe in the knowledge that God was my fortress. It was just the way they spoke the name of Saul, perhaps, that made me wonder . . . they want a new king, and if none is to be found from the line of David—the greatest of all Jewish kings who have ever lived— they will look to ours.

So when the prayers were over, I was somehow no longer in the mood for dancing. There were too many thoughts going round in my head, but I was too tired to think them clearly. Sitting for so long letting the priests' singsong voices wash over me, I'd got drowsier and drowsier, and there was a dull ache starting behind my eyes. When Deborah and the other girls went off in search of fun, I didn't go with them.

Instead I sat on my mother's knee, grown-up and made-up as I was, and tried to go to sleep with my head against her neck. She understood, for she always did, and stroked my wilting curls, and said she was glad I was still her little girl after all. We were sitting in a comfortable place in the shade, and in time a group of other women collected around us. They began to chat about the day, and how good it was to forget their troubles for a while and simply enjoy one another's company. But as women do, they soon fell to talking of the very troubles they said they

17

were glad to forget, and the things of which they spoke drifted in and out of my mind, and spread into my dreams, as I slept and woke and dozed by turns.

And so in place of the dusty courtyard I saw the exiles weeping by the rivers of Babylon, then tasted their excitement as they packed their bags for home. In place of the lengthening shadows I saw them forged into an army, singing songs of Zion as they set their faces towards the land of their fathers and drove their pack animals and ox-carts before them on the road. But then came the disillusionment, running so quickly to despair. For the glorious Restoration had turned out to be a squalid nightmare, as disease, drought and famine preyed upon the little flock. Harvests were destroyed by locusts, there was plague, blight, ruin.

Thus the faces of those plucky Pioneers were changed; as they buried their own children, the broken stakes they had in the future, the light in their eyes grew dim. The faith of some had grown so weak that they had turned their backs on Adonai, and indulged in the abominations of the very pagans who had taken them captive. Like the evil Babylonian witches, the women had baked bread for Ishtar the Mother Goddess. They had burnt their surviving sons and daughters as sacrificial victims in the fire of the Tophet, the place of the loathsome god of fertility. They had wailed and wept for Tammuz, the beautiful, beguiling god who dies each year, in the precincts of the Holy God of Israel. The priests themselves had been corrupted, offering blemished sacrifices to Adonai whilst keeping the best for the pagan tax-collectors. Adultery and fornication took place among God's people; they intermarried with the heathen, profaned the sabbath, lent to their poorer neighbours at exorbitant interest and sold them into slavery if they fell behind with their repayments. They had indeed become like the other nations, the Gentiles who scorned true religion and lived to gratify their lusts and fantasies.

But perhaps all that is now over, the women were saying when next I surfaced enough to listen. Perhaps the time of tribulation is behind us, and those of us who have passed the test and proved faithful will see our inheritance made over to us in full. This is the first year since the return when we have had enough food and to spare; the first year there has been oil and wine enough for us not to need to ration it out like beggars in the gutter. This party marks the beginning of something wonderful, something truly worth singing and dancing for.

'Amen,' I said, with my eyes still closed, and heard them all laugh at me kindly, as they might at the first halting words of a baby. And as though that were all I was, my mother stood up with me over her shoulder and carried me to bed; labouring with her own hands at the rebuilding had made her as strong as a man. I was asleep again before we were inside.

I was awoken sharply by the sense of movement somewhere close by. It didn't worry me at first; the whole family slept in one room, so I thought it must be my parents coming to bed. I lay stone-still on my pallet, blinking up into the darkness, but the pain behind my eyes was there once more so I closed them. It made no difference, so black was the blackness around me.

Then I started, as something moved again, and all of a sudden the night wasn't quite so dark. My pallet was nearest the doorway, and outside it there was a faint patch of lamplight, swaying and flickering.

I exhaled my relief. It was only one of the oil lamps which hung from brackets in the passage; they often banged against the wall if a breeze came. And it must have been left burning by mistake when the last ones to bed had retired for the night. Uriah and Ruth and their daughters were staying, as they'd offered to help clear up. So were some folk who'd come in from the countryside, since they wouldn't have had time to get home before dusk.

My relief was shortlived. The patch of light was moving, getting further away, but much more slowly than it would have been if someone were walking along with a lamp to guide his steps. Unless that someone was unsure of the way, or wanting to keep silent for fear of being found . . .

'Mother? Father!' a voice was hissing into the silence, and I realized it was my own. At once I felt foolish, and clamped a finger between my teeth lest I be tempted to call out again and betray my presence. Should this be an unwelcome intruder and not merely a sleepy guest who had lost his bearings, I must not let him know I was there. If my father had told me once to be careful, that we were living in a hostile and violent world, he had told me a thousand times.

So I slipped from my pallet and crawled towards the place where my parents would be sleeping.

There was no one there.

Rachael and Pithon weren't there either, and that truly frightened me. However special the occasion, neither Pithon nor I were allowed to be up at as late an hour as this must be. And I could hear no sounds of revelling; the party was long since over.

I crawled back and sat on my pallet, my heart thumping so loudly in my chest that I was sure the intruder would hear it. I couldn't think what to do, yet knew I should do something. I'd been brought up to use my head; Pioneers must show initiative, my father always said. They can't afford to be helpless—even children, even girls.

So I went to the doorway and stood staring out, my back and legs pressed against the cool plaster of the wall beside it. There was no door there, or even a curtain, for every piece of fabric in the house had been used to festoon the courtyard for the party, after Persian fashion.

But I couldn't see anything. Even the patch of light was gone, and it was so dark I couldn't even make out the doorway. I could only feel where the wall stopped and space began. I wished frantically that *I* had a lamp, but even if I could find one I would have no means of lighting it. There was nothing to do but wait: wait for someone to find me, or for the sun to come up.

A long, long time passed and neither thing happened. I stood there with every nerve straining, my eyes wide and peering, my ears alert for the slightest sound, and nothing came. Or that was how it felt, but I must have been alert in my sleep and asleep on my feet, because I shuddered awake when a hand gripped my mouth, and someone behind me said in thickly accented Hebrew, 'Do not move, do not scream, and you may live.'

I tried to scream with all my might, and struggled like a snared bird, but the hand on my mouth stifled me, then shifted to close off my nostrils too, so that I knew if I didn't comply it would be all over for me within moments. I left off wriggling, let myself go limp, and found myself sagging and gasping in the arms of someone not so much bigger than I was, but with vastly greater strength and much more idea of how to use it.

And twisting round I found that I could see him, for it appeared that he and the daybreak had arrived simultaneously. My assailant was a wiry youth with a grubby kerchief wrapped tightly about his head, revealing only rabid eyes and the bridge of a once broken nose. As I contemplated screaming again he must have guessed my thoughts, for he slapped my face so hard that I fell back around the doorpost onto my pallet. He threw himself down on top of me.

I had no idea what he meant to do. It was true that my mother had indulged my interest in boys, but she had told me almost nothing about the making of love, and much less about the abusing of it. She and my father had deliberately kept me innocent as long as they could in the harsh and violent world of which they often spoke. I lay panting and staring as he straddled me, his sinewy thighs and bony knees pressed hard against my sides as though I were a horse, his hands rough and heavy upon my shoulders. He started ripping at my garments, but he was awkward and fumbling in his haste; his fingers were sweating when they touched my breasts and he was breathing hard. His jagged nails scratched me, and he was swearing, with words I didn't know, because the fabric of my clothing didn't tear clean away at once.

Then abruptly he stopped, and I realized his own chest was heaving, and he was shaking more than I was. Suddenly he reached down and pulled a knife from his belt, and grasping my hair he prepared to slit my throat.

For myself, I had passed beyond fear. I lay motionless, waiting for the moment to come. My limbs were paralyzed but the speed of my thinking had gone wild: who *was* this boy? where could he have come from? was he alone? what did he want? And at the same time I was wondering what the stroke of his blade would feel like, or if I'd be gone before I knew.

Yet he seemed no more able to kill me than to do whatever he'd intended in the first place. The knife was jerking in his grasp, so that every now and then it grazed against my flesh, but he couldn't bring himself to stab me with it in cold blood.

So I forced myself to stay still. I lay without flinching, without even swallowing, lest the working of the apple in my throat against his blade should scare him into using it in spite of himself. Father had always said: self-control is a mark of the Shining Ones, and when death stares you in the face, as a Daughter of Zion you must resolve to meet its gaze.

I watched the boy grow calmer. His chest stopped heaving, and I noticed how hollow it was; he wasn't so much wiry as thin, under-fed. Now he looked exhausted and confused. All at once it seemed to embarrass him to be sitting there astride me. He moved off to one side and knelt on the floor with the knife across his lap and his head down. He dragged the kerchief away from his mouth to let his sweat run off, and brushed a hand furiously across his face. I knew he was angry with himself, and wretched, and deemed himself a coward. Briefly I despised him, and that gave me the courage to find my voice. I asked, 'Who are you? How did you get in here?' And I was pleased at how steady my voice sounded, and at how proud Father would be of me when all this was over.

The boy didn't answer. He didn't even look at me.

I repeated, 'Who are you? Did you come here alone?'

'No,' he said at once, and so savagely that he spat saliva in my eyes. 'No, I am not alone. There are many of us. They will kill you.'

'Then where are they? Why can't I hear them? Perhaps they have left you behind.'

Again he didn't answer, but my words must have disturbed him profoundly. For without warning he scrambled up and bolted from the room. That was when I found that the ordeal had exhausted me also; I sank back onto my pallet and was too shattered even to cry. The shock had caught up with me, I was trembling all over, and cold in the marrow of my bones though it was quite light now, and outside the dew would already be evaporating.

But still my parents didn't come. The whole house was uncannily silent. There wasn't even any birdsong. And still I lay shivering, as the sun climbed higher and cast its first rays through my tiny window. Fear began to build again, but dully; I was so tired.

I managed to sit up. Huddled in my cloak I looked around, and oh, God, how vivid the scene still is to me. How is it that we forget those things we yearn to remember, whilst we are endlessly haunted by images we ought never to have seen? The pallets on which the others slept were not rolled up neatly by the wall, as they would have been if their owners hadn't come to bed. They were spread out, but crookedly, one across another, having been abandoned in a hurry.

'Mother? Father!' I called as I'd called the previous night, but still there was no response and now my voice was all husky and cracked. I got to my feet but could hardly stand for shaking, and my throat was tight and dry as summer dust. I put up one hand to massage it, and when I brought the hand away there was dried blood on my fingers. Glancing down I saw a thin crusted trickle forking towards my chest; I didn't know he'd pressed so hard with the knife. And it was proof of what had happened, for I'd already begun to think I'd had a nightmare. Perhaps it was still going on, because everything seemed unreal, the light too bright, my thoughts too clear.

I stumbled out into the courtyard. Dazzled by the sunlight boun-
cing back from the whitened walls I almost fell, my ankles caught in a
collapsed awning. I shielded my eyes, blinked, and when I looked
again I saw the gate to the street wide open.

It was never left open. It was always closed and barred at night, and
in the daytime too if there was no one to guard it. Without knowing
why, I made my way towards it, and out onto the road.

I found myself standing at the centre of a company of bare-headed
women. They formed a silent half-circle around the outside of the
gateway; their clothes were torn and their hair cut, and their faces were
haggard with crying. Then one of them stepped forward; her young
face was lined and grey and there was ash on her forehead. She sobbed
out my name: 'Hadassah? Hadassah, it *is* you. Oh God. You're alive.'

She held me in her arms, but I felt no warmth from them any more
than I did from the sun. And she'd said, 'Oh God', not 'Thank God'.

Then all of them were crowding about me, hugging me, weeping
into my hair. I was suffocating; it was like feeling that rough hand
around my mouth and nose all over again. Panic overwhelmed me—so
much for my Pioneer's self-control. Flailing and gulping air and
shaking my head from side to side, I blurted, 'I want my mother.
Where's my father? What has happened?' I only felt to be asking but I
must have been screaming, for someone slapped my face to bring me to
myself.

'It's all right now,' they were saying. 'You're safe. Come, sit down,
you must rest.'

But they weren't answering my questions. Perhaps they hadn't
heard, so I shouted all the louder. I tried to tear myself free of them,
for they were flapping around me like so many vultures. I was
desperate to retreat to the sanctuary of the house but they said,
'Hadassah, stay here. You must not go back in there. You *must* not.'

They couldn't stop me. I was stubborn and accustomed to getting
my own way. When they imagined that they'd won me I slipped from
their grasp and fled across the courtyard. It was full of armed men; I
couldn't think how I hadn't seen them before. But they weren't
enemies. Those had long since got away. They were my father's
friends—the husbands, brothers and sons of the womenfolk in the
street. Two of them caught hold of me and I hung between them,
spent. They must have thought I'd fainted, because they made no
effort to prevent me from watching while the dead were borne out.

Kerchiefs and awnings had been used to cover them, but you could still see enough to know who they were. My parents were brought out first, then Rachael, then Uriah and Ruth his wife, Deborah and her sisters, and the guests who'd come in from the country. Lastly came the boy who had attacked me, the only one of his kind who hadn't got away fast enough. He'd been left uncovered, and there was an untidy sword wound in his hollow chest.

2

They carried me to someone's house, I didn't know whose. There they tried to make me take food, or at least drink something, but I should only have thrown it up. I lay on someone's bed on the floor, still shivering in the full heat of the morning.

In the afternoon they began to ask me questions, which I couldn't have answered even if I'd wanted to. They were anxious to know what I'd seen and heard, but I'd seen and heard nothing. I couldn't tell them how many the gang had consisted of, nor how they'd been dressed, nor how they'd got in. Whilst the women tried to soothe me, washing the blood from my neck and wrapping me in extra blankets to stop the trembling, their men stood about and in hushed tones exchanged their conjectures as to what must have taken place.

One or more of the guests must have been bribed by those who hated us, they reasoned; or perhaps some of our own number nursed secret sympathies for those whose lands we'd occupied. The gates must have been opened from within while the rest of us were sleeping. The family and guests had been rounded up and all killed in one place, then the gang had escaped.

'And Hadassah?' someone demanded, and was at once told to keep his voice down. He went on in a whisper, but still loud enough for me to hear, 'Why was she spared?'

'They mustn't have seen her. They came in the middle of the night.'

'But her parents and sister were taken from the very room she was sleeping in.'

'She still might not have been seen. Her mattress was right up behind the doorway.'

'You mean, she slept through it? Her family was taken prisoner under her very nose—and she slept through it?'

'They would have gone quietly, it was Abihail's way. It doesn't become a martyr to scream.'

'But they could have fought. They *must* have fought.'

'Not if they saw there was hope of Hadassah being spared.'

'It's a miracle. An utter miracle.'

'A miracle? It's a catastrophe. God Almighty . . . the poor child.'

There was a women squatting beside me on the floor, and she bent over me. 'You're sure you heard nothing?' she insisted; I'd lost count of how often I'd been asked that already. I made no reply; I felt weak as water, and everything was blurred and faint around me, like the sound of a distant ocean. I couldn't imagine how I'd heard nothing, any more than they could. But I'd had a lot of wine, and had always been a good sleeper. I was used to comings and goings in the night and not being disturbed. One time Pithon had dangled a spider onto my nose and I hadn't woken up . . .

'Pithon!' I shrieked, and sat up, clinging to the woman beside me. 'Where's Pithon? I didn't see him! They didn't bring him out!'

She held me, stroking my hair just the way Mother used to, and this brought my tears at last, torrents of them.

'We don't know,' she said eventually. 'No one has seen him. They must have taken him with them.'

'Taken him where? We must find him! I have to look for him!'

I stood up and tried to fumble my way outside, but one of the men restrained me while I beat against his chest with my fists. I wasn't used to being thwarted.

'We shan't find him now, my love,' the man said. 'He'll fetch too good a price in the markets of Persia.' It was a heartless thing to say, but already they must have been wearying of my raucous wilfulness. It never occurred to me that others might be worn out and grieving just as I was.

'They didn't take Rachael,' I blurted. 'Wouldn't she have sold well too?'

'Not after they'd finished with her,' responded one of the other men gruffly. 'And she wasn't so pretty.'

At this they all fell to bitter quarrelling. The women were incensed that such callous things were being said in front of me. My outbursts should be indulged for now, while my madness ran its course.

I didn't care whether they took my part or not. I hadn't understood the half of what the men had meant in any case. In particular I had no idea at all about what it meant to be a eunuch, which they reckoned would be Pithon's fate. Bewildered and drained, I lay prone on the bed once more, beyond crying and beyond caring, beyond anyone's reach.

The dead were buried the following day. Tradition and good sense demanded that we wait no longer; bodies could not be left to lie out in the heat.

I wished we could have waited. I wasn't ready to face being seen by people. Yet I wanted to be there; I should never forgive myself if I stayed away.

I'd worked out that I was in the house of one Gedaliah, an architect of comparable standing to my father. It seemed that he had assumed responsibility for the funeral arrangements, since we had no kin in Jerusalem, nor in the whole of the world for all that I knew. So it was to Gedaliah's house that the bodies of my family were brought to be rendered seemly.

I stood looking on, silent and numb, as the women laid them out side by side on their backs and peeled away what remained of the clothing from their stiffened and blood-spattered limbs. I wondered why they bothered. These weren't my loved ones any more. My mother was beautiful, rosy-cheeked, vivacious and generous; here was someone ugly, white and cold. My father was intelligent, cultured, consumed by a quiet zeal; here was someone inert and indifferent. I wondered where my parents had gone, for I couldn't imagine that souls so vibrant could be snuffed out as easily as the candles which were burning now by their heads.

But there was no one to whom I wanted to talk about such things. There was no one I wanted to talk to about anything, and after a while no one tried to talk to me. I watched them prepare the corpses for burial, washing and anointing them, dressing them in clean white robes as though they were dressing wooden dolls. I wondered where my own wooden doll had gone, and my trowel-charm, and all the other gifts. No doubt some flea-ridden Soil Child had won them, for Rachael's earlobes were split where her gold sleepers had been torn out, and her necklace was gone. So was Mother's. I put my hands to my ears and throat and discovered that my own jewellery was still in place. It was a wonder that my assailant hadn't snatched it, but he'd had other things on his mind. In a fit of confused anger I wrenched Rachael's ring from my finger and threw it out of a window into the street.

27

They tried to stop me going with the cortège but I howled until they let me. Once we'd left the house I neither screamed nor cried. I was determined that I wouldn't. I wanted to feel that my parents would have been proud of me after all. I marched dumbly between the keening mourners, picturing the victims of the massacre going just as dumbly to their fate like lambs to the altar, meeting death's gaze the way they'd taught me to do, and all because they wanted me to live.

Even Rachael had died like that for me. The confused anger returned, more intense than I could have imagined; and I wished she hadn't. I wished my parents had woken me and taken me with them. Why had they been so cruel as to leave me alone? Or why couldn't that hollow-chested boy have dragged me off to join them, instead of keeping me for some private purpose of his own which he then hadn't had the courage to carry out?

But *I* had courage, and I was resolved to show it. I walked with my head held high, directly behind the bearers of the open wooden stretchers. Relatives of Uriah brought their sorry burdens to join ours, and when I saw Deborah my resolve to stay quiet almost crumbled. No one brought the hollow-chested boy; perhaps he'd already been thrown to the dogs.

Crowds lined the streets and joined in the keening as we passed, or shouted Pioneer slogans. I knew that some folk were pointing at me, though I kept my eyes to the front, and I could imagine what they might be saying. But I didn't want anyone to feel sorry for me, not then. So far as I knew, I alone was left of the House of Saul, and I must act accordingly.

It wasn't as though I hadn't been prepared for this, all of my life. Since being a tiny child I'd been taught that we'd chosen a perilous path to walk upon. To be a Pioneer was to render yourself vulnerable; to be born into one of the most prominent Pioneer families was like being cast into Daniel's den of lions. Yes, the Persian authorities had granted permission for the return and the rebuilding, but they would do little to intervene on our behalf despite the fact that Israel was as much a part of their empire as Shushan was. Their policy for discouraging rebellion among their subject peoples was to allow them as much freedom as possible in their internal affairs; and if that meant freedom to torment one another, well, so be it. For as long as we all hated our fellow subjects, we were less likely to have any hatred left over for our Persian masters. Only if Persian interests were threatened would they do anything much to interfere.

Risk and uncertainty had always been a part of my existence, along with my parents' vision. The two went hand in hand; the cause which imperilled our lives also gave us our reason for living them. Even my own name was bound up with it all: Hadassah, or Myrtle, given to me because the prophet Zechariah had had a vision of an angel in a grove of myrtle trees. This angel had proclaimed God's abiding love for his holy city and promised its restitution. Also the myrtle is a symbol of peace, joy and life, for the prophet Isaiah wrote that Adonai will plant myrtles in the wilderness when he makes it blossom once more, like the Garden of Eden.

Yet today, for the first time, I began to be unsure that this would ever happen. To me, the Pioneer adventure had always been something exciting, the danger like a game, or like hot spice which makes an everyday dish taste special. Now that this spectre of danger had taken on flesh it was ugly, and I doubted I would ever have peace, joy or real life again. Yes, I was the sole survivor of a royal house . . . and I'd never known such loneliness. Once the great stone had been rolled into place, I should never look upon the face of a kinsman again.

When they bore my mother's stretcher inside its rock-cut tomb, I could cope no longer. I broke away to run after it; I think I must have conceived some crazed notion to give her my necklace to take with her, for I ripped it from my throat and it landed in the dust. Someone gave it back to me, reminding me that we enter this world with nothing, and with nothing we must go from it. Go where? I thought, go where? but I let them fasten the chain back under my loosened hair.

There were no speeches. These would be made at the wake, which would be held at the end of a week of mourning. We tramped homeward beneath the massing clouds of a sultry spring thunderstorm, and in the imposing shadow of the new Temple, rearing up defiantly from the platform of Solomon's which the armies of Babylon had razed. The new one was large, larger in some of its dimensions than Solomon's had been. But side by side they say it would have looked like a big barn next to a small palace, or a big bead of cloudy glass beside a clear crystal. Some of the treasures which the Babylonians had taken had now been returned, but there was no Ark of the Covenant, the symbol of the presence of Adonai. The oldest folk could remember the site when it had been desolate, before the rebuilding had begun, when bereft, bedraggled pilgrims had made their meagre offerings among the blackened ruins. But there was no one left alive who could actually remember the old Temple in all its glory, nor the appalling siege during which people had bartered heirlooms for bread, then eaten their own children and beheld their king being dragged away in chains.

The city walls, once breached and then destroyed, had never been rebuilt. That was something which the Persians would not allow, any more than they would allow us our own king. They didn't want a fortified city full of fanatics located within a province as volatile as ours.

I was taken back to Gedaliah's. During the week of mourning, a stream of visitors came to offer me their sympathies as custom dictated, but I wouldn't speak to them and after a while the stream dried up. I began to hear Gedaliah's womenfolk and their friends discussing in hushed tones what was to be done with me.

From one such discussion I learned with profound surprise and no little alarm that I did have at least one surviving kinsman. He was my second cousin Mordecai, and he lived in Shushan; his name had never been mentioned in our house. Holding my breath I stood outside the door of the room where the conversation was taking place; it hadn't occurred to them to involve me in it, because I was making it quite plain to everyone that I wanted to be involved in nothing.

'We cannot send her to Shushan!' someone was exclaiming. 'What would Abihail have said if he'd known his own daughter was going back to that hotbed of idolatry? The place is evil!'

'You're right,' agreed another. 'Spoilt as she is I would rather take care of her myself than have her go there. She's of the Remnant; she belongs here.'

Did I? I no longer felt to belong anywhere. The Pioneer vision was already blurring in my eyes. Even at the funeral there had been those who shouted their slogans and hailed the dead as martyrs to the cause, which could only become stronger through its suffering. Yet it was *I* who was suffering, not they. It was *my* family which had been destroyed, singled out by wicked men because of its eminence and the strength of its commitment to God's work. I owed it to the memory of those who had made the ultimate sacrifice, to fight on and never give up... yet for what? If God was on our side, why had he allowed this tragedy to happen? What had been the use of those prayers for my welfare? Granted, I had survived, but if this was Adonai's idea of looking after me, I didn't want to know. And if he was meant to be indwelling me, why did I feel so lost and alone?

'In any case, Shushan is three months' journey away,' someone else rejoined. 'How could we get her there? And if we did, suppose this Mordecai will not have her? What kind of man must he be, still living there amongst the heathen? At very best he must be the sort who loves money too much to come and rebuild his own nation.'

'Or else he's a coward and is kept away by the danger.'

'How can Shushan be any less dangerous than here? It is peopled by sinners and rife with shameful practices. The light of Adonai has never shone there. False gods hold it captive.'

And you see evidence of Adonai's light and power *here?* I thought bitterly. I'm sure *I* don't.

The debate about my future was settled unexpectedly and abruptly a few days later. Gedaliah and some of his colleagues had been going through my parents' documents and a testament had turned up to the effect that should anything happen to them, then Rachael, Pithon and I should be placed in the care of Cousin Mordecai since he had no children of his own and much regretted it.

I was distraught. Having lost my family and my best friend, I was now to lose everything else which had made me what I was. No amount of pleading or throwing of tantrums was going to change anyone's mind; my father had made his wishes clear.

That night I slept up on the roof alone—though it was much too early in the year for it to be warm after dark—and poured out my complaints to the stars. With his own testament my father had betrayed me. He and my mother had brought me up to believe I could always exercise some choice in what happened to me, as both of them had done, whereas in reality I was to be allowed none. Adonai too had betrayed me, letting me be sent back to the land of the pagans, where he had no power at all.

There was some further debate concerning how they could convey me to Shushan, but that too was quickly settled. A certain young Pioneer couple were due to return that way in a week's time because the girl's father, who was still living there, had succumbed to a slow but inexorable wasting sickness and she was anxious to see him before he died. Meanwhile, Mordecai would be apprised of my forthcoming arrival; Jehoazar the Governor was in regular contact with the administration in Shushan, and his couriers would take Mordecai a letter from Gedaliah explaining all that had happened.

I tried to find out more about Cousin Mordecai before we left, but no one in Gedaliah's household knew anything. All I could discover was that his name was a Hebrew form of Mardukaya, so his parents had named him for a Babylonian god. It scarcely boded well. I built up a picture of him in my head: he was rich and fat, with a courtyard full of rich, fat statues. I dreamed about him every night, and woke up begging Adonai not to let me be taken there. He didn't answer.

I contemplated running away, but there was nowhere I could think of to run to. Then when I met the couple I was to travel with, the madness in me began to subside. They were kind but firm, much better able to handle me than the others with whom I'd lately had dealings. The first time I said something spiteful, the young woman reminded me in no uncertain terms that I wasn't the only one to lose a father, and at least mine had loved me while he was alive. She hadn't heard from hers since the day they'd parted in anger, until the message came that he was dying. And she looked so near to tears, for once I had to acknowledge that others had feelings just as I did. Then she threw her arms around me, and when she said she knew how I felt, it was clear she meant it. From then on we were fighting on the same side. It was just as well, since we were about to spend three months in each other's company.

So while her husband went about sorting out the things which had to be done before they could leave, she and I spent many long hours together. Her name was Sarah, his Judah, and it was with Sarah that I began to face up to my grief and loneliness. We talked and we talked; I confessed all my bitterness because of the will, and my enmity with Rachael, and my pining for Pithon.

'If they took him as a slave, he may well be in Shushan,' she pointed out, waving my words aside when I asked her what a eunuch was. 'Don't you want to go and find him?'

But she couldn't answer my questions about Adonai. At least she didn't pretend that she could.

She did manage to answer some of my questions about Mordecai, however. Her father's elderly servant, who had brought the news of his master's illness, knew a little about my cousin. The servant was still in Jerusalem, for he would be returning to Shushan with us, so Sarah put my questions to him. Apparently Mordecai was the son of a certain Jair who had been my father's uncle; Jair's father had been Shimei, and his grandfather Kish. They were descendants of the Saulide Shimei who was famous for scorning King David and throwing dung at him, and this Shimei in turn had been descended from the Kish who was Saul's great uncle, and uncle of the Kish who had been Saul's father. The Kish who'd been Mordecai's great grandfather had witnessed the fall of Jerusalem to the armies of Babylon, and had been taken by them into exile.

All the names and convoluted relationships confused me utterly, though I knew I ought to make an effort to remember them. But they weren't what I really wanted to know. I wanted to know if Mordecai had a wife, and what sort of person he was. The servant said there was no wife so far as he knew, but since he hadn't met Mordecai in the flesh, he couldn't say what he was like. If I wished to find out more about my father's family, there were records kept in Shushan. But I knew that my mother's had been lost, burnt along with so many other priceless treasures when Jerusalem fell.

The day after the wake Sarah took me to the house to get my things for the journey. It was the first time I'd been back, and it was to be the last. I thought I wanted to be alone there for a while, and asked her to wait at the gateway, but I soon changed my mind. The trappings of the party were all still there. My chair still stood on its homely tribunal, and the curtains festooning the yard blew forlornly in the breeze, except for where they'd been torn down to do duty as shrouds. I couldn't bear to stay there any longer than it took to pile my clothes into a basket, along with the bronze mirror in which I'd admired myself and which I found still lying among the pots of perfume and kohl.

I can remember much of our epic journey quite clearly, even though a large part of me was still trying to pretend that none of this was happening. Early in the morning before we left, I'd had Sarah and Judah walk me around the familiar streets of the city which had been my home; together we'd stood high on the citadel where David's palace had once been, and I'd stared hard in every direction, striving to stamp the pictures onto my mind the way a king might stamp his seal onto all that he possesses. It was Jerusalem I wanted to take with me, not a chest packed with pretty dresses which I couldn't imagine ever wanting to wear again.

Sarah sensed my self-pity and hugged me briefly; Judah said, 'We must never lose heart, Hadassah. You were spared for a purpose and you must find it. Adonai doesn't waste his miracles.'

I couldn't think of anything to say in reply. I just went on staring at the jumble of sand-coloured cottages filling the valley below, and at the grey-green sheep-covered hillsides beyond.

Then the donkeys and the ox-cart were loaded and we were away, leaving behind us the newly-planted olive groves with their spindly trees, and the vineyards that were starting to look established, and the orchards and the myrtles and the bright spring flowers.

I have never been back.

To travel from Jerusalem to Shushan is an awesome undertaking. It's still more awesome when you consider that one man rules over every village and field and forest that we passed through; to walk from one end of the Empire to the other would take years, not months. We went north first, through Syria, a land of rock and wooded mountains; peering out between the cart's curtains as we jolted along I expected at any moment to be ambushed by bandits, or monsters. But bandits were never a problem, so said Sarah's father's servant. There were so many Persian guardposts along the way, no outlaw gang lasted long. As for monsters, he'd never seen one, but who could say? Then he winked at me and grinned, and I got cross because of his teasing.

The further we went, the hotter it became, as spring gave way to summer and the lush green turned to yellow. We held our simple Passover meal under the open sky, as they must have done with Moses in the wilderness, and I tried not to think of the previous year's.

'Cheer up, little one,' Judah urged me. 'We'll get there, don't you worry. This is the same route Abraham took, all those years ago, when there were no Persian garrisons to protect him.' That was true; but Abraham had been travelling the opposite way, with the Promised Land ahead of him.

We were making for the great Royal Road, built by King Daraya-vaush from Shushan to Sardis, and only recently completed. We had to veer a little out of our way in order to reach it, but the going would be smoother, there were decent inns along the route, and it avoided the arid desert that lay between us and our goal. The Royal Road ran east of the Tigris River; I thought it would be quicker to take a boat on the river itself. But that would have been expensive, and besides, Judah said, it wasn't navigable past Babylon. Babylon! I thought, with a jolt not caused by the ox-cart; Babylon, the harlot city . . .

After the mountains came pasture-land: day after day of hot, flat, stubbly grazing, with every now and then a field of corn or a clump of forest where we crossed a water-course or followed its reedy bank. Drab mud-brick hamlets squatted by the dusty track, each the same as the last, each with its gaggle of blank-eyed children who broke off their games to stare.

At night I would lie awake in the wagon, listening to the others talking as they huddled about their campfire assuming that I slept. Sometimes they talked about me, and then I would listen harder. Judah would sigh, and maintain that he'd never yet once seen me smile; would I ever get over what had happened to me? Could I ever be expected to? Then Sarah would entreat him not to upset himself. I was strong deep down, she could see it in my eyes. I would use the sticks and mud fortune threw at me to make a raft on which to rise above the tide of misery that threatened to engulf me.

Then I wept silently into my blankets, reminded of my father's counsel that the stones life throws at us should be built into city walls. What use were city walls, when my city was far away, in another world?

Yet I took a meagre comfort from Sarah's assurances. If she could see strength in me, I had to believe it was there.

The old servant must have seen it too. 'There are three sorts of folk I've come across in my time,' he said to me one day, as I walked beside him with the donkeys, skipping to keep up with the brisk pace he set. 'Those who let misfortunes pile up on top of them so they can't breathe—they will always be the victims. And then there are those who just manage to dig their way out—they survive. But those who climb up and stand right on top, trampling their afflictions beneath their feet . . . well, they are the overcomers, and they can see into the far, far distance because they're standing higher than everybody else. You belong with them.'

I was struck dumb, amazed that such pearls of wisdom should drop from the mouth of a slave. He must have guessed my thoughts, for he chuckled softly, and swung me up onto the least laden of the donkeys. He was sinewy and strong as a pack-animal himself, though he must have been almost seventy, and his wit-quickened eyes were faded to the colour of a weathered scroll. 'There are slaves and slaves in Shushan, you know, Princess. You'll be hard pressed to tell them from the free at times. After all, every citizen of the Empire is a bondsman of the King. And I've a good master; why should I want to give up my security? To be supplied with food and a roof above my head—that's all I need to render me content.'

I said, 'But your master is dying. What will happen to you then?'

'I shall serve his son, and the son of his son.'

Then I did smile, imagining this game old fellow running errands for successive generations until he was as ancient as Methuselah. But my sadness clouded in again at that; I asked forlornly, 'Why do we have to die *ever*, though? Where do we go, when it happens? Are the dead happy?'

He pretended to be shocked. 'Those *are* big questions for such a small girl.'

'I'm eight years old, and bigger than some who are ten.'

'True,' he conceded, pensive now. 'And you've tasted enough of sorrow for a woman twice that age. But it doesn't make your questions any easier to answer. They used to say that death was just like sleeping: a long, dreamless sleep in Sheol. Nowadays you hear it said that there's a judgment, and a future, all depending on how you've lived. But we shall each know quite soon enough; and some of us sooner than others.'

'Aren't you afraid?'

'Afraid to die? Not at my ripe old age. Whatever is to come, I shall commit myself to the Good Lord as I've always done. We don't need to know what he has in store for us, only that he loves us, and that he is never unjust.'

But my sadness only deepened. I said dejectedly, 'He wasn't being just when he killed everyone I loved.'

'Adonai didn't kill them, Princess. Adonai kills no one. It's sin that kills us, sure as the sky's blue. Adonai gave us to eat of the tree of life, but we chose the apple of knowledge we were never meant to have. Besides, I thought you said that your brother was still alive?'

'Perhaps. I don't really know.' My hope for Pithon was withering already. 'The people I was staying with said he would be made into a eunuch but Sarah won't tell me what it means.'

'If that's what's become of him, like as not he'll be in Shushan. The palace employs hundreds, maybe thousands.'

'The palace? You mean he'll be serving the Great King?'

'Not in person, I shouldn't think; though it's possible. Someone has to.'

'So it's something honourable, then, to be a eunuch?'

'There are eunuchs in posts of great honour, yes.'

But he wouldn't tell me what the word meant, either, for like Sarah he could see how dear Pithon had been to me. And from the glances they exchanged the next time it was mentioned, I gathered enough to know that it wasn't honourable at all, but something shameful. I resolved not to speak of it again, yet couldn't help wondering. Perhaps they had branded Pithon's forehead with a hideous pagan symbol, or welded a great heavy thrall ring round his neck, or given him drugs to make him obedient. Whatever it was, I was sure I'd still love him, and I said so to Sarah. But she tried to change the subject, and then said I shouldn't set my hopes too high; if he'd been taken to the palace, I should never find him.

'You said I would! That's the only reason I said I'd come with you! You're just like everyone else. Everybody lies to me!'

I stormed away and marched along ahead of them, fiercely alone; I spoke to no one the rest of that day. As usual, they paid no heed to my tantrum, knowing it was best to wait for me to simmer down.

The next day we saw Nineveh, and the servant grew excited. 'The Royal Road!' he exclaimed. 'That's where we pick it up. No more twists and turns and ruts full of dust after tomorrow.'

I whispered in awe, '*The* Nineveh?'

'One and the same. Capital of the mighty Assyrian Empire, long may it rot! The place is in ruins; you'll see as we get closer.'

And indeed it was; I was heartily glad that we didn't need to stay. In Jerusalem the ruins had an air of expectancy about them; Nineveh was desolate, its once-proud buildings crumbling to sand and subsiding slowly into their own foundations. Soon it would be no more than a shapeless mound, just like the multitudes of other shapeless mounds we had seen on our travels, which were the graves of forgotten cities of the past.

'Why so glum, Princess?' asked the servant, tilting up my chin. 'The place got no worse than it deserved, and no better than the prophets foretold for it. Babylon will wind up just the same one day.'

Thence we set out upon the last leg of our journey; in terms of distance we were barely more than halfway, but in time, perhaps a mere month from our destination. We'd now turned south, and the heat was becoming stifling. Away from the rivers and canals nothing grew but shrivelled thorns, and we had to stop a dozen times a day to replenish our jars of water from the stocks which were kept at intervals along the way.

The road got busier, except at midday when no one could do a thing but sweat and sleep. There were merchants and soldiers, and imperial officials who rode great horses and scarcely deigned to look at us except when they chose to check our documents and search our baggage. Now and again a liveried royal courier would pass, at break-neck speed; they rode in relays, so I was told, and could between them cover in a day the kind of distance which would take a single rider many weeks.

To my surprise, I found an eagerness stirring within me the closer we got to Shushan. Even though part of me was still futilely attempting to deny what was happening, the pictures of Jerusalem which I'd painted in my mind were growing dim, and I would catch myself wondering instead what this new and strange city would be like. Although I started to harry our poor patient servant with a barrage of questions, the fresh pictures I was painting for myself were mostly the product of my girlish imagination. I saw fine veiled ladies gliding down quiet, affluent colonnades with their children and handmaids in tow; there were columns of uniformed soldiers marching in step, street-hawkers peddling their wares, and marble-fronted buildings, temples, and stone gods everywhere. The Royal Road had by-passed Babylon quite a way off, so I'd seen nothing on the way which could truly prepare me for my first glimpse of the Empire's capital.

Then suddenly there it was ahead, like a shining crown upon a mound that reared up from the plain majestic and strong as the back of the monster Leviathan; beside it Jerusalem would have seemed no more than a village of mud and sticks built by children. I caught my breath, then Sarah said, 'That is only the palace, Hadassah. The city is beyond it, larger again, and the holy citadel where the god's fire is never put out.'

'Is that why it shines so? Are there fires all along the walls?'

'No, but they are faced with glazed bricks that capture the sunlight like jewels. They are covered in friezes, all different colours. Lions, gryphons, courtiers and soldiers—'

'And the Great King lives there all alone?'

'The Great King of Persia is never alone. He has wives and concubines and ministers and bodyguards. The palace is a city in its own right, with bankers and accountants and physicians and craftsmen of the same types that you'd find in a city anywhere.'

'And at this time of year, the King himself is unlikely to be there,' Judah added. 'When it's too hot he and his court retire to his palace in the mountains.'

The heat and humidity were such that it was hard to see anything beyond the gleaming edifice, but we'd had the lofty brown Zagros mountains to our left since joining the Road, and they formed half a circle around Shushan to its north and east. The heat-haze made them shimmer like reflections in a blue pool, and below them bright canals criss-crossed the plain like silver blades. In between there were cornfields and orchards, and date-palms: so many date-palms that at first you could hardly see the clusters of houses that crouched beneath them, craving their shade.

A little further on, the Road joined up with a river which flowed to the west of the palace, and as the two ran along side by side small craft of all shapes and sorts floated past us: rafts laden with fruit being punted along by sunburnt youths stripped to the waist; fishing boats bringing back their catches from downstream; and then an enormous river-borne litter draped with awnings beneath which some wealthy lord or lady travelled unseen. Along its banks, the river was fringed with reeds which swayed and rattled gently in the scorching breeze, and amongst them bloomed great white lilies, open to the sun. Every kind of lily grows at Shushan, they say, both on water and in the fields, so that its own inhabitants call it the City of Lilies. But away beyond the reach of the river and canals, all was dehydration and death.

We didn't enter the city at all that day, however. We repaired to an inn some few hours short of it, for Sarah insisted that we refresh ourselves thoroughly before presenting ourselves at the house of Mordecai.

But I was whining incessantly as she washed my hair and combed it, because it brought back so many memories, and because all at once I didn't want the journey to be over. I dreaded the moment when Sarah and Judah and the wise and kindly old slave would have to leave me in a house I didn't know, with a stranger who worshipped strange gods. I got angry, and yelped when Sarah pulled at a tangle in my hair; she snapped at me, but I was too taken up with myself again to think that she might be full of dread too. Once rid of me, she would have to go to her dying father, and she didn't know quite what was awaiting her.

I tossed and turned all night, the sweat running off me, and my head full of home. In the morning I wouldn't eat breakfast, and when Sarah wanted to bind up my hair and attend to my face I ran outside and sat in the courtyard of the inn. Except that it wasn't a courtyard; it was more like a small orchard, full of trees bearing orange or yellow fruit the like of which I'd never seen, and thorny shrubs weighted down with showy flowers of every hue from blood red to milk white. It was beautiful and dreadful and I didn't want to be there. I hadn't seen a single vineyard or olive grove or myrtle tree for weeks. The heavy morning air was stale with the smell of the reedbeds and swamps and there were itchy red swellings on my arms where insects had bitten me.

When at length Sarah came outside for me I was too miserable to defy her, and I let her lead me back in. There she dabbed at the blotches on my cheeks with tepid water—there wasn't any cold to be found—and made vain attempts to hide the bags under my eyes with powders and creams and kohl. She unwrapped my necklace and earrings, which had been stowed for safety among her belongings. Then she hung them in place, resignedly doing the same thing again when I'd sulkily taken them off. I lifted no finger to help while the donkeys and cart were reloaded, but the job got done just the same. Our departure could be delayed no longer. By noon we would be in Shushan.

3

From afar the sight of Shushan had amazed me; once within its walls I was utterly overwhelmed. I was a Daughter of Zion, with the blood of a royal house running in my veins, yet here I was surrounded by swarming multitudes to whom Jerusalem meant nothing. I moved among the crowds in a daze, holding tight to Sarah's hand, feeling dizzy and ugly and ignorant. Unsmiling strangers pushed past me, striding purposefully about their business; their elbows and baskets knocked against my face as though I'd somehow become invisible. It was almost worse than being jeered at or even stoned—at least then you felt you mattered.

I'd had to say goodbye to the old slave just outside the city, before we began climbing the steep road up from the moat to the gateway. It was his task to dispose of the donkeys, the oxen and the cart; pack animals and wheeled vehicles would be more of a hindrance than a help in the congested streets.

At my party I had revelled in the bustle and the noise. But milling crowds are one thing when their faces are familiar and friendly and flushed with exuberance, quite another when they consist of tight-lipped foreigners who are jabbering away to one another in languages you don't understand. And they looked so very alien—next to Sarah or Judah most of them appeared pale unto death, with their thin peaky features, and their hair and eyebrows fine as babies'. These I took to be the native Persians; but there were also red-skinned Egyptians and hook-nosed nomads, Assyrians, Babylonians, Phoenicians and Greeks—at least, these were the various nationalities I ascribed to them. Then there were the many whose origins I couldn't begin to guess, including some with faces as black and smooth as well-cured leather.

And the clothes! There was every kind of costume I could ever have imagined and many more I couldn't, such as the skimpy short tunics worn by some of the men, over curious garments I later learned were called trousers, that were sewn so they shamelessly followed the contours of their wearers' thighs and calves instead of hanging modestly to their ankles. There were bare-headed worker-women dressed plainly as any of the men, but comparatively few veiled ladies—though there were dainty curtained litters whose occupants couldn't be seen. Nor were there any soldiers; indeed, nobody appeared to be armed at all. There were no street-hawkers or stalls by the roadside either, and I hadn't yet laid eyes on one statue of a god.

There was plenty of marble about, and most folk seemed well-to-do, as I'd imagined. But then I was profoundly shocked to come upon a blind starveling with withered legs, hunched in a dusty corner and begging for alms in a thin reedy voice whilst thrusting a dirty cracked bowl right under my nose. For a moment I stood aghast; the man looked old enough to be someone's grandfather and I was appalled that he should be grovelling in the gutter, when all around there was evidence of such astonishing wealth.

Then Sarah dragged me away, and after that I saw crippled beggars everywhere, and flat-chested mothers each with a mewling infant under one arm and the other hand forlornly outstretched. Also there were the groups of despondent-looking labourers waiting to be hired; I wondered if they ever got work, and thought how much there would be for them to do in Jerusalem.

My curiosity was further aroused by numerous squat-looking, bald-headed fellows with soft plump bodies and ageless, beardless faces, whom I saw going about in groups of three or four, all richly dressed. And stranger even than these, perhaps, were the tall, spare, solitary individuals wearing long black cloaks which brushed the ground, and rendered them faceless by means of all-enveloping hoods.

The layout of the city was as alien as its population. Some of the houses were built of mudbrick like those at home, but everything was straight and square as though it had been planned and built in a single day, instead of evolving village-wise over centuries as David's City had done. And that single day must have been a relatively recent one; although Shushan had once been the capital city of Elam, a vanished empire almost as old as time itself, the Assyrians had reduced it to rubble—the rubble which now comprised the mound on which the proud new metropolis was standing.

Trees as well as buildings had been positioned carefully throughout; I found it bizarre to see them growing up all around as happily as they might have done in the depths of the countryside. Date-palms, figs, cypress and poplar grew in most of the yards as well as on the corners of the streets; but some of the walls around these yards were so high you could barely see the crowns of full-grown trees above them. Many of the humbler dwellings had curiously sloping roofs, whilst others had roofs made of reeds all woven together, so that some of the streets looked more like the banks of rivers. But the most imposing residences were hidden from view; you could only tell where they were because of the great bronze-studded gates twice as high as a man, set into walls which towered higher still. I fell to wondering what sort of place belonged to Mordecai.

It turned out that most of the Jews of Shushan lived together in one quarter of the city. There were no clear indications that we had entered it, but all at once the faces didn't look so exotic nor the fashions so indecent, and I began to see on the doorposts the familiar little boxes which contain our holiest prayer.

None of us knew where to find Mordecai's house, but when Judah enquired of a passer-by, the man knew at once who he meant and could give quite clear directions. We got lost all the same and had to ask someone else, and he too knew exactly who Mordecai was and where he lived. Perhaps the Jewish community was small enough for everyone to know everyone; yet I formed the distinct impression from these two encounters that my cousin was no ordinary member of it.

All too soon the search and the wondering were over.

Despite the universal awe which Mordecai's name inspired whenever we mentioned it, there was nothing special about his home, from the outside at least. A modest wooden gate, unadorned save for its discreet bronze prayer-box, was the only face which it presented to the street. Judah rapped boldly upon it while I fought to swallow the ache of fear which was rising in my throat. There was a fumbling of bolts and the gate opened. Behind it stood a wizened, wrinkled old woman dressed for housework, her robe girt up and a kerchief knotted firmly about her head.

She was momentarily puzzled, then caught on to who we must be and beckoned us hurriedly inside. All at once she looked more nervous than I felt; she kept glancing at me anxiously, particularly, so it seemed, at my earrings and neck-chain. Certainly their bright gold lustre made a marked contrast with the drabness of the small forecourt in which we found ourselves. It was as plain and empty as a drained cistern, and hot as an oven. There wasn't a scrap of shade, and the bleached mud walls trapped the sun and banished any breath of breeze. The woman left us standing there while she went to fetch Mordecai; her nervousness must have got the better of her manners, or else she was so used to the heat it didn't bother her and she'd forgotten that it might bother us.

It bothered me. My head was full of pounding like a blacksmith's forge, and my mouth was dry as a cinder pile. Sarah tried to squeeze my hand, but I'd made it into a fist. I felt trapped like the sunlight, and shut my eyes against its glare. When I opened them again, Cousin Mordecai was looking down at me.

Although part of me was expecting him to be a rich, fat idolater, there was another part which had supposed he must be at least a little like my father. The two of them had shared a grandfather, after all.

Mordecai certainly had Father's eyes: shrewd, intense, penetrating. Here the similarity ended. There wasn't the slightest flicker of mischief about Mordecai's expression, and because I associated mischief with kindness, I detected no trace of benevolence either in Mordecai's countenance. His mouth seemed to me to be just another taut line incised on a face which was etched with so many he must have carried all the worries of the world on his once-broad shoulders for years. He wore a sober, homespun, ankle-length robe with wide sleeves and a plain woollen sash, and an unpretentious but impeccably twisted turban from which emerged two perfectly matching forelocks coiled one in front of each ear. His frizzled beard was bitumen-black, and the longest and widest I'd ever seen.

He looked me up and down; he too seemed oddly perturbed by my jewellery. Then his eyes came to rest on my face, and he bestowed upon me what someone else might have interpreted as a smile. To me it looked like a grimace, and I decided that I hated him, unreservedly.

Inside the house it was cooler, but not much, and as bare and austere as the outside except for a few Hebrew texts inscribed in the cream plaster. I knew that was what they were, though I couldn't read them—at that time I wouldn't have been able to recognize my own name. We'd had priests to explain the Law to us; Pioneers had no time for books.

We sat down as requested, though coming from him it sounded more like an order than an invitation, and if I hadn't felt so weary from the heat and from my sleepless night, I might have refused and said I would rather stand. The wizened old woman went to fetch a plate of refreshments: candied dates and figs, honeyed biscuits and an assortment of intriguing sweetmeats, all set out with meticulous precision. Although they looked delicious, I did refuse these. I felt too sick to face them.

Then I noticed that Mordecai took nothing sweet either, contenting himself with plain bread and yoghurt, which we were told is what they have in Persia instead of sour milk. The old woman took the tray away, looking vaguely put out, and Mordecai looked disgruntled too. It didn't occur to me that they might be disappointed, having laid in luxuries which they normally denied themselves, in order to make a child feel at home.

Some introductions were made, during the course of which I learned that the old woman's name was Leah, and that she was employed as Mordecai's housekeeper. But I wouldn't answer any questions, and Sarah had to speak for me. I could tell that my rudeness was embarrassing her; I didn't care. With tears smarting in my eyes I let the conversation go right over my head, gathering only that although my father and my cousin had loved and respected one another as kinsmen, they had disagreed violently about almost everything. They had spoken neither to nor about each other since my father had announced his intention to join the Pioneers.

So *what* if Mordecai disapproves of us, I thought. He has no right to, when he is a Jew still living in Shushan.

But when Sarah and Judah began saying that it was time for them to be leaving, my contempt evaporated and panic set in. Not wanting to cry in front of Mordecai I ran outside, knowing that Sarah would follow me.

I wept and begged her not to leave me all alone with strangers who had already made it quite clear that they didn't like me. While she was trying to remind me that she must lose no time in getting to her dying father, I was whining and wailing, maintaining that she was just like the folk at Gedaliah's, and couldn't wait to be rid of me. I was wanting to hurt her, and I succeeded; we parted without making things up.

Presently Leah appeared and tried to coax me back inside. 'My lord Mordecai says you aren't accustomed to the heat, miss. It will make your head ache.'

'My head aches already.'

Although I was sure she was scared of me, she dared to come closer, and actually took me by the arm. But I shrieked, 'Don't you dare touch me!' and slapped her wrinkled face. She fled to Mordecai, and I relished the thought of her pouring out her indignant complaints to him—until he came out himself and slapped *my* face, very hard. I stared, too stunned to cry aloud, because no one had ever struck me in all the years I could remember.

After that I did as I was told, for the rest of the afternoon at any rate. Leah showed me to my room and stayed to help me unpack, because Mordecai told her to, and we worked in stiff silence. Presently Mordecai walked in without knocking, and picked up my bronze mirror which was lying on the mattress. He said, 'Vanity is a sin, Hadassah; and it is a sin to leave temptation lying in another's path. I shall keep this for you, along with that gaudery you're wearing.'

I knelt in abject horror while he unclipped my jewellery and stowed it in a pocket of his robe. Then he smeared away the kohl from around my eyes with the end of his sleeve.

Once my things were put neatly away, Leah set me to work chopping vegetables for the evening meal. I was all fingers and thumbs, partly through fear, partly because I wasn't used to doing kitchen chores. At home, Rachael and my mother had done them; Pithon and I were to enjoy our childhood to the full. Inevitably I cut myself and got blood on my dress; Leah tutted and said it was too fancy for everyday use in any case. She lent me one of hers, which was way too big, and the fabric so rough it chafed my skin where the marsh-insects had bitten me.

A little later Mordecai reappeared to see how we were getting on. Leah suggested that he take my pretty dresses and parcel them up with the rest of my valuables; some more appropriate garb could be procured for me in due course.

I hadn't cared about my dresses at all—until then. I hadn't even wanted to fetch them from Jerusalem. Now I didn't know whether I ought to care or not.

When the time came to eat, I still couldn't face anything. It was as hot as ever, and my head was so thick I thought it would burst. After Mordecai had made an elaborate blessing over the food, I asked to be excused.

Mordecai remarked, 'I see you are as stubborn as your father was, Hadassah.'

'I'm not stubborn. I don't feel well.'

'You will feel worse if you don't eat. You've had nothing all day.'

'I'm not hungry.'

Leah said, 'Don't argue with your cousin, Hadassah. You will make him angry again.'

'Leave me alone!' I blurted. It was her wheedling voice—it drove me to distraction. It was worse still when she kept appealing to Mordecai for support, as I knew she would proceed to do now. I was right; she looked at him and opened her mouth to complain about me once more, and I swept my plate of food into her lap. 'Go on!' I shouted, 'Complain about that!' and fled to my room.

I lay curled up on my bed sobbing my misery and fear into a cushion. I hadn't meant to do what I'd done; the heavens alone knew how Mordecai would react now. The merest hint of a sound outside my door convinced me that he was coming; when at last he did come, it was wellnigh dark.

I expected him to set about rebuking me at once. Instead he entered without drawing attention to himself at all, and stood in the doorway almost politely, as though waiting for me to invite him closer. I didn't; I didn't even get up.

He coughed, and stated, 'We have not made a very good beginning with one another, Hadassah.'

That was true enough, but I said nothing. Did he want me to apologize? There was no way I was going to do that.

He continued, 'I have to tell you that Leah has left. She has kept house for me for fifteen years. Have you nothing to say to that either?'

The note of quiet reason in his voice suddenly reminded me of my father after all; a little shamed despite myself I responded, 'She's left? I didn't know slaves could leave.'

'Leah was no slave, Hadassah. I paid her a fair wage. But she was nervous about your coming ever since she heard of it; older folk are wary of change. I assured her that you would be a help to her, since she is no longer as sprightly as she used to be.'

I muttered, 'I thought she was a slave. Everyone has slaves in Shushan, so they say. Hundreds of them.'

'Even if she were a slave, that would be no reason to treat her like a dog. And I have no slaves. We are all God's creatures and he alone is our master.'

I wanted to say, then why treat *me* like a dog? Why take away my mirror and my jewels and my dresses, the only things I have left to remind me of home? But I didn't quite dare, and sought refuge once more in a wretched silence.

'Well,' said Mordecai, 'No doubt it would be too much for me to expect that you might say you're sorry. I never once heard your father say it, when all is said and done. So I shall be content with your contrite manner.'

With that he went out, and he still hadn't blessed me with anything I should have called a smile. I lay down on my mattress again and tried to sleep, but the heat weighed down on me, pressing on my forehead and my chest, enveloping me like swaddling bands. No matter how hot a day was in Jerusalem, night was never like this, and the air was never so humid that you found yourself lying in a pool of perspiration. After a while I got up and went to the window—a tiny square hole cut into the otherwise featureless wall of the forecourt—but it was no fresher outside than in.

I must have slept eventually, and long—when I opened my eyes it was fully light, in fact the sun was high enough to be visible above the forecourt wall. I got up swiftly and guiltily; at home we had never lain in bed after dawn, but then, at home I'd never had a room to myself without the noise of others moving about to make me stir.

I'd slept in Leah's dress, and the sweat and the tossing had made it a mass of creases. Briefly I regretted antagonizing her, for I didn't relish the prospect of spending my days alone with Mordecai, or alone altogether.

In the event, I didn't have to do either. When I ventured from my room I was met at once by a tall, formidable lady who introduced herself as Mordecai's sister. She needn't have said so; I would have guessed in any case. I smothered a resigned sigh, and followed her to the living room, where breakfast was apparently waiting.

So was Mordecai; and he had the air of one who has been waiting for some time.

'My sister Ninlil has generously offered to stay with us for a while,' he informed me, without troubling himself to enquire whether I'd slept well, or even bidding me good morning. 'It isn't wholesome for a young girl to be brought up in a house without a woman there to give her appropriate guidance. Now, I trust that you will condescend to take food with us today.'

48

I nodded. All at once it seemed pointless to create unnecessary problems for myself. I wasn't going to better Mordecai for strength of will very easily—nor his sister, from the look of her.

Besides, I was ravenous.

Over the next few days, life rapidly acquired a pattern—which I suppose was good for me. I needed some stability after the upheaval of the three months gone, and although the routine which emerged was domestic and tedious, it could have been worse. Ninlil got me up early each morning—only on my first day had I been allowed to lie in late and sleep off the ill effects of my journey. Once up, she worked me hard: baking bread, sweeping floors, scouring dishes. But she wasn't unkind, and it seemed she wasn't scared of me, as Leah had been. Oddly enough, that made me feel safer.

In the afternoons we would spin or weave, or tend and water the herbs and flowering plants which Mordecai grew on a tiny plot of land at the back of the house. Ninlil called it a garden, and said that most folk in Shushan had one; Persians loved to bring nature right into their towns and cities. Despite myself I began to love it too; being there somehow made my heart feel lighter, and the leaden Shushan air less oppressive. Some of the flowers smelt sweet as perfume, and Ninlil allowed me to cut a few and put them in my room. She was almost as solemn an individual as her brother, but at least I didn't feel that she actively disliked me. I was sure that Mordecai did, and wondered if he regretted taking me in.

Most days Mordecai went out after breakfast and stayed away until sundown. I wondered what he did all that time; I couldn't imagine him working in the fields or on a building site. Then Ninlil told me that he was a banker—or to be more precise, a financial adviser in a Babylonian-owned banking firm, in which he was shortly to be made a partner.

I found it bleakly amusing that such a miser should be employed in advising folk how to manage their wealth. He was paid highly for his expertise, yet every part of his house was as drab and bare as the first room I'd seen.

In addition to his duties at the bank, Mordecai was a self-appointed spokesman for the foreign communities in the city, and Ninlil told me that he frequently went to the palace to present claims and complaints on behalf of clients. He was as highly respected in this role as in his financial one. Sometimes these clients would come to the house in the evening, and Ninlil and I would retire dutifully to another room. I tried to picture the sombre Mordecai being admitted to the great gleaming palace, and almost wished I could go with him. I hadn't set eyes on the palace, or the mountains, or indeed anywhere outside of my cousin's house, since my first afternoon in Shushan. That had only been a few days before, but already it felt like weeks.

'Can't we go *out* anywhere?' I moaned to Ninlil one morning, as we sat in the kitchen waiting for a batch of dough to be leavened.

She raised a sardonic eyebrow. 'And where do you propose that we should go? Respectable women do not walk the streets of Shushan like peddlars, you know.'

'Don't you have other kinsfolk or friends we could visit? You must have lived somewhere before you came here.'

She looked a little taken aback at my prying. 'I lived with another cousin of yours, and his wife and children and a widowed aunt. I *shall* go and visit them, come next sabbath. So you will be free from your chores for a day, and Mordecai will keep an eye on you.'

'Can't I come with you instead? No one ever told me I had all these kinsfolk in Shushan.'

'There are many things which the Pioneers don't tell their children, Hadassah. You may ask Mordecai's permission to come with me, but I can't see him granting it.'

Nor could I. He would probably be anxious that I might run away, and that would do his high reputation no good at all. I said, 'I've hardly seen him for days. He works much too hard to keep an eye on me.'

'Not on Shabbat, he doesn't; though he does teach a boys' Torah class some weeks. I think he gets lonely when he doesn't work.'

I considered that for a moment, but dismissed it; Mordecai was far too cold and aloof to derive enjoyment from company. I asked daringly, 'How come he never got married?'

'He *was* married, once,' she answered, then paused as if she wasn't sure she ought to go on. 'His wife died very young, of the summer fever. She was expecting their first child.'

I didn't know what to say. Nor did Ninlil, so eventually I asked whether *she* had once been married too.

It was clearly the worst way I could have chosen to try to change the subject. A change came over her which was so sudden and profound, it alarmed me. Her characteristic brusqueness was en-gulfed by chagrin; then her countenance became clouded, almost angry, like the sky before a spring storm. Perhaps her husband had died too, or else deserted her. But in that case I should have expected tears rather than something which more resembled fury. When I pressed the matter no further, she coughed, recovered her compo-sure, and enquired with false brightness, 'Well, young lady, what sort of thing did you do back in Jerusalem each sabbath, which was so much more exciting than here?'

I shrugged. 'Not so much, I suppose. I played with my friends. Or we used to go and watch the grown-ups and the older children rebuilding houses or working in the fields.' I swallowed hard. 'If I'd still been there, I'd have been working with them by now.'

'Well, be thankful you don't have to do spade-work outdoors in this heat. Don't you know that lizards and snakes burn to death here if they try to cross the street at noon in summer when the wind is from the south? And if you spread out barley to dry, it will pop like grain roasted in an oven.'

I managed a smile, seeing that she was trying in her own curt way to cheer me up with her exaggerations. But thinking about home had done me no good, because that night I had terrible dreams and woke up shivering even though the room was as hot as our bread-oven. I was back in Jerusalem on the night of my party, the hollow-chested boy was astride me once more—only he was heavy, so heavy that I feared I would be crushed. And this time the house wasn't silent. I could hear the shrieks and moans of the dying, and see blood running in through the doorway towards my pallet. Just as the stream reached me and started to stain my blankets, I awoke.

The whole of the next day I was more wretched than I'd been since my first afternoon at Mordecai's. Ninlil knew something was more amiss than usual and tried to talk to me, but I wouldn't be drawn. She had hardened herself inside too much to understand such things, I'd decided, and besides, it was talking which had brought on the night-mares. I would face them on my own.

However, this proved harder than I'd expected. I thought so much about them all day, and how to combat them, that they were already filling my head when I went to sleep that night. No matter whether I

51

slept or lay awake, they wouldn't go away. I kept remembering
Father's pronouncements about self-control, and Sarah's conviction
that I was strong deep down within myself. Yet what hope was there
for me if I couldn't even control what went on inside my own head?

So I sat up on my mattress in the darkness, hugging my knees, and
for the first time since coming to Shushan I tried to pray. Falteringly
to begin with, then desperately, I addressed Adonai aloud, begging
him not to forget me although I was an exile in a pagan land; and
begging him too not to forget the prayers which had been said on my
behalf on the day I reached eight. Afterwards I felt a little better, but I
wished I could see Adonai's face the way I could see Pithon's every
time I shut my eyes. Perhaps Adonai was reminding me that I ought to
be looking for Pithon—that was why I'd come to Shushan after all.

Rolling out the dough next morning I mustered all my courage and
asked Ninlil, 'What's a eunuch?'

Her eyebrows went up a little, but she could clearly see no reason
not to tell me. 'A man who has been gelded while he was still a boy, so
he isn't truly a man at all, and can never beget children.'

I was shocked to the core. I stammered, 'You mean—like a
bullock?'

'Exactly like a bullock. He becomes more docile, less hot-tempered
too.'

'And—does he look different from other men?'

'Of course. When he's young he stays slender like a girl instead of
broadening across the shoulders. When he's older his flesh runs to fat
just like a woman's does, unless he's careful.'

'And does he go bald?' Suddenly I'd remembered those soft,
plump, bald-headed men without beards I'd seen in the streets of the
city.

'Not necessarily. Eunuchs' heads are often shaved by their masters—so they *don't* look like women, I suppose, and to accord them
some respect. Eunuchs are highly valued here, but there were eunuchs
in Israel too once upon a time, when there were kings who could afford
to buy them. Why do you ask all this?'

I didn't answer. There was a lump in my throat so big I thought I
would choke. I worked on in silence, setting about the dough so
furiously that it wound up thin as a cobweb and I had to squeeze it up
and start again. Eventually I managed to say, 'I want to go out, Ninlil.
I feel like a prisoner here, or a slave. At home I could go wherever I

wanted, whenever I felt like it.' I was thinking, if Adonai wants me to find Pithon, I shall see him, out on an errand for his master.

Ninlil sighed, wiping flour on her apron. 'So you are still obsessed with tramping the streets like a washerwoman.'

'Tomorrow is Shabbat, Ninlil. Take me to see your kinsfolk. *You* could ask Mordecai for me.'

'As it happens, I already have done,' she said, with the merest hint of a smile, but it was more than I'd seen on her face or her brother's since my arrival. Spontaneously I threw my arms around her; she was patently embarrassed and for a moment so was I—all at once I realized this was the first time I'd felt the warmth of another person's closeness since parting from Sarah. But then Ninlil said, 'Don't get too excited yet, young lady. Mordecai insists that you stay here, for he wishes to spend Shabbat with you himself. He has cancelled his boys' Torah class in your honour, and the prayer meeting he hosts in the evening for their fathers. But he says you may come with me to market the morning after.'

I clapped my hands in delight at this concession, but couldn't for the life of me imagine what a whole sabbath day with Mordecai would be like, or how we would fill it.

As it turned out, he had meticulously planned our use of the time. I should have guessed as much, because he was meticulous about everything. After breakfast we would study the Torah, since that was how Mordecai always spent Shabbat morning. In the afternoon we would each go to our rooms to pray, then before Ninlil returned for the evening meal we would talk together of our family and our faith.

None of this constituted a prospect to be looked forward to. We took a painfully polite breakfast, passing things to and fro across the table and barely looking at one another; I gazed instead into the flickering flames of the sabbath candles which Ninlil had lit at sunset the evening before.

Our study of the Torah didn't go quite as planned, because it hadn't occurred to Mordecai that I might be wholly unable to read. He claimed it was a disgrace for *any* Jew to be unable to read the Law of God, let alone one of *his* relations. I smouldered quietly under his disgust; he said I need not worry, the situation would soon be rectified. From the tone of his voice I wasn't sure whether he intended to effect this by teaching me, or by disowning me.

Meanwhile he set about reading aloud to me the whole of the portion we were to have read out by turns. There was nothing in it about restoration or rebuilding, nor even about God's love and the bounty of his provision. It was merely a list of rules and regulations about not planting cereal crops in the same field as grapevines, not hitching an ox and a donkey side by side for ploughing, and not wearing cloth made of wool and linen woven together.

Mordecai sensed my bafflement and explained that the passage was really all about keeping ourselves pure, and not being sullied by the influence of the evil around us which might lead us to mingle idolatry with true religion. I didn't argue, so he went on to the next passage which was about how a girl must be a virgin when she marries; I understood precious little of it, but pretended it all made sense to me.

Then he came to a verse which said that no one who had been castrated could belong to the People of God, and after that all the rest of it washed over me without my hearing a word.

The time I was supposed to spend in my room, I spent in the garden. I no longer even tried to pray. Adonai seemed as distant and aloof as Mordecai, and besides, I didn't see how I could have dealings with a God who would turn his back on my innocent brother. I sat and sweltered in the blazing sunshine, seeking comfort from the beauty of the flowers, thinking that some other god must have made them, some god I didn't know. My family, my faith, my sense of meaning were all gone. I was nobody, and nobody cared if I lived or died. When Mordecai came to find me for our time of talking, the sun had made me ill; I hadn't even noticed until I stood up. I was so sick and faint, he had to let me go to bed, and for that at least I was thankful. We'd had our day in the house together, and understood each other no better than before it began.

The next morning I awoke with Ninlil's hand on my brow. 'It's as hot as a brazier,' she declared. 'There will be no trip to market for *you* today. You have the summer fever.'

I sat up to protest; and at once knew that she was right.

Summer fever is common in Shushan. Most folk catch it several times during the course of their lives; children and the elderly and those not used to the climate are especially vulnerable. Some forms of it can kill you, as Mordecai's wife had been killed, but my dose was a very mild one. In three days I was up and about; on the fourth Ninlil took me to market at last, and I began to learn at first hand about the city and the country I was destined to have to look upon as home.

I'd expected the experience to be wildly exciting, but it was so long since I'd been among crowds, I was more daunted than when I'd first set foot in Shushan. The market was all crammed into one tiny, half-covered part of the town, referred to as the bazaar; Ninlil told me that well-bred Persians look down on traders and don't like to see their business going on, so they herd them all together and then keep out of their way.

'Then how do the Persian city-dwellers buy their food?' I asked her. 'Do they send foreign slaves?'

'They do if they need to, but they would never admit even to that. Most of them own their own land outside the city and live off its proceeds. They employ men to manage it for them, and may never even go there themselves.'

'And their clothes? Don't they even buy cloth?'

'They keep their own sheep; and their servants make everything on the premises—or their wives do, if they aren't so rich. The King will not even buy treasures for his palace. If he wants Egyptian glass he commissions an Egyptian to make it for him; every glazed brick in his palace is made by Babylonian technicians, exclusively for him. I tell you, the Persians leave trade to the Phoenicians, just as they leave banking to the Babylonians and Jews, and religion to the magi.'

'Who are the magi?'

'A special priestly clan, and a very powerful one; you see them everywhere in their black cloaks and hoods. They go back to the time before records were made—in fact there were magi before there was religion in the sense that the Persians have it now, as practised by the kings.'

'But what do they believe? How come there aren't statues every-where?'

'Because the Persians aren't heathen in the way that you're think-ing, Hadassah. They worship a single, invisible god just as we do, only they call him Ahura Mazda, the Wise Lord. The magi were idolaters, in the old days. Now they administer the Wise Lord's cult, though not everyone approves of them. They practise strange rituals and drink haoma, the milk of a plant that gives them visions. In secret they may be pagans yet.'

I said, 'Ahura Mazda, the Wise Lord; Adonai, the Lord... might they not be different names for the same god?'

'Don't ever let Mordecai hear you say that,' Ninlil snapped, but before I could ask why, we'd reached the meat-market and the stench banished everything else from my mind. Flies buzzed among the chopped carcases, and all around the heads of the stall-holders, but they didn't seem concerned; they were far too intent upon their haggling. I saw one fellow who looked Jewish, yet here he was prattling away in some foreign language and selling meat with the blood in it. I said as much to Ninlil, but she answered, 'He's speaking Aramaic—it's the only language everybody here understands. And he isn't a Jew, or I would know him. He's probably from Northern Israel, a Samaritan. Many were deported here long ago by the Assyrians, and they've had little respect for God's Laws ever since.'

I said very quietly, 'It was the Samaritans who murdered my parents.'

'That is hardly fair, Hadassah. Mordecai was told that no one knows who was responsible.'

'The Samaritans will have been behind it. They were behind everything evil which happened to us.'

To take my mind off all this, Ninlil began telling me of the other nationalities represented in the bazaar. I'd been near enough right about which were which, except she told me that the men in the tunics and trousers were mostly Medes rather than Persians, though the two peoples had fused almost into one; strictly speaking the Royal House was more Median than it was Persian. The men with the black leathery faces were Cushites from Africa, for that was how far the Empire stretched south. In the west and north it stretched almost to Greece, and in the east to lands I'd never heard of, whose names I couldn't begin to pronounce.

'And all these different races live together in peace?' I exclaimed. 'I haven't seen a single man with a sword at his belt.'

'That is because they aren't allowed to have such things. Nobody but the Imperial soldiers may carry arms in the city.'

After the meat-market came fruit and vegetables, and Ninlil told me the names of most of those I didn't know. Among the fruit were apricots and melons, pink grapefruit, pomegranates, oranges and citrons—I recognized the kinds I'd seen growing in the garden of the inn outside the city. As for vegetables, there were cucumbers and garlic as well as many varieties I did know, and some which not even Ninlil could identify.

Finally we reached the fabric stalls, and here I lingered wistfully. There were so many vibrant colours and gorgeous textures, I couldn't resist touching them and comparing them with the coarse homely stuff I was wearing myself. Ninlil saw my guilty longing and for a moment there was pity in her eyes. It was *only* for a moment, but that was enough for me to exploit it.

'Couldn't I have just enough of that soft blue shiny stuff to make a scarf?' I pleaded.

'Don't be foolish, Hadassah. That's silk, from east of India, and costs a year's wages for a sliver you can scarcely see. They say it's spun out of clouds by angels.'

I giggled. 'Come, Cousin Ninlil, you can't really believe that.'

'It seems no more ridiculous than the other suggestion I once heard, that it's spun by worms. Either way, only kings and lords can afford to acquire it, and they have no choice but to pay money for it, since the method of its manufacture is kept so secret.'

'Couldn't I have some of that blue linen over there, then? I feel so shabby.'

'You have good dresses of your own.'

'But Mordecai won't let me wear them. He's taken the nicest ones away, and hidden them with my jewellery.'

'Then he wouldn't let you wear a new blue linen scarf, either.'

'I wouldn't let him touch it. I'd guard it with my life if it were a present from you, Ninlil.'

I'd only said that to make her give in. But to my amazement she took it for the truth, and more amazingly still, she was touched. Muttering, 'Don't you go telling him where you got this,' she hastily bought me a length without even bothering to bargain with the trader. I looped it delightedly around my shoulders, and preened myself all the way back to the house.

That evening Mordecai spent in conclave with a group of intense-looking gentlemen who turned up just after we'd eaten.

'Who *are* they, Ninlil?' I hissed as we made ourselves scarce. 'Are they more of his clients, come to see about loans?'

'No. They are the elders and scholars who normally come on the evening when Shabbat ends, to discuss the Torah. I told you about them. Their session was rearranged this week because of you.'

I smiled. It was gratifying to think that I'd interrupted the schedule of these august personages, and all for nothing because I'd been in bed with the fever. I said, 'I can't think what they find to discuss. Surely you either obey the Torah or you don't.'

'If only it were so simple,' Ninlil lamented. 'But in any case,' she continued, 'they don't confine themselves to discussion. They pray together, and some ask Mordecai to pray especially for them. Some come to him for advice about spiritual things, some for healing. He's a very holy man.'

'And he is also a doctor?'

'Not in the Babylonian sense. He knows nothing of medicines or powders. He heals in the way the great prophets did in olden times, though not so often and not so dramatically. Prophecy is not so powerful in our day as it once was.'

'So he will be shut away in the living room with them for many hours?'

'Yes, he always is.'

'Then, Ninlil...' I drew the scarf from where I'd hidden it down inside my clothing and smoothed it out lovingly on my lap. 'Let's go into his bedroom, and you can help me get back my things which Mordecai has put away.'

She was horrified. 'I should whip you for even suggesting such a thing! Stealing is a sin of the basest kind.'

'How can I steal what belongs to me?' I lowered my eyes, so she might think I was crying. 'My jewels are all I have left to remind me of my mother.'

'I'm sorry, Hadassah. When you've been here longer we shall go to Mordecai together and ask him to return them. He may just agree, if you are well-behaved and he's convinced that you mean no harm by your request.'

But that wasn't good enough for me. I had talked Ninlil into taking me to town, and buying me a scarf. I was beginning to get the things I wanted here as I'd done at home, and now I would not be thwarted. I bided my time, going to bed as usual once it got dark, and listening to ensure that Ninlil was settled too. Then I picked up my lamp—from my final week in Jerusalem until this very day I have never gone to bed without keeping one within reach—and made my way silently to Mordecai's private chamber.

I'd never been inside it. Excited rather than afraid, I looked about me. If anything, the room was more austere even than the rest of the house. There was nothing on the walls, and no matting on the floor.

The only contents comprised one rolled-up sleeping-pallet, and a plain wooden chest.

Biting my lip, I tried the lid. It wasn't locked, and came open easily. Finding my things was easy too, because there was little else inside: merely one spare robe and a few lengths of the cloth he used for his turban. My dresses were right at the bottom; I didn't attempt to get them out, for they weren't what I was most interested in, and I still had one or two in my room which I was permitted to wear on Shabbat. My neck-chain, earrings and mirror were wrapped up together in a piece of sacking bound with knotted cord; you couldn't see what the package consisted of, but you could feel the shapes.

Of course, I should have closed the chest at once and taken the package back to my own room to undo. But my heart was racing with the thrill of my daring, and the sensation was exhilarating. Besides, Mordecai's meeting wouldn't be finished for hours.

Clumsy with anticipation, I fumbled and fought with the knots, wishing I had a knife to slice through them. Eventually I worked enough of them free to slide the cord away, and my precious possessions tumbled out onto the floor.

When Mordecai came in, I was sitting cross-legged on the closed chest in all my finery, gazing at my flickering reflection in the bronze mirror.

I knew he would be angry. But he was normally so dignified and so self-restrained in everything he did, maintaining his equanimity even when I'd upturned my food in Leah's lap, that I supposed he would remain calm now too. His anger would be of the cool and withering type, a type with which I was quite familiar because my sister Rachael had been a talented exponent of it.

How wrong I was. Mordecai lost control immediately and utterly, flying at me like some fiend from a nightmare, all the while berating me so loudly that in a moment Ninlil had come running, in a state of half-dress. She stood aghast in the doorway, afraid to come near while her brother set about me, striking my face and wrenching the necklace from my breast so savagely that its wire broke, and the glittering beads scattered to the four corners of the room. He went for my earrings next but I managed to get away before he caught hold of them, for I was terrified that he would tear my earlobes just as Rachael's murderers had torn hers. I ran to Ninlil and clung to her; she tried vainly to quiet me, for I found that I was shouting and shrieking as loudly as Mordecai.

He strode towards us, and momentarily I feared he would strike his sister too, for protecting me. But one glance at the horror stamped on her face seemed to deflate his rage; he turned away and barked, 'Get out.'

Ninlil dragged me away in desperate haste, lest I should dare to disobey and choose instead to prolong the confrontation. She deposited me on my mattress and harangued me, wanting to sound reproving but instead betraying her own fear.

'What were you thinking of, you stupid, selfish girl? Look at you! Your cheeks are all swollen, your neck is red raw . . . oh, and your lip is bleeding; see, let me clean it . . .'

She took a loose fold of her dishevelled garment and licked at it, meaning to dab it on my face, but I was in no mood for fussing. I yelled, 'Whose fault is it that I look like this? I thought Mordecai was a holy man! A healer! He is worse than a Samaritan and has a temper like a mule!'

'Hadassah, be quiet, he will hear you!'

'I don't care! I hate him, and I hate his house, and I hate you! You should have come with me in the first place, then he couldn't have got so angry! I only wanted my own things! Why should he care what I wear anyhow? Riches are a sign of Adonai's blessing; my mother said so. I thought Mordecai was Adonai's servant. But he's evil! He ruined my necklace, the one Mother gave me for my birthday! Well he won't get my earrings, or my mirror, not unless he kills me first.'

Then I burst into tears, and Ninlil comforted me, rightly supposing that I didn't hate her at all.

After that, life at Mordecai's house deteriorated still further. There was an increased understanding between Ninlil and myself, but an increased tension too, as she found herself standing on the shaky middle ground between her brother and me. All she would say about his temper was, 'He knows he has his faults. They are a source of much sorrow to him.'

But he didn't apologize to me. Then again, I didn't apologize to him for rifling his room. But I dreaded the next sabbath, when I would be alone with him again. I'd failed to persuade Ninlil to stay at home with us.

'You will be all right if you're well-mannered and respectful,' she said. 'If you were as grown-up as you seem to think you are, you would use the time to try to put things right between you and your cousin.

After all, he has taken you in and given you a home, and you don't have another anywhere. You might as well make up your mind to be happy in this one.'

There was sense in what she said, and in my more mature moments I had to admit it. So I decided I would try, I really did. I was polite all through breakfast, I listened patiently when Mordecai read from the Torah to me, and when he went through the letters of the alphabet which he said I must learn.

Then in the afternoon, the boys came for the Torah class. I was told to go to my room and so I did, but through the little latticeless window I could watch them assembling in the forecourt, and it was so exciting to see other children in the house that I couldn't tear myself away. The smallest was perhaps six, most of the others were eight or nine, but a few must have been going on thirteen and in fact were not children at all. They arrived carrying tablets, and wearing little caps just as the boys often did back in Jerusalem. While they were waiting for some tardy classmates, they fell to teasing one another, knocking the smaller ones' caps off, sniggering and joking, and I realized that they weren't using Hebrew but Aramaic, the common tongue I'd heard spoken in the market. Mordecai wouldn't like that, I knew; I imagined him appearing at any moment and rebuking them.

Then one of the older ones saw me at the window. He gave me a slight sideways smile; soon one of the others saw what he was looking at and they all began nudging and pointing. Blushing scarlet, I withdrew, but they started calling to me, asking my name and inviting me to come out; they wouldn't hurt me.

And out I went. It was foolish, I know, but it was just so long since I'd spoken to anyone my own age, let alone a boy, that I forgot myself and everything else. They crowded about me besieging me with questions, and thoroughly enjoying the attention I told them I was Mordecai's cousin, an orphan, and had come to live with him.

Then simultaneously their voices trailed off, and their faces turned away in the same direction. A short distance from us stood Mordecai himself.

This time I honestly hadn't expected him to be angry with me. I hadn't been deliberately disobedient; at home in Jerusalem I'd still mixed freely with boys, and would have continued to do so for another two years at least. I thought he might well be angry with *them*, for their noisiness, and for using a language other than Hebrew in his house.

When I realized it was me he was glaring at, my heart sank. He told me to return to my room; he would deal with me when his class was over. And he called me a harlot.

I didn't know the word, but I knew the expression on his face; if the boys hadn't been watching, he would have beaten me there and then. I retreated to my room as instructed, and lay on my mattress awaiting his visitation. But the longer I lay there, the more worked-up I got, and the more my room began to feel like a prison.

Finally I made up my mind. I would pack my few remaining possessions and go. I had no idea where to, but whatever happened to me, it could be no worse than what would undoubtedly happen if I stayed. Somewhere out in the city were Sarah and Judah; and somewhere was Pithon. I would cast myself upon the mercy of Adonai, and if he proved to be as merciless as his disciple Mordecai, well so be it.

4

If I'd run away in Jerusalem, I wouldn't have got beyond the end of the first street before someone spotted what I was up to and marched me off home, Abihail's self-willed daughter or no. But the Jewish quarter of Shushan on a sabbath afternoon was deserted. So was the rest of the city, it seemed, for the day was far too hot for prudent folk to be out of doors by choice. Everything was silent as death, save for the shrilling of crickets and the slapping of my sandals through the dust. Already I wished I'd brought some water with me, but I hadn't thought.

The one thing I *had* thought to do was disguise myself as a boy, for Ninlil had made it abundantly clear that respectable young girls never go about alone in Shushan. This disguise I'd effected by making my blue scarf into a turban to hide my long hair, then tearing the bottom off one of the coarse woollen dresses which Mordecai made me wear to do my chores, and girding up the remainder into my belt.

But in the event the ruse did me no good. As I paused for breath in an apparently empty alleyway, a gang of ragamuffin street boys appeared from nowhere. Almost before I'd grasped what was happening, they'd jumped me, knocked me to the ground, and stolen my belongings. While they were working me over, they were laughing and crowing, calling me Jewboy and Hooknose, Nomad and Peddlar. As I sought to shield myself from their blows I found myself praying as I'd never prayed before; and the beating ceased. One of the ruffians had torn off my turban, my hair had spilled around my shoulders, and they'd seen I was a girl.

I'm not sure whether it would have been better or worse for me if they'd known from the beginning. But the shock rattled them enough now for them to scatter without doing me any further damage. I lay where they'd left me, dazed and faint and winded.

I don't think I was there long, though I could have fainted altogether for a while and lost track of time. Presently someone came

63

and peered into my face, then stooped and lifted me up. I didn't care who it was. I didn't care about the loss of my blue scarf, earrings, mirror and spare clothes, or the blood I could taste in my mouth from where the split in my lip had reopened, or where I was being taken . . . just so long as it wasn't back to Mordecai's.

I must have fainted then if not before, because the next thing I remember is waking up in some low dark room and hearing female voices conversing in a tongue which was neither Hebrew nor Aramaic. Struggling to sit up, I saw that the voices belonged to a woman in her thirties with two infant girls clutching at her skirts, and a girl of roughly my own age, presumably another of the woman's daughters. All of them had skin pale as Persians', but hair the colour of ripe corn. They could only be Greek.

They came and sat down next to me, no doubt asking if I felt better now, but I couldn't understand a word they said. I think they tried Aramaic as well as their own language, but I hadn't a single word of that either.

So they gave me water to drink, and sponged my face, then tried to get me to take food. Instinctively I refused, having been taught ever since I was weaned not to accept food prepared by Gentiles, and they didn't force me. By a mixture of speech and gestures the woman got across to me that her name was Helena, and that this was her eldest daughter Iphigenia; then they made signs to ask my name, and my parents' names, and where I lived.

I told them I was Hadassah and that my parents were dead; my guardian hated me and had thrown me out of his house so I was looking for my brother. They stared at me nonplussed, so I repeated everything more loudly and with bigger gestures, but this time made the mistake of mentioning Mordecai by name. I wouldn't have thought it could matter; surely no one had heard of him outside the Jewish community? But I'd forgotten that he acted as spokesman for the other displaced peoples as well. My blood ran thin as it dawned on me that they knew of him, and knew where to find his house.

I begged and begged them not to take me back. Even with no shared language my meaning couldn't have been clearer as I wailed and clutched at their garments. The girl Iphigenia must have had more sympathy for my distress than her mother did, for she began arguing with her, apparently on my behalf. But all the while I knew deep down that they would have no choice. Mordecai was a man of considerable influence, it seemed, and no good could come to a family which went out of its way to antagonize him. The man of the house came in—I deduced it was he who had picked me up from the gutter—and they began talking, no doubt making arrangements to escort me home.

So Adonai had delivered me from one beating only to condemn me to another—if indeed it *was* Adonai who had listened to my prayers. I lay back in wretched bewilderment with one arm across my eyes to hide the tears. I would never find Pithon. I would never find Sarah and Judah. I would live out the whole of my life as a domestic drudge for a man whose heart was as hard as the Temple rock. I'd often heard it said that Adonai was completely powerless outside the Promised Land; now I reckoned I'd proved that conclusively for myself. No wonder Mordecai looked so burdened all the time—it came of years spent trying to be heard by a distant godling, in a forgotten land where another deity held sway. The so-called Wise Lord Ahura Mazda was far from being Adonai by another name. He was Adonai's sworn enemy, and must be up in Heaven laughing at him, and at us. Perhaps he'd defeated Adonai even in Israel itself; after all, when you looked at them honestly, the Chosen People were no more than a boatload of peasants paddling a leaky vessel on a backwater of the mighty Empire of Persia.

My utter desolation must have spoken through my face just as powerfully as it had in my gestures, for suddenly Iphigenia, who was still sitting beside me, seized hold of both my hands and squeezed them tightly between her own. I was more confused than ever. She was a foreigner, a Gentile, a pagan, and yet hers was unquestionably the kindest face I'd seen since Sarah's. I wished with all my heart that I knew some Greek, or even Aramaic.

Then Helena her mother got me up, and gave me to understand that her husband would now see me home. I thought about feigning a relapse in my condition, yet it would merely deter the inevitable. Iphigenia hugged me when I left, and reminded me so unexpectedly of Deborah that I couldn't bring myself to respond.

Our journey back took much longer than I'd anticipated; I must have been dead to the world for quite some time after being rescued from the roadside. It transpired that the Greeks of Shushan didn't live in the city proper, but in a self-contained village outside the walls. The sun was setting when we reached our destination, and I was aching with fear.

But it was Ninlil who opened the gate. She embraced me, murmuring, 'Adonai be praised,' and it was so radically unlike her that I was startled rather than heartened. She thanked my saviour profusely in Aramaic, and I think she invited him in, but doubtless he wanted to be home while there was still some light.

And Mordecai didn't beat me. Ninlil took me through to the room he used as a study; it must have been where he'd taught the boys that afternoon, for one of their caps and a wax tablet lay where they'd been forgotten, on the floor. But now their teacher was quite alone, sitting at a table with his elbows upon it, and his finger-tips pressed against closed eyes which had sickly black shadows beneath them. He didn't even notice we'd come in, until Ninlil called his name softly, and he lowered his hands.

He looked so relieved that I actually felt a little guilty, for I was sure it wasn't merely the preservation of his good reputation that he was grateful for. But he said nothing, by way of welcome or rebuke; he merely nodded, and Ninlil took me away to tidy me up.

In the wake of my absconding, I expected things to be worse even than before. Of course I was punished: I wasn't permitted to leave the house at all for two whole weeks, even with Ninlil. Yet in other ways, Mordecai treated me no more harshly. When Shabbat came again and Ninlil went visiting, he read to me from the Torah and gave me another lesson in my letters, but made no reference to my little adventure whatsoever. Then the boys came for their class, and I saw no more of him that day.

When Ninlil returned in the evening, she brought me a new blue scarf and bronze mirror, whispering, 'Don't you tell Mordecai that I bought them on Shabbat.'

'As if I would.' I kissed her on the cheek and smiled at her ill-disguised embarrassment. 'I never talk to him about anything, and he never talks to me. He can spend a whole morning teaching me, but he never *talks*, not really.'

'He finds it difficult, Hadassah. He isn't used to children.'

'He teaches those boys every week.'

'Because their fathers wish it, and because he considers it his duty. But I don't suppose he "talks" to them either. He sees them as worldly and insolent; and so they are, most of them.' She paused for a moment, then said, 'It isn't that he doesn't like you, Hadassah. It's just that when you arrived here with your Pioneer friends . . . you weren't quite what he was expecting.'

'What *was* he expecting?'

'I don't think he really knows. A timid little waif who would do as she was told, I suppose; though he says himself that if he'd stopped to think about what your father was like, he would have been better prepared. But it was so long since they'd gone their separate ways, he'd almost forgotten.'

'Did they quarrel really badly? Before my father went back to Jerusalem? What about?'

'About the Restoration, and whether it was within the will of Adonai.'

'Mordecai thinks it wasn't?'

'He has considerable doubts, let us say. But he's quite a lot older than I am, Hadassah. The quarrel took place when I was too young to pay much attention. You'll have to ask him about it yourself.'

'I daren't, Ninlil. I daren't ask him about anything. He's so impatient.'

'Oh, Hadassah, I do wish you would try a little harder to see things his way. He *is* a good man, and you would find it so, if you weren't so stubborn. He has promised me he will do what he can to make you feel happier here. He won't take away your new scarf or mirror. He will return some of your dresses that he keeps, to replace the ones you had stolen. And he will let you come out with me whenever you like, once your punishment is over.'

'Will he let you take me *wherever* I like?'

Ninlil was right to become wary. 'It all depends on where you're minded to go, I suppose.'

'You'll find out, when I'm brave enough to ask him.'

I asked him over our meal one evening, a day or so after my fortnight's detention came to an end. I said, 'I want to take a present to the people who looked after me.'

There was a long, stiff silence. Then Mordecai said, 'They were Greeks, Hadassah. Gentiles.'

'I know they are Greeks. But they were kind to me. It's only right to say thank you.'

Brother and sister exchanged glances; I waited, almost enjoying the tension. Finally Mordecai announced, 'Very well. You may go there just once. What did you have in mind to take them?'

I'd had nothing in mind; I'd been too busy arming myself for the battle over my going there at all, and was surprised at how easily it had been won. So I asked, 'What do you think would be fitting?'

It was Mordecai's turn to be taken aback. He was well used to being asked for advice by all and sundry, but never by me. Ninlil said, 'All the Greeks in Persia are poor. A little gold might not go amiss. Shall we take it tomorrow?'

'No,' I said. 'Not yet. I want you to teach me some Aramaic first.'

Mordecai stiffened again. He suspected I was seeing how far I could go; and he was probably right. I pointed out that if I was meant to live in Shushan for any length of time, I would have to understand its speech; he concurred, but grudgingly. He no doubt considered it unnecessary for a woman, who would marry a good Jewish husband and never need to mix with Gentiles in her life.

'But *you* speak Aramaic,' I said to Ninlil afterwards. 'How did *you* come to learn it?'

Almost before the question was off my lips I was wishing I hadn't asked it. For the change came over her which I'd witnessed once before, on the only other occasion I'd ever asked her about her past. She looked angry, flustered, fearful and ashamed, all together, but eventually recovered herself enough to answer me.

'Our parents weren't renowned for their piety, Hadassah. Why do you think they gave us names like Ninlil and Mardukaya? They came from Babylon, and wanted us to be accepted by the people there. But my brother used to listen to the prophets and the rabbis, just as your father did. Perhaps they sat and listened together, and each became as zealous for his Jewish inheritance as the other, though in their different ways. And I ... I turned to Adonai later. Much later.' The expression on her face was so peculiar then that not even I was so insensitive as to pry further.

Over the next week, Ninlil taught me as much Aramaic as I could digest—which was quite a lot, because I'd always been quick-witted, and I was desperate to learn. An excitement grew within me at the prospect of seeing Iphigenia once again; I was haunted by my failure to embrace her when I'd left, because it reminded me of the bad terms on which I'd parted from Sarah.

We hired a burly escort first thing in the morning, from among the men who waited for work each day; Ninlil knew that the Greek village was called Arderikka, but wasn't sure how to get there, and I wasn't confident of being able to recall the way either. Besides, we were a defenceless woman and a girl, carrying gold. The escort we chose was a Greek himself—of that we made certain—and when we entered Arderikka it became plain that he was well-known there, for he kept calling out to passers-by and being hailed in return. The outlandish appearance of his temporary employers was manifestly arousing great curiosity in the neighbourhood.

Iphigenia herself opened the door to us, and I saw at once that she had friends with her. Jealousy rose up in me, but subsided straight away when she proceeded to greet me like a long-lost sister. I tried out my Aramaic on her, introducing Ninlil and explaining that we'd brought a gift for the family. Iphigenia's Aramaic was little more fluent than mine, but her eyes shone when she discovered we could communicate even slightly. Helena and her husband, whose name was Philos, entertained Ninlil, and I was drawn within the circle of fish-eyed girls. They stared at my swarthy skin—for so it appeared to them, if not to my fellow Jews—and wanted to touch my coarse dark hair and my strange clothing. I didn't much care what they thought of me, so long as they let me sit among them. After a while we were all talking, laughing at one another's broken Aramaic, and they began trying to teach me some Greek.

Towards noon the other girls went off home for the siesta, but the family wouldn't hear of our leaving; the gold we'd brought them was probably more than Philos could earn in a year. The adults and Helena's two baby daughters stayed indoors, while Iphigenia took me outside into their tiny yard and spread two pallets in the shade of a bedraggled vine which her father was trying to grow to remind them of Greece. We lay side by side, grinning and giggling, and Iphigenia said haltingly, 'You look happy today. All different. Last time, you were sad. You made me sad too.'

And it was true, I *was* happy; at least, I was happy if happiness is being able to forget the sorrow of your past just for a while, and daring to hope there may be some solace in the future. But I didn't have enough Aramaic to begin to say how I felt, so I simply smiled, and gave Iphigenia the hug I'd been saving for her. We were friends from that moment, though we were different in every way. I was a Jew, dark and Semitic, of a well-to-do house and once-royal blood; she was a pagan who lived in a dingy hovel but had skin like alabaster and hair like Mordecai's gold, and the most strange and beautiful face I'd ever seen.

When the time came for us to go, Ninlil had to drag me forcibly. Iphigenia said, 'You will come back? Soon?' And I said yes.

Over our meal that night I gathered up all my courage once more and said to Mordecai, 'I made a friend this afternoon. I'd like to see her again.'

'The Greek girl? No, Hadassah. It's out of the question. You took your gift. Let that be sufficient.'

'But I wouldn't so much mind being here in Shushan with you and Ninlil if I had a friend. She said I looked happy today, and it was true.'

'It isn't seemly for girls to while their time away gossiping. You will soon be a woman, Hadassah, and a godly woman spends her days keeping house for her husband and children. You must learn right habits now.'

'Cousin Mordecai, I shan't marry for *years*,' I protested; and that was true, too, but not *so* many years. It's not uncommon for a Jewish girl to be married at twelve. 'And I *do* work hard, almost every day. But I get lonely.'

Ninlil suggested, 'We could enquire among our neighbours and invite some of their daughters here from time to time.'

Mordecai opened his mouth to reject this, then closed it again; at least such girls would be Jewish. But I said, 'I don't *want* to be friends with just *any*one. My friend is Iphigenia.'

I suppose that the principle of the matter was as important to me as the person concerned; part of the reason that I wanted Iphigenia as a friend was that she constituted another challenge to Mordecai's authority. He said with enforced composure, 'She is not of our people. Adonai will be displeased.'

'But *you* have dealings with Greeks. *And* Babylonians, and Persians; and Samaritans! And if Greeks are so evil, why did Adonai create them? Why did he make *any* of the people who aren't Jews? I thought he made *all* of us in his image; that's what the Torah says.'

I think that Mordecai would have boiled over then, had Ninlil not laid a hand on his wrist. 'Go to your room, Hadassah,' she said quickly, and I obeyed. I knew they would argue the matter out when I was gone, and that Ninlil would plead my case.

After that, I lived for my visits to Arderikka. I was allowed to go with Ninlil once between each Shabbat, and if truth be told, I think she enjoyed going there almost as much as I did. She missed women's company, and would chat happily with Helena and help her with the babies.

Once a set day had been established each week for my visit, Iphigenia made sure that none of the other girls from the village were there. This suited me well. Much as I'd enjoyed being the centre of their attention, I wanted one real friend more than a crowd of playmates, and I think Iphigenia felt the same. She was a popular girl, being pretty and gregarious, but she liked to be free of her regular companions once in a while, and to make them envious because only she had a friend from the city.

We spent all our time talking at first, then as we got to know each other better, we combed each other's hair and arranged it in the styles of our respective peoples, and we tried on each other's clothes. Iphigenia laughed with delight to see me in her gauzy tunic, with a mass of curls wound up on the top of my head and hanging in tendrils over my neck, and cheap bangles with snake-heads around my bare arms. For myself, I'd never seen anything more lovely than Iphigenia in one of my Shabbat dresses—I'd sneaked it out of the house by wearing it myself underneath the plain homespun Mordecai insisted upon for weekday attire. To complete the picture I draped my blue scarf over her loose fair hair; it matched the blue of her eyes so perfectly that it brought tears to my own. I said, 'You can keep the dress, Iphigenia. I have others. And you look so beautiful.'

Gradually we learned one another's languages, so that before long we could say whatever we wanted to say, either in Aramaic or Greek or Hebrew, or a mixture of the three. I discovered that all the Greeks in Arderikka came from the same place, a city called Eretria, and that they had been deported to Shushan quite recently by King Darayavaush—whom they called Darios. This was because they and the people of another city, Athens, had helped some fellow Greeks who lived in Asia Minor to rebel against the Persians. It was rare for the Persians to practise deportation; indeed, they normally allowed already-exiled populations to return home, as mine had been permitted to do. But then again, it was rare for subjects to rebel against such beneficent—and powerful—masters.

The Arderikkans however didn't regard the Persians as beneficent at all. They rejoiced that Darayavaush's expedition against Greece had ultimately failed to bring that land under his control; but by the time his forces were defeated, it had been too late for Eretria. Those who were deported were the lucky ones.

I learned something of the Greeks' religion, as well as of their history. But there was no danger of my becoming pagan overnight, because their beliefs were an utter mystery to me. It appeared that there were almost as many gods as there were Greeks, and if you neglected any one of this astonishing array of deities when you made your petitions and offerings, you ran the risk of being struck down in any one of a hundred ways.

There were some lovely stories, though. Iphigenia told me one about a young girl who had sacrificed herself for her people. The girl's father had been the admiral of a great fleet which was to sail to a city called Troy to recapture his beautiful sister-in-law, who'd been kidnapped by a Trojan prince. However, the admiral had annoyed some goddess and been told that he must sacrifice his own daughter in order to obtain a favourable wind for his ships. He'd tried to keep the truth from the girl as long as possible, pretending when he sent for her that she was to be married to a handsome hero. But in the end she had found out the facts, and gone to the altar willingly; as soon as she was dead, the wind had begun to blow. The kidnapped woman was called Helena, and the girl: Iphigenia.

So I told her something about my own name, and why it had been given to me. It was the first time I'd spoken to her about my past, and she wept for me. But I didn't tell her about Pithon. Not even my best friend was to find out that my brother was a eunuch.

Punctuated by such weekly excursions, the summer drew on. I saw less than ever of Mordecai, because most sabbaths I talked Ninlil into taking me visiting with her. Yet too many days were still spent cleaning the house, or washing clothes, or preparing food, and this was little more than tolerable to me. I couldn't see the point of much of it, for it all had to be done again a day or so later. Spinning and weaving were preferable, but even though I could see some lasting result from this form of labour, it gave me little sense of satisfaction. I knew full well that Mordecai was quite wealthy enough to have bought any amount of the finest, sheerest fabrics from the bazaar had he so desired, just as he could have bought slaves to clean and cook. The unnecessary simplicity of our way of life seemed to me to be grounded in an upside-down

72

sort of pride on Mordecai's part rather than in a genuine desire to identify with the poor and needy.

Then one day dawned which was noticeably cooler than the last. Autumn was approaching, and with it the month of Tishri which contains three of the most important Jewish festivals. First there is Rosh Hashanah when we commemorate the creation of the world; then the Day of Atonement when we ask forgiveness for every sin committed during the course of the year. Finally there is the feast of Tabernacles, when we remember the wilderness wanderings of Moses and the Children of Israel liberated from captivity in Egypt; they had nothing but tents for shelter, and so we build temporary shelters in our yards and gardens or on our roofs, and eat and sleep in them each night for a week.

These were the first festivals to be celebrated since my arrival at Mordecai's, and true to form he ensured that we kept them scrupulously. While Ninlil prepared seasonal foods, her brother had me help him build our tabernacle in the little forecourt; it was a distinct novelty to see him working with his hands. But this wasn't physical labour to him. It was spiritual, to be carried out in an attitude of prayer and in accordance with Adonai's instructions as given in the Torah. Palm, willow and myrtle branches must be used, and citrus fruit; all of these could be obtained with ease, except the myrtle. We had to use thorny mimosa instead.

Working side by side for most of the day at something which occupied neither the mind nor the voice gave me opportunity to ask Mordecai questions I'd wanted to put to him for some while. It also gave me time to work up courage to ask them. I ventured, 'Why *don't* you go back to the Promised Land, Cousin Mordecai? Why build this shelter and mourn that *you're* still in the wilderness, when you could go home, and take Ninlil and me with you?'

'Because,' Mordecai replied grimly, without taking his eyes from the branches he was weaving together, 'when it is right for us all to return, Adonai will give us a king, and restore to us the Ark of the Covenant. What use is a Temple without the symbol of God's presence? It is empty—an abomination, no less! And it is only allowed to exist because the priests are prepared to offer prayers for the Emperor of Persia. But the Pioneers don't care, because they don't care about God. It is politics they care about, and nationalism.'

I said, 'But Kurash was sent by God to conquer Babylon and let us go home. All the prophets said so.'

'And if the first Pioneers had listened to the rest of what the prophets said, perhaps there would have been hope for their enterprise. But they neglected God's laws, and their offspring still neglect them. The Ark could have been melted down for bullion, for all they are concerned. So their aspirations will come to nothing and all their efforts will be wasted, when there is vital work they could be doing here.'

'What work?' I demanded, and my voice sounded sharper than I'd meant it to, because of all the doubts and deflated dreams I was battling with inside.

'The work of saving the Jews of Persia from themselves.'

'I don't understand.'

'I didn't expect that you would. The Pioneers think they know everything, but they are ignorant as infants. They imagine that Adonai is without power outside Israel's borders. They even think that they *know* Adonai; they fancy that they are Shining Ones like the hallowed kings and prophets of the past. They believe their own lies and are deluded by their own fantasies.'

There were tears of indignation smarting in my eyes. 'The Jerusalem folk *do* know Adonai! My parents did! *I* do!'

At last Mordecai condescended to look at me. 'Your face shines with nothing but anger, Hadassah.'

'So what? *You* get angry, angrier than *I* ever do!'

'But I do not pretend to be anything special,' he said quietly, and I could see that he spoke with rueful sincerity. 'I know Adonai little better than I know King Darayavaush, in that I have met him, I have even spoken to him and heard him speak to me. But when you are lying prostrate on the ground, it is difficult to become intimate. Adonai has reached out his sceptre to me and bidden me rise, but I'm only now beginning to find my own feet.'

I was more bewildered than ever. I muttered, 'If you knew Adonai even slightly, you would be kinder to me. Ninlil says you want me to be happy, but there are so many things you won't let me do.'

'You think it would be kind of me to let you become an indolent gossip who passes all her time with pagans, and paints herself, and decks herself out with baubles like the Queen of Sheba? It is as I said, Hadassah: God's people must be saved from themselves. They must be saved from assimilation; from becoming as the Gentiles are. That is just as much a danger in Israel as it is in Shushan. We need to be *different* from outsiders in every way. We must spurn their riches, their

luxurious living. We must dress modestly and cover our heads, and
refrain from eating unclean food. Yet I have watched the very boys I
teach taking off their caps as soon as they leave my house, and I have
even come across them in town wearing Median trousers. I know for a
fact that in pagan houses they eat whatever is offered to them, for fear
of being considered peculiar.'

'I don't know why they should fear it. There is less persecution here
than there was in Jerusalem. I never heard of Jews being stoned in
Shushan.'

'I heard of a Jewish girl who was beaten and robbed in the street,'
said Mordecai, with a meaningful grimace; and for the first time since
I'd heard them I remembered the nature of the taunts with which
those ragamuffin boys had assailed me. Mordecai continued darkly,
'Those who have eyes see that there is a great deal of ill-feeling against
us, under the surface, and that there are a great many people who
would make trouble for *any* of the city's minorities if they were given
the chance.'

'Why? We aren't doing any harm. Who are these people?'

'The landless and those without work, those you see waiting each
day for someone to hire them. They see the foreign contractors coming
in to work on the palace, and being paid from the royal treasuries, and
they resent it. Yet if it were not for the charity given them by many
wealthy Jews, they would starve.'

'You give them money? At home there were *Jews* who were
starving! Why don't the rich Jews of Shushan send charity to *them*?'

'There are some who do: those who would like to return themselves
if only they had the courage. They send gold to salve their consciences,
though I don't think much of it reaches its destination. But it is pure
hypocrisy. They are as misguided as the Pioneers they admire, and
they know Adonai no better.'

'So what *does* it mean, to know Adonai?'

'It means that you delight in every moment spent in his company,
Hadassah, and that when you are not at prayer, you yearn for it, as it
seems you yearn to be with your friend from Arderikka. And it is as the
prophet Jeremiah said: the Law of God becomes written on your heart,
and a joy to obey. Jeremiah knew the mind of Adonai better than any
other holy man who has ever lived. He knew that our God is the God of
all the universe, not merely one tiny country; thus living in exile need
not of itself cause us to despair. He knew that the Temple and the

sacrifices and the festivals and the rituals are important—but nothing like so important as the faith of the individual, the fragile, flickering flame of divinity coming alive within the human spirit.'

He spoke these last words with such fervour that I was afraid to ask more.

But after this conversation with Mordecai—the longest we'd yet had by far—I began to watch him more closely for evidence of the intimacy with Adonai which he claimed to be nurturing. Ninlil said that he did most of his praying early in the morning, though he observed the other traditional daily prayer times also. So one day when I chanced to wake before sunrise, I got up, and tiptoed to his bedroom where I hid just outside the doorway. I could hear him praying already, out loud, though I couldn't make out what he was saying. He sounded so engrossed that I risked peeping around the doorframe, and there he stood, with a shawl up over his head, rocking himself back and forth with closed eyes. The lids fluttered as though he were dreaming, and the customary frown lines on his face seemed smoothed—but perhaps it was only with the dimness of the lamplight. I was in no danger of being caught; he was lost to the world.

I crept back to my room, and wondered if you *did* have to be pious and morose and miserly in order to receive anything from God. If that were true, I would rather be godless. Mordecai's God wasn't at all like the one I'd been brought up to believe in.

It wasn't only Mordecai's words which confused me. It was Iphigenia too. I'd always believed that pagans were evil; they lied, stole, cheated, brawled and murdered without even knowing they did wrong. But Iphigenia and her family did none of these things. They were generous and honest and honourable; more so than many of the so-called People of God. I began to wonder whether being a Jew meant anything other than eating strange food and keeping strange customs. It was scarcely surprising that the boys hid their caps and ate pork when Mordecai and his kind weren't looking.

As autumn progressed, a wave of excitement surged through the city. I learned that the Great King and his entourage were about to return from Ecbatana, their summer retreat in the mountains. It was rumoured that the King's son, Crown Prince Kshayarsha, was extremely handsome, and I begged Ninlil to take me to watch the cavalcade approaching. However, she said there would be nothing to see; the King and his family travelled in curtained litters, for their faces are not to be looked upon by common people. 'Besides,' she added, 'The young Crown Prince may be good-looking, but he is also cruel. He's the satrap—that is, the governor—of Babylonia, and much hated there, so they say.'

Autumn turned to winter, and I couldn't believe that Shushan could be so cold, or so wet. Snowfall in the mountains and deluges on the plain turned the rivers to rampaging torrents, which regularly burst their banks and devastated the peasants' cottages which clung to them. We saw hailstones almost as big as pomegranates, and even one flurry of snow in the city. The wasteground between Shushan and Arderikka went from yellow dust to a morass of mud, then as spring stole upon us once again it became a riot of flowers and waving grasses. The acacias and tamarisks and poplars put on fresh mantles of green, and irises and lilies were everywhere.

My ninth birthday came and went, but Mordecai disagreed with observing such occasions. I was relieved; any sort of celebration would have been too painful. But it was ironic that I should be resident in Shushan yet living less like a Persian than I had in Jerusalem.

Passover at least was a more entertaining affair than the one I'd spent with Sarah and Judah in the middle of nowhere. The relations I sometimes visited with Ninlil all came to our house, and Mordecai led the mealtime service with passionate intensity, while everyone else ate too much and got shamelessly drunk. They all chanted in unison, 'Next year in Jerusalem!' with tremendous gusto, leaving me puzzled as to what they meant by it, if they had no intention of going there.

As summer returned, and everything but the oleanders lost its flowers and went yellow once again, a period of unrest began in Shushan. It was announced that the Great King was planning another expedition to Greece; understandably the population of Arderikka was plunged into fear and despondency. By Persian law, the King is supposed to name his successor before going off to war, but although Kshayarsha was referred to by everyone as Crown Prince and had been treated as such all his life, apparently Darayavaush had never had the legal documents drawn up which would establish him officially as heir to the throne of Persia. Now another of Darayavaush's sons, by a different wife, was claiming the right for himself, and fierce arguments had broken out at court.

Kshayarsha must have been confirmed in his position, but at the time I knew nothing about it because I went down with the summer fever again. This bout was a thousand times worse than the previous year's. Half the summer seemed to get swallowed up in it; all I can recall is sleeping, sweltering and shivering by turns, and the most dreadful dreams which I couldn't tell apart from reality. For days and days I was delirious; I couldn't face food, and anything I did eat came straight back up. Ninlil grew exhausted nursing me, washing the same bedclothes over and over again, and getting no sleep herself when I cried out in the night. Then one day I opened my eyes to find that at last I could see clearly, And what I saw was Mordecai kneeling by my side, his own eyes raised to Heaven and his hands poised over my forehead.

He didn't realize that I'd woken, so I lay in silence watching him. He was praying for me with an ardour as great as when he prayed by himself; there was perspiration on his brow so that I wondered if he had fever too. Then all at once he broke off and glanced down. Suddenly it wasn't only his brow that was moist.

'Ninlil? Ninlil!' he called. 'She is awake! Her spirit has returned to us ... thanks be to God.' And without a word to me, he rose and went to fetch his sister.

From that day on, part of me was unable to deny that he must love me, in some strange way of his own. But I didn't see any more signs of it. And despite his earnest desire to know God and to cast his burdens at the feet of Adonai, he did shoulder many anxieties for himself. He was anxious for his people's welfare, and for their very identity. This made him wary of any behaviour which fell outside the boundaries he'd drawn to define what was acceptable for a Child of God living amongst the heathen.

Once I became aware of things beyond the four walls of my sick-room, I realized that Mordecai had more reason to be fearful even than usual. The Great King Darayavaush of the glorious House of Hakha-manish would never again threaten Greece, because he himself was sick unto death.

The city was quiet as a tomb already, as folk came to terms with the truth that their mighty Emperor who ruled half the world was subject to disease and decay just like anybody else. Then one night we heard wailing up and down the alleyways, and knew that his hour had come. So loud and tortured did the keening become that there was no more sleep to be had; dawn was just breaking so Mordecai, Ninlil and I got dressed in silence and went outside.

At this ordinarily silent hour, the streets were thronged with people. Jews and Gentiles alike stood in stricken huddles by the roadsides, many with rent garments and some with shaven heads. By the time the sun was up, all of Shushan had taken to the streets, and the very stones echoed with their cries of mourning. I marvelled that they could summon up so much grief for a man on whom most had never set eyes.

It was only later that I learned it was themselves they'd been grieving for. Darayavaush had been kind to his subjects, merciful (on the whole) to his enemies, a champion of justice and a master of imperial administration. Above all, he had been tolerant of the many and varied religions practised within his empire and within the walls of its very capital.

But when the period of mourning was over, Kshayarsha the pitiless young Prince would be crowned, and who could tell what would become of us then?

5

The coronation didn't take place in Shushan, though I'd assumed it would. I discovered that the Hakhamanish Kings of Persia are always purified and invested in the ancient city of Pasagarda; though of course there was a period of holiday all across the Empire, and Shushan enjoyed more than its fair share of festivities and commemorative events.

The clamour of rejoicing rang hollow, however, and there can't have been many folk who failed to detect the undercurrents of apprehension that ran between the tables of those feasting in the streets and in the parks. Outside the capital, the uncertainty and the unrest bubbled up nearer to the surface; Egypt, which had never lain quiet, even under the benign hand of Darayavaush, was said to be on the brink of open revolt.

All in all there was plenty to give our new monarch cause for concern, but none of these anxieties showed on his face when he returned from the Pasagarda rituals to take his seat upon the great throne in the palace of Shushan. Not that we expected to see his face at all; although there were jostling multitudes lining the roads along which he would pass, they couldn't have been hoping for anything more than a glimpse of the royal litter, with its curtains tightly drawn. So Persian tradition dictated.

It appeared that tradition mattered little to Kshayarsha; he elected to enter the city in his battle-chariot.

This magnificent vehicle constituted an indispensable feature of any official procession. However, normally it was drawn along quite empty, as was the chariot of the Wise Lord Ahura Mazda. Any man who dared to step into the chariot of his king or that of his god would die for his audacity.

Kshayarsha cut an impressive figure. He carried a long golden sceptre, and wore a high, stiff, straight, battlemented headdress which made him seem taller even than he was. Beneath this, his hair and beard were elaborately curled, the way the long-dead kings of Assyria are depicted on their monuments. His crimson kilt and wide-sleeved cape were of swirling silk embroidered with rosettes of gold and purple; below the kilt I caught a momentary glimpse of silken trousers and blue leather shoes as his chariot swept by. As for his face, he was certainly young, but his expression was formally arrogant, and as stiff as his hat—for all that it gave away, he might as well have worn a mask, or hidden himself within his litter after all—so I couldn't decide if he looked cruel or not. I couldn't even be sure that he was handsome.

Once the procession had moved beyond us and the crowds had spilled into the street in its wake, Mordecai, Ninlil and I returned home. I resigned myself to the fact that we wouldn't be witnessing any more displays of imperial pageant for some considerable time, but almost as soon as the coronation holiday was over, another was declared: to celebrate a royal wedding.

Kshayarsha had taken as his bride a certain Vashti, the daughter of a prominent Shushan nobleman who was also a commander in the army. This Vashti was said to be very beautiful, but not even Kshayarsha was going to allow *her* to be seen in public. No aristocratic Persian is supposed to let any male outside his own immediate family look upon the faces of his concubines, let alone that of his wife.

The wedding afforded scant cause for celebration among the adults of the Greek community, but the children who had grown up in Arderikka and never known any different didn't harbour quite so much ill-feeling against the Persians as their parents did. Iphigenia herself was secretly entranced by the whole affair, and as we sat on pallets beneath the bedraggled vine in her courtyard we day-dreamed together about the romantic royal couple, whispering lest our fantasizing should reach disapproving ears. We tried to picture the glamorous robes and gorgeous jewellery which the bride and bridegroom would be wearing for the ceremony, and we wondered how long it would be before we heard that the young Queen was with child.

'Mother says that if Vashti doesn't conceive very soon, she may have a good while to wait,' Iphigenia informed me. 'The Great King will have to leave for Egypt shortly to quell the rebellion, or it will spread all over the Empire.'

'Must the King go and sort it out in person?' I asked, surprised. 'Poor Vashti! My people have a law that no man can be sent to war until he's been married for a whole year. That goes for the poorest peasant, let alone the King—if we had one.'

'Kings can't always do what they want. They have thousands of subjects to take care of, not just their own families. That's why most of the Greek states back in our homeland don't have kings at all, Father says.' Then she pursed her lips gravely, striving to recollect Philos' exact words: 'People should be free to take responsibility for themselves, not place all their hopes in a single man.' We both sat a while in reflective silence, then Iphigenia asked, 'Do *you* want to get married some day, Hadassah?'

'I suppose so. I hadn't thought about it.' And indeed I hadn't; among the Jews it is taken for granted that you *will* marry, for childlessness is regarded as a curse. 'Why?' I returned. 'Don't you?'

'More than anything,' she enthused, hugging her knees; above them, her face was glowing. 'I want to marry young, so I can have *lots* of children. But it depends on what the gods have willed for me. Perhaps the virgin goddess Artemis will claim me to be her priestess.'

I was perplexed. 'How will you find out?'

'My father will go to an oracle to consult about my future, when he can afford to.'

'An oracle? What's that?'

'Well, there is a priest or a priestess, and he or she will burn sacred herbs and go into a trance and . . .' Noting that I was more baffled than ever, she said, 'An oracle's a sort of fortune-teller, I suppose. Like the ones you see in the bazaar, only better.'

'There are fortune-tellers here in the bazaar at Shushan?'

'Of course. You haven't seen them? You have to pay them coins and they will throw sticks in the air and read a meaning from how they land. Or they will ask you when you were born, and read your future from how the stars looked on the day of your birth. Most of them are nomads from the desert, but the Babylonians are more skilful.' Then realizing I'd fallen pensive again, she leaned forward and demanded, 'Why? Do you want to know *your* future?'

I shrugged my shoulders, suddenly afraid of what I might find out. I answered, 'Ninlil wouldn't let me go into the city with you.'

'There's no need, if it's just an ordinary diviner you want to see. We have one here in the village, an old woman who's supposed to have been a priestess of Apollo, back in Eretria.'

'Has she told *your* fortune?'

'A dozen times. She says I'll have a wonderful husband and four lovely children, all of whom will live. But anyone can say that. She has the sight after a fashion, but she can't see things in detail, like the oracles do. Still, I can take you to her for fun if you like.'

A shudder ran up and down my spine. 'No, Iphigenia. No. I don't think so.'

Seeing how uncomfortable I looked, she didn't pursue the subject, and we spoke no more of it. But over the next few days I couldn't get it out of my mind. I hadn't really contemplated my long-term future at all before; surviving from day to day at Mordecai's had given me quite enough to think about. But now I began to wonder what it would be like to remain in his house for ever, sweeping floors and washing clothes. Perhaps he would try to find me a husband, but what kind of man would someone like Mordecai consider suitable for me? If one thing was certain, it was that I should get no say in the matter . . . All in all, the future seemed set to be as much of an ordeal for me as the past had been. At least if I had my fortune told and it was as dreadful as I envisaged, I could perhaps do something to try to change it before it was too late. And if the old village-woman could see things beyond the range of the natural eye, perhaps she would be able to see Pithon.

Thus I more or less decided that the next time I saw Iphigenia I would mention the old woman again. But on the day that Ninlil and I were due to go, I awoke to find blood on my bed-clothes.

Terror engulfed me. I wasn't yet ten years old, and no one had explained to me what it means to become a woman. I thought I was dying; kneading my aching belly with one hand, I struggled to fold up the soiled covers with the other, and Ninlil came in to find me trying to hide them at the bottom of my clothes-chest.

She guessed at once what had happened, and assured me that it was normal and natural and that without it I could never become a mother. But she seemed so embarrassed to be talking about such things that I refused to believe her. She went away, observing that I was in no mood to listen to sense, and I lay curled on my bed with a towel between my legs for the rest of the morning, waiting for the end.

It didn't come, and by noon I felt better and wanted to go out after all. But Ninlil said I must remain in my room for seven days, until the blood had entirely stopped, and after that I must take a special bath to make me pure again. During the period that I was secluded, I was to have no contact with Mordecai, nor indeed with any other man. Following my purification, life would return to normal; except that from now on I must never be seen outside the house without a veil. And every month, the affliction would come back.

I was distraught. I shouted at Ninlil, 'But *you* don't stay in your room for seven days every month! Neither did my mother!'

Ninlil responded softly, and with a hint of that strangeness which had come over her twice before in my presence, 'It is too late for me to have children now, Hadassah. I forfeited my chance. As for your mother ... the Pioneers have their own ways.'

Being confined in my lonely dark room drove me to distraction, when outside the sun would be shining on our little garden, and in Arderikka Iphigenia would be waiting for me and worrying. The Jews of Shushan were so strict about everything—at least, Mordecai was, and I became consumed by a fresh desire to defy him. So that evening, when I heard him conversing with Ninlil in his study, I crept out of my room and stood outside his, listening.

'She has started already?' Mordecai was asking. 'But surely this is very young! I thought most girls were eleven or twelve, some older still.'

'It's early, yes, but not unknown. I once knew a girl who was only eight.'

'No good can come of it, Ninlil. She is headstrong enough as it is, and she talks to boys without shame. Now she will give us more trouble than ever.'

'Why should she? Her behaviour isn't going to change overnight.'

'Her behaviour is quite disturbing enough already. Besides, she's uncommonly tall and comely for her age. You must watch her more closely from now on. These confounded visits to Arderikka, for example: does the Greek girl have brothers?'

'Not that I have seen or been told about. Mordecai ... don't put a stop to her going there. If you do, I fear she truly *will* become unmanageable.'

I smiled a smile of satisfaction and returned to my room.

As soon as my period of uncleanness was over I had Ninlil take me to Arderikka, even though it wasn't the usual day for our visit. Iphigenia was overjoyed to see me, having concluded I must have gone down with summer fever again. But the season was already too far advanced for that; it was that short but glorious time of year when the climate of Shushan is actually bearable, even pleasant. I told Iphigenia the cause of my recent confinement, and she regarded me with awe.

I beamed with pride at this, temporarily; then I was crestfallen. 'I haven't changed all *that* much, Iphigenia. I'm still the same Hadassah.'

'You don't—feel different? Not at all?'

'I don't know. How am I supposed to feel? I don't know anything about all this. Iphigenia . . . am I beautiful?'

'The Queen herself couldn't be prettier than you.'

'You really mean that? But I've felt so ugly ever since I came to Shushan.'

'You should have jewels and cosmetics and gorgeous gowns, then *everyone* would see how pretty you are. If your cousin is as rich as you say, he should give those things to you. How else will you attract a good husband?'

'I'm not supposed to attract anybody. I'm supposed to wait and see whether wise Cousin Mordecai decides to find a husband for me, then I'm supposed to grow to love this man after we get married.'

'And if you *don't* grow to love him? What will happen then?'

'Oh, Iphigenia, I don't know! I'm so mixed up inside! When I lived in Jerusalem I understood everything. I *knew* what life was supposed to be like when I grew up! Now I don't know anything! Sometimes I think I'd like nothing more than to marry a rich handsome Persian, live in his great house and have dozens of maids and slave-boys around me, wear and eat whatever I fancy, and forget I was ever Jewish; other times . . . Iphigenia, I want to see that old woman you told me about. I want to see my future.'

'I don't know how clear her sight is, Hadassah, I'm not sure—'

'But *you've* been to see her, you told me so! And more than once! Let me hear what she says and judge for myself. Let's go this afternoon, in the siesta, when everyone else is asleep.' I was on the verge of tears; coming into my womanhood so suddenly had brought everything to a head.

'Go on our own?' Iphigenia expostulated. 'Without Ninlil? Without even getting her permission? You'll be whipped when she finds out! You'll never be allowed to see me again.'

All the same, from the look on my face she knew there was little point in arguing further.

And it was all so easy, to begin with. Ninlil and Helena were both

sound asleep when we set out, as were their infant charges. No one
accosted us in the streets. Yet as soon as we stepped inside the fortune-
teller's house, I knew we shouldn't have come.

It looked just like any of the other houses—a squat mudbrick hovel
rubbing shoulders with its neighbours—but for some reason I couldn't
put my finger on, it gave me the shivers. The woman was as frightening as her home: shrivelled and stooping and exactly as I might have
expected a pagan sorceress to be, had I paused to think. However, she
threw no sticks up in the air, nor did she burn any herbs, nor go into a
trance or convulsions. She merely gazed at me very hard, and before
I'd even crossed her palm with silver or so much as said what I wanted,
she told me that a man whose seed had not gone into my making would
call me his own daughter; that I should become the Queen of Persia;
and that I should be the cause of the deaths of many thousands of
people. Then her eyes went very wide, and rolled back inside her head,
and she sank to the floor in a dead faint.

Iphigenia gave a little gasp and tugged at my elbow. But I was
rooted to the spot, rigid with terror, and had to be slapped hard on the
cheek before I would leave the house. All the way back Iphigenia kept
repeating that she had never known anything like this happen before
with the Arderikkan soothsayer; perhaps the woman was sick. But I
knew she wasn't.

When we arrived, Ninlil, Helena and the babies were still asleep,
and our disappearance had gone unnoticed. But a thousand lectures
from Ninlil or even from Mordecai would have worried me less than
the old woman's words. I couldn't get them out of my head, nor the
image of that shrivelled face with its eyes rolled back and its skin gone
slack with the stroke of her god. Iphigenia got me some hot mulled
wine and made me drink it, saying, 'Don't be scared, Hadassah. She
must be failing. She's entering her second childhood. How can you
become Queen of Persia?'

Her reassurances and the warm sweetness of the wine calmed me a
little, but I asked Ninlil to take me home when the sun was still high in
the sky. I said I felt ill and she believed me.

By evening I was more myself, however. The familiar routine of our
meal together, and helping Ninlil clear away and wash the dishes,
made everything seem normal and mundane again. For once I was glad
of the domestic round, and the vision of that dreadful face began to
fade.

Then when the pots had been finished, and I'd wandered out into the garden to savour the delicate scents of twilight, Ninlil came and touched my shoulder and said that Mordecai wanted to see me in his study.

I entered apprehensively, half-afraid that he'd somehow learnt of my act of disobedience after all. But it was on a different subject altogether that he wished to talk to me.

'Hadassah...' he commenced rather awkwardly, with a faintly benign expression on his face which was the nearest he seemed able to get to a smile; 'Hadassah, I think the time has come for me to tell you of a decision I have reached within these last few days. I've been considering the matter for much longer than that, you understand, but there were a number of factors which delayed my final verdict concerning it. To begin with, there was your behaviour, which I must admit I found extremely disturbing at first, and with which I am still not entirely happy. But I feel that you have made some effort to improve it. Then secondly, there are a large number of legal implications which arise in circumstances like these, and I have been compelled to investigate them thoroughly.'

He hesitated, his elbows on the table, and the fingers of each hand extended, tips touching, as though he were addressing his Torah class and wishing to stress some subtlety of doctrine. I just wished he would get on with whatever he was working himself up to tell me. Finally he clasped his hands together incisively and said, 'I have decided to adopt you as my own daughter.'

My head was swimming, and I had to grasp the edge of the table for support. It wasn't so much the wretchedness I felt at being forced to accept once and for all that my past was dead, and my identity with it. Nor was it my abhorrence at the prospect of being regarded henceforth as the offspring of this man for whom I had no love and little respect. (I would never call him Father, anyway; I was resolved upon that already.) It wasn't even the fact that *I'd* been given no choice in the matter. It was something much worse.

Mordecai asked me if I was all right; I said no, and I was so distraught with the secret I was carrying, I found myself telling him the truth.

He was more incredulous than angry. How could I have been so impious? he was demanding of me, while I just stood there and wept. Did I not know that divination was sin of the most heinous and perilous kind? It was worse, if anything, than fornication; arguably worse than murder! Many men and women who were much more saintly than *I* should ever be had been forgiven by God for moments of passion which had led them to defile their own bodies, or even take the lives of others. But divination! In order to consult such a person I must have made a deliberate decision, in advance, to turn my back on Adonai and his will for my future; instead of entrusting myself to his care I had exposed myself willingly to the powers of darkness.

I heard myself protesting through my tears that I'd meant nothing by it, that Iphigenia herself had told me that the woman's skills were limited; it was possible that she was nothing more than a charlatan out to separate people from their money. We'd gone to her as a joke, nothing more, and what she'd said wasn't to be taken seriously.

'But she told you that you were going to be adopted?'

'Yes ... I mean, not exactly, but—'

'What else did she tell you?'

'Nothing! Nothing, that was all!'

'You're quite sure?'

'Yes. Yes! I swear!' And I wept harder, because of course that *hadn't* been all; it had been the least of what she'd said, but Mordecai was taking this whole thing *so* seriously I didn't dare tell him any more.

'I must pray for you, Hadassah,' he said resolutely, and I nodded, sniffing and turning to go, thinking that our conversation was over.

'No; I must pray for you *now*. With you *here*. We must banish the powers of darkness and cast their evil influence from you before it has taken root.' Then he began calling for Ninlil.

I begged him not to; I was still futilely hoping she wouldn't find out that I'd given her the slip. But Mordecai said it was essential that she be present: encounters with the forces of evil could be appallingly dangerous and must never be undertaken lightly, or by yourself. This got me still more frightened, and by the time Ninlil appeared I was a gibbering wreck. I sat there on the floor with my head on my knees and my eyes tight shut while the two of them fell to chanting over me ... and I've no recollection of what happened after that. The next I knew, I was lying on my mattress with Ninlil watching over me, and aside from a desperate fatigue, I felt well. I wasn't shaking, my head was quite clear; and when I dared to think about the fortune-teller I was no longer afraid. In fact, I couldn't remember what she'd said. It was as though someone had raked my mind clean of any trace of the prophecy, which might as well have been written in sand.

I said to Ninlil, 'I'm sorry I went out without permission. I'm really sorry.' And so I was, though my remorse probably sprang more from relief and a desire to regain her trust than from genuine repentance. She soothed me, saying it was all right now, and there was no harm done. Clearly I looked as though I'd been punished enough. I whispered, 'Cousin Mordecai . . . where is he? What did he do to me?'

She answered briskly, 'He has retired to bed. Such prayer exhausts him.'

'What kind of prayer? What *did* he do?'

But she wouldn't answer, saying instead that I mustn't worry myself any more on that account, and adding, 'You need not fret about the future, either. Mordecai says that he will enquire of Adonai himself what he has in store for you, then you will be reassured.'

'How does he know I'll be reassured? It depends on what Adonai's reply is.'

'No, it doesn't, Hadassah. Adonai loves us, and *always* wants the best for us. Whatever sufferings we experience, he brings good out of them and transforms our sorrows into joys, if we trust him.'

I said nothing.

The next day I still felt calm about everything; in fact I was more at peace than I could remember being since coming to Shushan. Perhaps Mordecai's prayers had driven more than just the fortune-teller's words out of me. I stopped having bad dreams about the night of my eighth birthday. I managed a whole day, then a week, then nearly a month without arguing with Mordecai, or answering back, or feeling that I needed to run away. I helped Ninlil without complaining, and spoke civilly to both of them over our evening meals.

During the course of one of these, Mordecai informed us that King Kshayarsha was back in the city, having stamped out the rebellion in Egypt with rapid, highly efficient ferocity. Apparently there were some at court who considered he had displayed hysteria rather than decisiveness. For he had burnt temples and had statues of the Egyptian deities hacked in pieces in front of their own priests, as well as ravaging the whole of the Nile delta and reducing the natives to servitude.

'Well, they will not rebel again in a hurry,' Ninlil remarked. 'A little over-reaction now on the King's part may enable him to rule with a lighter hand later on.'

'You may be right,' conceded Mordecai. 'But from all accounts, that wasn't the source of his motivation. His zeal for the worship of Ahura Mazda knows no bounds, they say, and he is bent on making the piety of his father look like filthy rags in comparison with his own.'

'Then we can look forward to a decline in idolatry, Mordecai. The cult of the Wise Lord brooks no veneration of images.'

'You may be right in this too, and I hope you are. But it worries me, Ninlil. Once he has crushed the pagans, our devout King may turn upon the Hebrews next. Our ways may be as loathsome to him as those of idolaters.'

Ninlil smiled, and Mordecai asked what she was thinking; somewhat reticently she responded, 'I am thinking that for a man of faith, you are very quick to see the worst side of everything. Reality seldom turns out to be as gloomy as you have imagined.'

'In this you *are* right, I confess it. And no doubt the Jewish community here would benefit from a little persecution, were it not too severe. But there may be dark times ahead for us before we emerge into the full light of Adonai.'

'Perhaps you should seek his will as regards the future of *all* of us, not merely Hadassah,' Ninlil suggested; and Mordecai said he was doing so already.

We spoke no more on the subject until the meal was ended; indeed, we spoke no more on it for many weeks, or months even, so that I'd all but forgotten the conversation when at last Mordecai received the answer for which he'd been patiently waiting.

It came the following spring. I was just eleven years old, and had been in Shushan almost three years.

It happened that I was alone in the house with Mordecai for some days. This situation had arisen because the widowed aunt whom Ninlil and I used to visit had been taken ill and was near to death, and Ninlil wanted to be with her at the end.

On the fourth night of Ninlil's absence, I awoke to hear Mordecai screaming. It was the most blood-chilling sound I had ever heard. I'd never seen him smile, let alone weep, but now he was crying out in a tortured, anguished howl which gave no indication it would ever stop. Aghast, I sat on my pallet with my heart pounding as it hadn't pounded since the night of the massacre in Jerusalem. All my direst memories rushed upon me, and they were all the more terrible because it was so long since I'd been tormented by them; since the night

Mordecai had prayed for me, in fact. And still he was screaming, a screaming awful enough to stir up all the shades in Sheol. I knew I should have no choice but to go to him.

But when I grabbed my lamp and ran into his room he was quite alone. He sat upright on his mattress, bare-headed and bare-chested, his two grey-streaked forelocks uncoiled and splayed over his shoulders. There was sweat pouring off him, and he was rocking back and forth as he did when he prayed. He didn't seem to see me, though his eyes were wide open and staring in my direction.

With my heart in my mouth I crossed the room, as slowly as I could, all the while hoping he would emerge from whatever state he was in and grow calm. But he didn't, and I could no longer delay the moment of reaching his pallet, and stretching out my hand to touch him. He started convulsively, then cried out my name three times and clung to me, weeping against my breast. Mortified, I stood like a statue, neither holding him nor pushing him away, while he began amid juddering sobs to tell me his dream.

There had been thunder: thunder so loud that blood had run from his ears. Then there had been lightning, bright enough to strike him temporarily blind. After that the ground had begun to shake, so that buildings had collapsed into themselves like deflated wineskins—and not just the mud-brick hovels which will fall at the slightest tremor, but temples and porticoes and palaces. The very foundations of the earth were shaken, and no corner of it was spared from chaos; then from this hideous tumult had arisen two dragons, whose eyes, mouths and nostrils bled fire. They had reared up, poised for struggle, and all around them the peoples of the earth wailed in terror and anguish. Then the people were given weapons, fearful weapons of unspeakable destruction, and they too rose up to fight; not against one another, but all together against the Chosen People of God.

Mordecai was quiet for a moment when he had got all this out. But just when I began to think that the nightmare was over for both of us, he sat back from me and the shouting began again. 'Children of Israel, cry out to your God!' he roared, desperately, beseechingly, so that I realized he was still locked into his dream, and that it was no dream at all but a vision of the most awesome intensity. 'Return to Adonai!' he pleaded. 'Repent! Cast yourselves upon the mercy of the Almighty.'

Then abruptly he collapsed, just like one of the quake-ruined buildings he had described to me; so abruptly, indeed, that I hadn't time to catch him as he fell back upon his hard bed. He lay quite silent, so that I wondered if he was concussed, but fresh tears were spilling all over his face, and he was actually smiling. There was a stream of living water, he said, bubbling up from the ground, and it had quenched the fire of the dragons and the flaming arrows of the people. The wailing and lamentation had ceased, and instead there was the music of ten thousand angels singing, for Adonai had triumphed and the humble had brought down the proud.

I still didn't know what to do or say, but it didn't matter because once again he was wholly unaware of my presence. His eyes clouded over, then closed altogether. I decided at first that he'd worn himself out and gone to sleep, but he was in a far deeper and more tranquil place than we can ever travel to in our dreams. He was still smiling, an expression so foreign to his face as I'd previously seen it that he was utterly transformed.

I was in no doubt whatever but that his vision had been from Adonai, and that Adonai was working within him now in a way I could never have believed possible, nor begun to understand. Just as the fortune-teller from Arderikka had been possessed by a power outside herself, and much darker, so Mordecai was being overshadowed by a power so much greater, and at the same time so much lighter and gentler than anything I could have imagined, that the mere witnessing of it was making me light-headed. I had to sit down, but as I did so, Mordecai returned to himself.

I don't think he quite knew what had happened, for his eyes kept blinking and straying—perhaps the blinding light he'd seen in the vision was still dazzling him. He struggled to wrap himself in blankets, managing to mutter in gratitude when I passed him his heavy sleeved coat which lay in a tangle on the floor. He blinked still more at its crumpled condition; he must have thrown it off in his ecstasy, because in his right mind he would have folded it symmetrically. Realizing that the Mordecai I knew had gained the upper hand once more, I prepared to leave. But he called me back.

'Hadassah,' he said, 'I have seen into the future. It is fearful; but *we* must not be afraid, because we shall be conquerors.'

I mumbled something; this was hardly the kind of prophecy I was interested in hearing. I'd wanted to know if I would be rich and happily married with fine sons and comely daughters, and a house full of obedient servants eager to indulge my every whim.

'Hadassah ... don't go. There is something I must show you.'
Reluctantly, I waited.

'Go to the cupboard over there by the window; yes, the small one. There is a box inside it. Bring the box to me.'

I did as he asked me. The cupboard was let into the wall, and so small I hadn't noticed it when I'd raided his bedroom to retrieve my things. He took the box in one hand, and rubbed his eyes with the other. Then he loosened the hasp and took out a bundle of cloth swaddled around something hard. He gave the object to me to untie, since he was still too shaky to do it for himself.

I got the knots undone, and thus revealed an old dagger with a corroded blade. There had been gems set into the hilt at one time, but they were all missing now and you could only see the hollow sockets where they'd once been. I stared at Mordecai in bewilderment, having no idea what he meant me to do with it.

He said, 'This knife has been in our family for five hundred years, Hadassah. It was made for one of Saul's forefathers, and was used by Saul's Amalekite slave to cut his master's throat. If anything happens to me in the time of tribulation which is coming, you must take it from its cupboard and keep it, to pass on to your own children.'

I gazed at it, unable to speak. The solid weight of the ancient weapon in my hand suddenly made many other things seem solid and weighty too, things which had formerly existed for me only as dreams or fantasies, nebulous fears, or dry lessons from history. I saw myself as a mother, with half a dozen little ones sitting cross-legged at my feet, listening agog as I told them the stories of their ancestors. But then the children were gone; I was childless and friendless, running for my life as horrendous persecution broke out against the Jews of Shushan. I saw Mordecai clothed as a prophet and standing on a hilltop, a lone voice crying in the wilderness for his people to repent; many were pouring out of their houses and heaping up bonfires in the street, to burn their idols and their fetishes and their unclean foods and immodest clothing. But still more had barricaded themselves inside their homes, where they caroused and coupled in secret, and offered themselves to dark deities. Then I saw Saul's shattered army fleeing before the hosts of the Philistine heathen on Mount Gilboa five hundred years before.

I asked in confusion, 'How come Saul had an Amalekite slave, when he'd been told to wipe Amalek from the face of the earth? And how come you say this Amalekite cut his master's throat? I thought Saul fell on his own sword.'

Mordecai said, 'Saul compromised himself in many ways, Hadassah. It is the duty of each one of us to learn from his mistakes and from his tragedy. But we shall learn nothing from the past if the truth about it is covered up. Saul *did* fall on his own sword, but not cleanly enough to kill him. The Amalekite had been his companion from boyhood and couldn't bear to watch him suffer. Yet it was Saul who should have slit *his* throat—and that of the Amalekite king, whom he also wanted to spare. It is compromises such as these which have left our nation weak and pathetic. God's people are all too often seduced by their own distorted picture of what is merciful and what is acceptable in the eyes of the world, and are thus deflected from carrying out the injunctions of Adonai. Because of this, the Amalekite race lives on, and we haven't yet seen the last of its evil and destructive influence, you mark my words.'

I shuddered, and wrapped the knife up again. Mordecai took it from me and replaced it in its box, which he directed me to put back safely in the cupboard. I did so with relief, trying not to think that there might come a day when I should have to get it out on my own authority and save it and my family from the hands of violent men. When I turned around, Mordecai was already asleep. I picked up my lamp and left.

6

A short time after I turned twelve, Mordecai, Ninlil and I were invited to a banquet at the palace.

My experience of partying was still limited to the fateful occasion of my eighth birthday; but this was to be an event on an altogether different scale. To begin with, the festivities were to last for seven whole days, during the middle five of which the palace precincts would be thrown open to all the inhabitants of Shushan.

The first day would be taken up with a spectacular meal for satraps, government officials, generals and other dignitaries, both military and civilian, from every corner of the Empire. These officials had already been in Shushan for six months, engaged in high-level consultations on various contentious matters, legal, political and international. One of these was the planning of another expedition to Greece; any enterprise which Darayavaush had shelved or abandoned, Kshayar-sha was determined to undertake—regardless of its wisdom or the likelihood of its success, according to Mordecai.

There would then follow the five days during which any citizen of Shushan, however lowly, could wander about all but the most private quarters of the palace, be appropriately awestruck at the grandeur of its buildings, and marvel at the richness of its treasures which were being put on public display for the first time. Anyone who became jaded by the sight of so much gold could go out into the palace gardens, where there was limitless free food and drink.

Finally on the seventh day there would be another formal and extravagant meal—this time for the most illustrious members of Shushan society, in addition to the foreign dignitaries and imperial functionaries who had been guests at the first meal also. It was this seventh-day meal to which Mordecai had been invited, along with his close family. He'd been deemed worthy of this invitation on two counts: both his status in the field of finance, and his role as negotiator on behalf of the minority communities in the city.

The whole affair was an elaborate and wildly expensive exercise in public relations. Kshayarsha wished to lay on an impressive display of Persian power chiefly in order to stress to his subjects that he possessed near enough boundless resources to crush any rebellious ambitions they might be nursing. Therefore much was made of the exhibition of trophies taken during the subjugation of Egypt, and also of the plans for the massive campaign to be launched against the Greeks. In addition he wanted as many people as possible to admire the magnificent end-product of his enormous building programme; for all was now complete, and there was little point in possessing the grandest and most beautiful complex of edifices ever constructed if there was to be no opportunity to impress those who could never have seen such an astonishing sight even in their dreams.

Predictably, Mordecai was not looking forward to the banquet at all, and would no doubt have turned down the invitation altogether if he hadn't realized that it is always imprudent in the extreme to spurn the generosity of a man infinitely more powerful than yourself. And as Ninlil and I were at pains to point out to him, we wouldn't be compromising ourselves merely by attending; once there, no one would compel us to eat anything unclean, or drink more than we considered seemly.

In point of fact, I would have devoured all the pork in Persia sooner than forego the opportunity of sampling the delights of the royal table, or perhaps even that of meeting the King or Queen in the flesh. I think Ninlil secretly felt the same; and Iphigenia was as jealous as a cat among lions.

The meal itself was to be served after sundown, but we prevailed upon Mordecai to let us set out for the palace in the morning. For there was so much to see, and we were told that a wide variety of entertainments would be laid on throughout the day. I was beside myself with excitement; I'd never set foot on the palace mount before, because no one could pass the heavily guarded Propylaea without having some legitimate business on the royal citadel.

Feeling like royalty ourselves, Ninlil and I accompanied Mordecai across the bridge which straddles the moat between the residential hill and the royal one. Neither of these hills is natural, for both comprise the remains of the mudbrick dwellings of forgotten generations—as indeed does the third and least accessible of Shushan's citadels, where the fires burn perpetually for Ahura Mazda.

Before us towered the walls which surround the entire palace complex; every inch of them was covered with panels of glazed bricks in green, blue, deep red and gold. They depicted heroic figures stalking lions; or winged bulls; or gryphons, creatures with goats' horns, lions' forepaws and tail, and eagles' claws where the hindpaws ought to be. The line of the walls was interrupted every now and again by turrets, higher still, and the lofty gateway itself was flanked by two enormous statues of a Hakhamanish king being presented with tribute by his fawning subjects. You couldn't tell from the face whether it was meant to be Darayavaush or Kshayarsha because the sculptors and painters always make them look exactly alike. However, since the king was shown smiling and surrounded by cartouches and hieroglyphs, you *could* tell that the statues came from Egypt, since that is how they traditionally portray their pharaohs. Hence this serene-looking sovereign was unlikely to be Kshayarsha.

Once inside the perimeter walls, we found ourselves in a luxuriant terrace-garden which despite its formal layout was so large and so crowded you could easily have got lost in it. There were graceful statues here too, and glorious fountains; there were fruit trees and blossom trees of every kind, including some I'd seen nowhere else in Shushan, and all had been planted in perfect symmetry. Between them ran artificial streams bordered by lilies, with the lilies which grow on water floating peacefully upon them, their smiling faces upturned towards the sun. The air was heavy with scent and alive with wistful birdsong.

Even though the whole area was already thronged with people, everything was quiet and well-ordered. This was partly because anyone who hadn't been to the palace before was speechless with awe; but also, there were guardsmen everywhere—both real, and painted life-size on brick—all wearing colourful palace livery and standing to attention with one foot behind the other, spear-butt resting on the foot which was in front.

Clasping Ninlil's hand like a child half my age, I went about open-mouthed. All the guests wore their finest clothes—even I had been permitted to get out one of my Jerusalem dresses in honour of the occasion—and there was so much style and sophistication in the fashions being sported that I could have studied them all day. It was easy to distinguish the nobility from those of more modest birth, by the fluted hats which the noblemen wore, and by the noble ladies' veils which reached right down to their ankles. Some of the younger men looked so striking I couldn't take my eyes off them. They wore flowing capes and kilts like those the King had worn on his return from Pasagarda, and beneath their hats their hair was sleek and shiny as black silk.

And the nobility were present in such numbers! I hadn't realized how many fabulously rich and distinguished citizens Shushan could boast of; but Mordecai told me that many of them were courtiers known as the 'Royal Kin'. There were thousands of them, and many spent their entire lives at the palace. Comparatively few were literally related to the King.

After the formal gardens came another gateway, which opened onto the vast Service Court, the largest of the palace courtyards. The great bronze gates with their golden rosettes had been propped wide open, so the crowds could mill in and out freely. It was in this courtyard that the men's half of the banquet would be held, and it was laid out ready, with white and violet awnings fastened to the marble, lotus-topped columns by purple cords and silver rings. There were silver tables inlaid with ivory, gold and silver couches, and gold and silver cups, every one individually designed and crafted. Around the walls marched reliefs of spearbearers, dressed and equipped as Immortals, the King's own Military Division. Under our feet were paving stones of white marble, red feldspar, blue turquoise, and shining mother-of-pearl.

On the left hand side of the courtyard were the stables—a veritable palace in themselves, for no one loves horses more than the Persians do. No Persian will go on foot when he can ride, and the Great King never walks anywhere except within his own walls. Today, anyone could wander in and admire the King's fine stallions and mares.

On the right hand side of the yard was the Royal Treasury, and this too stood open to the public, though heavily guarded. Inside, there was so much worked gold, it was hard to believe it was real. There were examples of jewellery and ceremonial weaponry and insignia from Scythia to the Sudan; Ninlil and I were astonished by the beauty of it all, and Mordecai by its shameless extravagance. This went beyond what even he had imagined, for in all his visits to the palace on previous occasions, the Treasury door had been securely locked. The longer we stood there, with Ninlil and I feasting our eyes upon the stupefying wonders arrayed before us, the blacker his countenance became, until he could stand it no longer and propelled us outside. Under his breath he was muttering verses from the prophets about greed and injustice, and even I couldn't help thinking all of a sudden about the starveling grandfather and the flat-chested mothers with their mewling babies, whom I'd seen begging on my first day in the city.

Beyond the Service Court was the smaller Central Court. A graceful portico ran all the way around it, its gorgeous glazed brick designs all but obscured by the sumptuous awnings. One of the designs had been left conspicuously visible, however: it consisted of an elegant winged sun-disc hovering above two gryphons with human heads. Mordecai explained that the disc represented the Wise Lord Ahura Mazda himself; elsewhere, he said, you might see the disc with a human figure inside it, and this represented the King in union with his god.

After this second courtyard came a third, of similar size, known as the Private Court. But it was far from private today. It was thronged with cliques of chattering courtiers, men here, ladies there . . . and groups of podgy eunuchs who kept an eye out to ensure that all remained seemly. They couldn't prevent members of the various cliques making eyes at one another, however. Mordecai deemed such flirtatious conduct disgraceful, and said it was what came of their leading idle, indolent lives with nothing better to do than fall in and out of love—as if they knew what the word meant! I kept quiet, enthralled by the polished grace of the young women as they peeped coquettishly from behind their veils, as well as by the careless poise of the handsome youths they favoured. Just at that moment, it seemed to me that there could be no pleasanter way to spend one's days in all the world.

With me looking backwards over my shoulder, we passed on into the first of two long reception halls, where the women's banquet was to take place; Ninlil wanted to be sure that she and I would know where to come to, later on. I found myself wishing that the two sexes could have been accommodated in one place so that I could enjoy watching the young men as we ate; but since there would be hundreds if not thousands of guests, this would have been quite impossible. In any case, had the event been on a lesser scale, the women would probably have been entertained in the small courtyard of the harem.

But today the gates of the harem were locked as securely as they always were. The King's women would appear for the banquet itself, and that only.

The hall in which we stood was buzzing with activity. Palace serving-girls—dressed more like princesses, it seemed to me—bustled between the long low tables, laying places, putting out cushions, and adjusting decorations. There was a raised platform at one end of the room upon which a table had been set for the Queen and her ladies. The walls were of the loveliest soft red ochre, and were hung with the most exquisite, intricately knotted carpets, quite unlike anything I'd ever seen. Tapestries I was familiar with; I'd even embarked upon doing one myself back in Jerusalem, though I'd grown bored with it before getting halfway. But these carpets were different altogether, made with trimmed tufts of brightly coloured wool so soft that to touch them was like stroking the feathers of a bird. There were even carpets underfoot; I hardly dared walk upon them, imagining the labour which had gone into them, and the expense of the dyes.

Thence Mordecai took us to the Apadana, the throneroom of the King. He wasn't enthroned there today, to my disappointment; no doubt he was secluded in his private rooms, enjoying a little peace and quiet before the evening, when he would be on show for many hours.

But the throneroom was awesome enough even without the King's presence. You entered it by way of an immense stone staircase, for it was raised high above the ground-floor level of the rest of the palace. It was so lofty you could have stood ten houses in it, one atop the other, and it was longer and wider even than the Service Court. Thirty-six stone columns supported the roof, spaced at perfectly regular intervals, each with a capital in the form of two graceful horned bulls, back to back, and each ceremonially guarded by one of the King's Immortals. The floor was paved with marble and porphyry and seemed to extend for ever in each direction.

The throne itself stood at the far end of the room, raised up on a dais. It was a golden chair, armless but high-backed, with silver lions' feet, and it had a footstool with feet shaped like bulls' legs and hooves. In front of it were set two incense-burners on tall, ornate stands, but the incense was only burned when the King was present. Above the throne was a canopy made of silver inlaid with jewels, and held up by golden pillars. It was bordered with rosettes, and Ahura Mazda's symbol was there again, this time being saluted by two roaring lions.

By this time even I had seen as much splendour as I could appreciate, so we went outside again; but now into the gardens at the back of the palace. These were not laid out formally like the terrace-garden. They had much more the feel of a wild wood which had somehow been transported to the palace mount, but there were large clearings within it where Mordecai said that the King and his companions played polo. Here the entertainments for the common people had been going on all week.

Many of these were still in full swing although the commoners had departed, for the younger courtiers apparently enjoyed informal, market-place recreations as much as they relished the prospect of the altogether classier affair to which we could all look forward at sundown. Their desire to relax and behave for a while like ordinary folk was probably somewhat akin to their fondness for bringing natural things into their otherwise artificial surroundings; a life wholly encompassed by courtly etiquette could no doubt be stifling.

So there were jugglers, snake-charmers, fire-eaters and acrobats showing off their skills to applauding aristocrats—and some of the young male tumblers were even more pleasing to look upon than the noblemen, I decided, with their svelte bronzed bodies and sparkling eyes, notwithstanding that their finery was gaudy and their jewellery paste. Nearby, a motley band of travelling musicians had struck up with a wild peasant refrain, to which a handful of well-dressed, well-oiled youths danced along.

Despite the professed local aversion to trade, there were stalls laden with every kind of artefact from pottery to perfume—many craftsmen were working away right there in the open, making the products they were hoping to sell. There were silversmiths, engravers, lamp-makers, leather-workers; and it seemed you could make anything you wanted out of date-palms: candied dates, date cakes, date wine, date vinegar, and date honey; date-palm leaf baskets and fencing, cords, sacks, mats and even clothing. Elsewhere, the hot spring air smouldered with the gloriously mingled aromas of wood smoke and roasting meat: whole animals were being cooked on spits over roaring log fires, and smelt infinitely more appetizing somehow than the bloodless meat I was used to.

It was nearly dark when the banquet itself began. Scented lamps and torches were lit in the gardens, and inside the palace, and I doubted that Heaven could have looked or smelt more wonderful. Mordecai went off to the great courtyard in company with the men, whilst Ninlil and I headed for the reception hall with the womenfolk.

Many had already taken their places, and the air in the place was buzzing with expectancy, though there was no one as yet seated at the high table. We made our way to the opposite end of the room; but upon being asked our names, were sent to sit further up; Mordecai must have been even more highly respected than I'd imagined.

We sat down among the cushions, finding ourselves next to some other Jewish women whom Ninlil already knew; care had clearly been taken over the assigning of places. These were the wife, sisters and daughters of a certain Reuben, one of the partners in Mordecai's banking company; but they were got up just like Persians, in silk and gold. I reflected glumly that Ninlil and I could have been dressed just as richly and as fashionably as they were, had Mordecai so chosen.

However, they were much too cultured to show that they disparaged our simple attire, and struck up an animated conversation with Ninlil about the beauty of the furnishings, and about their impressions of the palace in general. But one of the sisters, a thin, sour-faced individual, did nothing but gripe about everything—the crowds, the heat, the flies—and the daughters were much older than me, so I kept quiet, looking about me and waiting to catch a glimpse of Queen Vashti.

Suddenly there was a blaring of trumpets, and she swept into the hall and onto the dais in one uninterrupted flow of movement, her feet, so it seemed, neither needing nor disdaining to touch the floor. She was accompanied by an older woman, tall and majestic, and followed by a dozen maids-in-waiting and another dozen page-boys, all clad in the richest purples, crimsons and yellows. The older woman was the Queen Mother Hutaosa, Ninlil whispered to me; she was Darayavaush's widow, and loved as much by the people as her late husband had been.

Vashti herself was more beautiful even than Iphigenia, I decided, with proud, flawless features, and a bearing so graceful and self-assured I should have known her for the Queen had she worn but sackcloth. Her hair was piled up in spectacular coils on top of her royal diadem, and there was so much of it I was sure it would reach to her thighs if she let it all down. She was wearing a veil, after a fashion, but it covered neither her face nor her neck; instead it was looped and plaited into her diadem and her hair, and bound with pearls. Her face was made up heavily but tastefully, and her figure was as shapely and rounded as an elegant amphora. As the members of her entourage took their places, I noticed that there were several bald-headed eunuchs bringing up the rear.

Once the food was brought round, I lost interest in the high table for a while. I was keen to taste anything, whether I could identify it or not. I would have done so, too, if Ninlil hadn't been deftly taking things off my plate as soon as I put them on it, whenever she remotely suspected that they might be unclean. But Reuben's daughters ate whatever they wanted, and no one tried to stop them. Much of the food was very salty or spiced, and I was surprised that no wine was served to wash it down. But I was told that Persians consider it common to drink whilst eating; the wine would be provided afterwards.

When I'd eaten my fill, I turned my attention to the Queen and her companions once more. Reuben's women too had begun to talk of her.

'They say she is with child again, you know, though you wouldn't think it to look at her.'

'Hmmph. She looks more like a courtesan than a wife and mother, all primped and painted like that.' (This was from the sour-faced sister.) 'Two sons, is it, that she has already?'

'I'd heard three. But either way, she has cause to be in good spirits—and indeed she is, so it appears.'

'The King is in a good mood too, by all accounts. Egypt is subdued, and they say that the negotiations over Greece, and imperial policy in general, have gone very well.'

'Who cares about imperial policy? *I* certainly wouldn't, if I lived in a place like this, and had all those girls and eunuchs waiting on me hand and foot.'

'Why do they do it?' I asked; and all of them looked at me at once, for it was the first time they'd heard me speak.

'Do what, my dear?' enquired Reuben's wife, affectedly.

'Make men into eunuchs. It's horrible.'

There was a silence among us; Ninlil was looking daggers at me, but had no wish to make a scene here.

'Well,' Reuben's wife said eventually, glaring at her daughters, who were tittering, 'If *you* were a king, would *you* trust your wives with men who were truly men? Especially when most of those wives are lucky to get one night with you in a year. A woman can become— *frustrated*, you know.'

The daughters were laughing less inhibitedly now, but I persisted: 'Kshayarsha has many wives? I thought there was no one but Vashti.'

'He is entitled to have as many wives as he pleases, my dear, according to Persian law. But as it happens, you are right: Vashti *is* his only wife, legally speaking. He has plenty of concubines, though.'

'Are they all here, at the banquet?'

'Of course; at the top end of each of these tables, along with his female relatives. They wouldn't miss tonight for the world, when they spend the rest of their lives all cooped up in the harem.'

'And the eunuchs live in the harem too?'

'Those who serve the women do, yes. Those who serve the men—'

She didn't complete her sentence, because one of her daughters became so helpless with laughter that she spilled her wine in the sour-faced sister's lap and we all had to assist in mopping her up. I'd been intending to ask why there should be any need for eunuchs to serve the men; surely boys who hadn't been gelded would do just as well? But I formed the distinct impression that the girls' laughter had to do with just such a question, so I didn't.

Ninlil said, 'Hadassah, the whole thing is quite simple. Men who cannot have children are regarded as more reliable, more loyal, because they won't always be trying to pull strings on behalf of their sons. Too many kings have been assassinated by men who desire to see their own dynasties established in their victims' stead. A eunuch can have no dynasty and therefore no ambition of that kind. He can only acquire honour by serving his king faithfully. That's all there is to it.'

The explanation made sense, but from the way Reuben's daughters were still giggling, I knew it wasn't the whole of the story.

I was distracted from this chain of thought, however, by an unexpected disturbance at the high table. Another group of eunuchs had entered, dressed differently from those who served the Queen, but they appeared to be trying to persuade her to allow them to escort her out of the hall. Although she was succeeding in maintaining her haughty composure I could see, even from where I was sitting, that her eyes were blazing with fury. Some of her own eunuchs began to argue with the newcomers, who eventually left, but not without physical encouragement. The Queen Mother Hutaosa remained entirely aloof.

After this brief interruption, proceedings continued as before; many of those present probably hadn't even noticed. But when the wine-course came to an end and we were shepherded with the rest of the visiting ladies back to the Service Court to be reunited with our menfolk, it was clear that the atmosphere here was markedly different: unmistakeably sour and strained. Persians seldom get obviously inebriated—uncontrolled drunkenness being one of the many things considered vulgar among them—but most of the men wore expressions so sober and grim they might have been considered more appropriate for a funeral than for a banquet. They were standing about in nervous huddles, talking in hushed tones, and there was no sign of the King.

But Mordecai would say nothing about this on our way home. Only when we were in the house, with the doors and shutters firmly closed, was he prepared to speak of what had happened.

He'd been seated quite near to the King's table, and had been in a good position from which to see him. Part way through the drinking-bout, Kshayarsha had despatched seven of his own eunuchs with orders to fetch Vashti to him at once. He wished to introduce her to his male guests.

'Whatever for?' exclaimed Ninlil. 'Surely it is anathema to Persians to display their wives before men?'

'It is now, among the ruling class at least. But you have to remember, things were different before Persia came into contact with Babylon and took over her empire. Persian women mixed flagrantly with men to whom they weren't related, before there were Semites among their subjects to show them the error of their ways; among the lower classes things are still as they used to be. It's as I said, Ninlil: Kshayarsha wants all foreign influence eradicated at every level of Persian society. He was making a point, though he couldn't have chosen a worse time or place to make it.'

'But what *kind* of point, for pity's sake? Anyone would think he saw his wife as some pretty piece of jewellery, to be flaunted like the items in his Treasury. Did he announce his intentions aloud?'

'Yes, he did; and yes, that's *just* how it was. It's as important for the Great King of Persia to have a beautiful wife as it is for him to have a splendid palace; but why have either if no one sees them or admires them? The young men who have his ear were teasing him, saying that for six months he'd been showing off his wealth but he hadn't brought out his finest exhibit. They were behaving very loudly, and their remarks were suggestive, even lewd.' Mordecai shuddered visibly in disgust. 'I could hear their every word.'

'Wasn't the King angry?' I asked in amazement. 'He could have had them impaled for such insolence, couldn't he? He *should* have done.'

Ninlil said, 'He must have had too much wine. So must his companions.'

'I don't know about that. Kshayarsha can hold his liquor well; he's been bred and brought up to it, like all his kind. But he was certainly flushed about the face; and more flamboyant than usual in his conduct. If truth be told, I think his cronies were getting him aroused, with all their curiosity about Vashti's charms. You know the tale which bards tell of a king who ruled in Sardis before it was part of the Empire, who was so excited by his own wife's beauty that he induced one of his personal guards to glimpse her naked.'

'Kshayarsha would have done well to recall how the story ends,' Ninlil observed. 'Didn't the woman find out what had happened, and tell the guard he must kill her husband and marry her, or else be executed? There was a new king in Sardis before the day was out.'

'I don't think Kshayarsha was any more mindful of the lessons of history just then than he ever is. The rumour was going about that he'd been drinking haoma before the banquet got started.'

'Haoma?' I enquired. Ninlil had mentioned it to me once, but I hadn't paid much heed.

'The sacred drink of the magi. They use it in their rituals; it makes a man see things which aren't there, like dreaming while awake, and he supposes himself invincible, irresistible and immortal. No one is meant to drink it except in worship, and then in very small amounts. But our sagacious Kshayarsha cannot abide being bound by law or tradition, Hadassah. He thinks that a king should do whatever he wishes, and he flouts convention at any opportunity. Among the Persians that is an extremely hazardous thing for *anyone* to do—the King included—and now he may have done it once too often. There were some older counsellors there, relics from the reign of Darayavaush, who tried to caution him not to insist upon Vashti's being summoned. But he wouldn't listen, any more than he's listened to the voices of reason which have sought to deter him from moving against Greece.'

'What happened when the eunuchs returned with the Queen's refusal?'

'The King stormed away in a temper, and didn't come back. It's not surprising. He's about to attempt the conquest of an entire people, and he can't even control his own wife.'

The following day, the news was all around Shushan that the official court advisers—one representative from each of the seven noblest families of the aristocracy—had prevailed upon Kshayarsha to depose the Queen and relegate her to the ranks of the harem. These were all young men just like he was, for it was the Great King's prerogative to choose his companions and chief advisers for himself. They were rash just like him, too; apparently he wasn't the sort to value the wisdom and experience of his elders, no matter how august they might be. He probably hadn't taken much persuasion to do the bidding of his contemporaries, however; his dignity and authority had been appallingly slighted.

Yet it was well known that he'd chosen Vashti for himself, just as he'd chosen his advisers, and it was generally assumed that the couple were deeply in love. No one seemed to know whether he had technically divorced her, but a proclamation was duly made throughout the Empire, and in all its languages, that she was never again to appear before the King, and that in every household over which the House of Hakhamanish held sway, the husband was to assert his authority over his wife.

All this gave Iphigenia and me a great deal to talk about on my next visit. Among the adults of Arderikka, even to speak the name of Kshayarsha—or Xerxes, as they called him in Greek—was now taboo, because everyone knew of the expedition he was preparing, and the threat of it hung like a storm-cloud over the village. But I whispered to my eager friend about what I'd seen at the banquet, and what Mordecai had told me of it from his own point of view.

Iphigenia shuddered visibly, simultaneously outraged and intrigued. 'How could Vashti have dared to defy her own husband like that, and in public too? Even if her husband hadn't been the King, he would have had to divorce her.'

'I admire her,' I retorted. 'Why should men be allowed to treat their wives like horses or something? Why should they make all our choices for us? It wasn't like that in Jerusalem. Well, not for my mother anyhow.'

I'd spoken too loudly in my fervour, for Iphigenia's mother had overheard. 'You don't want to model your behaviour on that viper Amestris,' she snapped. (This was the closest most of the Greeks seemed able to get to pronouncing Vashti's name.) 'A more spoilt and vicious woman never walked the face of this earth. You know that it's because of her inordinate possessiveness that the King—may he be accursed!—has taken no other wives. It has nothing to do with love; she's just too jealous for her own pampered sons and is utterly determined to see one of them inherit her husband's throne whether they are equal to the task or not. Well, I am *glad* he has deposed her.

Apart from anything else, her father is Otana, who is to lead the native Persian contingent in the Expedition.'

I asked, 'Are Vashti's sons *still* first in line for the throne? Aren't they in disgrace along with her?'

'I don't think her disgrace affects them. By Persian law, a man's sons are his own. If he sends his wife away, she must leave their children with him. And *he* has no other legitimate heirs. A concubine's son cannot inherit the throne.'

'Maybe he'll take another wife and get new heirs,' I suggested. 'Vashti won't be able to stop him any longer.'

'Perhaps not,' agreed Helena. 'She must certainly have misjudged how far she could go with him. The King's word is law—if he summons *any* of his subjects they must come running, whatever custom dictates. But he has three sons already, of whom he's said to be very proud. It will only cause strife later on if he has more by another woman.'

I thought back to the day when I'd watched Kshayarsha enter Shushan in his chariot. He'd seemed so majestic, so unassailable, and he ruled the greatest empire of all time; but what was he really like, underneath the battlemented headdress and the precisely symmetrical beard? There seemed to me to be something faintly pathetic about a man who had to invoke the power of law against his own wife. And if he'd wanted to depose her, why had he had to wait for his youthful advisers to give their approval? I voiced my contempt aloud.

'He listens to his advisers and his magi too much on everything, according to Father,' Iphigenia declared. 'Father says that Ksh... I mean, that *he* wasn't even interested in making war on Greece at all until his hot-headed cousin started nagging at him. Mardonios, that's the cousin's name, Mother, isn't it?'

'Mardonios in Greek, Marduniya in Persian,' Helena answered, and spat on the earthen floor. 'But I won't have either of his names spoken in this house again, Iphigenia. He is the worst of all of them. Why don't you two girls go and gather some flowers for the table? We should make the most of beauty and freedom while we still have them to enjoy, and not defile our tongues or our minds with talk of evil men.'

Of course, I was by no means alone in regarding Kshayarsha's conduct towards Vashti as a sign of weakness rather than strength.

Shortly after the news of her displacement had been broadcast throughout the Empire, a major rebellion broke out in Babylonia. This was the most serious revolt to erupt since Kurash had made the Hakhamanish dynasty great; it had begun in one of the wealthiest satrapies, and one frighteningly close to Persia itself. Two pretenders arose in quick succession; the first of them butchered the rightful satrap and styled himself 'King of Babylon', then the second despatched him, in similar fashion.

Kshayarsha's armies moved in, crushing the uprising, and proceeding to oppress the province with the utmost brutality. The young King hadn't forgotten the hatred which the population had reserved for him when he'd been satrap there, and he wasn't going to let them forget his reputation for cruelty. The fortresses of their once-great and long dead sovereign Nebuchadnezzar were torn down, temples and holy ziggurats were pillaged, the estates of the richest citizens were confiscated and granted to Persians. Babylonia lost its privileges, indeed its very identity, and was ferociously taxed. No longer did Kshayarsha call himself King of Persia, Babylon and Egypt, a title which had allowed the latter two nations, once imperial powers in their own right, to retain some of their self-respect. Now he was King of Persia only, but Emperor of everywhere else.

This severe policy of Kshayarsha's was in stark contrast to that of the benevolent Kurash, who had demonstrated special respect for Babylon's illustrious past and for its religion. Darayavaush for his part had watered the seeds of goodwill which Kurash had sown, even giving money for the building of temples to his subjects' gods. But Kshayarsha seized the most sacred statue of Marduk, which was three times the height of the tallest of men, and had it melted down for scrap. A priest who protested at the sacrilege was summarily put to death.

'How dare he?' I breathed in awe when Mordecai told me of this. 'Has he no fear of Heaven at all?'

Mordecai saw things differently. 'Marduk is nothing, Hadassah. An idol is merely a creature of man; but man is a creature of Adonai. Kshayarsha's blasphemy is not what matters. The important thing is that the prophecy has now been fulfilled. Babylon is laid waste; it is desolate, not merely defeated. Adonai is Lord of all the world, Hadassah; he doesn't only see into the future—he controls it.'

That night when Mordecai retired to bed, I heard him singing aloud. It was an ancient psalm my father had once sung, about the triumphs of Adonai and the destruction of his enemies and their graven images. Now that Marduk was no more, it was as though Mordecai had at last eradicated anything which remained of his own polluted upbringing. His parents had given him an idol's name, but now its associations were exorcized for ever.

It soon became clear that rooting out idolatry in Babylon wasn't going to be enough for Kshayarsha. There were still shrines to false gods within the land of Persia; the time had now come to demolish these also, and promote the worship of Ahura Mazda in their place. The symbol of the winged sun appeared everywhere, along with inscriptions in praise of Kshayarsha's piety. One of these read, 'Among the rebellious nations was one where demons were worshipped. Through Ahura Mazda's favour I destroyed their sanctuary, and in that very spot I worshipped the Wise Lord.'

Having thus set his house in order, Kshayarsha trained his gaze fully upon Greece. The preparations for his campaign took three whole years. A great canal was dug, and great bridges were built, so that the fleet and the land forces could make the enormous journey in safety, and remain within sight of each other as they followed the coastline. Elaborate negotiations were entered into with the peoples whose territories would be traversed, and arrangements were made to induce Carthage, the most powerful state in the west, to attack the Greek colonies of Italy and Sicily to prevent them from coming to the aid of their fatherland. Stores of provisions for the enormous Persian host were established all along the route, lest supply lines be cut off by enemy action.

This prodigious feat of organization was designed to avoid the pitfalls encountered by Kshayarsha's father Darayavaush when he had invaded Greece ten years earlier, and been almost entirely unsuccessful. Marduniya, the King's bellicose cousin, knew all about such things, because he'd subsequently been in command of a Persian fleet which had been miserably wrecked off the coast near Mount Athos before it got anywhere near Greece. This was the place where the great canal was now being engineered, so that ships need not negotiate the lethal promontory. Marduniya was desperate to rebuild his reputation, and it was rumoured that he wanted to be satrap of Greece once it was conquered. He would likely get his way, for he and Kshayarsha were closer than brothers.

It seemed that the organizers had thought of everything, and made contingency plans to cover any conceivable eventuality. Yet still there was a cloud of foreboding massing above Shushan, which grew thicker and blacker as the date of the expedition's departure approached. It was well known that many of the elders at court were opposed to the enterprise, the foremost of them being Artabazush, an eminently prudent and cautious man. He and his colleagues felt that the rash young King was biting off more than he could chew.

In the autumn after I was fourteen, Kshayarsha left Shushan to winter at Sardis in Asia Minor, the most far-flung of his royal seats, and the one nearest to Greece. In Sardis and to the north of it, his army began to muster—a process which would take many months. His seven advisers were left behind to rule in Shushan, and engineers and builders were despatched to bridge the Hellespont, the straits which divide Asia Minor from the mainland to which Greece is appended. Their first efforts were ruined by an almighty storm; it was reported at Shushan that Kshayarsha had proceeded to behead the engineers, then commanded fetters to be thrown into the sea and three hundred lashes to be inflicted upon the waters.

Iphigenia and her parents were encouraged. Philos said, 'The gods are not dead after all. It is hubris for a mortal man to suppose he can tame the elements. Now his presumption has been punished.'

'Hubris?' I enquired.

'Arrogance, Hadassah,' Iphigenia explained. 'Thinking you are better than you are, better than others, better than the gods themselves. It makes you mad, and then the gods destroy you.'

I thought that Kshayarsha must indeed have been barking mad, to execute his best engineers; but perhaps it was insecurity rather than capriciousness which led him to do such barbaric things?

New engineers built a new bridge, all made out of ships. They lashed together two lines of them, with three hundred vessels in each, then laid cables and planks and a road across the top of them. It took the army two whole days to get across; for it was the largest host ever assembled, numbering hundreds of thousands—some said even millions—and comprising divisions from forty-six nations. Kshayarsha watched the crossing from a white marble throne—from the security of which he would also watch the forthcoming battles—and during it an eclipse was observed. The magi conducted some ritual and claimed that the omen portended the eclipse of Greece; but who was to know for certain quite *what* was going to be eclipsed?

As time drew on and Kshayarsha's host pushed further and further into the unknown, the reports we received in Shushan became less frequent and less reliable, and the rumours wilder. For example, it was said that a well-respected man from among the Great King's allies had asked permission to keep his eldest son at home while the rest went off to fight. Kshayarsha had ordered the son in question to be cut in half, and the two parts of his body to be displayed on either side of the road along which the land troops must march, as an example of what His Imperial Majesty would do to all double-minded men. Then at a place called the Nine Ways, the magi had recommended that nine children be sacrificed, and Kshayarsha had done so, despite the fact that the cult of Ahura Mazda sanctions no such practices.

Conversely, and confusingly, stories were told of Kshayarsha's clemency as well as of his cruelty. Two Spartans were sent to him for punishment because their countrymen had treacherously killed two Persian envoys. The Spartans are the boldest and proudest of all the Greeks, but although this pair of scapegoats refused to prostrate themselves before him, maintaining that only a god was worthy of this kind of homage, the King would not harm them. He claimed that he ought not to lower himself to behave as his enemies behaved.

At first, on the whole, things went well for him. His crack troops, the Immortals, defeated a heroic band of Spartans at Thermopylae, a mountain pass which was the gateway to Greece; the Persians advanced through the country, destroying anything that moved, and reducing temples and altars and holy precincts to dust and rubble. Athens was captured and sacked, and some of its most famous works of art brought back to Shushan. Most notable of these were the statues of Harmodios and Aristogeiton, two friends who had once slain an Athenian tyrant in the name of democracy. Many of this tyrant's friends had also wound up in Persia, and were among those who had encouraged Kshayarsha to conquer Greece. Now they were exultant: so much for Greek freedom, and the power of the people!

But in the autumn when I was fifteen, the Persian fleet lost a terrible battle near the island of Salamis. Its commanders had been tricked by the Greeks into fighting in a place which didn't favour them, and thousands of Kshayarsha's best men perished in the blood-darkened waters. The flower of Persian youth had been dashed against the rocks, bruised and broken; while the folk of Arderikka danced in the streets, the heavy sultry silence of the Shushan nights was shattered by keening; by the anguish of mothers who knew not whether their sons lived or died; by the agony of young brides whose pillows were cold, and would never again be warmed by the kindling of love. As if it were not enough for Kshayarsha to have lost so many in the tragic battle, he went on to execute the surviving captains of his ships, for cowardice.

Only gradually did the true scale of the disaster become known. For it wasn't just that Greece hadn't been won; almost all of Thrace, a Persian province to the north of it, had revolted and been lost. Kshayarsha himself was reputed to be desperately depressed, and to be on his way back to Sardis. He intended to remain there for a while ensuring that the Greek cities of Asia Minor didn't rebel again also, as they'd done in the days of his father.

His seven advisers, still in power in Shushan, were allegedly seriously concerned about him—and not only for the state of his mind, but for his physical well-being too. He and the troops which remained to him would have to reverse their enormous overland journey, this time without the support of the fleet, and without stashes of supplies waiting them at each stage along the route. The one thing no plans had been made for was a retreat, because none of the campaign's designers had imagined for a moment that Persia *could* be defeated by a nation of puny and disparate cities whose leaders couldn't have agreed on the price of a flea under normal circumstances. Disease, dysentery and starvation would be Kshayarsha's only escorts on the long march home.

Against all the advice of his fellow generals, the headstrong Marduniya remained in Greece with as many divisions as the King would allow him to keep, intending to winter there and renew the campaign when spring came. But almost before the new season had begun, he was defeated in battle near the city of Plataea; they say he died a hero's death. At about the same time—perhaps on the very same day—what was left of the Persian fleet was annihilated.

It was perhaps just as well for Kshayarsha that he didn't return at once to Shushan. Public opinion was running high against him; he had sacrificed a generation of Persian men on the altar of his own ambition, out of a perverse desire to prove himself the equal of Kurash and Darayavaush. There was widespread fear among the native population of Shushan that their mighty Empire was on the brink of collapse— rather an overreaction, admittedly, but hardly a surprising one when you think that Greeks and Babylonians and a whole motley assortment of displaced people had taken to the streets to boast of how their various gods had brought the oppressor low.

The jubilation of the minority communities was pitifully short-lived however. The poor of Shushan, fearing that Kshayarsha's defeat would mean hard times ahead and an even smaller bite of the economic apple for them, began to look back fondly on the days of their grand-parents and before. Then, Media had been Media, and Persia Persia, and the peoples of the world hadn't been all mixed up and competing for the same land and the same food. The labourers who waited each day to be hired hadn't had to watch contractors from Cyprus or Syria or Scythia stealing their work, or beg for loans from affluent Jewish bankers, merely to survive. I began to see their scowls when they passed me in the street, and once there was abusive graffiti on the wall outside a Jewish bakery in the bazaar. I told Mordecai about it, and he could think of nothing reassuring to say to me, save that we must place ourselves in the hands of Adonai. For these disaffected elements could cause trouble even when acting in isolation, and as the mood took them. If someone were to arise with the ability to unite them, the fulfilment of Mordecai's horrific vision could be just around the corner.

All in all, those three years following Vashti's demise were not good ones for me. I can remember little about them, and what I *can* still recall, I would rather forget. I worked with Ninlil in the kitchen, I washed clothes and cleaned rooms, I mastered my letters, and I learned great chunks of the Torah by heart, though they meant nothing to me, and moved me still less.

Then just when I was starting to think that my life was going to drag on in the same way for ever, Mordecai summoned me to his study one day and said the time had come for him to find me a husband. When he launched into a list of the qualities he would be looking for in any hopeful candidate, it was precisely as though he were assessing some client's credit rating, and I could take no more. I ran out to my room and beat my fists against its walls. I was nearly sixteen years old, and he was still treating me like the submissive orphan waif-child he'd always wanted me to be, having no mind of my own, no dreams, no feelings except for grovelling gratitude to him for taking me in and bringing me up as his own. Nor would this ever be any different, because I was a woman, and a Jewish woman in Shushan was never allowed to grow up.

7

Soon after I turned sixteen, Kshayarsha returned from Sardis to Shushan. But it was a while before anyone knew it; he entered the city in secret and proceeded to live like a hermit in the private quarters of his palace. In all but name, his seven advisers were still the rulers of the Empire.

They weren't happy in this role, however. From his clients who had regular business at the royal courts, Mordecai gleaned that the seven were deeply anxious. The mighty Persian Empire required a mighty monarch at its head, and ever since Kurash founded it, it had always had one.

It wasn't merely the failure of the campaign against Greece which was responsible for Kshayarsha's depression, though that was undoubtedly the major cause. When his surviving generals had slunk home with their tails between their legs, they had at least had wives to welcome them, for whom it was almost enough that their husbands still breathed. But Kshayarsha had only his mother, Hutaosa; and she'd been the wife of Darayavaush the Great, whose magnificent statues looked down their long proud noses at him whenever he passed through his own gateway, their hieroglyphs and cartouches serving only to remind him that he was hated in Egypt, loathed in Babylon, and despised in Greece.

Therefore Kshayarsha's hard-pressed regents advised him to marry again as soon as possible, and to install his new bride in Vashti's place as Queen of Persia.

It ought to have been simplicity itself for him to procure a suitable woman. The King was young and handsome as well as unimaginably wealthy and powerful—in theory he could have had his pick of every beautiful, well-born maiden in the Empire. Yet in practice things proved much more problematic. It had been laid down by Darayavaush that the Persian kings should choose their wives from among the seven noblest Shushan families—the families of his seven advisers—but it soon emerged that relations between the heads of these families and Kshayarsha were not at all good. Because of what had happened to Vashti, who was a daughter of one of them, they were all at loggerheads with their younger representatives who advised the King, as well as with the King himself. If Kshayarsha had humiliated one of their daughters, what was to prevent him from doing the same to another?

In addition to this, Kshayarsha made it known that there wasn't one available female among any of the seven families with whom he would want to share his bed for one night, let alone his throne for the remainder of his reign. It seemed that he hadn't yet learnt his lesson about flying in the face of convention—but Vashti had been proud, beautiful and intelligent, and he *had* loved her passionately; finding a worthy replacement for such an ideal consort would be all but impossible in the eyes of a man as besotted as he had been.

When it came to *un*available women, things were different entirely. There were rumours going about that he had taken his own brother's wife as a mistress while in Sardis, and that this wasn't the first time he'd sown his seed in another man's field. Although these rumours were never confirmed by palace sources, they must have given those in government an additional reason to be apprehensive. For the King to get sons on his concubines was one thing; to have carriers of the royal seed littered all over the Empire was quite another. A king's bastard sons can be carefully watched so long as they are living in the harem, but there is no knowing what ideas those outside it may take into their heads.

For a while no progress was made, and it was hard to see how the deadlock could be broken. Then it was announced by the palace that Kshayarsha had consulted with the Wise Lord Ahura Mazda and had been shown the correct way to proceed. Agents of the imperial court would travel the length and breadth of Persian territories in search of freeborn, unmarried, undefiled girls who possessed beauty, intelligence and good reputation; wealth, social standing and even nationality were to count for nothing, for it was the individual's personal appearance and qualities which mattered. Girls who satisfied these criteria were to be brought to the palace, and those who found favour in the King's eyes would each spend a night in his bed. From these, Kshayarsha would make his choice of bride, thus ensuring that he married the most desirable maiden in the whole of

Asia and North Africa. For how could the King of Kings ever be truly content if he suspected that somewhere in his realm there was a man with a lovelier wife than his own?

Predictably, Mordecai found this announcement distasteful in the extreme. 'Adonai made us male and female!' he thundered over dinner. 'That means, one male to one female! Who is Kshayarsha to think he can take and deflower the daughters of a hundred different men, even a thousand? He is mortal like the rest of us, and subject to the wrath of Adonai.'

I said peevishly, 'Israel's greatest king, David, had half a dozen wives, and scores of concubines, and the Scriptures say that he was a man after God's own heart.' But Mordecai ignored me.

'What will happen to the poor girls Kshayarsha rejects?' ventured Ninlil. I thought she sounded troubled and looked unusually pale: almost the way she sounded and looked when asked about her past.

'Those who fail his initial inspection will go back home—much mortified, I don't doubt, but they will be the lucky ones. The rest will remain in the harem as his concubines; no man will marry them once their maidenhead is gone. And if there is any chance of their being pregnant by the King, they must not be allowed to go where they cannot be closely supervised.'

'And if a father is not willing for his daughter to be taken?'

'How many fathers will dare to stand in the way of the Great King? Besides, Kshayarsha will pay a high price for his pleasure, and expect no dowry. Many parents will be only too grateful to have one less daughter on their hands.'

Whiter still, Ninlil asked, 'How will the King's agents find these girls in the first place? Are they to go from house to house and demand that any virgins there parade before them? Is every girl in the Empire to pay for Vashti's sin by being examined and appraised like a brood mare, just because the Queen refused to be?'

'I can't see it coming to that. Many fathers will be clamouring to put forward their daughters' names; I should be surprised if Kshayarsha's agents aren't trampled underfoot in the stampede. Then there are the uncles and grandfathers who will take the initiative when they see their relatives being too modest about their own daughters' attributes. And there is the neighbour who will do it for spite, or for a bribe; the mother who will submit the name of her daughter's rival for the hand

HADASSAH

of some eligible nobleman, to remove her from the running. The
possibilities are endless.'

'And when a girl is chosen, will she be taken at once to the King?'

'By no means. The Great King of half the world isn't going to risk
soiling his sheets or his flesh with something his commissioners may
have picked up straight from the gutter. She will have to have baths,
and more baths; and then "beauty treatments" as the royal perfumers
call them ... but why a girl can't be beautiful enough the way God
made her, I can't imagine.'

Ninlil relaxed a little at this; she couldn't help but derive some mild
amusement from her brother's excessive intolerance toward all things
cosmetic or decorative. She smiled at me, meaning me to share this
amusement, and I smiled back—partly to oblige her, but mostly so that
it wouldn't occur to her to observe how withdrawn I'd become all of a
sudden. I didn't want her to ask me what I was thinking.

For I was no longer speculating about the quest in merely a
general kind of way. Far from it; it was as though my mind were
doing cartwheels inside my head. The fact was, my own betrothal
arrangements were proceeding apace, and there had been little I
could do about it. Several pompous businessmen had expressed
interest and visited the house to look me over, sometimes with
their mothers; I'd said something impertinent to each of them, or
picked my nose, or pretended to have nits, and succeeded in
dampening their ardour.

But the most recent of them, one Benjamin ben Caleb, would not be
put off. He understood full well why I was being objectionable, yet was
smugly convinced that I would grow out of it in time, once I was used
to the idea of marriage. He was the worst of the lot, with his patience
and his patronizing; he seemed to find it inconceivable that I would not
grow to dote upon a man as beneficent, indulgent and generous as he,
especially since his bank-balance was in equally fine fettle. As for me, I
would have found an oily rag more attractive, but I'd been unable to
see any way of staving off the inevitable.

Until now.

When Mordecai had left the table, to chant his evening prayers, I
said to Ninlil, 'I want to go to Arderikka tomorrow.'

'It isn't our usual day, Hadassah.'

'I don't care. I need to talk to Iphigenia. If you take me I promise I
won't be rude to Benjamin next time he comes. And if you don't, I'll

119

speak Greek all the time and tell his mother I don't know the Ten Commandments, and that I've never baked bread or spun or woven in all my life.'

I got my way.

Iphigenia had heard all about the palace announcement, and I expected she would find it just as intriguing as I did. She too had lately been plagued by suitors, most of whom constituted no more attractive a prospect than Benjamin ben Caleb. But the more I talked, the more fidgety and abstracted she became, until finally I asked her what was wrong.

'Nothing is wrong, Hadassah. Something is very right. I'm going to be married.'

'I know you're going to be married. But—'

'No, you don't see. I'm going to be married *soon*. The pledges have been exchanged. His name is Nikias, and I think I'm in love with him.'

I was dumbstruck. I was jealous, too, and desolate, and angry, all at the same time. Eventually I blurted, 'Why didn't you tell me? I'm supposed to be your best friend! I've never even heard of this Nikias; you've never even mentioned him!'

'I didn't meet him myself until yesterday. He came here with his aunt, because his parents are dead. That's why he's moved to Arder-ikka—the only kinsfolk he has left are here. But he's lived in Greece until now, Hadassah! He could take *me* back to live there! And he's so shy, and gentle, and quiet—'

'He sounds more boring than a fish! *They* are shy and gentle and quiet.'

'Hadassah, please don't be cross with me. I'll still be your friend, you'll still be able to visit me, we shan't be able to go back to Greece for years, we couldn't afford the boat fare—'

'I don't believe this! You're going to marry a strange, soft-headed man you've met only once, and you say you're in love with him? How *can* you be?'

'Nikias is hardly old enough for me to think of him as a man. His beard hasn't started. And he isn't soft in the head, or strange. We only talked for an hour, but by the end of it I felt as if I'd grown up with him, right here in the village.'

My eyes were smarting. I clenched my fists and looked away;

Iphigenia leaned forward and touched my wrist, but I thrust off her hand and sat with both my own, still clenched, under opposite armpits.

'Poor Hadassah. I do so wish you could marry who you want to. Is this Benjamin ben Caleb really so awful? Couldn't you learn to love him, in time? Or is there someone else? Someone you haven't told *me* about?'

'I don't want to marry *anyone* if it means spending every day squatting in a cramped little kitchen, or fetching water, or sweeping floors! I want to do something that *matters!*'

'Doesn't having children and taking care of them matter, Hadassah?'

'Of course it matters—if you have any sort of life to offer them. But what would *I* have to offer?'

'I—don't know.' Iphigenia looked confused; it was clear she hadn't the remotest idea what I was talking about, and I wasn't sure that *I* had. She asked, 'What did your mother offer you?'

'A vision!' I retorted, 'A vision I could believe in and be part of, to rebuild our city and our nation.'

'Well, you could still do that. You and your husband could go back to Jerusalem together.'

'But I don't want to *do* that any more! I don't see the point! It was all for Adonai, and he doesn't answer my prayers. And his followers here are all like Mordecai... or else they are just like Persians, and don't trust God in their hearts any more than *I* do. Oh, Iphigenia... I want to *be* somebody again. I want to be happy.'

All at once she understood what I was driving at. She said, 'You want to be Queen.'

I stared at her. 'I didn't say that, Iphigenia. Don't be ridiculous.'

'It's what you meant, though. It's why you're so taken with the idea of the Great King scouring the Empire for a bride. You want to be chosen.'

'How *could* I be chosen as Queen? *I'm* not the most beautiful girl in Asia. I'm not as pretty as *you* for a start.' Hearing her voice the thing aloud had punctured my excitement; and in any case, I *hadn't* really thought I could ever become Kshayarsha's bride. One night in his bed and then a life of luxury in his harem where I should never have to spin or sew or clean again, and could while away my days wafting about the exquisite colonnades and gardens of the palace was more what I'd had in mind—if indeed I could be said to have had *anything* in mind beyond vague shapeless dreams and escapist yearnings.

But now even those seemed to evaporate, once exposed to the harsh light of day. I said miserably, 'I can't even see how I could be chosen to go to the palace in the first place. Mordecai thinks it's all an abomination: the harem, the extravagance of the court, everything.'

'But it was foretold that you would be Queen, don't you remember?' A mischievous smile played on Iphigenia's lips. 'The old witch-woman in the village, who was priestess of Apollo . . .'

'What?'

'You *must* remember! It was years ago, mind, not long after you started coming here.'

'I—don't know.' I shook my head, trying to clear it; there were so many things revolving, sinking and rising inside it, that it was starting to throb. Summer was coming: the air was heavy, the insects were biting, and I still couldn't take the heat sometimes. I said, 'I remember going to her, yes. But after that . . . I think I was frightened, and Mordecai prayed for me to forget.'

'And you've forgotten? Just like that?'

'No; I mean . . . yes, but . . . oh, I don't know! Do *you* remember? Is that what she said, that I'd be Queen of Persia?'

I must have looked even more baffled and awestruck even than I felt, for Iphigenia's smile at once vanished and she said, 'It was just a bit of fun, Hadassah, nothing more. You mustn't set your hopes on silly dreams. We have to live *here*, in the world where the gods have placed us. We can't live in dreams.'

However, over the next few days I thought more and more about Kshayarsha, until my fantasies turned to obsession. If I'd had a mother I could have talked to, she would have told me that what I was experiencing wasn't love at all, nor was it something unique or prophetic. It was merely infatuation, of the kind almost every young girl conceives sooner or later for a figure who is powerful, scornful, distant and unattainable.

But I had no mother, and would never have shared such thoughts with Ninlil. My passions were too strong and ungovernable within me to be shared with *anyone*, I thought; and attaining the unattainable had always excited me, the more so since I'd occasionally managed it. Lying sprawled on my pallet in the heat of midday, I imagined that it was a great canopied bed with lions' feet and horned bulls' faces at each corner, and graceful gryphons at its head; Kshayarsha was reclining beside me in silks and jewels, and my whole body ached with a yearning for it to be true.

Whenever I went to the bazaar with Ninlil I wished for the King's litter to pass, and me to catch a glimpse of his face, and he mine, as though he might decide on the spot that his search was at an end. I would persuade Ninlil to go home by a way which had a view of the royal citadel, in case he might be standing on one of the towers surveying his realm; I studied the face of every passing stranger, lest one might be Kshayarsha going about in disguise to see what really went on in the streets of his capital.

At night I began to dream of him, though he never did more than kiss me softly on the lips, for the ecstasy of that was enough to wake me up. Not that I really knew in any detail what lovers did beyond that. Iphigenia and I had whispered and giggled, but she understood little more than I did.

Throughout my early years in Shushan, Arderikka had been the place I would go to in order to forget reality for a while. Now I escaped into my fantasies, sleeping or waking, and it was there that I was drifting at noon one day when Ninlil came into my room and told me that Benjamin ben Caleb was here, and both his parents with him.

'I won't see them. Tell them that I'm ill.'

'Hadassah... you *must* see them. His father is here, not just his mother. It can only mean one thing.'

I stared at her.

'For the love of God, Hadassah! You are sixteen years old; you cannot put off marriage for ever! They have come to arrange the betrothal, if Mordecai will give consent.'

'If *Mordecai* will give consent? What about *my* consent? I don't consent! And what about you? *You* put off marriage until it passed you by for good!'

I had grazed her sorest point, and had done it on purpose; but it hadn't been a wise moment to choose for exposing her wounds, whatever they were. White with mortification and helpless anger she shrieked, 'You wicked girl! If you had taken the slightest notice of *any* of the men who have come here, your father might have taken some account of your views! How can he be expected to treat you as a grown woman when you act like an infant in a tantrum?'

'I *won't* have you call him my father! He's *not*, and he never will be!

But if you want me to see Benjamin, I'll see him. I'll see him this once, and he'll never want to see me again!'

So much for the promise I'd made to Ninlil about behaving myself the next time Benjamin came. I leapt up from the bed, and went just as I was. I was unveiled and wearing nothing but a thin home-spun shift which Iphigenia had given me as a birthday present; it was cool to sleep in, it left my arms, shoulders and ankles quite bare, and little else to the imagination.

Thus attired, I burst into the reception room where Benjamin and his elderly parents sat, sipping fruit juice and conversing politely with Mordecai. They broke off at once when they saw me, hair swirling, eyes and cheeks ablaze. The poor mother's mouth dropped open as if I were stark naked; but then I practically was.

I said nothing; I didn't need to. Benjamin was so embarrassed he didn't know where to put himself, though I could have given him a few ideas. His aged and venerable father, who had never seen me before, knew *exactly* where *he* wanted to be, and got up to leave forthwith.

I could have felt quite sorry for Benjamin if I hadn't found him so pathetic. The unfortunate man must really have taken to me on his previous visits, despite the honeyed sarcasm I'd been wont to pour on him; perhaps he was too gullible to recognize it for what it was, and it had been wasted on him. He stood up too, all flustered like an adolescent twenty years his junior, and began striving to pacify the old man, saying I wasn't really like this, truly I wasn't; there must have been some misunderstanding. There certainly had, his father retorted: Rabbi Mordecai's daughter had the manners of a whore, and how *that* could have come about was beyond *anyone's* understanding. But they'd been made to look fools, all three of them, and would not forget this outrageous affront to their dignity for a long time.

Only once before had I seen Mordecai lose control the way he lost it the moment his scandalized guests had left. I'd expected a lecture about immodesty and impropriety, and to be told that Benjamin and his father were valued clients; had I no concern for my adoptive father's reputation whatsoever?

Instead, he went for me physically. He hadn't done that since I was a little girl; now I was almost as tall as he was, for as the years passed it became clearer and clearer that I *had* been blessed with Saul's stature, as well as carrying the blood of his house. Not only was I tall, but I was filling out already into the mature shapeliness of my womanhood;

holding me pinned against the wall Mordecai can't have been unaware of it, as I struggled and screamed, limbs thrashing and breasts heaving. Somewhere far off Ninlil's tremulous voice was beseeching him, but he paid no heed. He was frantically trying to slap my face to allay my hysteria—as if he were any less hysterical than I was—but my hair was all over it and getting in his own. Before he managed to strike me, I struck him, and he was so appalled, he released his grip and I got away.

I ran straight into the street, for if I'd gone back to my room to dress properly first, I should never have succeeded in quitting the house. Dishevelled and distraught as I was, the few people I passed must have thought I'd been raped at very least, but at that time of day there was hardly anyone about. Those who were didn't attempt to come near me, for I was cursing Mordecai at the top of my voice like someone mad, and mostly in Greek or Aramaic because I'd never heard Hebrew used for swearing. I'd no notion in my head as to where I was going, as I fled past bronze-studded gates and around palm-graced corners, but my feet took me to Arderikka.

Even in my frenzied state, I realized at once that something was very much amiss at Iphigenia's. No one came to comfort me when I burst into the cottage and sank to my knees, my nails clawing into the earthen floor. Looking up through the tangle of my hair I saw Helena, her own hair loose and more matted than mine, her clothing torn, and her face streaked with dust and tears.

I tried to ask what was the matter, who was dead, but the words wouldn't come. Then Helena stammered, 'You must leave here, Hadassah. Please. Go now, and don't come back.'

I rose unsteadily to my feet, letting go the soil which I'd unwittingly scraped up with my grasping fingers. I managed to whisper, 'Where is Iphigenia?'

'She is in the bedroom, but you must not go through. She will not see you. She will never see you again, nor will we.'

I broke down in tears; my best friend, my only friend was dead. There could be no other explanation, and I blurted my abject misery aloud. But Helena said, 'You know very well what has happened, Hadassah. That's why you must leave. Please, go now, before Philos comes back and finds you. He's so angry; I'm afraid what he may do.'

Bewildered, I backed away towards the door and stumbled out into the scorching noontide sunshine. Having nowhere left that I *could* go, I sat down in the dust of the deserted street. Flies buzzed about my streaming eyes, and the shrilling of crickets seemed louder than the blasting of shofars in my ears. Presently a shadow fell across me, and someone pushed a cup of water into my hands.

Glancing up, I saw it was a young girl, one of Iphigenia's village friends. She said quietly, 'You *must* know what has happened.'

'Why must I know? How could I know?' My voice came out all hoarse, for the heat had made my throat as dry and my lips as cracked as the mud in a summer river bed.

'The King's commissioners came to her house. She's going to be taken away. She is blaming you, and so are her parents.'

My throat had turned to fur and I gulped down the water all in one go. No matter how many hours I'd spent fantasizing about the King's search for a bride, that was all it had been: a fantasy. I tried to protest: how could I possibly be to blame? Did *I* have contacts at the palace? And why would I want to bring Iphigenia to their notice even if I had?

But before my parched lips could form the questions, I knew the answers. *Mordecai* knew people at the palace, and it wasn't unknown for me to succeed in manipulating him. Nor was it beyond me to be utterly callous when in the grip of spite or jealousy. Iphigenia knew me well; if I could not marry a man I loved, I would make sure somehow that no one close to me could do so either.

I seized the girl's hands in desperation. 'Please, go in and tell them it wasn't me! Please! Tell them I want to talk to them. Please—'

In the end she agreed, because I wouldn't let go of her, and because my public display of distress was beginning to attract unwelcome attention. Half a dozen village children had slipped out of doors and were gawping at me with their fingers in their mouths. It was some while before the girl appeared again and told me I could go in.

There was still no sign of Iphigenia, nor of her father nor her two little sisters. But Helena took me in her arms and kissed me and said she was sorry, so sorry she'd blamed me without speaking to me first; but her daughter had been so upset by my reaction to her forthcoming marriage, she was convinced it was all my fault.

I cried like a baby, and my unrestrained weeping made Helena realize at last that Iphigenia wasn't the only one who faced a wretched future; as coherently as I was able, I explained what had just happened at Mordecai's, while she told me at the same time what had taken place in Arderikka the day before.

The King's agents had appeared in the village not long after sunrise and made directly for her house. They had conducted themselves with the impeccable politeness which is the mark of any well-bred Persian, but their message came across clearly enough. It had been brought to their notice that Helena and Philos had a daughter of surpassing beauty, and they would like very much to see her, and, depending on the outcome, to arrange for Lord Memucan, Chief Privy Counsellor to the Great King, and Shaashgaz, the Warden of His Majesty's Harem, to meet her. Memucan was the one who had recommended the dethroning of Vashti, and apparently he knew the King's tastes well.

The formula the agents used in requesting the pleasure of Iphigenia's company was exactly that which any suitor's go-between might use; but *any* suitor could have been refused without undue offence being caused, if care had been taken over the choosing of words. Kshayarsha was *not* any suitor, so Iphigenia had been duly brought out, her younger sisters—now eight or nine years old—hanging agog about her skirts. She'd been inspected and interrogated, and inspected some more. Notes had been made, then the men had bowed low and promised to return on the next morning but one bringing with them their aforementioned superiors who were empowered to make the necessary arrangements for her conveyance to the palace.

As soon as they were gone, Helena had struck up with her keening; the neighbours had come running and passed on the news and the mourning cries like torchfire one to another. Once Iphigenia was taken to the palace, she would never again be seen by her family and might as well be dead; it had happened already to a girl from the village, and she'd never been heard of since. Nor had it ever been proven who had given her name to the imperial marriage-brokers; but within a month the boy to whom she'd been betrothed had been married to her cousin, to the sleek satisfaction of her aunt.

I said, 'Helena, it must be the same with Iphigenia. She cannot be the only girl in Arderikka who has noticed Nikias. But surely there is something we can do?'

'No one can do anything to save me, Hadassah.'

I hadn't heard her approach; she must have followed the whole conversation from the family's bedroom. I drew back from her mother's embrace and beheld my friend, dry-eyed and deadpan; it was as though all life had drained out of her already, and all the keening seemed horribly appropriate. I sprang towards her and grasped her by the shoulders, shaking her as if to arouse her from sleep. But she was

listless and unresponsive against me, and her empty eyes stared right
through my skull. I heard myself berating her, urging her to fight back
before it was too late.

'It's too late already,' she said, still looking through me, not at me.
'This is what the gods have ordained. I was so happy. Too happy. I
made the gods jealous, just as I made *you* jealous. It is they who see to it
that the sharpest pain comes swift on the heels of the sweetest pleasure.
We cannot fight against Heaven.'

'Who is to know what Heaven has ordained? Kshayarsha *hates*
Greeks; *anything* could happen to you if you go to the palace. Haven't
you thought of that?'

'Of course I have thought of it. Do you think I care? I should *rather*
go to my grave than to that butcher's bed. To betray Nikias will kill
me, Hadassah. I would kill myself *now* were I not sure that my parents
would pay for it dearly tomorrow, when the commissioners return
with Memucan.'

Exasperated, I thrust her aside. How could she be so resigned, so
passive? In her place, I should have fought the armies of Persia single-
handed before giving in to a destiny I dreaded. It was all so hideously
ironic: that she who loved another was to be taken to the King, whilst I
was about to be betrothed to one I despised, when in my dreams I'd
pictured myself with Kshayarsha.

Suddenly, everything fell into place; my mind became clear as
running water. I announced, 'You won't have to betray Nikias,
Iphigenia. I shall go to the palace instead of you.'

There was an incredulous pause, as they tried to take in what I'd said.
Then Helena snapped, 'You foolish child! You shall do no such thing! It
would be the death of poor Ninlil, and of Mordecai to whose care your
own father entrusted you. Besides, it is Iphigenia they have chosen.'

'You're saying *I'm* not beautiful? *I'm* not intelligent and of good
reputation?'

'Of course I'm not saying that. If they saw you, they might take you
as *well*, and then where should we be?'

'They won't take Iphigenia if she is no longer a maiden,' I retorted,
wishing I were a little clearer in my mind as to what this meant. 'And
they won't be angry provided that they don't have to go back empty-
handed. I *have* to get away from Mordecai's. You don't know what
he's like. If he makes me marry Benjamin, *I* shall die.'

'Surely he won't *make* you,' Helena argued, but she didn't sound so sure of her ground any more. 'Can't you ask Ninlil to speak to him?'

'Ninlil doesn't feel sorry for me any more. Believe me ... I shall be making no sacrifice if they take me to the King. Iphigenia, does Nikias know what is to happen tomorrow?'

'Of course.' Suddenly her eyes were no longer dry. 'I saw his sister. She says he is heartbroken. Oh, Hadassah, *he* loves *me*, too.'

'Then fetch him here today. Lie with him today. *Marry* him today.'

'I dare not! Even if it could be arranged, the King's men would kill me *and* my parents as soon as they found out we'd tricked them.'

'You could say it wasn't your fault. Say Nikias forced you.'

'Then what would happen to *him*? Hadassah, I would sooner die a thousand deaths than see any harm come to Nikias.' She choked back her sobbing. 'If I go quietly he will forget me in time, and find happiness with someone else.'

I shook my head in helpless frustration. I found it incomprehensible that she could be so selfless at a time like this. So I said, 'Why don't you spare a thought for *me* instead of your precious Nikias? You said yourself that I secretly wanted to be Kshayarsha's bride.'

She could think of no response; it was Helena who asked quietly, 'And what would you say to Mordecai, Hadassah? Have you considered *that*? How would you talk him into making arrangements with the commissioners?'

'He wouldn't need to make any arrangements. You could do it. You could say I was your daughter.'

Iphigenia laughed bitterly through her tears. 'You could no more be my sister than could a crow-black Cushite. Besides, I don't think the King likes Jews much more than Greeks. And such tales are told of his cruelty to *any*one he doesn't respect. We are *all* infidels to him; it is only Aryans who honour Ahura Mazda. Don't you know he's giving gold to pure-bred Persians who marry pure Persian women and get pure Persian children? He could hardly take a Semitic woman for himself.'

'Ahura Mazda told him to get himself the loveliest woman he could find, don't you remember? He said nothing about her race or her religion. Anyhow, you could tell him I'm adopted. That's true, after all. And you could pretend I *am* Persian—my father always said I could pass for one.' I turned to Helena. 'If we do it this way, you get to keep the bride-price you would have got for Iphigenia. Mordecai is certainly in no need of it.'

Iphigenia whispered, 'You would go to the palace without even telling him? How? Would you stay here until tomorrow, and not go home?'

'No; I shall have to go home, to get my good clothes. In any case, he and Ninlil will know I have come here, and they will send someone tonight to come and fetch me and everything will be ruined. And I shall have to tell them that I've been chosen by the commissioners, or they will spend weeks and months searching for me, and when they find out where I am the King's men will get to know the truth about me, and we shall all be punished.'

I paused to scan their faces. I could tell that they were at last beginning to wonder if there was sense in what I said, and daring to hope. Growing excited I continued, 'I shall tell Mordecai that the King's agents saw me and will be coming again to take me to the palace. But I'll tell him I lied about my name so they wouldn't know I was Jewish, and that he must come to Arderikka in disguise to receive the money for me. I'll say I lied because I didn't want to give them cause to enter the Jewish quarter, lest they start looking for other girls there too. And I'll tell him that my appointment with Memucan is for the day *after* tomorrow. That way, when he comes here I'll be gone, and it will be too late. Don't worry about the bride-price; his pride wouldn't allow him to ask it from a family poorer than he is. He'll be too angry to think about it anyway. He won't hurt *you* though. You can just tell him that the commissioners came early, fearing we might trick them if they allowed us too long to think of a way of saving me from them.'

But my tongue had been working too quickly. I hadn't thought the business through carefully enough, and even as I finished speaking I watched Helena's dim spark of hope sputter out. It was the anticipation of Mordecai appearing in a rage on her doorstep, I'm certain; I ought to have said that I would make sure he didn't come near Arderikka at all. She said, 'No, Hadassah. I forbid it. I should have forbidden you even to speak of such foolishness. Iphigenia is right; we must all accept what the gods have ordained for us.'

But I could see that Iphigenia herself was still clinging to the hope I'd ignited within her. I took her to one side as I prepared to leave, and said, 'Don't give up. I shall come back tomorrow, and we will find a way to persuade her. Tell her that Mordecai *won't* come near. I'll see to it.'

I was so convinced I would succeed that as soon as I got home I went ahead with what I'd planned. I banged on Mordecai's wooden gate like someone being chased by a lion; when Ninlil opened it and set about reprimanding me for acting so wickedly yet again and then running away like a worthless slave, I feigned hysteria and beat my fists against her chest, howling that something dreadful had happened, something worse than I could ever have imagined. I refused to tell her what it was, but kept up my wailing and kicking until she went to fetch her brother. When they returned together I was lying on the ground in the forecourt, my bare arms and legs flailing, and my loose hair caked in dust. I had no intention of permitting them to suspect for a second that I wasn't completely distraught.

I still wouldn't tell them what was wrong, so Ninlil hauled me to my feet and dragged me inside. They laid me on a couch but I sat up and clung to Ninlil, my face buried in her garments so it wouldn't be apparent that my eyes were quite dry. I had no doubt I'd be able to conjure tears if I gave myself time; I only had to think of Benjamin ben Caleb, and they came.

In between bouts of sobbing I got my story out. The imperial commissioners had selected me, there was nothing to be done about it; they had come while I'd been at Iphigenia's, and that was where they would come for me again, on the next day but one.

Just as I'd hoped, Mordecai and Ninlil were both as distraught as I was pretending to be. Predictably, Mordecai's distress came out as anger; he paced about the room hurling question after wrathful question at me, none of which he allowed me to answer. Why in Heaven's name couldn't I have been civil to Benjamin and his parents, as any normal girl would have been? If I hadn't run away half-dressed like a hussy, none of this would have happened. And what business had the King's commissioners to make provision for the future of a man's own daughter when the man concerned wasn't even there? Why hadn't I told them my name, and his name, and invited them to come to our house and speak with him and sort it all out in a proper fashion?

I told him I'd been too frightened; they'd assumed I was Iphigenia's sister, and we'd all been too stricken with panic to say otherwise. I was aware that my explanation was less than convincing, but I knew it hardly mattered because Mordecai was too agitated to think rationally or even to take in exactly what I'd said. This became patently clear when he began raving about the disgrace I was bringing upon my family and my people; I told him again that the commissioners knew nothing about my real background and were assuming I was Greek. This afforded him no comfort; he merely accused me of perfidy: was I so ashamed of my ancestry that I could cast it off like an unwanted cloak? But since I *hadn't* admitted I was Jewish, on no account must I admit it later. That way, his name and that of our family and people would not be dragged through the mud along with my own when I became polluted with the wanton immorality of the harem.

Once his anger had worn itself out, he took his leave; no doubt only grief remained to him, and he wished to work through that alone as was his wont. But I was afraid to be left with Ninlil lest somehow I might give myself away. So I pretended to cry myself to sleep on the couch, refusing to speak to her at all; presently she carried me to bed and I let myself go limp enough to keep her from studying me too closely. By now I was so confident of my success that I was beginning to enjoy myself. I decided to feign a touch of fever, though nothing too serious; that way she would leave me to sleep in the morning and not check on me too early. Thus I should have sufficient time to make my escape before they looked for me. The commissioners were due to return to Arderikka before noon, therefore all would be sure to work out provided that they didn't come later than they'd promised.

So I moaned and tossed on my mattress for a while after Ninlil had lain me down; peeping through half-closed eyelids I perceived that I'd worried her, for she settled herself to watch me instead of leaving straight away. I think she *did* feel sorry for me then, for the first time in months. She knew I didn't want to marry Benjamin, but she could never have suspected in a hundred years that I should prefer to take my chance in the harem. At length I fell silent, but didn't allow myself any real sleep until she'd slipped away.

I had no fear of sleeping too late the next morning; I was far too worked up. I awoke well before dawn and packed my two newest sabbath dresses, together with the blue scarf and bronze mirror I'd got long ago from Ninlil. I made a hasty attempt to get the dust out of my hair, then gave up and packed my comb. I threw an everyday dress on top of my soiled shift. The rest of my things I made into a bundle, and laid them on my mattress with a blanket spread over them; from a distance at least it might fool someone. Then I found a wax tablet and wrote a note. It said that I had gone to Arderikka, and that there was no use in coming after me because I would have been taken to the palace already.

Even so, as I crept past Mordecai's bedroom, I came close to abandoning the whole scheme. He was weeping; I could hear him full well from outside. Imprudently I hesitated, and around the edge of the doorway I could see that his lamp was lit, and he was on his knees with his shawl up over his head as he wore it to pray. But I had resolved upon what to do, and now I must go through with it.

That didn't stop the guilt which rose unexpectedly to nag at me on the way to Arderikka. *Was* I bringing disgrace upon my family name? What would my father have made of what I was doing—my *real* father, not Mordecai? The path I was treading was certainly not one he would have chosen for me. Yet he and my mother had always told me to hold my head high, to think for myself, to remember that I was special. So they couldn't truly have wanted me to squander my youth and my beauty in drudgery, either in Mordecai's house or in Benjamin's. The blood in my veins was royal blood; perhaps by means of my deception I might indeed wind up with a throne to sit on. What better way to do justice to Saul's memory than to pass on his blood to generations of Persian kings? For Israel was merely a backwater, obscure and doomed to be eclipsed more and more by the brilliance of the Empire which had subsumed it. In contrast, Persia was mighty, glorious, peerless, and her kings were rich beyond belief. Yes; I was doing the right thing.

However, as soon as I entered Iphigenia's cottage I saw that my problems were by no means over. Not only had Helena remained adamant that I should not go with the commissioners, but she had also brought Iphigenia herself back to that way of thinking. I walked in to find her already clad in her only half-decent garment—the dress I had given her so many years ago. It was loosely cut and therefore still fitted her, though it was rather too short now. She wore bangles and earrings, the only ones she had, and paste jewels around her neck. Her hair was bound up with ribbons on the crown of her head, with wispy tendrils brushing her pallid cheeks; around her temples she wore a garland of Shushan lilies. She looked for all the world like a victim going to the altar; yes, like her namesake in the old Greek story she'd told me once herself.

She said, 'Help me make up my face, Hadassah. If I'm to meet my fate, I must meet it looking my best. That way my parents will get a better price for me.'

I argued and argued, but there was no changing her mind. I tried everything, including telling her in so many words that she was being thoroughly selfish because she was deliberately depriving her best friend of her one hope of freedom, and because she had made me provoke Mordecai's wrath for nothing. I had told him a lie; whatever would he do to me when he learned that I hadn't been selected at all? How could I go back home to him after this?

But I might as well have pleaded with a stone, and in the end I helped her paint her face just as she'd asked me.

After that, there was nothing to be done but wait. And that waiting seemed to last for ever, for with every hour that passed, I feared that Mordecai would appear, or that some hired servant would come in his stead. Finally, when the sun had climbed to its zenith and we thought perhaps they weren't coming, the imperial commissioners arrived.

Iphigenia's two sisters had been outside to watch for them; they burst breathlessly into the cottage and announced that the royal procession had entered the village and was approaching the end of their street. I crept to the door to look.

A procession it certainly was. There were guardsmen with spears, in front and in the rear, a veritable regiment of them; and in between, four mounted noblemen, and half a dozen litters being borne upon the shoulders of richly-robed slaves. Trumpeters went before all the rest, advertising the mission's importance and clearing the road of children and dogs.

I went back inside as the visitors drew near, and stood beside Iphigenia, holding one of her hands while her mother held the other. Philos her father was there too, his face set and unreadable. Outside the door a clipped, cultured voice proclaimed in impeccable Greek the presence of the imperial deputation. It then requested permission for Lord Memucan, the King's Privy Counsellor, to enter, along with Shaashgaz, Warden of the Harem.

Philos granted it, and they swept in at once, followed by their pages and by the three commissioners who had been responsible for bringing Iphigenia to their attention. A handful of the guardsmen came in too and formed up on either side of the door, one foot forward, with spear-butt resting on it. The dark, low-roofed cottage became suddenly and incongruously illumined with gold and purple, silver and saffron; it was as though a profusion of bright flowers had burst open upon a barren plain. But there was no joy to be got from the brilliant display.

Memucan was exceptionally tall, and quite young, of an age with the King whose confidant he was. He wore the fluted hat and crimped beard characteristic of Persian nobility, and a rich purple robe complete with cape and long wide sleeves. He wore the robe with justifiable pride; a peasant would have had to work for five years to buy so much sea-purple wool, and only the Great King may give a man leave to wear it.

Shaashgaz hovered at Memucan's shoulder: an ugly fellow with a plump, beardless, ageless face, sagging flesh, and a flabby figure the shapelessness of which not even his flowing garments could disguise. I realized with a shudder that he was a eunuch, and once I'd become aware of this, I couldn't stop gawking at him. It was such a long time now since I'd seen Pithon or even thought of him. Suppose he *had* been taken to the palace when my parents died? Might Iphigenia be able to find out? Dare I admit to her after so long that I had a brother who still lived—maybe—but who might look like this fat, formless half-man...

So absorbed was my mind with such thoughts, and so drawn were my eyes by the odious spectacle of Shaashgaz, that I failed for some few moments to grasp what was happening. I only emerged from my reverie when Iphigenia hissed in my ear, 'Answer him, Hadassah! Have you gone deaf?' and I tore my eyes away from the eunuch to see Memucan standing right in front of me, caped arms folded, feet planted firmly apart, and narrowed eyes staring me in the face.

'I—beg your pardon, my lord. I didn't hear what you said.'

'Your name, child,' he barked, in Greek. 'I asked you your name.'

I opened my mouth to say Hadassah, but checked myself just in time. For they were *all* staring at me now, even Shaashgaz. While Memucan stood awaiting my reply, the eunuch walked around behind me and put his hand on my head, then trailed his fingers through my hair, traced the line of my neck, my back, my rump. Something exploded inside my head; I thought, this is it, this is my chance, I have been granted it after all, in spite of everything and everyone. Willing myself not to flinch at what Shaashgaz was engaged upon, I met Memucan's eyes and said steadily, 'Myrsine.' It is Greek for Myrtle. And I willed Helena and Philos and Iphigenia to stay silent.

They were too stunned to do otherwise. Memucan asked my age, and I told him; and whether I had ever lain with a man, and I said no. Then he asked me the names of my parents, and I said, 'If you please, sir ... I am the sister of Iphigenia here. Her parents adopted me at birth.'

There was a dreadful silence, broken only by Helena catching her breath. Memucan swung round to face her, demanding to know why he hadn't been told of me before; his subordinates had noted down all details of the family on their preliminary visit. Helena gabbled some nonsense, being too terrified by his manner and by his stature to string anything meaningful together. So I said, eyes averted, 'My lord, I have been away visiting friends in the city. My mother didn't know when I would return. She was afraid you would ask to see me, and that she wouldn't be able to contact me.'

Memucan nodded. He was stroking his beard and his brows were knit together, but there was a smile at one corner of his mouth. He cupped my chin in one hand and tilted my face so our eyes met once more. '*You* aren't afraid,' he observed. 'That is remarkable. As remarkable as your face, and everything about you. You could be Vashti, ten years younger, could she not, Shaashgaz? I can scarcely believe it.'

At last I understood why they had passed over Iphigenia as though she were a spider on the wall. My face was unpainted, my hair was loose and still matted with yesterday's dust, I wore no jewellery, and my dress was as plain as a grain-sack. But none of that mattered. Memucan knew the King's taste in women as he knew his own; indeed, from the way he looked at me I saw that the King's taste *was* his own. He wouldn't have dared soil his master's goods by touching me as Shaashgaz was doing, for Shaashgaz had never been a man, thus his touch meant nothing. But Memucan would have derived considerable enjoyment from participating in the examining of me; that much I could see clearly.

There was some more talk after that, and there were more questions, addressed to Philos and Helena. I was rather dark for a Greek: could that be explained? And it was strange that a girl as well-formed and womanly as I was hadn't been married off already; were they *sure* I was a virgin? (There would be serious trouble for them later if I turned out not to be.) They had no alternative now but to confirm my story, for to make me out a liar would have meant immediate trouble for us all. Yes, I *was* dark for a Greek, but they had found me exposed; my parents could have been Persian for all they knew. And yes, they had tried to find a husband for me, but I was headstrong and had turned down every suitor who had shown interest. That much at least was true, and Memucan's eyebrows went up when he heard it. I wasn't sure whether it made him less keen to take me, or more; Vashti's strength of will was one of the qualities which Kshayarsha had found most appealing about her, but in the end it had led him to reject her.

I needn't have worried. Memucan's mind was already made up, as was Shaashgaz's, though that didn't prevent him from examining me further just to be sure. I endured it impassively, while Memucan spat out orders at his guards and slaves: the designated litter was to be brought to the door and made ready. There was only the one; Iphigenia would remain at home, and no, her parents must not be anxious, she would be left in peace from now on and so would they. It wasn't Kshayarsha's way to take two sisters into one bed, nor to deprive a mother of both her marriageable daughters one after the other. Another slave entered, bearing a golden casket on a plush purple cushion, and the bride-price was paid.

I don't know to this day how much I fetched, but Helena looked as though she might faint at any moment, and even the stony-faced Philos had to sit down. Then another two eunuchs came in; one wrapped a saffron cloak about my head and shoulders. Iphigenia threw her arms around me, thanking me, blessing me, kissing me, wishing me luck and saying how desperately she would miss me.

But I was already looking beyond her, over her shoulder, at the golden litter which waited with curtains drawn back, outside the open door.

BETH

*'But my people stubbornly closed their
minds,
And made their hearts hard as rock.'*

ZECHARIAH 6:12

8

Borne aloft through the streets of Shushan, I felt like a queen already. So well trained were the bearers of my litter that it hardly rocked at all, and never jolted. I lay among cushions stuffed with the softest of feathers; it was like riding on white clouds on a breezy day. Peeping between the curtains, I could watch folk scrambling out of our path as the trumpeters sounded the royal fanfare. Even the most dignified merchants and money-lenders had to make way—for me, an orphan from the back of beyond, in my homespun clothing, with dust still matted in my hair.

In front of my litter rode Memucan and his three subordinates; behind in the other litters travelled Shaashgaz and his eunuch attendants and pages. We were soon descending from the hill upon which the residential part of the capital was built, and still my carriage remained steady, and exactly horizontal. Then as we set about the climb up to the royal citadel, I began to be nervous for the first time since embarking on my rash enterprise; but it was a frothy kind of nervousness, almost delicious. As we passed the immense statues of Darayavaush with their trains of tribute-bearers, ripples of excitement washed over every part of me, each stronger than the last, until they were grown to waves which I feared might become too strong for me to bear. Through the terrace garden we went, and I glimpsed the fountains and the channels of bright water threading amongst the beds of flowers and between the exotic fruit trees, and the spring lilies, and the water lilies with their innocent faces open to the sun.

We traversed the three courtyards I'd visited as a wonder-struck sightseer four whole years earlier; today they weren't crowded with Shushanite revellers, but empty and vast and quiet, their tranquillity broken only by the plashing of fountains and the echoing footfalls of palace servants going about their work, and sweetened by the gentle calls of birdsong.

140

I'd expected to be conducted at once to the harem, whose securely-locked gate I remembered from last time. Instead, I was taken through a warren of cool cloistered passageways and tiny open courtyards to an area at the extreme south west of the palace, beyond the reception halls where Vashti's fateful banquet had been held. It transpired that this was the wing in which new and temporary women's quarters had been installed: new, because they had only existed since the King's commissioners had begun their collection of the Empire's most eligible virgins; and temporary, because each girl who slept with Kshayarsha would thereby attain the rank of concubine and be transferred to the harem proper. None had gone there yet, for none had completed their period of preparation, though some had already been at the palace for many weeks. Once a new queen had been crowned, any remaining virgins would be sent home.

Presently my litter was set down; the curtains were opened, and one of Shaashgaz's eunuchs invited me to step out. Shaashgaz himself was no longer anywhere to be seen; neither were Memucan nor his men, nor the guards and trumpeters. The eunuch beckoned me to follow him, and we penetrated further into the complex of corridors. One wall was always half-latticed, with the sunlight streaming through its honeycomb perforations to cast stippled golden patterns onto the floor; shining motes of dust floated through the sunbeams, in and out, passing invisibly through the darkness between each ray. Here and there in the same wall were doorless, curtainless openings onto the little yards about which the corridors were built.

The opposite wall had doors all along it, some open, some shut. Through the open ones I saw poky dark rooms, each barely long enough to accommodate one bed, and more like prison cells than sleeping chambers. Here it must be that the favoured maidens lived; and there began to be undercurrents of foreboding mixed with my nervous excitement. At least the girls weren't shut in during the day, or so it appeared. As yet I had seen no one.

The eunuch led me into a room much larger than the rest, which had upholstered couches around three sides, the fourth giving onto its own yard. This was the reception room, I was told, where I must await the pleasure of one Hegai, Keeper of the King's Virgins, who would assign me quarters and an attendant. He might be some time in coming, however, for his duties were many. The eunuch bowed himself out, and I was alone.

For a while I stood without moving in the middle of the room, the saffron robe clutched about me—though it didn't quite cover my dirty clothes. The floor was of polished marble upon which I dared not walk about, for my leather sandals looked so dirty and shabby against it; the eunuch had worn soft kidskin slippers which made no sound and left no mark. The cushions on the couches were so clean and uncreased, they looked as though no one had sat on them ever, and certainly I didn't dare to.

But the Hegai I was awaiting didn't come, and didn't come, so after an interval I bent to unstrap my sandals and stepped gingerly in my bare feet out into the courtyard, where a pair of iridescent butterflies danced about a neatly pruned bush covered in purple blossom. The place was so beautiful and yet so silent: where *was* everybody? Where was this Hegai, and why was he keeping me waiting so long? I hadn't even been offered food or drink... And yet Memucan would have had me believe I was something special. Did he lead *every* girl he chose into thinking that way? Was it his way of ensuring they co-operated meekly? Had I simply exchanged one life of lonely incarceration for another?

Then gradually I became aware that I wasn't alone after all. I had a profound intuition that I was being watched; I wheeled around, expecting to see the Hegai whom I'd been told to wait for. Instead, there were three girls in the reception room, not standing, but draped upon the couches, regarding me disdainfully down their long, straight, Persian noses. They were dressed in layers of sheer trailing garments, sewn with jewels and embroidered with spun gold. Their hair was fine and glossy as black silk, and their long-lashed eyes were sultry with kohl. I felt coarse and clumsy beside them; and ugly, and ignorant, the way I'd felt on my first day in Shushan. I tried to tell myself that I was the daughter of a royal house, and that I could have been mistaken for none other than Vashti when she'd been a girl—but it didn't work.

They greeted me correctly, in Aramaic as highly polished as the marble floor, but there was no friendliness in it. Before I could respond, they began exchanging studiedly nonchalant remarks at my expense, saying that I must be the new girl, and rather dark for an Aryan, wasn't I, and why was there dust in my hair, and was this truly the finest attire I'd been able to find for such an auspicious occasion? They didn't actually address any of their questions to me, however; they behaved as though I were some raggedy doll, incapable of comprehension or of speech.

I tried to make overtures, asking their names and how they had come to be at the palace, and how long I should have to wait before being presented to the King. But this drew nothing from them at first except peals of contemptuous laughter. Then one of them deigned to inform me that there were many, many girls in front of me in *that* particular queue; they couldn't be sure of *how* many, but someone had said it was over a hundred, and perhaps nearer two. The queue could be jumped by no one, however beautiful; strict protocol must be observed in this as in every aspect of courtly life, and the King would see us in precisely the order in which we had been registered. As for me, since it would clearly take such a great deal of time to make me presentable—if indeed this should prove possible at all—I need not expect to set eyes upon His Imperial Majesty for two years at least.

After that, they fell to bickering amongst themselves as to which of them had been at the palace the longest; I didn't know whether to be relieved or dismayed to discover that they apparently loathed one another as much as they'd decided to loathe me. So much for my mental picture of palace life as an endless round of convivial banquets, baths and siestas taken in fellowship with blithe, gregarious, pleasure-loving ladies all of whom shared my interests and relished my company. The King's Virgins were as jealous of one another as nestlings all squawking and fighting over one worm. Perhaps the harem itself would be pleasanter?

Then without warning their carping voices broke off; they twisted themselves smoothly as cats from their couches, and vanished in silence on their slippered feet. I gazed in some surprise at the doorway by which they had left; and through it walked the most dazzling creature I'd ever seen, short of Kshayarsha himself.

I hadn't really formed any expectations of what Hegai would look like, but had I done so, they wouldn't have remotely resembled the reality. Dripping with gold and swathed in silk, he was willow-thin, and graceful as the girls who had melted away upon his arrival. Indeed, I might have taken him for a girl, but for his broad, gold-studded belt and the ornamental dagger he wore at his hip.

Excluding his saffron slippers, he was clothed from head to foot in darkly flowing magenta embroidered with gold and silver thread, and his slender wrists, fingers and ankles were adorned with jewellery more extravagant even than the pieces I'd seen long ago in the Great King's Treasury. His hair and ears were hidden beneath a loose

conical cap whose crown fell coquettishly forward, and about the cap
was wound a flamboyant turban which went right around his mouth
and chin, looped over his narrow shoulders, and ended in a streaming
pall down the length of his back. All I could see of his face was his
eyes with their finely plucked brows and kohl-thickened lashes, and
part of a sublimely aquiline nose; the eyes were smoky and smouldering and made-up more heavily than the girls', and he seemed no older
than I was.

However, from the richness of his raiment and the effortless poise of
his bearing, I could see he was a polished and perfect product of the
court, and that he was haughtily proud of it. No wonder that months of
treatments were needed before a girl could appear before the King;
even his male officials had to be exquisite, if they ranked highly
enough.

He came towards me, moving languorously as a sated lion, regarding me affectedly down the line of his nose just as the girls had done.
Perhaps the acquisition of such an expression was a part of the training
I would have to undergo. But he hadn't truly *seen* me; because as soon
as he did, I noticed the expression change. The difference was almost
imperceptible, tempered as it was by his cultivated manners. But it was
real; the tilt of his chin shifted, along with the crown of his cap, and he
was looking at me now with his head cocked slightly to one side, his
sculpted brows arched so that they disappeared beneath the pleat of
turban which swept his smooth forehead. Not sure how I was meant to
show my deference towards him, I bowed my head, but only a little,
and I didn't take my eyes from him. I couldn't.

He greeted me courteously, introducing himself, enquiring after my
health and trusting that my journey had been comfortable. Then just
as Memucan had done, he asked my name; but his voice was sonorous
and lilting, and languid as the rest of him. I gave him the answer I'd
given Memucan.

'Myrsine?' He laughed aloud, tossing back his head in a gesture of
apparently effortless elegance, though it must have been calculated and
practised for hours. 'There have been a dozen Greek girls standing
where you stand, at the very least, and not one of them looked in the
slightest like you.'

I said nothing. What *did* this paragon of proud beauty think I
looked like? Did *he* think I was anything like Vashti?

He continued, 'If you have a reason to conceal your true identity, assuming a Greek one was scarcely prudent under present circumstances. Almost *any* other nationality might have been better.'

I maintained stubbornly, 'They took me from Arderikka, my lord. No one lives there but Greeks.'

He inclined his graceful head. I knew that he knew that I was out to deceive him, but he didn't accuse me outright. Instead he said, 'Well, you will not last long among the other girls if that is what you tell them. Most of them are Persian through and through, and many lost fathers or brothers in the expedition against your troublesome fellow-countrymen. We shall have to find you a new name and a new background—Myrsine.'

I nodded, again without speaking. He asked me if I were hungry, or thirsty, or tired, and clapped his slim, gem-encrusted hands to summon a slave-girl, who came scurrying. She was as ugly and homely as he was stylish and beautiful, but younger than either of us. He instructed her to fetch wine and sweetmeats, addressing her politely, but she bobbed and scampered in such a way as to make it quite plain that she was terrified of him. He seemed to regard this as normal; although his manners were urbane and over-fastidious he was well used to being obeyed, even grovelled to, and wanted me to know it. As he turned back towards me, I saw his painted eyes flick lazily up and down, appraising my figure. I felt coarser, clumsier, uglier and more ignorant than ever.

Presently the slave-girl returned, bowing and fussing, and set down her tray, taking care to straighten the items upon it before scuttling away. Hegai poured wine for us both, but refrained from tasting his. Instead he passed me the sweetmeats. 'Make the most of these,' he advised me. 'Once your treatments begin, such things will be scrupulously rationed.'

As soon as I tasted the wine, I knew it was mixed much stronger than I was used to. By the time my cup was drained, I had told Hegai my real name, though I still didn't say I was Jewish.

'As I thought,' he observed with relish. 'A Semite. The name *is* Semitic, is it not?'

I nodded.

'And yet you are as pale for a Semite as you are dark for a Greek. And I'm afraid a Semitic identity is little preferable to a Greek one.'

'Why?'

'There are people here who would disapprove.'

'The Great King himself?'

But he didn't reply to me directly, saying instead that there were many men in influential positions who had cause to fear the Semitic race; the intellectual and insurrectionary Babylonians were Semites just as surely as the people of the southern desert-lands were. I saw he wasn't used to answering questions; he considered it his rôle to ask them. Yet he didn't seem displeased.

'Hadassah is a pretty name despite its associations,' he remarked, pouring me more wine. 'What does it mean?'

'It means Myrtle.' And when he arched his brows again quizzically, I explained, 'Myrtle trees grow upon the hills around my home town. They have little white flowers shaped like stars, and blue berries which are used to make perfume.'

But by the wry smile I could trace through his turban I saw he'd known exactly what a myrtle tree was all along, and he said, 'So that rules out Egypt and much of Mesopotamia.'

'I beg your pardon, my lord?'

'As the place of your birth.'

The wine had begun to restore my confidence, in addition to making me less cautious. I said provocatively, 'I thought the Great King's quest was for girls who were beautiful and intelligent, and that their nationality was of no consequence?'

His smile broadened. He knew full well that I was almost teasing him, yet for all his airs and graces, he wasn't annoyed. 'They have to be beautiful and intelligent *and* of good reputation,' he reminded me. 'How am I to assess your reputation if I know nothing about you?'

'You could decide who you would *like* me to be, and believe that.'

'Very well. Your name is Esther, since it is a Persian name and it means Star, the shape of a myrtle flower. It is also akin to the Babylonian Ishtar, the name of my favourite goddess. You are the youngest daughter of a noble but impoverished and unsung family, and you are as Persian as King Kshayarsha himself, may he live for ever.'

'Esther.' I spoke the name aloud three or four times, accustoming myself to its alien sound, and to the strange shape my tongue had to curl into in order to get it to come out right. I said, 'But I shall never speak like a Persian.'

'You may well do, by the time you are ready to meet His Majesty. And there are many other things about you which will interest him far more than the purity of your accent.'

Now it was he who was doing the teasing, but I was no more displeased than he had been. I ignored the suggestive overtones of his remark, and said, 'Ishtar is a Semitic goddess, my lord, and Hegai is a Semitic name. Do you think that perhaps *I* should create a new personality for *you*?'

But he'd evidently decided that things had gone far enough. Still smiling, he rose to his feet and said, 'Enjoy the rest of these delicacies at your leisure, Lady Esther. I must go and check that all your surly sisters are back in their rooms and that they have been behaving themselves acceptably this afternoon. I shall have a room prepared for you, and I shall assign you a maid who will escort you to it.'

'Where *are* all the other girls?' I enquired, finding myself sorry that he was preparing to take his leave. 'I only saw three. And they were hardly welcoming.'

'Oh, they will have been sleeping, or visiting in one another's rooms. But none of them should have been in here; I shall deal with those three later. However, I shouldn't go out of my way to make friends among them were I in your place. The fewer dealings you have with such disagreeable females, the better. The majority are terrified of their own shadows and see poison in every cup and a rival's knife behind every curtain. The remainder are bitches. They will fit into His Majesty's Harem very well.'

I was mildly shocked at the strength of his language—particularly since his expression was still one of benevolence—and also at the implication that life among the concubines was no happier than that among the virgins. Before I'd got over my surprise, he had bent, kissed my hand most unexpectedly through his turban, and departed.

I resigned myself to another lengthy wait, but had only tasted two more of the sweetmeats when there entered not one slave-girl, but seven. Each was as plain as a bullrush, and either as skinny as one or else too stocky or fat. The handmaids of the King's Virgins were as carefully chosen as the mistresses they served, but for precisely opposite qualities; no potential bride of Kshayarsha was to feel threatened by the charms of her own attendant. Nor was her attendant's cleverness to give her any reason to be on her guard: these seven didn't look to have half a shekel's-worth of initiative between them, and I'd seen more life in a pebble than I saw in their eyes.

They all bowed simultaneously, with fingers to their foreheads, then one of them introduced herself as Farah and invited me please to follow her to the room allotted to me; where were my things, and she would carry them? I realized with a stab of self-reproach that in my excitement I'd forgotten to bring them; they must still have been at Iphigenia's. Ah well, they would perhaps be more use to her than they would be to me in this place. My finest robe would look like a beggar's rags at court.

I replied that I had nothing except my sandals, which I put on again, and set off to follow my guide, with the other six girls falling in behind. Expecting to be shown to one of the cramped little cells I'd seen earlier, I was surprised once again when Farah led me up a stone staircase to a room all by itself on a higher storey, complete with its own little balcony, to which I ran at once. It overhung a tiny yard, scarcely more than a stairwell, but it was open to the sky and bathed the room in sunlight. I had my own carpet, couches around the walls, a low table, and glazed clay bath, in addition to the cedar-wood bed which was raised from the floor on carved legs—never before had I slept on anything more pretentious than a pallet.

I caught my breath, and said, 'Farah, why have I been given a special chamber? And why are there seven of you, when Hegai said there would be one?'

'I don't know, my lady. You must have found favour with him.'

'Aren't there *any* other rooms like this?'

'None, my lady.'

'And this hasn't ever happened to a girl before?'

'Never.'

Mulling this over, I went to one of the couches and sat down, giggling in delight as the down-filled cushions absorbed my weight and puffed up around me. I twisted myself about as I'd watched the three conceited maidens do, and lay on my back looking up at the painted ceiling and imagining them confined to their cells, being upbraided or worse by the sophisticated Hegai. I wasn't sure what I'd done to impress him—unless it was merely to resemble Vashti—but clearly I must make sure I did more of it. He was evidently the person most worth befriending of those among whom I should be living for the foreseeable future. Certainly I should have little chance of being befriended by the rest of the King's Virgins now, even if I'd had any before.

Glancing down, I saw that Farah and her six comrades were waiting patiently about my couch, and it dawned on me for the first time that they would do or say nothing without my requesting it. So I ordered Farah to fill my bath with heated water and fetch oil and perfume, and the others to find me clean garments to put on afterwards; they obeyed without question. I hadn't been bathed or pampered by anyone since the death of my mother, and I decided that if the souls in Sheol have any knowledge of what passes on earth, today she would be happy for me.

So I stepped out of my coarsely woven dress and my soiled shift, cast aside my new saffron robe, and spent most of what remained of the daylight hours in my bath, watching the dust float out of my hair, and sending my slave-girls one after another to fetch fresh hot water. After luxuriating there long enough, I lay damp and naked on the couch, and had them rub scented oil all over my body and into my hair to make it shiny and sweet. As dusk fell and they lit my lamps, someone knocked upon my door; Farah ran, and told me it was Hegai.

I had her go and ask him to wait, while the other girls dressed me hurriedly and got my hair up after a fashion. Discarded gowns which had been brought for my appraisal lay all over the bed and the carpet, but there was no time to tidy them up. Hegai was duly admitted.

He'd changed his own clothes since leaving me; now he wore wide flowing trousers, nipped in at his bangled ankles, a loose tunic over the top of them, and an embroidered turban fastened with an emerald over his brow. But his garments were all of dark magenta as before, and I could still see little of his face but his eyes.

It seemed to startle him that I'd impressed myself upon my surroundings so quickly, and asserted my authority over the seven slave-girls with no apparent awkwardness. My dusty hair and dirty clothes had perhaps led him to think I'd been little better than a slave myself; though at least I was now clean and sweet-smelling, I was hardly any tidier. I apologized for my disordered appearance; he passed no comment on it, merely suggesting I should not spend so long in the bath in future, at any rate, not in hot water. For, strange as it might seem, too much exposure to water would dry out my skin and give me wrinkles, especially if the water was over-heated. I wondered how he knew what I'd been doing, then saw that the tips of my fingers were pink and puckered.

Having reassured himself that everything about the room was to my satisfaction, he proceeded to enlighten me as to my daily routine which would commence the very next morning.

I should begin by taking breakfast, then a bath—but a short one, and in milk rather than water, because it contained fat and its properties were thus less drying. Then I should engage in some gentle exercise, to tone my muscles without building them; Farah had been carefully trained and would show me what to do. Next there would be massage, using oil of myrrh; after three to six months this would be replaced by the much more expensive oil of balsam. Massage would be followed by manicure, and pedicure.

Then I should take a long and compulsory siesta, not only to avoid the worst of the heat, but to accustom me to sleeping in the afternoon so that I should not be tired at night, when I must get used to being at my best. While I slept, cosmetics would be burned next to my bed, and slices of cucumber placed over my eyelids.

Upon waking, I should have a light snack, dress at last and have my hair arranged, in case anyone should choose to visit me. If I wished, I could leave my room and go visiting myself, were I to consider it necessary to seek out feminine company more stimulating than that of my attendants. Male company I should be denied utterly, lest I be tempted. While out of doors I must ensure that I be protected from the sun at all times, for its heat would age my skin as well as darkening it, which would never do.

Early in the evening I should take my main meal of the day—a meal which would consist of plenty of fish, raw fruit and vegetables, but no fatty meat, nor sweet things, nor more than a sip of wine. My diet would be carefully regulated, and closely supervised. After my meal I would be given lessons: in elocution, courtly etiquette, deportment, cosmetics and the like. He was sorry that the regime was so prescriptive, but it was in my best interests to co-operate.

I thanked him, and assured him that I would, and that such a way of life would be sheer bliss after where I'd come from. I expected him to excuse himself then and let me sleep, for I'd had no siesta whatever that day and so much had happened in it that I was exhausted. But he was in no hurry to go; it seemed that I wasn't to be denied *his* male company. Perhaps it wasn't considered healthy for a girl to see no man at all, and he alone was for some reason to be trusted? However, I was prevented from speculating further, because once again he began questioning me.

'You didn't *mind* coming here, Esther, did you?'
'No.'

'Might I ask you why not?'

'Because I was about to be betrothed to a man I didn't love.'

'Was there someone else you *did* love?'

He was looking right into my eyes, and for a moment I couldn't reply. His own were so enigmatic, and liquid with gentle amusement; had he perhaps got in mind to tempt me himself? Was this some kind of test of my fidelity to Kshayarsha, before I'd even had my night with him? Deeming it wise to change the subject as rapidly as I could, I answered, 'No,' and added without really thinking, 'And I thought I might find my brother.'

'Your *brother* is at the palace? What is he doing here?'

Inwardly I cursed myself; how could I have been careless enough to say that? I mumbled, 'I don't know that he *is* here. But I had nowhere else to look.'

'You lost him? But how? Was he sold as a slave?'

'He might have been.' Then desperate to get it said, since it would have to be, I gabbled, 'There was a break-in at our house when I was eight years old, and Pithon was nine. They took him away and I never saw him again. But he was very good-looking. Everyone said he'd have been sold for a eunuch.'

Hegai wasn't shocked in the slightest, though for a moment I thought I discerned a real sadness in those limpid eyes. He said, 'It is possible he was brought to the palace then, yes, and quite likely if he was as lovely as you.' I started, taken aback that so peerless a creature could find anything attractive at all about me. However, he went on without waiting to assess my reaction: 'I cannot say that I have heard his name, but that means little. There must be more than a hundred eunuchs serving the harem and another hundred serving the men, and two dozen work under me among the Virgins. I only hope for your sake that he survived the knife. Many don't.'

I didn't respond. I thought of asking him to make enquiries, but didn't quite dare; mostly because I was afraid he would find out nothing, or worse. I wanted to be able to go on hoping.

The next morning, Farah woke me early; I was not to get into the habit of lying in late, lest I be unable to sleep at noon. Hegai had left me almost at once after our conversation about Pithon; he'd said that he could see I was tired; but I thought *he* seemed a little worn too. I wondered how he had come to be carrying such a weighty burden at his tender age.

Another of my handmaids brought my breakfast: a very light affair consisting of bread, fruit and yoghurt. I ate it still wearing my night things, for Farah was already supervising the filling of my bath with milk. I asked her if all the girls got milk, or was this another of my inexplicable privileges? She said no, milk was for everyone. The King owned enough cattle and goats to provide milk-baths for several thousand girls, if he so desired. And many thousands of beasts were slaughtered every day to furnish food for his table and for the countless employees and servants at the palace.

All in all, Farah was tolerably well-informed about palace life, but knew less than nothing about the outside world, never having been there. She was a house-bred slave, as were her six subordinates; since they'd known no other life they were by nature subservient and content. But this made them dull companions, for they didn't speak at all except when addressed directly, and even then could only converse for a matter of seconds without returning to the topic of cosmetics. Not that they used make-up themselves; it wasn't permitted. When I suggested to Farah that I might anoint *her* hair and put kohl around *her* eyes just for fun, she was speechless with horror. I sighed, and began to miss Iphigenia.

After a time I gave up trying to talk altogether, letting them all get on with pumicing the rough flaky skin from my elbows and feet, and smoothing oil into the delicate flesh underneath. Then there were the exercises; Farah showed me how to bend and stretch and twist, to make my body supple and my muscles taut. After that came the massage; I had to lie full-length upon the floor, with them all kneading and pummelling me with their practised hands as though they were bakers and I a lump of dough. I enjoyed it nonetheless; it was so wonderful to be able to take delight in my own body rather than regarding it as some sort of pagan temple of dangerous passions and lusts which must be repressed at all costs. I smiled with pure pleasure as Farah worked upon my breasts—to keep them firm and round, she said—and I imagined what Mordecai might say if he could see me. By now he would know that I'd deceived him—actually outwitted him—and the thought of that made me feel better than anything.

Next came my manicure and pedicure; Farah and three of her assistants attended to both my hands and my feet simultaneously, shaping the nails with tiny files, and pushing down my cuticles to reveal the moons.

As noon approached, they laid me once again upon my bed, and I went to sleep straight away, dreaming of scents and silks, and Kshayarsha... or was it Hegai perhaps? Certainly when I awoke I was already wishing he would come to see me again, because Farah and the others were as shallow and unattractive as lakes in drought; whereas he, for all his surface polish, had begun to intrigue me. He *did* have a Semitic name, so how had *he* come to be in the King's service? And how *had* he achieved such high rank so young? Was this the only reason why everyone seemed to be so in awe of him? Perhaps he was a son of the deposed royal family of Babylon, in training for government of his province?

But he didn't come, and there were many hours to fill before I could expect my evening meal. Farah brought me a little bread and fruit for lunch, then dressed me and did my hair. I might have gone out, had I not felt daunted because of my unpleasant encounter with the three obnoxious girls, and because of what Hegai had said about them and their kind. Besides, if by any chance he *did* come, I wanted to be there.

Presently there was someone at the door, and my heart leapt, but it wasn't him. It was another of the Virgins, one I hadn't seen before. Unlike her three sisters—for thus she referred to all of our number— she had a smile on her face, and she brought me a gift in a little jewelled casket. Deciding that Hegai must be wanting to deny me any friends for some selfish reason of his own, I opened it in delight, and found a pair of earrings, exquisite as they were expensive.

The girl told me her name, and how old she was, and how long she'd been at the palace, and that she came from a family of Medes, who are practically indistinguishable from Persians since their two kingdoms were fused into one such a very long time ago. We chatted amicably for a while, but the longer she was with me, the more obsessed she appeared to become with the privileges I'd been granted so far by Hegai, and with what she called my dark desert beauty. She admired the robe which Farah had dressed me in, and wanted to feel the texture of the fabric from which it was made, which I permitted her to do despite the fact that I couldn't see how it differed from that of her own. Then she admired the styling of my hair and wanted to touch that too, but when she began to trail her fingers through my curls and thence along the line of my neck, I grew alarmed and told her to leave. She wasn't at all keen to do so, and if I hadn't had seven attendants, three of whom were built more like oak trees than cypresses, she might have refused.

When she had gone, I found I was breathless and my heart was pounding. I seized hold of Farah's hand to calm me down, and stammered, 'Farah, what was she doing? What did she want?'

Farah seemed frankly baffled that I didn't know. 'Why, my lady, she must want some favour from Master Hegai, and she thinks you may get round him for her.'

'So she brought me the earrings as a bribe?'

'I suppose so, my lady.'

'But the way she touched me . . . why did she do that?'

'Because you are very beautiful, my lady. *Anyone* would think so. She must want to be your friend.'

I still didn't understand; Farah must have thought me as green as the spring grass. She had to explain to me in words of one syllable before I saw what she meant by 'friend', and then realized how the girls in the House of the Virgins and in the harem proper survived for such long periods of time without men. It no longer surprises me but it still saddens me, and back then I was shocked to the core. I said, 'You must never let her in here again, Farah. You mustn't let *any* of them in. And I don't want these earrings either. Take them away.'

For the rest of the afternoon I felt all shaky inside, and would do nothing but sit on my balcony and look at the sky. Then when Farah and her companions brought my meal—a veritable feast on silver trays, with silver dishes and plates and finger-bowls—there was a note along with it written on a sealed and scented wax tablet and addressed to me. The style of the script was immaculately neat and controlled, and the Aramaic letters are much like the Hebrew ones. So I had no difficulty in deciphering it and ascertaining that it was a request from Hegai to dine with me.

Thrilled, I told Farah to go and find him and say yes. Her companions adjusted my hair, and were still fiddling about with combs and slides when he walked in. He must have been on hand already, and confident that I wouldn't turn him down; I wasn't sure I'd have been allowed to, in any case.

He was dressed differently again, but still in magenta. I wondered how many of these sumptuous suits of clothing he possessed, for everything he wore looked to be worth a skilled craftsman's earnings

154

for a year at the very least. We sat down on cushions beside the low table, with all seven of my women hovering ready to attend to our every need. He unwrapped the lower part of his turban ready to eat, and I caught my breath.

I'd never imagined that such beauty could exist in any face but a woman's. His olive-brown skin—most certainly too dark to be Persian—was smooth, quite hairless, the line of his chin flawless but firm, his reddened lips full and his white teeth perfect. So entranced was I by the sight of him that it didn't occur to me to question why a male should be permitted to dine in my room; nor whether I ought to be permitting myself to eat unclean food.

For unclean it certainly was, by Jewish reckoning. There were oysters and crabs, shellfish of every kind, and we are not to eat anything fished from the sea except that which has fins and scales. Hegai had to show me how to eat them, deftly removing the crabs' shells, and jerking back his head to swallow the oysters whole after prizing them open and loosening the meat. I wondered if my initial clumsiness would betray my ancestry without my saying anything, but he didn't remark on it, and I made sure I ate enough of the things to make him think again if he did have his suspicions. He said that seafood like this was brought from the Persian Gulf every day, because it was the Great King's favourite kind of dish, and he alone in all Shushan could afford such luxury for his household. So as a commoner I wouldn't have been expected to know how to deal with it however Gentile my background.

After the meal Hegai excused himself, explaining that tonight he was busy because another new girl had arrived and he must ensure that she was settled. I found that I was unreasonably but fiercely jealous, and must have shown it. For he kissed my hand and said, 'Don't be troubled, Lady Esther. She is timid and homesick and barely speaks; and certainly cannot read. Anyhow, you will have no time this evening to think about anything but your lessons. Anahita will be here shortly.'

'Anahita?' I wanted to ask more, but he wasn't for letting me detain him.

When he'd gone, I said to Farah, 'Is he not charming, and gorgeous? Have you ever in your life seen such fascinating eyes?'

Farah however would express no opinion, seeking refuge in clearing up our plates, her face scarlet. I started to tease her, making out that her embarrassment must be the mark of a guilty conscience, then assuring her that she needn't worry: *every* girl fancied *someone*. But in a while she implored me in some desperation, 'Please, my lady, don't ever say such things! Master Hegai has great power; he has served as King's Chamberlain and would be so still, were it not for Lady Vashti's disapproval. It would get me into trouble if someone should hear and take such talk the wrong way, and mention my name along with *any* boy's. He would have me killed.'

'*Hegai* would have you killed? You can't mean it.'

'Oh, but I can, my lady.' She glanced about to check that none of my other six girls were listening; they weren't, for they had taken away the trays of left-over food, of which there was enough to feed a small family for a week. Then she whispered, 'One of the kitchen maids was caught speaking to a young man, who had been brought into the Virgins' House to repair a water-pipe. Hegai had her impaled—and the man along with her. It was horrible. It took them hours to die; everyone was watching, and they were watching each other. And it wasn't only because she was a slave. He would've done the same if she'd been one of your Sisters, and even if the man had been a eunuch.'

I laughed aloud. 'I don't believe it. Hegai is as gentle as a dove; he wouldn't hurt anyone. And why on earth should a girl be punished for speaking to a eunuch?'

'There are eunuchs and eunuchs, my lady, surely you must know that? Some are capable of things which others are not. Only those with no manhood remaining at all can mix with the palace women; a stranger could be any kind. Master Hegai can be as cruel as he needs to be, and sometimes he *does* need to be. If he were known to be lax about his duties it would be *he* who finished up on the stake. The eunuch who was Warden of His Majesty's Harem before Shaashgaz was impaled because one of the women in his charge was got pregnant by someone other than the King.'

I didn't want to dwell upon the subject any longer, not least because I was afraid of showing my ignorance. So I asked, 'Who is this Anahita, then, who will be coming to take my lesson? Will she come every day?'

'She is a powerful person too, my lady. She was senior concubine of King Darayavaush, may he rest in peace, and when he died she vowed never to bed another man. She has charge over all the concubines of His Majesty King Kshayarsha, and she is the harem's chief midwife.'

'Does she give lessons to *all* the—"Sisters"?'

'She gives all of them their first.' Farah averted her eyes as she spoke, but I thought nothing of it. 'After that, she will assign you someone. You had best make yourself ready to receive her, my lady; she is very strict. I shall tidy up your things.'

Nevertheless, it was quite some time before the said Anahita appeared; easily long enough for me to have grown almost afraid of meeting her. Farah had requested permission to leave me, and for her companions to stay away too until the lesson was over. I had granted it, not troubling to ask why she should deem this to be fitting. I sat on my balcony, for the first time seriously doubting whether I had done the wisest thing in taking Iphigenia's place.

So my thoughts were far away when Anahita came in. She didn't even knock or beg leave to enter; the first I knew, she was stalking about my room as though it were her own, setting out jars and phials, tongs, razor-knives and tweezers, and instruments whose use I couldn't even begin to guess. Then she spread a linen sheet over the cushions on one of my couches, and ordered me to strip and lie down.

I was aghast, unable to imagine what she might be going to do to me. She was tall—taller even than me—and strongly built, with thick wrists and ankles, large hands, and the hardest face I'd ever seen. I backed away against the balustrade of the balcony, but she summoned me again, with such authority that I obeyed her. 'You must be examined,' she announced, without even looking at me, but continuing to attend to her equipment. 'We must be sure that you are healthy; and as sure as we can be that you are a virgin. The welfare of His Majesty the Great King of Persia is not something to be left to chance.'

If Shaashgaz's examination had made me feel cheapened, Anahita's made me want to die. I lay with my eyes screwed shut against the tears, the fear, the degradation. I couldn't think how she could be so rough, after years of experience in delivering babies; perhaps she wished to ensure I didn't imagine that she was enjoying it.

When she'd finished she allowed me to get dressed again, and proceeded to lecture me on the importance of personal cleanliness and good sanitation in a large and intimate community—the principles of which I was perfectly familiar with already because we Jews know such things better than anyone, having rules about them in our Torah. But it was just as well that I *did* already know, because I couldn't have taken in a word she said. I still felt naked, as though when she looked at me she could still see everything I had, right through my garments. In a while she pronounced that I'd learnt enough for one day, and she left me.

After she had gone I wept and wept. I wanted a bath, to wash away the pollution of this pagan woman's touch, and I was sore where she had shaved me, and inside. If it was going to be like this when I lay with Kshayarsha, I should never dare go near him, and instead of looking forward to it with romantic naivety as before, I was already beginning to dread it utterly. But Farah didn't come, and I didn't know where to get water from, let alone milk.

After the misery came tears of anger; how could I have let this hateful she-monster near me? Why hadn't I screamed, or fought? I had come to the palace to escape Mordecai and Ninlil's domination, yet neither of them would ever have treated me so brutally, and if they'd tried, they wouldn't have succeeded. There was so much I didn't understand: about the complex and bizarre workings of palace life; about the meaning and demands of marriage, or rather of the nearest thing to it which I was ever likely to get; about my own body itself. Yet all of this mattered so very much now, and there was no one to whom I could talk about it without confessing my own callowness.

Suddenly a knock came at the door. Sick with fear that Anahita had returned, I broke off weeping and sat with my hand between my teeth, willing her to go away. But I should have recognized the knock, and remembered that Anahita wouldn't have bothered. It came again, then the door was pushed open, just a little, and I saw it was Hegai.

There was no time to try to hide the fact that I'd been crying. In fact my face felt so red, and my eyes so puffy, that all the make-up in the world couldn't have helped me. When he approached my couch I was sitting huddled up in a ball with my arms around my knees and my head pressed upon them. But he didn't speak, so I had to look up; and he had sat down beside me. For a split second I saw through a crack in his polished veneer, and there was a core of molten pity behind it. Although his long delicate fingers were folded in his lap, I had a disconcerting but profound sensation that he would rather have put an arm around me, had he dared to.

'Please, Lady Esther. You must not be discouraged. Anahita was very pleased with you. You are the first girl who has waited until afterwards to do her crying. You hide your feelings well; that is important at court.'

I didn't know what to say; I was all confused, all churned up. Finally I spluttered, 'You should have warned me of what was going to happen. Farah should have warned me. Both of you knew; don't pretend you didn't. I hate you. I hate her. I hate Anahita. I hate this whole place.'

'Nothing quite like that will happen to you again, I can assure you. Still, if you would prefer to return to Arderikka and marry the man you do not love, I could try to arrange it.'

I didn't know what I wanted. I said no, then yes, then no again, then I got up in a fury and strode out onto the twilit balcony where the evening air was fresh and smelt of jasmine and roses. Of course, Hegai couldn't send me back what*ever* I wanted; he would have no more say in the matter than I now had. He came after me, promising, 'You will get soon get used to Anahita when you have seen a little more of her. *No* girl is warned about her examination; what would you have gained by spending your day in dread of it? You impressed her, though, and that is not easy. Not easy at all.'

I wasn't looking at him, but could sense his eyes fixed on my face; reluctantly I glanced his way, and realized that he too was still impressed by me, and more than before. I growled, 'I have no intention of seeing *any* more of Anahita.'

'You won't be able to avoid it. She has decided to undertake your education herself.' He paused, waiting for the shock to sink in, then said, 'Believe me, Esther. You don't know what this means.'

Hardly caring, I muttered, 'What *does* it mean?'

'It means that she thinks you could be the one we are all looking for. She was Chief Concubine of Darayavaush, Esther. She knows what is needful in a royal consort as much as Memucan does. As much as *I* do.'

There was a gentle breeze blowing in the half-darkness; it caught the swept-back tail of his turban and wafted it about his narrow shoulders. He suddenly seemed frail rather than graceful, and almost vulnerable. Unlike Anahita, he was no taller than I was. I tried to imagine him giving orders for a man to be impaled, and almost made myself laugh despite everything. But I found myself saying, 'No, my lord Hegai. It wouldn't be possible. I don't think I can go any further with this. I may not have spent my day in dread, but I'll be in dread worse than ever till my night with the King.'

I bit my lip then lest I give away any more, and appalled at myself
for having said even what I had said, in front of a man. But he merely
smiled—I could see it in his eyes—and touched my hand; I was
gripping the balustrade as though in fear of falling. 'Please,' he
soothed me, 'You are worrying yourself over nothing, I swear to you.
It will be many months before you need even think about Kshayarsha.
The gods deal our days out one at a time, Lady Esther. And that is the
only way for us to live them.'

9

Thus I walked away from the dull routine of life at Mordecai's into the decadent daily programme of the House of His Majesty's Virgins. Being the pleasure-loving person that I was, I ought to have enjoyed it, and had thought at the outset that I would do. Yet I did not.

I was expected to eat thick, strong-smelling yoghurt for breakfast every day, and it began to make me feel sick. My milk-bath afterwards only reminded me of the yoghurt, and more than once I actually *was* sick.

After my bath, lotions would be applied to my skin immediately to eliminate the slightest risk of its turning dry and scaly; except on the days when they put wax all over my arms and legs to strip off the hair. As for the hair on my head: they washed it one day in three and rubbed oil into my scalp; they said that this prevented brittleness, stimulated growth, and would go some way towards promoting a glossy shine in it and making its texture smooth to the touch, coarse as nature had made it.

Then came the exercises, which were repetitive and tedious. As for my morning massage, this became a torture instead of a delight. For whenever they were even slightly too rough it was like being examined by Anahita all over again, and when they were too gentle I imagined the unctuous maiden from Media running her fingers over my neck.

At siesta-times I missed Iphigenia, and the giggling girlish conversations we used to have lying on our pallets beneath Philos' puny vine. The cosmetics they burned next to my head—which were supposed to improve my skin-tone and make me relax—gave me strange dreams, and the cucumber laid on my eyelids meant I had to lie face upwards all the time and I invariably awoke with back-ache.

Once I'd been dressed and my hair had been put up, there was nothing to do until the evening meal came, for there was no one I wanted to visit, and no one to visit me. Excepting the Median, and the three cat-like creatures I'd encountered on my arrival, I'd spoken to none of my Sisters, though I had seen some of them. They had access to the little courtyard under my balcony, and would sometimes go there to gossip in the afternoons. Now and again they glanced up to see if I was there, and if I didn't withdraw in time, they would call out some disparaging comment. I thought of complaining to Hegai, but didn't want to cause him trouble.

After my meal, Anahita would arrive for our lesson. She began with deportment and elocution: how I must carry myself in order to make the most of my enviable stature, and how I should pronounce my vowels so as to sound like a Persian lady and not some foreign scullery-maid. Thence she progressed to the use of henna, and the correct way to paint it onto my fingers and feet; although I would always have servants to attend to such things, it was important for me to be able to give them appropriate directions.

Next came instruction in the enhancement of my complexion: various creams could be used to remove dead skin or tighten my pores, and there was even a noxious-smelling substance which she claimed would make my skin lighter in colour if I used it each day for a period of months. Then she explained how to paint my face according to the latest Persian fashion, and how to wear my hair in the way that the most admired of the concubines wore it. I wasn't sure that I liked the result, however—I considered it rather too formal and elaborate.

In any case, all this advice seemed ludicrously incongruous coming from a woman who never used make-up, and who wore her hair dragged back severely from her brow and mostly covered by a veil even within the privacy of the women's quarters. But rendering herself attractive to men no longer concerned Anahita; her one lord and master was seven years dead.

She undertook also to familiarize me with the vast and bewildering subject of Persian courtly etiquette. It seemed to me that if one learned it well enough, one would never need to think of anything original to say or do in one's entire existence. There was a correct way to address every single individual, in accordance with his or her rank; one must always bow before a noble man or woman, and genuflect before a satrap, and one must always enquire after the health of whoever one chanced to meet, before proceeding to discuss any other matter. If that person should already be known to one, then one must kiss him or her: upon the hand if one wished to show submission, upon each cheek to show equality or near-equality, on the brow for superiority, and upon the lips for close friendship or something more. I remembered that Hegai had kissed my hand.

If one were offered a gift, one must refuse twice, and then accept. One must never go about immodestly dressed, and a woman must always be veiled anywhere a man might be encountered; one must never be drunk in public, nor vomit nor relieve oneself in the presence of any other person. One must never consciously tell a lie, nor make a promise one could not keep. One must never pollute water by washing or relieving oneself in a flowing stream, nor even by swimming in one.

I couldn't imagine that I should ever set eyes on another flowing stream in my life, but the rules had to be assimilated, no matter how irrelevant.

However, regarding the person of the Great King himself, there were twice as many regulations as there were about everything else put together. Every second of his day was circumscribed by a predetermined formula or ritual; there were rituals associated with his getting up, his bathing, his dressing, his eating, even the cleaning of his teeth and his retirement to bed. Most important of all were the regulations concerning audience. One must invariably prostrate oneself fully before him, and kiss the ground at his feet. One must always address him as Your Majesty, King of Kings, and if one presumed to come into his presence without being summoned, one would incur the penalty of death unless he were gracious enough to raise the tip of his sceptre and extend it in one's direction. Only his very closest relatives were exempt from these procedures.

When I had been at the palace four days, Hegai sent another request to share my company at dinner. My heart leaped in my breast; I forgot everything I'd learnt about etiquette, and declared outright how glad I was to see him. He rebuked me gently and indirectly, saying that Anahita must have been negligent in her instruction, but he couldn't hide the fact that he was touched. We talked of this and that during the meal, for I didn't want to overstep the mark again. If my ignorant curiosity about him—or about life at court in general—should cause him to take umbrage, then he might never return.

Not that I could be confident of his intention to return in any case, but I was reasonably certain that he was at least enjoying being with me. The whole thing was mystifying; I couldn't imagine that so influential and desirable a youth didn't have a host of high-born cronies he would prefer to consort with. As soon as we had eaten, he was gone; but the lingering sweetness of his perfume remained, and that of his smile.

And he did return. In fact, we dined together every evening, though he never failed to seek my permission with scrupulous courtesy. But despite the hours we spent in genial conversation, I found out nothing whatever about him, and he found out very little about me. The conventions of Persian manners enabled us to talk and talk but say nothing; only in his eyes could I hope to glimpse the real Hegai, but he was rarely so far off his guard as to allow even a hint of his inner self to show through. As for my own feelings, I hardly dared examine them. I was at the palace for one reason only, and that was to share a bed with Kshayarsha, perhaps once, perhaps for ever. Even to think about any other man was like dancing with death.

But surely Hegai must *know* that, I thought, as I watched him dip his fingers so elegantly in the finger-bowl, or wipe them on the towel which Farah held out for him. Can he not see that he is tempting me himself, he whose task it is to keep temptation from my path? Why does he come here night after night, and associate freely with me, as though he were my brother?

For the whole of each day I would look forward to his visits, and only the prospect of them made my life bearable. As the days and weeks dragged on, my listlessness must have begun to show, for Hegai took to questioning me again, and with some concern; so did Anahita, but about as sensitively as a bull might interrogate a worm. I told her that I was perfectly contented, but confessed to Hegai I was bored to distraction when he wasn't there, and I was missing my friend from Arderikka.

He asked more about her, and I realized too late that I should have said she was my sister. But he'd known all along that I was no Greek, and that I'd lied to the Royal Commissioners, so it scarcely mattered. He enquired solicitously, 'Would you like to see this girl again? I'm sure I could arrange it, if it might restore your spirits. You were so vibrant, so alive when you first came here, Lady Esther. *I* am almost missing *you*, though you're sitting here beside me.'

'Iphigenia could come here to visit me?'

'Yes, if she were willing. I could send some of my subordinates to escort her.'

'I think I should send her an invitation in advance first of all, so she can get used to the idea. She may be afraid that she won't be allowed out of here once she's in.'

'She too is beautiful, then, and intelligent, and of good reputation?'

'Yes.' A wave of jealousy rose up in me again but I quelled it. So Hegai and I composed the invitation together, and had it translated into Greek by a eunuch who could write five languages. Another eunuch conveyed the little tablet to Arderikka, and many days passed, but Iphigenia made no reply.

'We shall send another message,' Hegai soothed me. 'You may be right: the poor girl is terrified. Perhaps she suspects a trick of some kind. This time you must include something more personal, something which no one else would know about, so she can be sure the letter is from you.'

I nodded, and obeyed him, but more days passed and still she didn't come. We sent a third and final message, and Hegai promised that if she didn't respond this time he would have her brought whether she liked it or not.

'Do I matter so much to you, Master Hegai?' I asked provocatively. But he only said that *all* of the King's Virgins mattered to him overwhelmingly, and it was his business to see that the loveliness which nature had lavished upon them was magnified by his staff's ministrations, rather than worn away. I said it was so long since I'd *seen* anything of nature, it was a wonder I hadn't shrivelled up altogether, like grass without rain.

'You find natural things attractive?' he exclaimed, as though such an idea were ridiculous. 'You like gardens, and flowers, and butterflies, and birds?'

'Of course. Don't you?'

'You are more of a Persian than I imagined. Kshayarsha will adore you. Tomorrow I shall take you for a walk in the palace gardens, if you will permit me, and show you His Majesty's botanical collection.'

'*Permit* you? I should love every moment of it! Would you *really* take me there? Would it be allowed?'

'Anything which is of benefit to one of my charges is not only allowed, but obligatory.'

'When shall we go?'

'In the afternoon, after you have taken your siesta.'

'But the other Virgins will be about, doing their visiting. They will see us, and be more envious of me than ever.'

'Not so envious as they will be when they learn that you have had a friend to visit from outside.' His eyes smiled at me above the mask of his turban. 'I didn't think their envy worried you, Lady Esther.'

'It doesn't.' I looked straight at him and added, 'I care nothing for their approval or for their friendship, so long as I have yours.'

I knew I'd unsettled him with that remark, because he began to talk very matter-of-factly about arrangements for our promenade, how I must wear a hat as well as a veil, to shade my face from the sun lest we undo all the work done to lighten my complexion, and about how good it was that I could rise above the resentment of others, for this was the key to success and sometimes to survival itself within the harem.

The following day, he arrived before I'd even been awoken from my midday sleep. I cursed Farah's painstaking slowness as she dressed me, enjoining her to leave my hair alone; I would throw a veil over it and should have to wear a hat anyhow. She showed Hegai in, and for once he too chose to ignore the conventional mode of greeting, announcing instead, 'I have a surprise for you, Lady Esther.'

From behind his back, he produced a broad-brimmed hat made from straw; and a wax tablet. I sprang towards him, and ignoring the hat I seized the tablet and broke the seal. But the script being Greek, I couldn't understand it, and squealed in frustration. He sent Farah to fetch the eunuch translator, and in the meantime positioned the hat over my veil, adjusting its angle, and appraising it with his own head tilted to one side. 'Exquisite,' he declared. 'And your complexion is lightening by the day, I swear it.' He put out one hand and touched my cheek—professionally somehow, like a baker testing his bread. But the caress was ever so slightly gentler, and lasted ever so slightly longer, than it need have done, I was sure.

However, at that very moment the eunuch came, and told us that Iphigenia would be able to visit the next day if someone could fetch her. Hegai said it would be done; and we set off for the palace gardens.

I had thought he would insist upon Farah's coming with us, for seemliness, but when I ordered her to ready herself it was Hegai who asked in surprise whether I really wanted her to be present. I opened my mouth, unsure what to say, and before I could think of anything he'd dismissed her and taken my arm.

Silently ecstatic, I floated beside him like someone borne along on a cloud. We passed several of my sisters going about in ones and twos; they suspended their conversations to glare at me in stony deprecation, but I merely smiled sweetly, not so much gloating, as in love with all the world.

He took me through cloisters and courtyards, and out into the gardens where it was as hot as the desert. Summer was drawing on, and down on the plains below, the vegetation would be parched and yellow. Here, an army of gardeners bearing huge jars upon their shoulders kept everything watered, and lush as an oasis. The scent of blossom was heady, overpowering.

I quickly realized that a love of nature was certainly not something which Hegai regarded as amusing. On the contrary, he was passionate about it, and as we walked, his disposition grew more animated than I'd ever thought to see it. He'd been overjoyed, not disconcerted, to find that I shared his enthusiasm. But whereas my own liking was of a general sort, and largely ill-informed, he knew several names for every tree and every flower which we passed, and most of the birds and butterflies as well. Not only that, but he knew which region of the Empire every kind of plant was a native to, and when he told me, I could see he was watching my face for a reaction; he was still trying to work out my own provenance. I was glad of the hat's wide brim, for I only had to incline my head slightly to plunge my face into shadow.

However, it was entirely my own fault that I was almost found out. I stopped to admire some flame-red poppies growing by the path, and he said that although they were common enough in many of our satrapies, the King himself had grown these particular ones from seeds sent him as a gift by the governor of Judah. It was the richness of their hue which had so appealed to Kshayarsha, as well as to me. I tried to express a polite interest and then move quickly on, but Hegai wouldn't have it.

'Do you know,' he said, 'The flowers of this variety last only a day, or two at the most? And you can eat the seeds . . . Look.' He bent, and shook out one of the graceful scarlet heads; a light shower of seeds dropped into his upturned palm and he held them out for me to taste. I wouldn't; I knew that renegade Pioneer-women back in Jerusalem had made a potent drug from unripe poppies to deaden pain. I wasn't sure that they'd used this particular variety, but I was scared that these seeds might have magical qualities too—such as the power to loosen the tongue.

Hegai was visibly crestfallen. 'It's a shame you don't like them, Lady Esther. Poppy seeds are one of Kshayarsha's favourite delicacies.' He smiled suddenly, a slight, almost wistful smile, but not slight enough for the turban to conceal it. 'We used to shake them out together when we walked here in the evenings. He used to say that there was nothing on earth which made him happier and sadder than the Judah poppy: happy, because no man could be so hardened as to fail to find joy in its beauty, and yet sad, because that beauty is so short-lived. He said it reminded him of his own mortality; that he, the greatest man in all the world, must die like everyone else, and that human beauty is even more fleeting than the spark of life itself.'

I was astounded, but not by the poignancy of this piece of philosophy; the theme was a familiar one from snippets of Greek poetry which Iphigenia had been able to remember and repeat to me. I exclaimed, 'You used to walk here with the Great King himself? Just the two of you?'

'It was one of my pleasanter duties, yes.'

'I—had no idea.'

'No idea of what?'

'That you knew the King personally.'

'I was his Chamberlain. How could I not do?'

'I . . .' But all at once I didn't want to go on. I was suddenly afraid of showing my ignorance again; I'd no idea what the office of Chamberlain entailed, though Farah had indeed told me that the post had once belonged to Hegai. Yet if Hegai *did* know the King, he had presumably been acquainted with the King's wife also . . . I gabbled, before my courage failed me, 'So you must have known Queen Vashti then, also. Lord Memucan said I looked like her. Is it true?'

Hegai allowed the poppy seeds he hadn't eaten to trickle through his fingers onto the ground. He stood facing me and took hold of both my hands. 'No,' he answered. 'You have her eyes, her nose, her mouth. But you don't look like her at all, and for that you should be grateful.'

'I don't understand.'

'Vashti isn't beautiful, Lady Esther. Oh, she was once. She was incomparable. But jealousy has tightened her lips, and furrowed her brow, and soured her expression. That must never happen to you. Never.'

It was the first time I'd heard him make such an emphatic pronouncement about anything. Surely, this had to have *some* meaning? I found myself gazing into his eyes, imagining him saying that he loved me, or, at very least, that it mattered to *him* that I should remain beautiful. But he merely said, 'If Kshayarsha is to make you his bride, you must remind him of Vashti as she *was*, when he first wed her, not as she has become. In fact, it would be better if he didn't think about Vashti at all in connection with you, or rather, that the connection is

made in his heart but not in his head. In his head there is someone else
he should perhaps be thinking of when he sees you.'

More confused than ever, and knowing I was getting into deeper and
deeper water, I mumbled, 'I don't think I want to be his bride, Hegai.'

'Because of Anahita, and the way she hurt you?'

'No. Well, yes, but . . .' How could I possibly explain the turmoil of
my feelings, to him? He still had hold of my hands, and his own were so
warm and yet so dry, so firm and yet so light; and his eyes looking
straight into mine were so dark, so deep, so concerned. What were we
doing here together, unchaperoned? Why had he brought me, if I was
no more to him than any of the other Virgins, albeit one with a greater
chance than most of being chosen Queen? Yet I only needed to put one
foot wrong, to misinterpret his concern only slightly, and I should
finish up impaled on the stake which Farah had so graphically
described to me. In the end I just said lamely, 'I don't want to think
about being his bride lest I raise my hopes in vain.'

'If that's what you fear, then your fear is groundless. You have no
serious rival here.'

'Not yet perhaps. But Lord Memucan and his men are still out
hunting.'

'No, they are not.'

'I beg your pardon?'

'I have recommended that the quest be curtailed. There is no need
for any more girls to have their lives ruined by being brought here
against their will, no need for any more families to be wrenched apart.
I will not be responsible for unnecessary cruelty, and I am hated by
quite enough young females as it is.'

All of a sudden, the sky above me felt very heavy, and it wasn't just
with the torrid afternoon heat. The mingled scents of the flowers
became sickly sweet, my head began throbbing, and I said, 'Hegai, I
need to sit down.'

There was a fallen log just near to where we were standing—we were in
that part of the gardens which is allowed to grow wild, like a real forest.
Hegai sat me down and asked if I were ill; the heat must be affecting me,
we ought to go back inside. No, I said, it wasn't the heat. It was
everything: being severed from my kinsfolk and from the life I'd understood, even if I'd hated it; existing in this in-between world, not knowing
whether I should be going on from it to obscurity and futility in the
harem—without his being there any longer to protect me from the

jealousy and bickering of those around me—or to glory; and if by some
miracle to glory, whether I would be able to bear the strain of it, being
pampered and pandered to for the rest of my days by fearsome women
like Anahita, or by fat ugly eunuchs the like of Shaashgaz the half-man,
whose flesh wobbled when he walked, who was an abomination in the
eyes of any respectable person, and who would remind me perpetually
and painfully of what Persian oppression had done to my own brother.

I got the whole lot out in one incoherent sentence, and finished up
breathless and distracted. Thus I didn't at first appreciate how quiet
Hegai had gone, or how he was no longer looking at me, but at some
invisible object far away among the trees. By the time I'd emerged
from my self-pity enough to notice, he'd stood up and was already
striding back the way we'd come, instructing me to follow him, for it
was almost time to eat.

It wasn't, anything like. I ran and caught him up, asking in
trepidation what was wrong, how I had offended him. But he
wouldn't answer, keeping his eyes firmly fixed ahead of him, and he
was walking so quickly I had to skip to avoid being left behind. In this
fashion we proceeded all the way back to my chamber; the girls who
had watched us with disapproval when we'd left now curled their lips
sardonically, and I was mortified, fervently wishing that some magic
might transport me to the privacy of my room without my having to
pass amongst them. Once we reached our destination Hegai left me
without another word, and that evening I ate alone.

The next morning I refused to get up. Farah tried rebuking me,
reasoning with me, coaxing me, jollying me along, but none of it worked;
she was my servant after all, and I wasn't compelled to obey her.

I wasn't consciously wanting her to have to resort to summoning
Hegai. I was too despondent to think strategically, or to think at all.
Just about the time I ought to have been lying down for my siesta there
came a knock at the door, and Farah was stricken with panic, fearing as
I suppose that it was Hegai, and that when he saw how things were he
would be angry because he *hadn't* been summoned. I realized without
much interest that Farah must feel at least a little loyalty towards me,
for she'd kept my wilfulness quiet at grave risk to herself.

But it wasn't Hegai. It was a eunuch, saying that my friend was here
to see me, and ought he to show her straight in?

Iphigenia! I'd forgotten all about her. 'Yes,' I said, 'Send her in at once,' even though I was still attired for sleep and my hair was like a bird's nest. I'd tossed and turned all night, which was partly why I hadn't yet got up.

She came in dressed in her best—my old robe from Jerusalem—wearing all the jewellery she possessed, but she still looked like a forlorn little waif come to beg at a rich man's table. She stood in the middle of my room, her face white as mist, overwhelmed. Then she saw me and gasped in Greek, 'Hadassah, are you ill? May the gods forgive me, I should have come sooner. I didn't know.'

I tried to tell her I wasn't ill, and that there was no need for her to worry, but she patently didn't believe me. And I tried to tell her to call me Esther, for it *was* almost as bad to be Jewish here as Greek.

'I ought never to have let you take my place,' she blurted, wringing her hands. 'I knew it would be like this for you. It is terrible.'

'It isn't. Honestly, it isn't. You have come on a bad day. Let me explain to you.' But the more I tried to tell her about my beauty routine and my lessons, then about Hegai and how I thought I must have offended him in some way, the more I seemed even to myself to be describing life in a prison run by a capricious governor whose rules were incomprehensible, yet spelled out death when contravened. All the time I was talking she kept attempting to interrupt, yet I wouldn't let her; so desperate was I not to admit that I might have made a wrong decision. But when at length I paused for breath she said, 'Hadassah—I mean, Esther—it isn't just all that. It's Mordecai, your cousin. He's distraught.'

My train of thought faltered, and collapsed. I whispered, 'What do you mean?'

'He came to our house the day after you left, though he knew he'd be too late; he knew you'd tricked him. He says his life is ruined.'

'His reputation, more like.' I was beginning to feel better; I was going to find out how sweet my revenge had been upon him. 'His own adopted daughter, and a daughter of Abraham at that, run away to a pagan king's palace—'

'No, you don't see. It's not his reputation he's concerned about. He says he would give up all the wealth and status he has, if it were possible to get you back by doing it. He must love you very much.'

I laughed out loud. 'That's what Ninlil used to tell me. And what of her? Wasn't she with him?'

'No. My mother asked after her and he said she was sick.'

'I can well believe it. She's sick of having no one to help her with all the boring and dirty jobs around the house; no one to torment and criticize all the time.'

Iphigenia said nothing; she stood staring down at her twisting hands, for I hadn't even invited her to be seated. I apologized, sliding off my bed at last and leading her to sit beside me on a couch. Farah brought a tray of sweetmeats; I hadn't ordered her to do so. But I ought to have done, and resolved not to scold her; for once she'd shown initiative, and it was just as well. I teased Iphigenia for her wan silence, asking her what she was thinking, and after some goading she stammered, 'I'm thinking that perhaps you *are* as selfish as Mordecai says you are. You should have seen his face, Esther. It was greyer than his hair or his beard; and he's so thin. Has he always been thin?'

I shrugged. 'Not especially. I don't know; I suppose he might have been.' I couldn't even recall whether his beard had turned grey. 'Anyhow,' I added vehemently, 'It's too late for me to go back now, and he knows that as well as I do. The search for maidens is over, because Hegai thinks I shall become Queen. He thinks Kshayarsha will be entranced by me, and take me as his bride.'

Again Iphigenia fell silent.

'Well, have you nothing to say to that? Aren't you excited? It isn't like you, not to share in my happiness.'

'Esther, I wanted *you* to be there when *I* got married, but it's too late now. You missed it. Why else do you think I'd have taken so long in answering your invitation?'

It was my turn to be lost for words. Iphigenia had turned her face away, and brushed one hand abruptly across her cheeks; something seemed to congeal inside me. But I fought to disregard it, whatever it was, and said at last, 'You're married already? To Nikias? But you hardly know him, and your parents can't possibly have had time to make proper enquiries about his family. God give me strength.'

She rounded on me, so uncharacteristically bitter that she didn't even look like herself. 'What was the point in waiting, when I knew what I wanted? You said so yourself. And we only had the word of a Persian that the Commissioners wouldn't come back for me as well, after they'd taken you.'

'A Persian gentleman's word is his bond, Iphigenia. Lying is one of the most serious crimes a man can commit in their eyes, almost worse than murder.' I swallowed hard, thrown by the way she was shaking her head in consternation at what had come over her, dismayed at having caught herself reacting with the same kind of self-centredness she claimed to have discerned in me. No doubt she was wishing she hadn't come; it was all going so horribly wrong. After a long and wretched hiatus I asked in a small voice, 'Iphigenia . . . what is it like?'

'What is what like?'

'Getting married. The first night, I mean.' I swallowed again. 'Does it hurt a lot?'

She wiped her eyes and nose; my implicit admission that I lacked her experience and craved her advice had brought her back to herself. She sniffed, and replied, 'Not so badly. And hardly at all after the first time. Mother says it has to hurt a little, to prepare us for the pain of childbirth.'

'But bearing a child must be exciting as well as painful. Was this not exciting too?'

'Exciting?' Plainly she had no idea what I meant; it hadn't occurred to her that the thing *ought* to be exciting. I don't think she'd ever truly felt the way I'd been accustomed to feel when I used to fantasize about Kshayarsha siesta after siesta; or the way I might feel about Hegai even now, were I insane enough to allow myself to do so. All she could find to say was that it gave her pleasure to think that she could bring Nikias satisfaction. He was so kind, and loved her so much, and they could hardly wait for him to give her a child to make their love complete.

I tried to imagine Iphigenia as a mother; the idea was ludicrous, I decided—she was far too young. And yet in truth she was not, and neither was I . . . We sat and regarded one another without speaking, knowing too certainly for words to be necessary that if we ever had been close, it was all over now. Her life would already be taken up with cooking and cleaning, spinning and weaving, each morning hoping to wake up feeling sick, as Nikias' life quickened her womb. Our aspirations were as different as those of two girls the same age possibly can be, except that hers were simple and clear-cut, whilst mine were as tangled as uncombed wool.

Presently she made her excuses and left, and I wasn't sorry. I sat out on my balcony, staring up at the cloudless Shushan sky, and felt lost, more rootless than ever, and knowing less than ever who I really was.

10

It was more than a month before I saw Hegai again to speak to, and my life became a burden to me which was heavier than I thought I could bear.

Summer waxed hot and fierce, and the Great King and his immediate entourage left for the cooler mountain palace at Ecbatana. This immediate entourage, so called, consisted of many thousands of courtiers, eunuchs and women; advisers, magi, physicians, masseurs, perfumers, garment-makers, laundry maids, scullery maids, food-tasters, cooks, and cooks who cooked for the cooks. But none of the Virgins went with them, for none would be ready to be introduced to the King before his return. Kshayarsha himself was said to be more depressed than ever, according to Farah; perhaps the clear mountain air would do him good.

Then one evening Farah brought my meal as usual, and out of the blue there was a message with it: written in immaculate script, on a scented and sealed wax tablet.

Hegai's words made not the slightest reference to our misunderstanding in the garden—whatever its nature had been—nor to our protracted separation. They merely requested my permission for him to dine with me in my chamber, using just the turn of phrase which he'd always used.

I didn't bother to send a reply; I leapt up and went to the door myself, knowing he would be waiting outside. So he was, with his arms crossed nervously over his chest and the fingers drumming on opposite shoulders. When he saw my joy, relief spread across his face like the rays of the early morning sun bathing the plain of Shushan. Yet still he made no reference to our estrangement, and throughout the meal we talked of trivialities; I didn't dare raise the subject if he didn't, for it must mean he didn't want to discuss it. But as he prepared to leave I asked anxiously, 'You'll come again tomorrow?' and he said yes.

174

It was the same for the next three evenings; on the fourth I decided to risk all and ask him what had been wrong. But he wouldn't answer, and left early, saying he felt unwell.

'What do *you* suppose is wrong with him?' I enquired of Farah. 'He used to be so composed, so cool about everything. Now he's as tense as a harp string and timid as a lizard.'

'With respect, my lady... to the rest of the Virgins he's harsher than he's ever been, and to his eunuchs too. He caught one of the eunuchs shirking his duties, and flogged him himself—thirty strokes.'

None of this made any sense to me. All the same, I wasn't going to say anything else to Hegai about it, not if it meant I wouldn't see him for weeks on end again.

As things turned out, however, I was destined to see much more of him, not less. When the tide of summer had turned, and some of the sting had begun to go out of the midday sun, Hegai announced that from now on he would be taking my lessons instead of Anahita.

'But why?' I exclaimed, incredulous. 'Have I offended *her* now, too?'

'Far from it. You have learnt all that she can teach you. You must now receive instruction from someone who is better acquainted with the present King than she is, that is all.' He spoke so starchily that I didn't dare press him further.

And curiously, I found that I enjoyed his lessons no more than Anahita's. Each session we spoke about increasingly delicate matters, yet he grew more and more distant in his approach and it was as though he wished he were somewhere else entirely.

'You must have Farah use a deeper colour on your lips and your cheeks,' he told me brusquely. 'Our lips and cheeks redden when we are filled with desire, and that is the impression which you will want to give to Kshayarsha. You must use more kohl on your eyelids, because our pupils dilate when we are aroused, and thus our eyes appear darker; cunning use of kohl will convey the same message. Don't wear such a delicate scent, either; it doesn't hold enough promise. Try something spicier, more sultry, like balsam. And you must soften the style of your hair—it may be fashionable like this but it doesn't suit you, and the King will not like it. The same sort of thing goes for your dusting powder: forget what is supposed to be in fashion. You need paler powder along your cheekbones to emphasize their structure, and darker along your jawline lest it seem too square and strong.'

All the while that he was speaking, he was reddening my mouth and the hollows of my cheeks, applying kohl and perfume, loosening my hair and brushing creamy powder over my cheekbones and chin; but you would have thought he was giving a lecture on the mixing of plaster whilst rendering a mudbrick wall. Listening to him discoursing on desire, and yielding myself to the artistry of his skilful fingers as they flew over my face and through my hair was churning up my already turbulent feelings towards him the way the wind whips up a storm on a lake of invisible currents; yet his expression remained infuriatingly impassive throughout.

When he'd finished, he stood back to survey the result, then declaring that my coiffure still wasn't quite right, he unwound his turban, took off his cap, and let his own hair fall free. He told me he would put it up in the style he was aiming for; if he got it right on himself the way he'd achieved it in the past, the technique would come back to him and he could do mine the same. I watched transfixed, because his hair was as long as mine, and shone like a pool of sweet water in the evening sunlight. He took golden pins and slides, back-combed and braided it; and when he was satisfied with it, and with my own, he passed me a mirror. I cried out with my hand to my mouth, for we could have been twins.

That night I lay awake for hours. I couldn't even say Hegai's name to myself without feeling the blood rush to my cheeks and lips as he'd described, and imagining my pupils expanding until my eyes turned quite black. Yet the friendship I'd once thought we enjoyed had become as dry and barren as the parched fields outside the city, silently begging for the first of the season's showers. I concluded that things could not go on as they were, and once I had made my decision, lunatic as it was, I managed to sleep.

In the harsh light of dawn, things looked a little different. Surely it was better to resign myself to making the most of my relationship with Hegai just as it was: detached and professional perhaps, but at least without danger attached to it? Thus my head was arguing; yet my heart was urging me to drink a little wine to bolster my confidence and to restore my view of the situation to what it had been the night before.

My heart won; when Hegai arrived for our evening meal there was a healthy flush about my face which didn't owe its existence to cosmetics. I kissed him once on both cheeks as custom permitted; then

176

twice, for which there was no such provision. He didn't pull away, so I kissed him again, for a little longer. I asked him to take me walking in the gardens the next afternoon; he agreed, a trifle reluctantly perhaps because of the last time, but not without a wistful pleasure that I'd suggested it.

As the hour set aside for our promenade approached, I took wine again; when he came for me I kissed him on the lips through his turban. Once in the seclusion of the gardens I held his hand instead of linking his arm, and every so often I would squeeze it just that little bit harder. When we sat down to rest upon the fallen log, I moved up so close that the arm on which he supported himself was half around my back. I drew it gently the rest of the way, and he left it where I'd put it.

In short, he resisted none of my tentative advances in the slightest; but instead of relaxing he grew tenser by the moment. I didn't care; I was on fire with daring, and with the knowledge that he wouldn't be able to maintain this tension much longer without something breaking inside him.

I couldn't hold his hand once we were among people again, but after we'd returned to my chamber, and eaten, I sent Farah and the others away with the trays and dishes and told them not to come back until I summoned them. Then I sat beside Hegai and put my arm about his shoulder. He was shaking like a man saved from drowning in icy water.

I said softly, 'I don't wonder that you didn't feel well the other night, Master Hegai. You *aren't* well; you have a fever. You need to lie down.' And I pulled him closer, and around, until he lay with his head in my lap. What showed of his face was as white as death. 'Don't be anxious,' I soothed him. 'You're doing nothing wrong. You are sick, and it seems that there is no one but me to care for you.' I loosened the turban from around his mouth, on the grounds that it restricted his breathing; then I unwound it slowly from his head as well, removing his cap and stroking the hair back from his brow. But he didn't stop shaking. I said, 'I do wish you would tell me what the trouble is.'

He closed his eyes and hid them with his hand. I laid my own upon it.

'Your hand is cold, Master Hegai, and you are shivering. Perhaps some wine will warm you.' I lifted a goblet which I'd already filled and positioned within easy reach; propping up his head I held it to his lips.

At first he wouldn't have it, then changed his mind and drained it to the dregs. The fire of daring within me flared up afresh as I saw that I was winning. The smooth red heat of the wine was melting the tension from his face even as I watched; but no drug-induced contentment came in its place. I whispered, 'Why are you so sad, my dearest Hegai? Is it my fault? If you say yes, you will make me sad too, beyond endurance.'

I moved his hand away from his eyes and he opened them, searching my face. Then he said, 'I'm not sad, Lady Esther. I'm happier than I thought I could ever be again. But it cannot last.'

What did he mean? If only I could be sure enough of what I thought he must mean, to risk saying that it could last as long as we wanted it to last—if we were discreet—and to risk kissing him properly, the way I longed to. But before I'd made up my mind, he was speaking once more.

'Esther is the only name I could have chosen for you. You *are* like Ishtar, the goddess who risked all to follow her beloved Tammuz to the House of Darkness and restore him to life. Yet she knew what she was doing, and you do not.'

Mystified, I waited for him to go on, stretching out the tips of my fingers to caress his fine cheekbone—finer than mine—and then the downless cheek itself. He asked me if I knew the story and I said yes; the women of my homeland had re-enacted it every year at our Temple, though the practice went against our traditions and my mother had said it was vanity, and its celebrants apostate. I wasn't thinking what I was saying; I couldn't think about anything, for the fire in my heart and in the rest of me was steadily devouring all in its path.

'How can it be vanity?' he persisted, as though I cared a jot. 'Each year the fields lie dead, while Tammuz is dead and Ishtar searches for him in the Underworld. Then the lovers emerge triumphant, and there is new life for crops and for mankind, just as you have sought to bring new life to me.'

'Then I shall be Esther, and I shall call you Tammuz from today, if it makes you happy,' I declared, not understanding why all this talk of pagan deities should so suddenly matter to him. In the end I threw all remaining caution to the winds and said, 'The Great King can wait, and he can wait for ever, for all I care. It's you I desire, my lord Tammuz. I love you.'

178

After that, for one fleeting moment, I knew ecstasy. Hegai didn't leap up from the couch, or even turn his head to one side as I raised it to mine and our lips brushed together. I unclipped one of the brooches at his shoulders and slid my hand around his back inside his clothing, feeling the perfect line of his collarbone against my arm. By then I had closed my eyes for joy, but when I opened them again to see if he was truly happy too, his own were streaming.

I held him to myself in consternation; and then in an increasingly erratic voice he began to pour out to me the answers to all the questions I'd been wanting so much to ask him: the entire story of his life. But the more he told me, the less I wanted to listen.

He was the son of a Babylonian brickmaker, which made him as Semitic as I was, but also a member of the pitiless heathen civilization which had long ago destroyed Jerusalem and carried off my ancestors into exile. His father had been rich, for it wasn't mud-bricks that he manufactured, but the costly glazed and decorated ones which go to make up the friezes in the Great King's palace. Indeed, the family had been resident in Shushan for a while, because at the beginning of Kshayarsha's reign the finishing touches were still being put to the mighty complex of edifices, and Hegai's father had supervised some of the work.

But then Babylon had rebelled against Persian domination, and any Babylonians living in Shushan had found themselves in mortal danger. Hegai and his parents had fled back home, but it soon became obvious that the revolt could not succeed. Doom over-shadowed the once-proud nation, then crushed it. The destruction of the city of Babylon itself had been absolute, more horrific than anyone could have credited. Neither Kurash, the founder of the Hakhamanish Empire, nor the great Darayavaush would ever have done such unspeakable things, for Persians by nature are tolerant, respecters of religious tradition and admirers of beauty and culture wherever they find them. But the beauty of Babylon was ruined, the elegant buildings razed to the ground, the glorious gateways and friezes with their yellow-tiled lions stalking in procession along the blue-tiled sacred avenues were defaced and plundered. There was wholesale massacre too; it seemed that the only people left alive were those who could fetch a good price in the slave-markets. All the booty became the property of the Great King, so he received the proceeds of every sale. Not that he ever laid eyes upon his wretched human chattels—only upon the gold he got for them.

Hegai's own parents had been tortured and then strangled before his very eyes. He himself had been fourteen years old, still a child in so much as his voice hadn't broken, and he'd never done a day's work in his life. He'd been his mother's only son, and the joy of her advancing years; pampered and protected, he dreaded being set to menial tasks almost more than he dreaded being killed.

In the event neither fate had befallen him, but he couldn't bring himself to tell me what had. Throughout his anguished account the pitch of his voice had been rising; now it failed him altogether.

Even then I didn't guess the truth about him. It astounds me now that I could have been so naive, but I'd been cossetted by my parents as surely as Hegai had by his, and since coming to Shushan no one with any qualification to do so had seen fit to talk to me about things which might be deemed unseemly. Even Anahita, who had gone into great detail about my forthcoming presentation to the King, had told me nothing of what would happen once he took me into his bed. Yes, I knew what a eunuch was, and how one might be made, but I'd thought they all had to be fat and bald and revolting. I'd forgotten entirely what Ninlil had once told me, that eunuchs when young stay slender like girls. And I never had worked out what Reuben's daughters had been giggling at when I'd asked about eunuchs at Vashti's banquet.

So I just sat there speechless until Hegai was forced to spell it out to me.

'They took my manhood, for God's sake! Can't you see? I'm like Shaashgaz, whose flesh wobbles when he walks, who is an abomination in the eyes of any respectable person . . .'

Sick at heart, I recognized the words I'd spoken to Hegai on our first visit to the gardens. All I could think was: oh my God, oh my dear God, and I was saying it to myself in my mind, over and over again. I didn't know whether to be angry or distraught or disgusted. Hegai still lay with his head in my lap, both arms flung up to hide his face as though he felt himself too abhorrent to be looked upon; certainly I couldn't look at him, and I no longer cradled him in my arms. I would have moved away from beneath him if I could have done, but he was like a dead weight across my knees.

I heard myself asking him why he hadn't told me, but even as I spoke I knew I shouldn't have needed to. I could only have been so obtuse because I'd wanted to be.

'I thought you must have known,' he wept. '*Everyone* knows that ungelded males past the age of puberty aren't allowed to go about the women's wings of the palace unescorted—if at all—except the King and his own sons. And you must have seen that I hadn't even the shadow of a beard, and heard that my voice was still high, even though I do my best to deepen it.'

It was futile to attempt to excuse myself for my foolishness, and yet I did. How could I have been expected to know all about who was allowed access to where, and with whom, in an environment as alien to me as the Persian royal residence? And there had been no eunuchs where I'd come from.

There was no need for me to explain myself, he said; for it had become more and more plain to him as time had gone on that I *didn't* know; though only when I'd openly expressed my contempt for Shaashgaz had he been forced to face up to it. Until then, he'd been deluding himself far more certainly than I had. He'd deluded himself into supposing that I *did* know, but that unlike every other girl, who was repelled by the sight of him, I could look beyond the superficial and want to befriend the person inside. He'd been terrified of telling me the truth, however, lest I should never want to speak to him again, and then his beautiful illusion would be shattered.

'I was frightened, Lady Esther. I didn't want to lose you. I was afraid you'd be disgusted, or at the very least angry that I'd deceived you for so long. And the longer it went on, the worse it got. That day out in the garden ... I knew I was just being stupid, it all had to stop. But in the weeks that followed, I missed you; I missed you so much. So I had to come back, but then I realized you didn't just want me for a friend. You found me—attractive. I didn't think it would ever be possible for a woman to want me, and it was like paradise. But it cannot go on. I can never even feel for you the way a man should feel, much less make love to you. They cut me too young, and too close.'

Without warning he sat up and tried to dry his eyes. He straightened his clothing, fastened his brooch, and began to put on his cap and turban with fumbling fingers. Relieved of his weight across my lap I edged away from him, shuddering involuntarily at the dreadful thought that I could ever have been stirred by desire for a man who wasn't even a man; that I could have allowed myself to be polluted by his touch.

But he looked so lonely; it was little wonder that he'd been grateful to find someone with whom he could share a table, let alone his soul. The Virgins for whom he was responsible either feared him for his cruelty, or reviled him for his aloofness, or despised him for his condition, or were fiercely jealous of his dark, fey beauty. Yet all at once it came quite clear to me that his aloofness wasn't a sign of arrogance, but of fear; his acts of cruelty were born of a need to prove to himself and to others that he wasn't weak; his polished manners were a shield which he used in order to protect himself from the barbed tongues of those who hated him, and from his own crippling sense of incompleteness and inferiority.

So I took him in my arms once more, for the first time in my life experiencing the joy of offering genuine comfort to another; and this other was a gelding, an aberration, an abomination in the sight of Adonai... While he cried his heart out on my shoulder, I began to tell him all there was to tell about my brother and how I had loved him, and then about my parents and my sister, and our idyllic lives back in Jerusalem, where we had been God's Remnant, the rebuilders of the holy nation. I told him I was Jewish, because it seemed so wrong to keep anything from him after what he'd been willing to reveal to me, and it was all so incongruous, because our two peoples had been bitter enemies for more than a century.

But even stranger was the fact that the more I told him about myself, the more I felt to be speaking about someone else. For weeks I'd been eating unclean food without thinking twice about it, I'd lost count of when sabbath was, and in all that time it had never once occurred to me to pray. Worse still, I knew from what Mordecai had read to me out of the Torah that the wretched creature I was embracing was just as unclean as the oysters and lobsters and shrimps and prawns which we had devoured together at my table; a eunuch was never to be accepted as one of God's people. I lost the thread of my story and fell silent, so he went on with his own.

He'd been drugged and castrated amidst the smouldering ruins of his city, by a dealer who'd bought him from those charged with the profitable disposal of the Great King's booty. At least the instruments had been clean, and his wounds had been well dressed afterwards; for handsome boys are expensive, and the making of a eunuch is a dangerous operation. He'd been in agony for days, the physical pain so acute it was some time before he could appreciate that this was only a minor part of what he was destined to suffer. He'd healed up well, and was henceforth an exceptionally valuable commodity: a good-looking gelding, and a virgin at that, therefore he carried no infection.

He was sold, for an exorbitant price, to a rich Median merchant who was eager to ingratiate himself with the King. Hence the merchant brought his prize purchase back to Shushan and made a present of him to Kshayarsha, who was known to have acquired a taste for boys from the Greeks who intrigued at his court. It came as a surprise to many folk to discover that His Imperial Majesty should associate intimately and by choice with natives of a land he had determined to subjugate. Yet this was Kshayarsha all over: he was fascinated by the very things and the very people he claimed to despise, and found beautiful non-Aryans irresistible.

Thus Hegai became the property of the King for the second time, and whereas before he'd belonged to him merely in a legal sense, now he belonged to him personally—very personally. He was at once made Chamberlain—in other words, eunuch of the bedchamber—and slave as he was, he became responsible for all of the King's domestic arrangements. These included putting Kshayarsha to bed at night and getting him up in the morning; and keeping him company in between.

At this point in his story Hegai paused, to assess my reaction. But I said nothing; I was well past being shocked now. So he continued, and he was no longer weeping. It seemed to be doing him good to get his misery out in the open.

Kshayarsha had been pleased with him; in fact, more than that. It soon became manifest that he was infatuated with his pretty attendant, and he began giving him gorgeous clothes and jewels, riches the like of which Hegai had never seen in his wildest dreams. Although in theory he was still a slave, in practice he rapidly grew to be one of the wealthiest and most influential personages in the entire Empire. It wasn't only his besotted lover who showered him with gifts, either; he received twice as many again from people who wanted favours from the King and hoped that Hegai would exercise his influence on their behalf.

Inside, however, his emotions were in ferment. He found himself having to come to terms with the fact that he, who had been brought up to expect that he would marry and beget his own children, was sharing a bed with a man. Nor was this just any man, but the most powerful man in the world, and the man who had been responsible, albeit indirectly, for the murder of his darling's own parents. Yet Kshayarsha went out of his way to treat him tenderly, so that Hegai was unable to hate him, and indeed often wept in his arms. For since the operation tears had come all too easily, and he was gradually forced to accept that it wasn't merely the physical aspect of his manhood which was gone.

Thenceforth he'd resolved to fight against the onset of effeminacy with all the determination he could muster. He wore a full turban to conceal his beardlessness, and deliberately deepened his voice. He hid his softened emotions, and sought desperately never to cry in front of another human being; in this he'd succeeded until today. If any of the courtiers mocked him, he would no longer run to the King, but shrug off the insult with such aplomb that it was unable to stain him, being repelled like water from an oiled fabric. And if he chanced to be mocked by an inferior, he would have the wretch flogged within an inch of his life.

But no sooner had Hegai started to make peace with himself and with his perverse new existence than everything was upset again. It transpired that he'd aroused the jealousy of Vashti because he was evidently so close to her husband.

It wasn't so much Hegai's sharing of Kshayarsha's bed that she resented; after all, the King had hundreds of concubines and was entitled to several wives, though because of Vashti's possessiveness he'd never exercised this right. He also had plenty of other pretty eunuchs; the vanquished Babylonians were ordered to supply the court with five hundred every year. In Greece, his boyfriends wouldn't have needed to be emasculated, or even to be slaves, but the deflowering of freeborn youths who would go on to have freeborn wives and sons would never have been acceptable in Persia, and not even Kshayarsha would dare ride roughshod over that particular tradition. No, it wasn't her husband's sexual infidelity nor its peculiar orientation that so upset Vashti, but rather the fact that he was patently in love with Hegai on some much deeper level.

Therefore she'd made up her mind to get rid of her beautiful, bewildered young rival. She spread lies about him: that he'd been selling his body on the streets of Babylon for years and was riddled with the diseases of promiscuity; that he'd seduced the Great King in order to gratify his own twisted lusts, and thereby brought into disrepute the honourable status of eunuch, the employment of which venerable species of creature had been advocated by the glorious Kurash for fundamentally different reasons.

There was just enough truth in Vashti's claim concerning Kurash for some very influential people at court to swallow the malicious fabrications which she'd put about along with it. Kshayarsha was constrained to dismiss Hegai from his post for the purpose of salvaging his own reputation.

I said, 'But surely Vashti herself had been relegated to the harem by that time? Why should Kshayarsha have continued to listen to her?'

'It wasn't her he was listening to. It was the concubines and courtiers she'd corrupted with her lies about me.' Hegai wiped away the last of his tears and dared to look me full in the face for the first time since launching into his confession. All the kohl on his lower lids had run onto his cheeks so he looked as though he'd been struck. 'Lady Esther, you must never make the mistake of thinking that Vashti lost her power along with her throne. She is a clever and formidable woman who pulls many strings, and you'll do well to watch out for her. Though the King's concubines were bitterly jealous of her when she was Queen and were only too glad to see her brought down, once she was their equal they transferred their jealousy to me. They begrudged *me* the time I spent with Kshayarsha, when they were lucky to be summoned to his pleasure any more often than a poor farmer can afford to allow his cow to be serviced by a bull. And they begrudged me my looks, because I was comelier than some of them were.'

'Comelier than *all* of them, I shouldn't wonder,' I told him, and reached out tentatively to touch his kohl-blotched cheek. He looked down at my hand, then raised his own to clasp it in place, and closed his eyes. Swallowing hard, he took up his story once more.

Kshayarsha had loved him still, knowing that all the rumours were false. Therefore he couldn't bring himself to have Hegai killed, or sold to some slobbering sodomite, or even set free and turned out onto the streets where the only sort of living he could have hoped to make was the one from which Vashti was maintaining that he'd come.

So he'd had various lowly jobs at court, being regarded by all with whom he had dealings as an anomaly: neither slave nor free, neither courtier nor commoner, neither man nor woman; not exactly in disgrace but no longer deserving of honour because of his closeness to the King. Then when the quest began to find a new bride for Kshayarsha, Hegai had been the obvious choice of overseer for the girls whom the Commissioners found, and to train up the most promising of them. After all, no one but Vashti herself knew better than he what the King found appealing in a bedmate.

At this juncture his voice trailed off. He still held my hand pressed against his cheek, which was hot as a live coal. As gently as I knew how, I ventured, 'And did *you* still love *him*, my poor lonely Tammuz? Did you *ever* really love him? Have you ever stopped?'

He shrugged helplessly. 'I don't know. I was so confused. But part of me loved him, yes; how could it be otherwise, when I'd lost everyone else I'd ever cared about, and half of my own self too? What other chance did I have of finding love, or peace?'

I made no comment, thinking that I'd had little more love in my life of late than he had; and as for peace, I'd never really thought in those terms since being a child. He added, 'And Kshayarsha *was* kind to me, he didn't just use me. *He* had a pet name for me, too. He used to call me Tishtrya, the brilliant white star which is the overseer of all the other stars, and which appears for ten nights at New Year in the form of a beautiful youth. They say he only stole the statues of Harmodios and Aristogeiton from Athens because the lovely Harmodios reminded him of me. When he hears that your name is Star, he'll be reminded again. That's what we must hope for.'

I whispered, 'The Great King *can* wait, Tammuz, as I said. Let's pretend just for tonight that none of this ever happened.' And I kissed him long and lovingly on the lips, exactly the way I'd wanted to.

Summer mellowed into autumn; Kshayarsha and his retinue returned to Shushan; autumn turned to winter, and the rains brought new life to the thirsty plain. Hegai and I continued to spend our evenings together on our own; he was my Tammuz, and I was Esther, his Little Star. I grew to love him more and more as time went on. For a while my feelings towards him perplexed me: how was it possible for me still to be drawn to him, now that I knew what he truly was? Surely it was senseless, and not only senseless, but improper, unhealthy?

Yet not many days had gone by before I came to see that the nature of my love for him had changed. I no longer desired him; but it was so long since I'd conceived anything remotely resembling selfless love for anyone, I'd forgotten what it was like. In a curious way, it was liberating: for me, and also for Hegai. According to Farah he was no longer dispensing punishments glibly all around whenever he saw his dignity threatened. There was a new confidence about him which percolated much deeper than his urbane facade, and he'd begun to command the respect of those for whom he was responsible, instead of their fear and their suppressed contempt.

And our mutual love was far less senseless than it would have been if Hegai *had* been fully a man. We could have had no future together in any case; the best we could have hoped for would have been a sordid, clandestine affair—most probably a very short one—and then to be impaled simultaneously to watch each other die.

But as things were, we both tasted happiness, and it was so much the sweeter and more poignant because a time was all too quickly coming when we should see each other no more. Our friendship blossomed like the King's Judah poppies, and there was a sparkle in Hegai's eyes which ironically made him more alluring than he'd ever been. Sometimes I would tell him so, and he would smile, and blush; and he said he was reminded of the day many months ago when I'd offered to create a new identity for him just as he had done for me. It seemed that somehow I had achieved this.

Gradually over the weeks I told him more about myself, as and when things occurred to me, and about the life I'd led at Mordecai's as well as back in Jerusalem. When I told him the name of my guardian's sister, his eyebrows went up so far that they were lost in his loosened hair.

'Ninlil? But Ninlil was a temple prostitute from childhood, who gave up her living to join the peculiar religious cult which her grand-parents had belonged to, and which her brother still practised. The whole city heard about it. Do you suppose we're talking about the same person?'

'No,' I answered with a laugh, but immediately thought again. Ninlil had freely admitted that her parents were not pious Jews; both she and Mordecai had been named for Babylonian deities. If her parents had involved her in indecent rituals it would certainly explain why she could not then marry in accordance with Jewish law; and why she was so reluctant to discuss with me sexual matters, or her own past. All at once I felt acutely sorry for her, and for the way I'd treated her, and I wondered if she'd recovered from the sickness to which Iphigenia had said she'd succumbed.

Then one evening Hegai informed me that the first few girls had received notification of the dates on which they must report to the King, and suddenly all of that seemed very close, and very dreadful. Each subsequent day flew by like a petal blown away on the breeze, rather than lasting for an identical eternity; every moment spent with Hegai was precious as wrought gold. Each evening after we had dined, he would excuse himself for a while, and return later for our lesson, looking wan and hunted somehow. I deduced that he must be taking my Sisters one by one for their carnal appointments, though he never said so, and I never asked. Little by little we began to talk more about Kshayarsha, however, although at first I would try to change the subject in a futile attempt to deny reality.

'What is he *really* like?' I asked, once I'd accepted that there was to be no running away. 'I've heard so many conflicting rumours. I've heard that he's cruel, but soft; stubborn, but vacillating; headstrong, but too much under the influence of his advisers; rash yet overcautious; brutal yet tender. Where does the truth lie?'

'All of those things are true, and none of them. He is the richest and mightiest and least private man in the world—and he feels it keenly. He is anxious to be judged as great as his predecessors, and to do what is right, but knows he is neither as intelligent as they were, nor as popular with his subjects. So sometimes he thinks he must demonstrate the firmness of his control, other times that he must win his people's affection. And he is much more fanatical in his devotion to Ahura Mazda than his predecessors were. He considers that the Wise Lord has given him the Empire, and that this god alone can help him preserve it. So he believes it his duty to wipe out all traces of paganism, and he is right that there is much wickedness involved in its practices. But there is also much beauty; and repression of religion seldom achieves what it sets out to do, as far as I have seen.'

'What of the Jews, then? We are not idolaters. Does he want to stamp out our faith too?'

'I couldn't say, my Little Star. But you need have no fear for yourself. Be assured I shall pass on to no one the secrets that you've shared with me.'

Paradoxically, his assurance caused me to fear for the first time on this score. I hadn't realized that Kshayarsha's repression of paganism might involve the destruction of the pagans themselves, not merely their altars.

As my introduction to Kshayarsha drew inexorably closer, Hegai began to speak more freely about the duties he'd had as the King's Chamberlain, and to drop hints to me about the steps I could take to awaken His Majesty's desire.

Each night, before Kshayarsha retired, Hegai had had to undress him according to a preordained procedure: he would first stand close behind his royal master and loosen his cape and sash, then the King would sit on the bed while Hegai knelt and took off his slippers, holding Kshayarsha's feet upon his lap. Next Hegai would avert his eyes whilst removing the imperial trousers, and help the King into his night robe, after which Kshayarsha would slip off his tunic and drawers for himself. I giggled at the crazy idea of it all: at the lengths to which these Persians would go, to avoid being seen unclothed even by those with whom they were intimate. I exclaimed in amazement, 'Must *I* do all that for Kshayarsha, on the night when I am sent to him?'

Hegai smiled a mischievous smile. 'You won't be expected to, no. He has a new Chamberlain now who will ask you to wait outside until his master is in bed. But the Chamberlain is a slave and you are not; you can send him away before the King is ready rather than after, and perform his role yourself. Then Kshayarsha will know that you have my approval.'

I nodded thoughtfully, letting the implications of his words sink in. Then I ventured with some hesitation, 'Tammuz, aren't *you* jealous of me? How can you prepare me so ungrudgingly to take on a role which once belonged to you? You ought to hate me more than anyone.'

Hegai blinked and glanced away. 'Perhaps I love him enough to want him to be happy. And I know he could be happiest with you.'

'That's why you befriended me, right from the beginning?'

'Yes.'

'You could see it even then?'

'Yes.'

'But what if one of the girls whose turn comes before mine appeals to him too? What if I never get my chance with him at all? What will happen to me then? Will I be sent back to Mordecai's?'

Hegai tilted my chin up and kissed me, very lightly, on the lips. He said, 'Never since you came here have I seen you nervous, Little Star—until these past few days. You mustn't grow timid. It's your spirit which has most distinguished you from your Sisters, all along. What is upsetting you?'

189

I shrugged and made no reply; a large part of the truth was that although I'd come to the palace of my own free will, I had no more control over my own fate now than I ever had done.

Thankfully, however, he let the question go unanswered. Instead he said, 'You should know that there is no need whatever for you to trouble yourself. None of the other girls will dare to send away the Great King's Chamberlain. They won't even think of it.' He smiled again, and I should never have thought to see a single smile combine such roguishness and such loss at the same time. 'It's as I explained to you, Little Star. In the palace, influence can be exercised in a thousand ways, and power wielded from a prodigious distance by those who are cunning. Vashti keeps me from the King even though she is no longer Queen, whilst I can send him messages without the need of any tablet or errand-boy.'

I reflected on this momentarily, then asked with not a little apprehensiveness, 'What will happen to Vashti, Tammuz, if I—if someone is enthroned in her place? What will happen to her children?'

Hegai threw up his hands. 'Who can say? Perhaps there will be bloody civil war when the time comes. Such things lie in the lap of the gods, and must be left there.'

This brought me little comfort. I said, 'There *are* no gods, Tammuz, or else they care nothing for their creatures. The gods of the nations are nothing but lifeless lumps of wood, and the God of Israel has less substance than the wind . . .' I let my voice peter out, for he looked more bereft than ever. But he didn't contradict me; how could he, when he considered the course that his own life had taken? Instead he turned away, and spoke his next words to the wall.

'It's my belief that Kshayarsha loves Vashti still, deep inside him, in spite of everything. He only loved me because I was so much like her.' Then he pulled himself together enough to look back at me. 'He will love you for the same reason, Little Star. Of that we have to be confident.'

The following week, the first rains fell. I stood out with Hegai on my balcony in the twilight; arm in arm we leaned backwards over the balustrade, laughing, our palms and faces upturned for joy at the piquant coolness of the droplets that splashed on our cheeks and in our hair and down our sleeves. Secure in the innocent bliss of our friendship, it was almost possible to believe, for that exquisite fragment of time, that no one else in the whole world mattered, that nothing else existed, that we could go on being carefree and together for the rest of our lives. But in the midst of our laughter an urgent knocking came at the door and a haughty youth I didn't recognize—but whose very presence meant that he had to be a eunuch—walked right into my room without waiting to be asked.

We must have looked guilty as children caught pilfering at the bazaar; not even Hegai could compose himself so quickly. He didn't try; he merely leaned further back against the dripping balustrade, his half-unwrapped turban trailing from his shoulders and his rampant wet hair all mingled with mine, and called, 'What is it, then, Ashpamithra? Could you not have waited and seen me tomorrow?'

But before our shocked visitor could find words to explain his mission, Hegai's laughter died in his throat. He strode inside from the rain and swept his colleague into a corner, where the two of them whispered while I hovered, cold with foreboding but not knowing why. Then Hegai sent the youth away, ignoring the latter's attempts to stand upon his dignity, and said, 'Esther, come and sit down.'

I approached him uncertainly, searching his eyes, but he would say nothing until we were seated side by side on one of my couches, the moisture from our clothing spreading dark like blood on the plush upholstery. Then he said softly, 'You must surely know who that was.'

'No. How could I know?'

'Then you must be able to guess.'

'Guess? Look, Tammuz, I—'

'That was Ashpamithra, the King's new Chamberlain.'

'So?' I still didn't see what his visit had to mean; either that, or else, like so much that had gone before, this was something else which I simply didn't want to see. Hegai grasped both my hands.

'You are to go before the King on the first night of Tebeth, less than a month from today. This is it, Esther. The waiting is almost over.'

'No, Tammuz. There must be some mistake. It can't be my turn yet. There must be scores of girls to go before me—'

'Kshayarsha can take whom he chooses, *when* he chooses, Little Star, whatever we may have been told to the contrary. Reports of your astounding beauty may have reached him already.'

I might have rebuked him for teasing me then, except that I suddenly noticed how sick he looked. He embraced me, and I clung to him, fretting: the King's personal attendant had seen me unveiled, with my hair and my clothes all bedraggled, and my face-paint no doubt all blotches and streaks. And he'd seen the pair of us larking about and touching like children, like lovers... What kind of report would Ashpamithra be relaying to his master now? All the preparations I'd undergone and all the lessons I'd been forced to sit through would be wasted after all. Yet none of this was what I really wanted to say.

Hegai only murmured, and stroked my hair until I fell silent. Then he said, 'The more Ashpamithra says, the better Kshayarsha will look forward to meeting you, Little Star. He will be intrigued; he'll be excited. If he knows you are close to me, he may be smitten before he even sees you—if he isn't already. Everything will be all right, Esther; it will. You have to believe it.'

But I didn't, because I knew he didn't entirely believe it himself; I had seen how pale he'd gone. Also, I knew full well that he needed me just as much as I needed him.

So our final weeks together were a nightmare of pretence, as each of us tried to protect the other from despair by concealing the extent to which we knew we should pine once apart. Never had I felt the pain of imminent loss anything like this; when I'd feared being parted from Iphigenia by her betrothal to Nikias it was only myself I had cared about, whereas now I was terrified for Hegai. He would go back to being lonely and aloof; to cowering behind his cool, cultured veneer; to hardening himself against the hate of those around him, and taking it out on his charges or their servants regardless of whether they deserved it, when everything threatened to become too much.

And I would go back to thinking only of myself, to pursuing my ambitions, whatever their implications for those around me. Kshayarsha would never need me the way that Hegai did; I should never feel that I mattered to him except as a bed-mate and a mother for his sons.

But we spoke of none of this. We spent our evenings going again and again over details of protocol and the finer points of Hegai's theories on beauty and seduction. I cannot bear to think what must have been running through his mind as he divulged to me so many intimate confidences: hint after tender hint about the things which Kshayarsha liked his beloved to do. I wondered how many nights of bitter-sweet experience lay behind the techniques he'd learnt and earnestly sought to remember and pass on to me.

Yet in spite of all our good intentions, as the fateful night drew closer it seemed that everything conspired to go wrong. My monthly flow didn't begin when it should have, and I was terrified lest its coming should coincide with my presentation to the King. Some nasty little mite got inside my clothes and bit me all down my neck, and a crop of pimples broke out on my forehead, which no combination of potions or ointments would either cure or cover up. With only one week to go, Hegai caught a chill and made himself stay away from me lest he pass this on to me along with everything else. So I had no one but Farah with whom to share my mounting fears.

Then two days before my turn arrived, and three since I'd seen Hegai, a sealed tablet was brought to me which had come from outside the palace.

It was written in Aramaic and full of mistakes; I couldn't work out why she hadn't used Greek, knowing as she did that I could have it translated. But once I'd digested the contents, it was painfully obvious why Iphigenia hadn't wanted any eyes to peruse it except my own.

She'd heard that Mordecai had been appointed to the position of financial adviser to the palace Treasury, and she guessed that I might not have been told. In other words, he had traded his lucrative partnership in the most prestigious private banking firm in the city for what was in comparison a modestly salaried post in a government department, everything about which he despised. Presumably he'd done it in the hope of gaining access to me, Iphigenia reasoned, because he loved me.

Cursing out loud, I crushed the tablet in pieces beneath my feet. Mordecai didn't love me. He loved to *control* me, that was all. Even *now* he imagined he could ruin everything I'd done to create for myself the life I wanted.

But he wouldn't succeed. Of that I would make sure.

The first day of Tebeth dawned cold, damp and grey, but even the leaden winter sky was not so overcast as my soul. I lay for the last time upon my cedar-wood bed with its ornately carved legs, and looked about the room which had been mine for almost a year. I'd never come to love it, but now it seemed the most beautiful place in the world, and I never wanted to leave it.

No one had told me how this day would differ from any other, as far as the hours prior to sunset were concerned. I still hadn't seen Hegai since he'd gone down with his chill, but I'd received a message the previous evening, to say that he was better and would come to me before noon to ensure that everything was in order.

In the event he arrived before I'd even breakfasted, and I invited him to share it with me, but neither of us could eat a thing. He dismissed all seven of my attendants, but was no more familiar with me after they'd gone than he'd been when all of them were there. I realized that I'd lost him already; he'd used our time apart to gird himself against my going. I was faced with the cool professional, the polished, painted eunuch whose experience of love was his trade.

With our breakfast still untouched on its silver tray, he proceeded to bathe me, in gloriously creamy milk brought in gilded amphorae by a whole train of his minions. Then he applied to my skin some lotion silkier and more viscous than anything which had previously been squandered on me. He worked without speaking, and his touch was no more sensuous than a physician's. His turban was wound in a style even more forbidding than usual, with barely enough gap for his eyes to look out. These were made up so heavily, his turban might just as well have covered them entirely for all that they gave away.

My exercise routine was dispensed with; instead he insisted on examining me minutely for the slightest flake of rough skin, or a single stray hair on my legs or arms, or the least little chip in one of my nails. Miraculously, my bites had gone down and my forehead was clear now of blemishes, though by the time Hegai had plucked my eyebrows punctiliously it had turned temporarily pink. He readied me for my siesta early, and said that I should rise from it late; it was of paramount importance that I be able to last the whole night, if need be, without craving sleep.

I said sulkily that I should be quite unable to sleep now, but he made me drink some ghastly bitter infusion, and there must have been poppy in it or something similar because I slept like the dead for hours. When I awoke, he spent what little remained of the afternoon explaining to me the procedure for my introduction to the King. I listened, and took most of it in, but there was a griping in my belly which grew worse with the inexorable approach of the hour of my departure. After I'd eaten, Hegai said, I should be made up; and then—according to Lord Memucan's directive—I should dress in my favourite garments: His Majesty liked to see that his women had good taste, so they weren't to be told what to wear. Finally Hegai himself would escort me and my seven handmaids to the Apadana.

'The Apadana?' I gasped. 'I am to be taken to the King in his throne-room? Why not to his private chambers?'

'Every Virgin is taken first to the Apadana, for His Majesty's approval, my lady. No one but he can be the ultimate judge of whether or not a girl is fit to share his bed.'

My anxiety increased. 'Has he rejected many at that stage?'

'No, not many. Memucan and his Commissioners have done their job well; as have I, or so I like to think. But some have had their appointments put back to a later date.'

Perhaps I should have welcomed the chance of a respite, but I didn't. The last thing I wanted was to re-live this day with its tension and uncertainty all over again. I asked, 'Why? Had they not been adequately prepared?'

'Of course they had been adequately prepared.' Hegai bristled. 'But you know as well as I do that His Majesty hasn't been in good spirits of late. Sometimes he is physically sick. There are nights when he is too weak or weighed down to want a strange woman in his bed, or to want *any* woman.'

'Why didn't you tell me this? I shan't be able to bear it if he turns me away like a beggar. Why didn't you tell me I should have to go before him in the Apadana?'

'There is always a veil of secrecy surrounding the movements of the Great King, my lady. It is a matter of prudence, of security. Official secrecy is pandemic in Persia; you must have deduced that.'

'Why must I? Why does everyone here think I must have seen this, I must have realized that, I must have known the other? Stop speaking to me in such obnoxious high-flown language! And stop calling me your lady. My name is Esther; you gave it to me yourself. Or had you forgotten?'

He responded with forced evenness, 'I have told you not to be afraid, my lady. As soon as he sees you he will want you. We shall make sure of that. Come; I must show you how to make the prostration more gracefully.' He linked my arm and drew me to the floor beside him, our foreheads side by side on the ground as we kissed it. Then he got up and pushed my shoulders and rump further down, eventually declaring himself satisfied. I moved to rise, but he warned me that on no account must I do so in the throne-room until the King extended his sceptre towards me, at which moment I should touch its tip to acknowledge His Majesty's graciousness.

Dinner was served to us earlier than usual, for we had to leave time afterwards to attend to my face, hair and apparel, and besides, I must not enter the royal presence drowsy on a full stomach. But there was little danger of that, since I still couldn't bring myself to eat at all.

As the winter sun sank low in the sky and cast its mellow dying rays across my balcony, Hegai began to make up my face in exactly the way he made up his own. He brushed out my hair, remarking that our efforts to soften the texture of my locks had proven singularly successful. He pinned my curls up loosely, with golden slides he'd brought with him for the purpose: they were crafted in the shape of butterflies, their wings inlaid with brightly coloured enamel, and with jewels for eyes. Then he announced that it was time for me to change into the garments I would wear to meet the King.

But while I went to the coffer and began to look through it for what I considered most appropriate, he strode to the door and snapped his fingers just outside. One of his eunuchs came in with a bale of clothing in his arms, and laid it on the bed.

'You want me to wear these?' I demanded of Hegai when the boy had gone. 'I thought I was supposed to choose for myself.'

'You may choose for yourself if you so wish, my lady. But you would be better advised to wear these.' He coughed uncertainly, and added, 'They are my wedding present to you.'

I said nothing; I merely crossed to the bed and began to examine them, holding the items aloft one by one.

The fabric was the softest, the sheerest and the most expensive I'd ever laid eyes or fingers on. The weave was so fine it looked to be the very work of angels, and the embroidery on it must have taken a lifetime's hours to design and execute. There were loose trousers, gathered at the waist and ankles; the waistband and ankle cuffs were stiff with gold thread, and extending away from them were fronds and tendrils of stitchery as delicate and lovely as the foliage of any of Kshayarsha's exotic botanical specimens. Then there was a thin, sleeveless shift, and a loose-sleeved robe to go over the top; from the gold-stiffened neck band cascaded more coils of embroidered foliage, to match that on the trousers. There was a trailing collared cloak, there were kid-skin slippers pointed at the toes, and finally came a veil so light that it floated out upon the still air as soon as I raised it to my face. And the colour of every article was deep, dusky magenta.

Hegai went out onto the balcony while I undressed, as if it mattered; I'd been naked in his presence for half the day. But the distance between us was growing by the minute; it was as though when the time came for him to lead me to the King, he wanted us to be total strangers. I could stand the strain no longer; once attired in all his finery I ran out after him and threw myself into his arms. I wasn't weeping, which was just as well because we should have had to start again with my face, and would have angered His Majesty with our lateness. But I was beating on Hegai's chest, wailing that I should never cope without him; couldn't he see the King and arrange to be transferred to my service?

'Don't make this worse than it is,' he implored me, and the pitch of his voice was high and cracked because he was losing the battle to control it. 'Please, my lady. We must go now. The sun has almost set.'

So saying, he lowered the veil in front of my face, then sent for my seven attendants, and we began our stately progress to the Apadana, Hegai walking in front of me, Farah and her companions behind. I put into practice everything Anahita had taught me about deportment, and kept my eyes fixed unswervingly on the tail of Hegai's turban. I could sense the probing stares of the bystanders quite well enough without having to see them for myself. There was little point in my taking offence from their curiosity, or expecting that things would be otherwise. I had set out purposely to place myself in the public eye, and must accept the consequences.

At the entrance to the Apadana we were confronted by a formidable detachment of spearbearers, all kitted out in identical royal livery, all standing grimly to attention, spear-butt planted on forward foot. Commanding them was the Hazarapatish or Chief Minister, by name Artabanush, whose task it was to announce visitors to the King. Hegai apprised him of our business—as if he didn't already know—speaking in ceremonial Old Persian rather than everyday Aramaic, and presumably repeating a formula he'd used in identical circumstances many times. Artabanush made some equally formal and unintelligible reply, to which Hegai responded in turn; no doubt the entire exchange was as futile as it was formal, since both Hazarapatish and Keeper of the King's Virgins would have known exactly what each other's role entailed without one word being uttered.

Artabanush ascended the vast stone staircase which gave access to the Great King's presence; at the top a pair of heavy curtains of intricately woven, richly textured tapestry were swept back to receive him, then swiftly closed once more. Hegai continued to stand in front of me, presenting only his tensed narrow back to my view.

I was well prepared for it to seem like an eternity before Artabanush returned. But that eternity passed, and another besides, and still the great curtains remained staunchly closed. With the spearbearers' eyes boring into me, I didn't dare seek to attract Hegai's attention. I stood statuesque, fervently hoping that my multiple layers of trousers, shift, robe and cloak would succeed in disguising the heaving of my breast and the juddering of my knees.

Then the curtains opened and Artabanush reappeared. He descended the steps more hurriedly than propriety dictated; at once Hegai sprang forward to meet him and the two of them conferred, in Aramaic now, but too quietly for me to follow closely. I caught enough, however, to learn that the King was indisposed, and would see me at his later convenience.

Black pinpricks stung my eyes, and the faces of the spearbearers, already oddly coloured because of the magenta gauze in front of my eyes, appeared stranger still, and began to blur and swim across one another like clouds in a dream. I must have been swaying, for Hegai took one glance at me and caught my elbows to steady me while someone brought a chair. Once I was ensconced he left Farah to tend me, whilst himself continuing his whispered altercation with Artabanush. This grew steadily more heated, so that I couldn't fail to grasp what was being said, and its implications. Artabanush was flatly refusing permission for Hegai or me to see the King or send any message to him, via any intermediary; so Hegai announced that he would go in without it.

I knew full well what Hegai was volunteering to risk on my behalf. Anahita had explained the matter to me with perfect clarity: anyone who presumed to enter the presence of the King without being summoned stood to forfeit his life unless the King for some reason of his own deigned to spare it. There was precious little chance of that happening when he had expressly denied access to either of us. For all my desperation to get this whole thing over with, I couldn't sit by and allow Hegai to endanger his very life because of me. I called out to him, and when he ignored me I struggled to my feet to go after him. But Farah restrained me, and I was compelled to watch in abject horror as the one who meant more to me than anybody had since the massacre of my family in Jerusalem slowly mounted the steep stone steps which led to his certain death.

But the next thing I remember is Hegai himself raising my chin from my chest and saying, 'Come, my lady. How often must I remind you not to be so anxious?' And for one brief moment his lovely eyes smiled, the way they must have smiled at His Majesty as he rose trembling from the prostration, his fragile life spared by the extended sceptre whose tip he was touching. Kshayarsha must indeed have been besotted with him still, and Hegai had lost none of his powers of seduction by sharing his secrets with me.

Together we climbed the stairs, arm in arm now, with Farah holding the train of my cloak, and her six assistants mutely following. The curtain drew aside for us, and we beheld the gracious countenance of the Great King of Persia, though at such a distance it could have belonged to anyone. Reverently we advanced through the forest of soaring, bull-headed columns, all of them guarded by liveried spear-bearers, and made to seem loftier even than they truly were by the pall of blue smoke hanging between them. This drifted upward from the incense burners smouldering in front of the throne, and shrouded the elegant capitals as mist shrouds the summits of mountains. There was a golden glow about the person of the King, created by a thousand burning candles set into the walls and the floor; then I saw that in addition to this aura of light, he was surrounded by a halo of courtiers, eunuchs and pages who waited on him whenever he sat there, doing him homage and enhancing his glory by their doting proximity.

But I couldn't see their faces. As we ventured closer, I could look at no one and nothing except the Great King himself, majestically enthroned upon a raised dais. Kshayarsha sat motionless as rock, his feet planted firmly on his footstool. He was holding in one hand the ceremonial lotus, emblem of the House of Hakhamanish, in the other the sceptre which had saved Hegai's life. The pleats of his garments and even the stylized curls of his beard could have been carved from solid granite. I had a brief but disconcerting impression that his eyes were closed; but then Hegai tugged at my arm and we went down for the prostration, magenta veil beside magenta turban, magenta robes and cloaks fanning out upon the polished marble and porphyry of the Apadana floor.

Soon the jewel-encrusted tip of the royal sceptre was stretched out towards me; I touched it and rose to my feet, the sceptre rising just ahead of me as though it drew me up by some magical power. Hegai was already standing, and as I came up beside him, he took my hand. I grasped his own harder than I should have done, knowing there was scant hope of my ever being able to hold it again. But the King didn't see; he didn't see anything, for his eyes were indeed closed, and his face pale, even for a Persian, and even for one whose skin was caked in paint.

For a long time no one spoke. The right to do so belonged solely to the King, and unless he saw fit to exercise it, the rest of us could be detained at his silent pleasure until the end of our days.

I let my eyes wander from his face to examine his attire, fabric dyed with real sea-purple, a hue so rich and so deep that there was nothing in nature to which I could have compared it. It seemed that every fold in his rosette-studded cape and great wide sleeves had been accurately measured and arranged in deliberate symmetry. Upon his head he wore the tallest and most extravagant headdress I'd ever seen—not the battlemented war-crown he'd worn for his entry into Shushan immediately after his coronation, but an elaborate affair more like an enormous stiffened turban, with the royal purple mitra encircling it.

Hovering at his shoulder was a pretty slave-boy who couldn't have been more than ten years old; I wondered if he'd already lost what might one day make him a man. He held a fringed parasol, which he would open and hold above the King's head should the latter choose to move out from beneath the canopy which hung above the throne. Another boy stood beside him with a ceremonial baton for swatting flies, despite the fact that it was winter and there wasn't a single one to be seen.

At last I permitted myself a stray glance at the rest of Kshayarsha's entourage: there was the disdainful Ashpamithra, Hegai's successor as eunuch chamberlain, and beside him stood seven more of his kind; all young, all conceited, all comely, but probably they wouldn't have looked quite so youthful had their boyish beauty not been artificially preserved.

In addition to them, there were Kshayarsha's seven advisers, one from each of the seven leading families of Shushan; and one black-cloaked, black-hooded figure lingering in the background, who could only have been one of the mysterious clan of the magi.

And still the King hadn't spoken. At long last Ashpamithra, who stood closest to the royal ear, bent down and whispered into it, having exchanged glances with his predecessor. Kshayarsha's eyes fluttered open, and he saw me for the first time.

From that moment, everything began to go the way Hegai had hoped and believed it would. Whatever malady was afflicting the King, his attention was wrested from it with sufficient violence for the heaviness to depart from his eyelids and some of the colour to return gradually to his cheeks. He glanced from me to Hegai and back again—perhaps he imagined he was sick enough to be seeing things double. He beckoned the pair of us closer, then closer again, until we stood at the very edge of the dais on which the throne was positioned. Then Hegai was left where he was, while Ashpamithra was directed to bring me up the steps to the throne itself. I was now standing near enough the King to feel his breath upon my face; it smelt very slightly stale, and it was oddly comforting to know that His Majesty the Great King of Persia might have putrid breath when he was ill, just like the least of his subjects.

Although my veil was sheer enough for him to discern my features quite clearly through it, he handed his lotus and sceptre to Ashpamithra, and drew it slowly away from my face. Some of his attendants appeared profoundly disturbed; removing my veil was not an element of the prescribed procedure. Nor was touching my face with his bare fingers, nor reaching for a ringlet of my hair and admiring its texture the way a merchant delights in a costly swatch of cloth.

Without taking his eyes from me, the King said something in Old Persian; one of his eunuchs translated it into Aramaic as 'Chamberlain, you may proceed,' and Ashpamithra, all in Aramaic now, launched into what was manifestly a standard liturgy extolling the sublimity of His Majesty Kshayarsha son of Darayavaush, King of Kings, Sovereign Ruler of Persia and its Empire, Chosen Vessel of Ahura Mazda, and then recounting the divine decree of the Wise Lord that his royal servant should choose out and take unto himself the most beautiful and virtuous maiden in his vast domain, to be his bride. All the while Kshayarsha continued to study me intently.

As for me, I was well aware that I was meant to keep my eyes averted, but I couldn't. I gazed directly into those of the King, and I knew he wasn't angry at my doing so. On the contrary, my boldness appeared to please him; faint as I'd felt before meeting him, now that the waiting was over I felt myself once again to be in control. Indeed, I was more than in control; I was becoming quietly excited.

For Kshayarsha was as handsome in reality as he'd been in my girlish daydreams. Here was no middle-aged, podgy, pot-bellied sluggard of the kind they say some of the old pharaohs were, whose wits grew dull and whose muscles turned slack from sitting in state every day, being waited on hand and foot. Kshayarsha was young, and underneath his fine raiment was built sparely, like a huntsman—which of course he was. He rode horses for sport, and played polo; and he despised convention if it threatened to stifle him. Granted, he'd been sick ... but what man wouldn't be, when his marriage-bed was cold, and he was hemmed all about by jealousy and intrigue? Since banishing his wife from his presence, he'd taken lovers where he chose; and now I was determined he should choose me.

Ashpamithra's speech was drawing to a close; he concluded it with a lengthy question, couched and obscured in magniloquent language, and addressed to Hegai. The gist of it was: had the illustrious Keeper of His Majesty's Virgins brought to the King an eligible candidate for his appraisal, and could the said Keeper vouch for the girl's worthiness as regards the unique honour for which she was to be considered? I don't know what Hegai was supposed to have replied, but all he said was, 'Yes,' and he said it so simply, so directly, so certainly, that an audible gasp went up from those grouped about the throne.

Then Kshayarsha commanded, 'Come here, my darling,' and he wasn't referring either to me or to Ashpamithra. Hegai ascended the dais to stand beside me again, and must have read a secret look from the eyes of the King, because he knelt and laid his head in His Majesty's lap. The gasps swelled to mutters, and I watched the eclipsed Ashpamithra turn scarlet with mortification. Kshayarsha tilted Hegai's chin up, and caressing his cheek through his turban said, 'You haven't failed me, have you, Tishtrya? What is the maiden's name?' And Hegai, whose love-name meant Star, said that my name was Esther, which means Star also, and the spell he'd worked upon the King was complete.

Kshayarsha rose portentously to his feet, drawing Hegai up with him, though Hegai stood barely as tall as the royal shoulder. Then he snapped his fingers at one of his seven eunuchs and ordered, 'Abagtha, fetch the gifts we have set aside. Go quickly.' And while the said Abagtha scampered to obey, Kshayarsha parted Hegai's turban and kissed him softly on the lips. 'You're the most precious jewel in my crown, Tishtrya. Despite the harsh blows which fortune has dealt you, you bear me no grudge, and even go out of your way to bring me happiness. Ashpamithra? Pay close attention; I want you to feast your eyes upon this boy, and adopt him as your shining example.'

Ashpamithra looked sideways at Hegai, not quite scowling. Abagtha's rapid footfalls approached once more and he mounted the dais, prostrating himself before Kshayarsha, then presenting Hegai with yet another bale of magenta clothing and also a small golden casket. Hegai made the obligatory two refusals, then accepted the clothing but handed the open casket with a winning smile to Ashpamithra, declaring that he wished to honour his worthy successor. Ashpamithra's lips curled into a smile of their own, for the casket was full of priceless jewels. Kshayarsha clapped his hands and commended Hegai's generosity with grandiose eloquence. I suppose everybody present knew perfectly well that Hegai had acted from prudent diplomacy, not munificence.

Seemly words of admiration and congratulation were exchanged among the King's associates; he turned to me, and announced that a special gift had been reserved for me also, and I should receive it in due course. However, he must have turned too quickly, because he held one hand briefly to his middle, grimacing all but imperceptibly. He sat down abruptly upon his throne once more, and ordered Ashpamithra to lead me away.

I tried to snatch a last glimpse of Hegai over my shoulder as I left, but he wouldn't look at me. Farah took hold of my train as I stepped down from the dais; her companions fell into line behind her, and we made our solemn way towards the private apartments of the King.

This entailed retracing our steps across the entire palace complex, for the King's rooms were located in the southern wing. I had passed the first test, but there were many others to come, and more demanding ones. We crossed the Central Court, and the Private Court, then the long, red-ochre banqueting hall where I'd once sat with Ninlil for Vashti's great feast. Thence I found myself entering unfamiliar territory.

Two more eunuchs, of the plump and ageless variety, stood on guard at the entrance to Kshayarsha's quarters. I was not a little shocked to note that one of them had had an ear removed, and the other a couple of fingers. I'd heard tell of such brutal sentences being passed by Persian courts but seen no unequivocal evidence of their having been carried out, prior to this. No doubt the one had heard too much on some occasion, and the other had probably had his hand in the royal coffers.

Ashpamithra greeted the pair of them as we passed, calling them by their names: Bigthana and Teresh. They grunted back indifferently, and we were taken through an antechamber into a spacious reception room. Here Ashpamithra invited us to wait. It struck me all at once how high and fluting his voice was, and that unlike Hegai he was perversely proud of this.

On a low table just inside the door sat a golden casket much like the one Hegai had received and passed on to Ashpamithra. This second casket contained the gift set aside for me: a delicate necklet of gold and precious stones, whish Ashpamithra hung about my throat, explaining how it signified that I'd been awarded the honour of a night with the King. If I did well, it would be the first gift of many.

Then he bowed himself out, and once he'd gone I was free to study my awesome surroundings.

If my chamber among the King's Virgins had been luxurious, this one was opulent beyond imagining. It was lit up as bright as day by a plethora of lamps and candles. Every inch of wall-space was covered with vibrant, intricate carpets worked in blue, purple, saffron and scarlet; every column and every piece of furniture was plated with gold, if not solid gold right through, and the seats of the couches were upholstered in stuff as downy and flossy as billowing clouds. The marble floor was buffed so highly that it was like standing by magic upon the surface of a lake on a still summer's day, and the air was thick and sweet with frankincense.

Kshayarsha's love of nature was as evident here as his love of beauty and opulence, for there were bowls of cut flowers everywhere, and also bowls full of soil with live plants growing, as though he wanted to make a garden in his very chambers. In addition to plants, there were gaily-coloured finches in silver cages, which sang to one another in no apparent distress at the curtailment of their freedom. Most astonishing of all, two great blue birds almost as big as eagles, with tails like extra wings, strutted about unchecked, as though they owned the place.

'What *are* they?' I hissed at Farah, shrinking backward as one of them ventured closer to take a look at me.

'Peacocks,' she whispered, but since she was even more wary of them than I was, I concluded she knew of them only by repute.

I was half-expecting another lengthy wait, but very soon there were voices coming through from the ante-room, of which two were certainly Ashpamithra's and the King's. Whoever the others belonged to, their owners were pertemptorily dismissed, and then all I could hear was the Chamberlain's reedy soprano offering to help Kshayarsha out of his ceremonial garb, and enquiring in wheedling tones whether His Majesty felt better now, or whether he wished the importunate girl to be sent away after all?

No doubt the earnest young eunuch wished to appear concerned only for the welfare of his ailing lord and master, but he'd overstepped the mark and underestimated the shortness of Kshayarsha's temper and the intensity of his attraction towards me. I'm not sure what Kshayarsha did to him, but I heard the eunuch yelp in sudden pain as he was told to get out and not return until he was sent for.

I presumed that the King would come through to me at once, but he didn't; after some while I began to wonder what he could be doing, or whether he was iller than I'd thought and had either forgotten about me or passed out altogether. I glanced apprehensively at Farah, hoping she might be able to enlighten me as to the correct behaviour to adopt under the circumstances. But she did nothing but stare at me vacantly, intimidated utterly by the situation in which she found herself.

Just as I was deciding that I should have to gather up all my courage and go to him, Kshayarsha appeared in the doorway. I caught my breath, for not only had the ceremonial crown and cape been discarded, but the beard too; it should have occurred to me that there aren't many young men—or indeed many men at all—who can grow a beard of their own as long and thick and regular as the one a Persian king is meant to have. I knew that Kshayarsha had to be thirty years old at the least, though being almost clean-shaven he looked younger.

He was certainly no eunuch, though. There was a dark shadow about his jawline, and dark hair on his chest where his loosened tunic hung open at the neck. The hair on his head was long and lacquered, and still fell in perfectly symmetrical curls almost to his shoulders, which were muscular and broad—twice as broad, or near enough, as his hips, the litheness of which was blatantly perceptible through his sheer silken trousers. He wasn't beautiful in the way that Hegai was, but he was proudly handsome in a way of his own, and uncompromisingly male.

He leaned on the doorpost and regarded me for a long time, without moving or speaking; then my hand went to my mouth as I recalled that I ought to have prostrated myself once again. I fell to my knees with my head on the ground, hoping fervently that I was doing it with grace, as Hegai had shown me. Behind me, I sensed my attendants copying my example.

But this time Kshayarsha held no sceptre which he could extend to raise me up. Instead he came and stood over me, and remarked almost casually, 'You know, the incomparable Hegai risked his life for you just now. Apart from my favourite wife, my mother, my seven counsellors and the Hazarapatish himself, no one may safely approach the Great King of Persia uninvited. You must be quite an exceptional girl.'

I had no idea what he expected me to say or do. The tests had begun again already; there were no rules of etiquette to guide me in making a response to an unorthodox greeting such as that one. I said, 'So he has told me, Your Majesty, and not infrequently.'

'Ah, so you and he know each other well? How intriguing; how *very* intriguing.' But he still didn't invite me to get up. Rather, he walked around me in a circle three times, now and again stopping without saying why, then as soon as I began to worry that he'd identified a defect in me, he would simply walk on. Eventually he commented, 'You *are* exceptional, to look upon at least. Exquisite. You could be his sister. To think that my agents have scoured the entire Empire, scaling mountains and crossing deserts, journeying to the farthest corners of the earth where the winds have their homes, when such a flawless specimen as you has been living here in Shushan all along. Yet perhaps that is *all* you are: an exquisite shell, just like the sea-shells I have in my collections, dry and empty as a picked skull inside. *God*, how I am weary of beautiful women.'

Startled at the sudden vehemence in his voice, I looked up; he had flung himself supine on a couch and closed his eyes once more. Not even Hegai could have predicted that the King would behave in such an unceremonious manner in front of me, nor could anyone have devised a fitting response for me to make. Then as I watched him, Kshayarsha grimaced again as he'd done in the throne-room, and moved his hands to his stomach. I ventured dubiously, 'Can I get you anything, Your Majesty?'

The pain passed off, and he relaxed. With an exaggerated sigh, he answered, 'How about a peaceful night's sleep? Or a whole day when I don't have to listen to the whining of peevish courtiers? Or aren't you quite that exceptional?'

I didn't react, and he sighed again yet more deliberately, as if to say, alas, you *are* like all the rest. But I wasn't going to make a fool of myself by apologizing for my existence as Ashpamithra had done, and I certainly wasn't going to give away anything about myself until I'd worked out exactly what game he was playing.

There was a jug of wine on a table nearby, and some goblets. So I got up without waiting to be invited, and went to pour him an unmixed draught. From the corner of my eye I saw Farah, still hunched up on the floor like a scolded puppy, staring in horror because of my audacity, but I ignored her. I carried the filled goblet to Kshayarsha and knelt by his couch; he opened his eyes to find me smiling at him, a gentle, wry smile which I hoped resembled Hegai's. I said, 'So there are some things which even a king cannot procure simply by wanting them.'

It was his turn to be startled now. I was still smiling, and I held the wine to his lips; he took the goblet from me and eased himself up against the back of the couch until he was sitting rather than lying. Sipping at his drink, he studied my face reflectively and then observed, 'You have a singularly fluent grasp of Aramaic for a foreigner, my dear.'

'Your Majesty?' All at once, my mind was turning somersaults: precisely what had Hegai told the King about my background? The official story he'd invented for me was that I was as every bit as Persian as the royal family itself, from a once-distinguished but long-forgotten house. Surely he'd remembered to alter my records, and they didn't still say what Memucan had written, that I'd been adopted and raised among Greeks? Or was it my likeness to Hegai, whose roots were in Babylonia, which had given me away?

So I didn't say anything; Kshayarsha gave a low chuckle and asked, 'How old were you when you were adopted? Come now, it's a straightforward enough question, isn't it? Or can you only cope with subtle ones? Do you consider it strange that I should show a genuine interest in you and your past?'

For one dreadful moment I thought that perhaps he'd met Mordecai in person and knew *everything*; the meddlesome wretch was employed at the palace now, after all. But no; the last thing Mordecai would want even at this stage was to admit to anyone that his own adopted daughter, a Jewess, had run away to join the harem. So I whispered, 'I don't know how old I was, Your Majesty.'

'You were too young to remember your real parents? A baby, perhaps?'

'Yes, Your Majesty. I—think I was found exposed, and those who rescued me became my adoptive parents.'

'You were exposed? Here in Shushan?'

'I—yes, Your Majesty. I think that's what happened.'

'Even *more* intriguing.' He took another sip of his wine, then licked his lips, provocatively somehow, almost seductively. 'Because, you see, exposing babies is not a Persian custom. They have a tiresome tendency to die, and pollute the earth with their decomposing bodies. It is the kind of barbarism practised only by such as the Greeks, so far as I am aware, and even then, only by the poorest and most ignorant.'

I was more flustered than ever, especially because he was sporting a wry smile just like the one he'd wiped from my face with his questions; it was almost as though he'd stolen it from me and was now parading it flagrantly before me. I set my lips in a tight line, lest I be tempted to say something I should later regret.

'Oh, there is nothing to be ashamed of in being Greek,' he announced breezily. 'I don't hate *all* Greeks, by any means. There are many at my own court, some of whom are prominent philosophers, the most intelligent individuals I know. They are even wise enough to realize that there are no such things as gods with physical bodies like mortal men. No; it's only the Athenians and the Eretrians I hate, because they induced subjects of my illustrious father to rebel against his benevolent sovereignty.'

I shuddered, knowing all too well that Kshayarsha could raze Arderikka to the ground and massacre its every inhabitant on a whim if he so desired. But his manifest enjoyment of my discomfiture was beginning to make me angry rather than afraid. I withdrew slightly from his couch, sitting back on my haunches.

Then quite without warning, he sprang forward and seized me around the throat. I gagged and spluttered, my eyes watering; he hissed into my face, 'Don't you know that I could have you flayed alive for lying to the King, you little hussy? I know perfectly well that you were brought here from a hovel in Arderikka whilst your records claim that you're as Aryan as I am. Not only that, but some flea-ridden wench from there has been to visit you. The name given as belonging to your father has no existence in any of our files outside of the ones relating to your ancestry—which have in themselves clearly been tampered with since your arrival at the palace. Do you take my agents and my spies and my clerks for fools?' When I didn't offer him an answer—because he was rendering me physically unable to—he demanded, 'Or is it *me* you consider the fool?' And he cast me away onto the floor with all his sportsman's strength.

I crouched there rubbing at my neck, but I didn't cry; I was too angry. I thought: if your spies weren't fools, they would know my identity for certain. And if you were truly a great man of authority like your father Darayavaush, you wouldn't need to bully me bodily like a scurvy slave-dealer.

I was concerned that my refusal to weep might have angered *him* further also, but one look at his face told me that it hadn't. He hadn't been angry at all, even when he'd made as if to throttle me; it had all been part of my testing, and his cheeks were flushed with arousal. He said softly, 'So, my clever and persistent Tishtrya was right in this too: that there is precious little in this world which is capable of frightening you. Come here, my dear, and share my wine, since it seems that your serving-women are too daunted to pour you any. There isn't a great deal of point in having seven of them if they cannot see to your simplest needs, you know.' He held out his goblet; I rose, walked to his couch with all the dignity I could muster, and knelt again for him to hold the wine to my lips.

When I'd taken a dainty mouthful—and it was the richest, sweetest, strongest stuff I'd ever tasted—he continued, 'They say that there are still Persian families who can't afford even *one* slave, though there cannot be many left now, since they don't have to pay so much as a daric a year in tax. Still, it is one of my burning ambitions to bring it about that there are *none* so poor by the end of my reign. It is not fitting for Aryans to perform menial tasks. The other races were specifically designed for this purpose by the Wise Lord Ahura Mazda. Babylonians, Egyptians, Greeks and Jews ... they were all created solely to minister to the incomparable people of Persia, and to utilize their skills in our service. It is a grave pity that so many of them fail to recognize this, and conceive ideas way above their station. However, it is of no consequence. They will be rightly educated in time.'

He was still trying to break me, I knew that; if he couldn't cause me to fear for myself, he would have me afraid for my people—whoever he thought they were. It did occur to me briefly that I no longer had the remotest idea of what life in the streets of Shushan was like for its displaced, minority communities; I'd had no meaningful contact with the outside world for ten months or so. I knew there had begun to be serious resentment against non-Persians long before my voluntary incarceration, because of economic difficulties as well as because of Kshayarsha's own campaign to eradicate paganism and every kind of foreign religious practice. Yet I had no idea whether things had got worse in the meantime. I *was* starting to get some idea of why Vashti at the banquet had been unable to tolerate her husband's arrogance a moment longer and had felt herself compelled to defy him. I wondered how Hegai could ever have loved such a swine.

But he read my thought somehow, from my blazing eyes and the set of my jaw perhaps, and said it out loud to me word for word. Then finishing up with the promise that I was about to discover Hegai's reason for myself, he wrapped his well-muscled arms about my back, and kissed me hard on the mouth.

I was outraged at his presumption, but only for a second. The wiry strength of his arms and the heaving of his taut breast against me unlocked a door in the depths of my soul, and released a flood of excitement such as I'd never experienced even in my wildest dreams of him.

Before I'd even thought what I was doing, my own arms were round his broad back, my nails cutting into his flesh through his silken tunic as his lips devoured mine and I fought to snatch enough air to kiss him in return. I was instantaneously convinced that my whole being had been preparing itself all my life for that one glorious moment, and had found its true purpose and wanted nothing else but him, ever again, beside me, all around me, within me. The fear induced in me by Anahita's examination and by my own ignorance evaporated like morning mist on the Shushan plain.

There was certainly no room in the manuals of Persian courtly etiquette for any description of the kind of kiss he was giving me now; there was no tenderness about him whatever, but a hunger to which I responded with all that I was. I didn't care that Farah and her companions were still grovelling there on the floor, watching; indeed, I wished that Mordecai and Ninlil could have been with them. I didn't even care that somewhere, out of sight and out of mind, Hegai would be mourning alone.

Then all at once the thing ended as suddenly as it had begun. He tried to lift me up onto the couch beside him, but when he took my weight his pain returned, and he cried out loud, letting me fall back on the carpet. For a moment or two I could do nothing but lie there panting, on fire with frustration. Then I wobbled up onto hands and knees, and looked through the tangle of my hair into his contorted face. I croaked, 'You *are* ill, Your Majesty. Dear God. Let me send for Ashpamithra.' But he shook his head and put out a hand as though to restrain me.

'It . . . will pass. It always passes. There is . . . medicine in that bottle . . . on top of that chest, by the door.'

I scrambled to fetch it, then held the bottle to his lips the way I'd held the wine before, and he took two enormous draughts. It seemed to bring some relief; he lay quiet for a while with his hands pressed to his stomach, and I laid my own hands on top of them. Then he blew out his breath between his teeth and said with unguarded rancour, 'After all this time, I have found a woman with the grace and subtlety of my beloved Tishtrya, and the spirit and passion of my Vashti . . . and I cannot take her. I, the Great King of Persia and Emperor of half the world . . .'

He spoke as though to himself, or perhaps to his god, but it was I who sensed the depth of his inner sorrow, and responded by kissing his brow and asking, 'But what ails you, Your Majesty? Has it been like this with you long?'

'Oh, a long time, my sweet Esther, so long . . . ever since I was forced to retreat from Greece with what remained of my army, and we had little but grass to live on for days at a stretch. That's when it's worst even now—when I don't eat wisely.' He gave a bitter laugh. 'Yet my Babylonian physician says that I worry too much, and it's my anxiety poisoning the humours in my belly. Can you believe that? These quacks will say anything, and we have no choice but to swallow what they say—and their noxious potions to boot. Give me some more of that wine, my dear, though I'm not supposed to drink it. It may do something to take away the vile taste.'

I held the goblet to his lips again; they'd been full and red when they met mine, but now they were white and cold. I cradled his head in the crook of my arm as he drank, and I said softly, 'You will get better, Your Majesty. You look better already.'

'Yes, the pain is passing now . . . But it will return. I have good days and bad days. This had been one of the worst; until it became full of you.' He smiled again, if rather wanly, and added, 'You have the gentleness of my own mother, to crown all else that you possess. Do you know, whenever I was ill as a child she would hold me just as you are holding me, with her arm just where yours is, and concern just like yours on her face? Such perfection . . . and you have to see me like this.'

'Your Majesty, please forgive me. Perhaps I shouldn't have come today after all. It was selfish of me, and inconsiderate of Hegai to let me have my way.'

'No, my dear. It is *I* who should ask forgiveness of *you*. And Tishtrya is never inconsiderate—not towards me. He knew that you would do my heart good, if not my belly, even today. And as to your selfishness: surely you aren't telling me that you *wanted* to come here?'

'Of course, Your Majesty. This is what they have been preparing me for, all these months.'

He seemed a little disappointed to be given this as my reason, and only then did it strike me that although he was possibly the only man alive who could have virtually any girl he wanted, the enjoyment he derived from this must be considerably diminished when not one of those females went with him by choice. So I said to comfort him, 'I take it that Hegai told you I came to the palace of my own free will.'

Plainly Hegai had done nothing of the kind, for momentarily the Great King of Persia was rendered speechless. I was well pleased with his reaction, and continued, 'Though I might perhaps have been glad of some of your medicine to settle *my* stomach earlier today, even so. It is still a rare honour for a girl of humble background to be granted a night with a king.'

212

'And look how you are spending it! They have trained you to seduce me, and here you are acting as my nurse.'

'There will be time enough for seduction later on, Your Majesty, when the pain is gone entirely. The night is young, and I can be patient.'

However, even as I spoke I saw that there would be no consummation of our mutual desire on this particular occasion. Hegai had seen to it that I was well rested, and ready for a whole night of love had the King required it of me. But Kshayarsha's eyelids were heavy and closing already; he muttered something about having forgotten how drowsy his confounded medicine made him, especially when taken with wine against his doctors' orders. Presently he succumbed to a troubled half-sleep, under the cloud of which he seemed to see himself once more on the nightmare journey home from Greece to Sardis, for he was talking with slurred speech about lost battles, the violent deaths of his kinsmen and friends, and the privations of that long, miserable march where one man after another had fallen by the wayside. Then he began to speak of futile longing, of lost love, and of Vashti.

After that, he stopped talking altogether. I tried to withdraw my arm from his neck without waking him, but his eyes swam open and he struggled to sit up. With the heels of his hands pressed against his cheeks he said distractedly, 'There is no need for you to stay here, child; I don't want you distressing yourself for nothing. Send one of your women to fetch Ashpamithra . . . he will find you suitable accommodation for the night. I shall send for you again tomorrow, when I am better. I need to sleep now. Ashpamithra will see to me.'

That was when I realized that at last I knew *exactly* what to do; Hegai's careful preparations were not to be wasted after all. I said, 'You won't have to summon Ashpamithra, Your Majesty. I can do all that is necessary.'

There was another door leading out of the reception room, set in the opposite wall to the one I'd come in by. Deducing that it must give access to the King's bedroom, I helped him up, and motioned Farah to help me. We had quite a way to struggle, because there were dining rooms and sitting rooms and dressing rooms and a room especially for washing and bathing to pass before we found what we were looking for. Eventually we got him to his bed, and I told Farah to return with all her comrades to their own quarters: their services wouldn't be required again until the morrow. They left gratefully enough, and I was alone with Kshayarsha.

I went through the whole ritual of disrobing him, precisely as Hegai had described it to me, though the royal cape and sash had already been disposed of. He was too drugged to resist me, and could barely sit upright, but he performed his own part in the procedure to the letter; it must have become as a reflex with him. Once he was lying down I thought he would sleep at once, but paradoxically he revived somewhat and called me back as I made to slip out the door. I knelt obediently by the high bed, which was crowned with a great golden canopy just as I'd once imagined it, and he asked with disarming simplicity, 'Esther . . . is Tishtrya happy?'

'Your Majesty?'

'Oh, come now, my dear. He risked his life for you; he shared with you his most private secrets. You must have been closer to him than anyone else has been since he left me. You must know whether or not he is happy.'

'I'm—not sure, Your Majesty. I think he was happy when he was with me.' I suppose I could have petitioned the King at that very moment for Hegai to be assigned to my service. But my thoughts were all bound up with Kshayarsha himself now; I'd consigned Hegai to my past, just as he'd tried to consign me to his.

But Kshayarsha said, 'You truly *are* an extraordinary girl, Esther. Never before today have I encountered a woman who was neither jealous of my Tishtrya nor disgusted by him. Nor did you merely accept him for what he was, but you actually befriended him; even when you knew full well what he'd meant to me.'

He paused, waiting for me to say something in acknowledgement of his praise for me. Yet there was nothing I *could* say. His words had made me out to be some kind of paragon; how could I admit that I'd only befriended Hegai in the first place for my own advancement, and because he'd been winsome, and because I *hadn't* known what he was?

However, Kshayarsha chose to interpret my cowed silence as modesty, and he was more impressed with me than ever. He whispered, 'Esther, you gave Tishtrya the love he deserved and so much needed, and which I was prevented from giving him. For that alone I would love you.' (I found myself thinking: had you not crushed Babylon with such unwarranted viciousness, Hegai would still have been enjoying the love of his own parents.) 'But you are beautiful and vivacious and passionate besides. You came to my palace and to my bed because you wanted to; because you knew that you could truly love me, and restore to me the joy which the years of anxiety and failure have taken from me. Esther—under the bed there is a chest; the key for it is in the fruitbowl on the table by the window. I want you to pull out the chest and open it, and hand me the box which is inside.'

I did as he bade me, though disconcertingly reminded of the occasion when Mordecai had long since asked me to do something so much the same. When I'd found the box inside the chest, and got up to hand it over, the King was sitting up in bed. His eyes were glittering; and not with fever.

He opened the box; it contained a golden tiara inlaid with sapphires and emeralds, enamel, and deep blue lapis lazuli bright as the plumage of his peacocks as it glowed in the lamplight. There was a heavy necklace crafted to match; and bracelets and earrings and anklets, all fashioned in the same eclectic Hakhamanish style. Before I could make even one of the obligatory two refusals, Kshayarsha had taken the tiara and placed it on my head among my dishevelled curls.

'Esther,' he announced, 'This crown and these ornaments were made for Vashti and I presented them to her on the day I chose her as my wife and my queen. Now they, and I, shall belong to you—if you accept us.'

My heart took wings. It was of no interest to me at all now why the King had favoured me, or whether his delight in me was justified. I clasped his hands and exclaimed, 'Your Majesty, I accept,' for how could I not do, especially when it seemed that for once in my life I was being offered some kind of choice.

'In that case,' he said, 'We need have no regrets about the way this evening has gone, for pre-marital chastity is so important to my subjects. Nothing could please them more than to learn that I had mastered my manhood and kept my bride a virgin until the night of her wedding. And so I shall do, my dear; in this at least I shall be adhering to custom, and no one will be able to point an accusing finger in my direction. I have waited so long for the perfect bride, and you have waited so long to be brought to me; it will do us no harm now to wait a little longer.'

12

We never did send for Ashpamithra that night. Once he'd bestowed his betrothal gifts upon me, Kshayarsha slept.

For a while I remained where I was on my knees, watching him, partly because I was worried for him that he'd had too much medicine, and whether it was really very dangerous for him to have mixed it with alcohol. But more it was because there was a fear in me that if I left his bedside and sought sleep myself, I would wake up to find that I'd dreamt the entire episode. Every so often as I knelt there I would put up my hands to touch the tiara, then the earrings, then the necklace; I would gaze at the bracelets and the anklets lest they vanish before my eyes. And I would tell myself that they could mean nothing other than that I, Esther who had once been Hadassah, was to become Queen of Persia and Empress of the mightiest domain the world had ever seen.

But as the night drew on, and the lamps sputtered out one after another, I could keep awake no longer and lay down on one of the couches in Kshayarsha's reception room. Thus it came about that I did indeed get my night with the King, but ended it as chaste as I'd begun.

It was Ashpamithra who woke me, way after dawn. Light came streaming in from the King's private courtyard, which had been curtained off the previous evening so I hadn't known that it was there. The birds in the cages were singing brightly, and the two peacocks pecked happily at seeds and crumbs which Ashpamithra had scattered for them on the floor. He said to me, 'His Majesty would have me assure you that he is much better this morning, my lady, and has gone to the Apadana to attend to the business of the day.'

'Shall I see him later on?' I enquired eagerly, for nothing Kshayarsha had said the night before would have led me to believe we would be separated again so soon. But it seemed that everything had changed since then.

'No, my lady. You will not see him again for quite some time. When you have breakfasted and refreshed yourself, I am instructed to take you to the suite of rooms which has been prepared for you. Your servants will be brought to you there, and you will have everything you require.'

A dart of apprehension pierced my euphoria. I caught Ashpami-thra's hand instinctively, as though he were Hegai, and stammered, 'His Majesty hasn't changed his mind about me? Last night...' I touched the tiara; it was still there, I had slept in it. 'He'd had wine, and medicine. You don't suppose...'

'No, my lady. He hasn't changed his mind.' Ashpamithra spoke with conviction, but also with a certain bitterness which was under-standable. He had more reason to be jealous of me than he was of Hegai, for much as the King might still feel affection for the latter, that relationship was over. The new Eunuch of the Bedchamber extracted his effete hand from my grasp and continued stiffly, 'His Majesty can hold his drink, my lady. It never causes him to make ill-considered decisions.'

I thought: *something* led him to summon Vashti to parade herself before his lascivious friends, but I didn't say it. Ashpamithra pro-ceeded to offer me somewhat grudging congratulations, as though as an afterthought; I accepted them as graciously as possible, knowing that it would be even more foolish to alienate the present Chamberlain than the one he'd replaced.

After that he brought me yoghurt and fruit for breakfast, and delicious iced water sweetened with honey and flavoured with citron. He told me that this was sherbet, made with ice from the Zagros mountains. Then he handed me a voluminous cloak with a heavy veil, which I had to put on over what I was wearing. I could remove it, bathe myself properly and dress my hair once I was in my own chambers, he explained; but custom dictated that no one save the women of the King's immediate family, and her own female atten-dants, should set eyes upon His Majesty's betrothed from the time of the engagement's being formalized until the day of the wedding.

So when I was ready, he took me from the royal apartment to another suite of rooms to the west; which although not strictly speak-ing a part of the harem, or of the House of the Virgins, was apparently connected to both, and lay in between them. Here I was to be kept while arrangements for my marriage were being made.

My seven attendants were already there awaiting me, having been summoned I suppose just after sunrise. All of them were more in awe of me than ever before, and they bowed low, as though I were Queen even now. When Ashpamithra had gone I scolded them, and forced Farah to embrace me and wish me luck, but she could only repeat words which I gave her to say. So I set her and her companions to sorting out my things; all that I possessed had been brought for me from my room among the Sisters. Meanwhile I explored my new quarters.

They were situated on the ground floor. I had two separate rooms— a reception room and a bedroom—and my own tiny courtyard, scarcely bigger than a stairwell. Everything was sumptuously decorated, but space was limited and I hoped I shouldn't be confined there too long. Once my things were in order, my dresses hung up or folded away, and my jewels and cosmetics stowed in caskets, I ordered the girls to proceed with my daily routine as normal. Although the King had expressed himself well satisfied with my appearance, I couldn't afford to relax my attention to it before the wedding. Nor could I think of anything else to do with myself. For my frustrated desire for the King still burned within me, all mixed up with a queasy excitement and a vaguely resentful apprehension because once again it seemed that control of my fate had been whisked from my hands.

I took my siesta at the customary hour, afterwards having myself dressed and prepared to receive visitors. It was just as well that I did all this, because no sooner was I ready than an authoritative knock came at the door.

Farah went to answer, and there entered a tall, elegant woman; or perhaps I should say lady rather than woman, since that was the impression most eloquently conveyed by her proud carriage, her expensive but unobtrusive clothing and her quiet unpretentious dignity. It wasn't until she removed her veil that I realized she was old enough to have been my grandmother, standing as she did as straight as a girl a quarter her age, and having kept a figure which many a girl might have been willing to die for. She'd kept her facial looks too, for although her hair was all but white, her features were noble and strong.

Her two attendants were little younger than she was, and perhaps had served her as long as they could remember; they took her veil and cloak without being asked, and by the slightest nod of her head she made it known to one of them that she wanted the high-backed chair from the farthest corner of the room, and to the other that she wanted also the gift-box which this maid was carrying, and which had, as it transpired, been brought for me.

She said that her name was Hutaosa, and all at once I half-recognized her from Vashti's banquet. She was the mother of Kshayarsha and widow of Darayavaush, and was worthy of honour in her own right, commanding by sheer strength of her personality both respect and affection from her late husband's people. Looking at her, it was quite easy to see why. She wore authority like a subtle perfume, and though her expression was grave and her age-lines honed by the patient endurance of suffering, to me her eyes seemed to speak peace and a profound serenity; her very being radiated tranquillity, warmth, and a lifetime of wisdom and experience.

I bowed, almost to the floor, and kissed her hand; she took me in her arms and kissed me on each of my cheeks.

I said, 'So it is true, my lady. I am to be married to your son, and to become the Queen of Persia.'

'Most certainly you are, my daughter; and you shall call me mother from today.' Then she kissed me again, with endearing spontaneity, and squeezed my shoulders. 'Words cannot express how happy I am for you, but all the more so for him. He pines for Vashti still, yet can never take her back, for which I have to say I am not sorry. He so much needs a woman who can make him forget. You may be able to achieve that, from what I have heard.'

'You've heard tell of me already? But from whom?' I couldn't help but ask her outright; her openness caused me to be candid in return.

'From Hegai, whom you so generously befriended. He has brought me reports of you and your progress twice a week at least, ever since you came to the palace. We both had high hopes of you from the beginning, and I don't think we shall be disappointed.'

'I hope not, my lady.'

'You mean, "I hope not, my *mother*",' she reminded me; and made me repeat it. I did so, aware that I was blushing.

'Now you must accept my betrothal gift,' she announced, and handed me the box; I declined it twice as I'd been taught to, then took it and thanked her profusely. I was half-expecting more jewels, but it was filled with honeyed sweetmeats, the like of which I hadn't been permitted for months. I exclaimed in delight and ate one at once, knowing full well that when these were gone there would be no more until the wedding. But today was a special day.

I devoured a couple more, before thinking to hand them around; my own maids dared not take any, but Hutaosa and her two accepted. Then Hutaosa said, 'Your servants may be wiser than you are, my daughter. From now on you must never accept food or drink from anyone, unless you know and can trust that person implicitly. Suppose I were not who I said I was? You have never met me before in your life, so you could not be sure. Or suppose I *was* who I claimed to be, but maintained an allegiance to Vashti?'

My mouth was already open to receive another of the delicacies, and my hand was halfway to it, with the morsel in my fingers. Hutaosa smiled slightly at my manifest horror, but then grew grave again.

'You may eat it, Esther; it is safe enough, believe me. I supervised the making of these myself, from beginning to end. But you cannot be too careful, now that your election has been made public through your installation here. By this evening it will be all around the harem that the Suite of the Betrothed has an occupant. Then every concubine in this citadel will hate you, and Vashti more than any of them.'

But I didn't eat the sweet; all of a sudden I no longer wanted it. Its aroma had become cloying rather than tempting.

'We shall find you a taster,' Hutaosa continued briskly, as though she were planning on getting me something as everyday as a house-keeper. 'And you will eat nothing which she hasn't sampled first. But in any case, I shall spend the greater part of each day here with you. You have much more to learn now, such as the formalities of the wedding ritual itself, and what your role in it will be. Until that time you will set eyes on no man, nor even a eunuch, so that your ardour will be strong on the night that Kshayarsha beds you.'

'And will that night come soon?'

'Your wedding will take place on the ninetieth day from today; and your coronation will form a part of the same proceedings. It will be the greatest state occasion witnessed in Shushan since my son returned from Greece. The people are sorely in need of a pretext to celebrate.'

'Ninety days! But that's so long! I'm to be kept here like a prisoner for three whole months? How shall I bear it?'

'You will bear it because you must, my sweet daughter; and because it is a simple fact that kings and queens enjoy less freedom than their own subjects in a vast and unwieldy empire like our own. It is our adherence to tradition, our willingness to submit to its fatherly guidance and to walk within the boundaries marked out for us, that keeps the great edifice from falling. The common folk have certain expectations of their lords, and those lords in turn have expectations of their sovereign. Provided that those expectations are fulfilled, our walls will withstand the assault of the fiercest of storms.' She sighed heavily. 'I wish only that my beloved son would accept the good sense of this. It takes a great monarch to preserve intact the inheritance bequeathed to him without losing armies, territory or his very reputation, but a greater one still to expand it successfully, or introduce innovations without bringing disaster upon his own head or on the heads of those millions for whom he is responsible.'

'And you don't consider your son to possess this degree of greatness?' I ventured daringly.

But I'd pushed Hutaosa as far as she was willing to go on our first meeting. She dismissed my question with a wave of one hand, and instead began to enumerate for me the reasons behind the ninety-day period which must pass before the wedding.

The first and most significant one concerned the time it would take for invitations to be sent to the satraps of the farthest-flung provinces and the regional governors who served under them, and for these august personages then to make their way to Shushan with their caravans of courtiers, their harems, their servants and their hangers-on. Every satrap's court was designed as a replica of the central Imperial one, and although these replicas might be less grand than the original from which they'd been copied, the organization required to transport them was almost as elaborate.

Secondly, the New Year Festival must apparently be celebrated first, for there was no time to plan and bring off a royal wedding before it. New Year is the most important event in the Persian calendar, and has been so for centuries, ever since the days when the magi and most of the people were pagan and the worship of Ahura Mazda was hardly known. Several weeks before the festival itself, Kshayarsha would travel to Parsa, his religious capital, along with pilgrims from all across the Empire. There they would establish a huge tented city, centred on the sanctuary. Those people important enough to receive an invitation to the wedding would proceed from Parsa directly to Shushan once the New Year festivities were over, and would have to pitch their tents once again on the plain below our city.

Thirdly, my wedding garments had to be designed and made up, and there was the equivalent of several scrolls' worth of information for me to absorb as regards etiquette and protocol, in comparison with which what I'd learnt already would seem like the few words a child has to learn on his first day of schooling.

So I gritted my teeth, and said that I *would* bear it all, since I had no alternative; and thus began another tedious eternity of waiting, made tolerable only by the wisdom, the gentle wit, and the quiet approval of Hutaosa. My vanity and my selfishness didn't appear to perturb her in the least; to her these were but minor flaws in my character, merely symptoms of my immaturity, and would be balanced out by experience as time went on.

Balance, it seemed, was important to her, as were righteousness and purity; and honesty above all else, for like her son she was a fervent devotee of the Wise Lord. But in Hutaosa there were no visible undercurrents of self-pity, or cruelty, or insecure viciousness to disturb the surface of the pool of serenity I seemed to perceive within her soul. I thought she was perfect in every way, and what little belief I had left in Adonai began to crumble.

The first measurements for my bridal garments—and for those of my seven attendants—were taken the following day by one of Hutaosa's sisters. The two of them discussed with me at great length the design of my apparel, what kinds of fabric it should be made from, and how it should be embellished. I had little idea of what I wanted, except that I insisted on wearing magenta. Hutaosa's sister protested that it wasn't a feminine colour, and certainly not suitable for a virgin. But Hutaosa understood my insistence very well and I got my way, because there was no rule governing the matter and I should be causing no offence to tradition.

Once this decision had been made, I was happy to let the two sisters draw up the rest of the details themselves since I had but meagre understanding of the subtleties of Persian bridal fashions. I couldn't see why I shouldn't wear some of the things Hegai had given me for my presentation to Kshayarsha, but apparently it would never do for the future Queen to be seen wearing the same outfit twice. This went for the day-to-day domestic round as well as for great state occasions; Hutaosa informed me that the entire populations of several towns were responsible for supplying funds to stock the Queen's wardrobe, and I would be expected to make full use of these. Far from begrudging the wealth of their royal family, Persians take pride in it, for it enhances their nation's status in the eyes of the world.

The better I got to know Hutaosa, the more I came to like her. She had an uncanny way of appreciating how I was feeling, without my ever telling her, and sometimes when I didn't even understand myself. I suppose now that it came of so many years spent as the wife of a king; she knew the frustrations and tedium of palace life like no one else. Whenever I felt lonely she would be there to talk to me; whenever I felt plain and unlovely despite the hours devoted to my toilette she would spoil me with some frivolously feminine little gift—a phial of some exotic perfume, or an arm-ring, or a decorative comb to twist into my hair.

When I was bored, which was a commoner complaint of mine than all the rest, she would have her attendants play the flute or sing to me. Once they'd exhausted their repertoire, Hutaosa herself would challenge me to a board-game, draughts or checkers or senet. Mordecai had never sanctioned the playing of such games, regarding them as a sinful waste of the time our gracious Lord had given us. But Hutaosa said that they toned up the mind just as exercise toned up the muscles and the figure. And in the emotional cut and thrust of life in the harem, a flabby mind is as much of a liability as a flabby body.

I quickly realized that little went on in the palace of Kshayarsha of which his astute mother was unaware. But she did not use her intelligence to manipulate her son or his advisers, or to scheme for the gratification of her own ambitions. Her father had been none other than the noble Kurash, benevolent founder of the Hakhamanish Empire, and he had brought her up to behave nobly as he did. Despite his glorious conquests he'd maintained an abstemiously simple court; in wartime he'd led his troops into battle in person, and had voluntarily subjected himself to the hardships endured by his common soldiers. When the time had come for him to die, he was buried in a simple tomb; by then Hutaosa herself had been married to his successor Kambujet, and when he also died she was given to Darayavaush who'd come to power at the end of a bloody civil war. It seemed that she'd had little say in these dynastic matches, but she harboured no bitterness, and though she'd been widowed twice had never let sorrow get the better of her. I, who had always fiercely resented being bridled by anyone, found it baffling that a woman so self-assured as she could have allowed herself to be used and neither fought it nor let it crush her spirit. I found myself wondering if faith in her Lord Ahura

Mazda gave her some inner contentment which I'd never thought could be got from Adonai.

As Persia's power had increased and its people had prospered, so the Imperial court had grown steadily more luxurious—or decadent, as Mordecai would have said. In this respect I was reminded of the history of the Jews, and only just stopped myself in time from saying so to Hutaosa; it was hard to keep secrets from her. For Saul, my ancestor, the first of our kings, had been content with the rustic simplicity of his father's modest fortress at Gibeah, whilst each of his successors had lived more ostentatiously than the last. The third of them, Rehoboam, had seen his kingdom fall apart, because he himself lacked the qualities of statesmanship required to hold it together. This was precisely the kind of fate which Hutaosa thought might lie in store for Kshayarsha.

Not that she ever criticized him directly. He was her son and she loved him unreservedly; she would never have admitted even to herself that he was a disappointment to her.

But it was his ill-fated expedition to Greece which had caused his mother more grief than anything else he'd ever done. She told me her side of its story one chill winter evening a month or so after I met her; we were warming our hands at a small fire-stand which Farah had brought us.

'It was an indescribable relief to see him back safe, after everything we'd heard,' Hutaosa sighed, her eyes drawn towards the fire yet focussed somewhere in the past, way back behind it. 'But when he *did* get back, he was so wan and gaunt; and that was after I don't know how many months supposedly recuperating at Sardis, where the Wise Lord alone knows what he got up to.'

'It's true, then, that he seduced the wife of his brother the satrap?'

'He tried to, at least. And he tried to seduce her daughter too, a poor unsuspecting girl younger than you are. But who am I to blame him? He no longer had a wife to come home to, and he'd lost all belief in himself and his capabilities. It's a constant source of sorrow to him to think that he's failed to live up to the standards his father set for him. Darayavaush was so over-bearing, so dominating. He kept all his sons on too short a rein, and never left them room to grow. The first real responsibility he ever gave to Kshayarsha was the governorship of Babylonia, and it was too much for him when he hadn't been ade-quately prepared for it. It made him diffident and grasping and

destructively selfish, and brought out a cruel streak in him which I
hadn't seen since he was a child and I had to punish him for pulling the
legs off spiders.'

I giggled. 'He really used to do that? Pull spiders' legs off?'

'That and worse. He used to bring live snakes into the harem and
cut off their heads with his dagger when he was only seven or eight. He
claimed he'd heard a magus say that it was the duty of God's servants
to destroy all poisonous or harmful animals, and I know, I've heard
them say it too. But Kshayarsha was always intense about religion,
from a very early age, and his zeal hasn't always been channelled in the
wisest directions.'

I contemplated this for a moment or two, propping my chin on my
hands and gazing into the softly glowing embers; there are few days in
any year when it's cold enough to light a fire indoors in Shushan, so it
always feels special, magical somehow. And I was thinking back to
when I'd been a child, and zealous for my faith too, looking forward
with naive enthusiasm to taking part in the work of rebuilding
Jerusalem. But my eagerness had sprung from a desire to make my
parents proud of me, rather than from any religious belief of my own; I
asked Hutaosa if that had been true of Kshayarsha.

'No, I don't think so. His father was never particularly pious,
though he favoured Ahura Mazda rather than the gods of the Old
Religion. The prophet Zarathustra, who spread the knowledge of the
Wise Lord among our people, stayed for a while at the court of
Darayavaush's father Vishtashpa when Vishtashpa was a satrap—
though I've actually heard more than one priest try to claim that
Zarathustra lived hundreds or even thousands of years ago, in the
days of legend. So Darayavaush was brought up to follow his teachings, but it never ran deep with him, and he was happy enough to let
other religions be practised openly within the Empire, as was my
father Kurash. Both of them believed that the gods of the nations
were aspects of Ahura Mazda by other names. As for me: I have
worshipped Ahura Mazda all my life, but not as Kshayarsha does.'

'So where did his piety come from, then?' I was frankly intrigued; I
couldn't imagine that anyone could become excessively religious all by
himself, and almost from the cradle.

'The seeds of it were always in him; perhaps Ahura Mazda sowed
them in his soul when I conceived him. But he listened to various magi
as a boy, some of whom were more dangerous than others. I remember

one in particular who told him he would never be great unless he eradicated the evils of paganism from his domains; Ahura Mazda had been prepared to overlook the ignorance of Kurash and Darayavaush, but he'd been gracious enough to impart full knowledge to Kshayarsha, and would therefore expect his complete obedience.'

I said nothing in response to this, and Hutaosa must have sensed that I'd gone unusually quiet. However, she proceeded to explain to me something of the teachings of the prophet, since I was manifestly unaware of them, and this would never do if I was to wed her devout son. It seemed that the cult of Zarathustra involved no animal sacrifices; no temple ritual; no idols, of course—in fact, little that could be recognized as religion at all. The only ceremony which was obligatory to his followers was the worship of fire, the purest symbol of God; Kshayarsha would visit his fire-altar in the citadel south of the palace every other day at the least.

'And the magi?' I asked when I could get a word in. 'What of them? I heard tell that they were once pagans themselves, yet you say they want the Old Religion wiped out.'

'There have been magi as long as there have been men, my daughter. They have their origins in the priestly clan of the Medes which existed long before records began. And they have been priests to every god who has ever been venerated. But when Ahura Mazda's light began to eclipse all the rest, they were afraid that their influence would wane along with their ancestral deities', and they announced their conversion to his cult, all to a man. Thus their yeast leavens our society at every level; they even claim to have secret knowledge about the Wise Lord which he has revealed to them alone, and other men must consult them if they wish to be enlightened. But I should not care to guess what most of them believe in their hearts, nor what rites they practise in the privacy of their own homes. I would trust very few of them; neither would Kshayarsha, on his better days.'

'Then why doesn't he get rid of them? I've seen them here at the palace; there was one with him in the Apadana when I was presented there.'

'Because he fears them, my daughter, just as everyone does. Their eyes are everywhere, their meddling fingers are in every pot, and they possess arcane powers against which weapons of bronze and iron are useless. They can read the stars and see into the future, or sentence a person to death by their black arts, or merely by a curse.'

'They can *really* do that? You really believe it?'

'I believe that their powers would be much reduced in their effect if honest men and women did *not* so fear them. But Kshayarsha is too impressionable; he is too ready to listen to *anyone*, because he is profoundly unsure of himself. He listens to the rash and violent young knaves who call themselves his advisers; it was they who persuaded him to wage war upon the Greeks. And on the way there he sacrificed white horses to the spirit of the river Strymon when he was about to cross it, because the magi counselled him to do so, even though sacrifice plays no part in the Wise Lord's true worship. They say he even sacrificed nine *children* to the gods of the Underworld, at a place called the Nine Ways; he swears to me that he didn't, but I don't doubt that someone among his generals did it, and was never punished because his sin was sanctioned by the magi.'

Hutaosa shuddered suddenly, and for one brief moment the glassy surface of her serenity was shattered. She said, 'You know, my sweet Esther, my recurring nightmare is that some evil schemer of a politician will arise from within Kshayarsha's government and promise him greatness by some other tortuous route; and my poor gullible son will take it, provided that it is couched in pious terms and can be construed as the will of Ahura Mazda. Then who knows how many thousands of innocent people will suffer; and Kshayarsha himself will ultimately suffer more than any of them.'

Unexpectedly she reached out her hand and laid it firmly on my wrist. 'You must restore his faith in his own judgment and his own worth, my daughter. You must show him that there is no need for him to prove himself to me or to anyone, and certainly not to the Wise Lord, who sees what is written on our hearts in any case, and cannot be fooled. Esther . . . who is *your* god? Don't *you* want to be a Daughter of the Light?'

She meant, didn't I want to worship Ahura Mazda? But what could I say? It was so long since I'd prayed to any god at all. Prayers to some disembodied phantom were no substitute for taking action yourself, in my experience, if you wanted something badly enough. No, there was no response I could have given to Hutaosa which wouldn't have been a lie, and to lie to an eminently righteous woman who was kind to me would have constituted the grossest injustice and base ingratitude.

So I tried to change the subject, asking if there was anyone at court who might conceivably rise to the kind of position of influence with the

King which Hutaosa had described, and who was evil enough to exploit it.

'Several,' she replied grimly. 'Take Haman, for example, the son of Hammedatha. He's only a junior minister at present; he's assistant secretary for taxes. He's ruthlessly ambitious, though; I've had men watching him. But you haven't answered *my* question, have you? To which god, or goddess perhaps, do you ascribe *your* good fortune?'

Unable to see any way of escape, I confessed that I was confused about the whole matter; that my guardian had encouraged me to worship *his* god, but that this religion wasn't quite the same as the one I'd been born to, so now I was like a boat tossed on the sea, not knowing what harbour to make for. However, I didn't give away which god or religion I was talking about.

Hutaosa shook her head solemnly. 'It isn't good to be adrift without a god you can turn to in an hour of need.'

'I know.'

'Ahura Mazda is the one true god, Esther. You could turn to him. He welcomes disciples from any and every race of men—and women.'

Yet weak as my faith in the God of my fathers had become, I felt certain I should never be able to forsake him altogether for another. I was like a wife who no longer loves her husband, nor even speaks to him from one week to the next, but nevertheless would be horrified should someone suggest that she elope with another man. Even for the goodly Hutaosa I could never betray my parents' memory so flagrantly; nor even for Kshayarsha himself.

As my thoughts devolved upon the King and the extent of my desire to please him, my expression must have softened and some of the perplexity been smoothed away, for Hutaosa somehow read what was in my mind. She asked with genuine concern, 'Esther, do you believe you will grow to love Kshayarsha? Your task will be so much easier, and your future so much more congenial, if the affection you show towards him springs up from the well of your soul and doesn't have to be forced or faked.'

I answered honestly, 'I think I'm in love with him already. I have dreamed of him off and on for many years.'

Hutaosa nodded, unsmiling, but I was sure she was well pleased and deeply relieved by this reply. 'That is good,' she said. 'Very good. Because sometimes when I've been talking to Hegai, I have been a little anxious that you were rather in love with *him*.'

I was taken aback, not knowing whether she was baiting me. She apologized, saying she hadn't meant to be cruel; nor had Hegai meant to spoil things between us by breaking confidences and discussing our friendship with her. It was just that, for once in his short and pitiful existence, he'd been so happy he hadn't been able to help himself.

A wave of guilt washed over me, swiftly engulfed by a wave of confusion, and I couldn't look Hutaosa in the eye. The guilt ought to have been there because I, who was betrothed to her own son, had wantonly sought out the love of another under my fiancé's very roof. Yet in a curious way she was rather making me feel ashamed of casting Hegai back into the pit where I'd found him.

I muttered, 'Perhaps I *could* have loved Hegai, if our pasts had been different. But because of them we had no future. We both knew it. And Kshayarsha—'

'Kshayarsha is a man,' interjected Hutaosa, softly but very pointedly, and I felt meaner than ever. Yet I looked up to find her now smiling. 'There is nothing wrong or shameful in conceiving desire for a man,' she reassured me. 'When the Wise Lord made us, he placed an unlit candle in each of our hearts which he called longing, and he placed it there on purpose, not only within us—men and women both—but within every creature that moves upon the earth or flies in the sky or swims in the sea, so that they might long to be joined with others of their kind and fill the earth, skies and seas with life. Each candle waits only for a tiny spark of opportunity to set it alight, and then it burns bright as the sun.'

I didn't know if this was the teaching of Zarathustra which she was expounding, or some heretical doctrine of her own; but certainly it put me in mind of certain words of Moses which I'd read with Mordecai: that in spite of Eve's sin in enticing Adam to eat from the tree of the knowledge of good and evil, she would continue to experience desire for her husband. Yet the way Mordecai had read the passage, this desire had sounded to be a part of God's curse on his wayward creatures, and no doubt this was the way Mordecai had intended me to interpret it. Now for the first time, the notion occurred to me that Mordecai might have taken Adonai's meaning the wrong way. And if he was wrong in this, what else might he be misguided about?

'You seem uncommonly troubled all at once, my daughter.' Hutaosa's knowing voice cut off my chain of thoughts. 'Come, you must not be embarrassed to speak about such things. They are perfectly good and healthy; but it is not healthy to cover them up. Having lived among Greeks I should have thought you would know that.'

'I'm sorry?'

'Well, the Greeks say that Love is a boyish god, do they not, who pierces us with his arrows and makes little wounds in our flesh? Such wounds heal quickly if exposed to fresh air and light. But covered up, they tend to fester and become infected, until they poison us and we die.'

So I smiled too, and crimson with mortification began to try to tell her how I'd felt when Kshayarsha had kissed me: as though some secret door within my soul, whose existence I myself had scarcely suspected, had suddenly sprung open and released what had been contained behind it. And yet that release had remained incomplete, because Kshayarsha had been ill; and then he'd explained to me that in any case we must wait, because the King's bride is supposed to be a virgin on the night of her wedding.

Then Hutaosa clasped my hands in hers and said that I need explain no more, for she too had known love like that with Darayavaush; and would that more women could know it. So many were forced into wedlock with men they could never love; others failed to find our strength of feeling within themselves even when they did love their husbands after their own fashion. Yet how was a wife to fulfil her role of giving her husband pleasure, if he knew that she took none from him?

Thence the former Queen of Persia proceeded to talk to me for hours about love and its consummation, about being a woman in all its many aspects. These were all the things which I was sure my mother would have told me, had she been granted a few more years, and which Ninlil had run away from discussing. By the end of it, I felt I had understanding in place of superstition; and best of all, I knew that the feelings I'd had for Hegai and for Kshayarsha weren't merely not evil, but actually to be envied.

And then of course there was the matter of children, Hutaosa went on: for if I was ready for marriage I must be ready also to bear and raise children—preferably sons—for my lord the Great King. Could I see myself as the mother of a future emperor?

I hadn't seriously thought that far ahead, but as soon as she broached this question I realized that I might have to be able to say 'yes' to it in the very near future indeed. So instead of answering her, I asked: 'What will happen to Vashti's sons, if I bear the King others?

Will hers be passed over in favour of mine? Won't that cause her to hate me even more?'

'Naturally it will, if that is what happens. But even if you *are* blessed with sons—and I pray the Wise Lord that you will be, for all of our sakes, and for Persia's—we cannot be sure that Kshayarsha will choose any one of them to be his heir, much as you and I may wish it. It would bring me little pleasure to see any one of *that* viper's brood installed upon the throne of Kurash, but they are Kshayarsha's sons as well as Vashti's, and he loves them dearly, all three of them.'

'How old are they now?'

'Darayavaush is seven, Tithraushta six, and Artakshathra nearly four. But there is no hard and fast rule of succession in Persia, my daughter. It is enough that the heir should be a son of the reigning king, and preferably one born when his father was already crowned. Children belong legally to their fathers here, not to their mothers. Even if Kshayarsha were to divorce Vashti officially, her children would remain at the palace and continue to be brought up as his.'

'So he hasn't divorced her up till now. I am merely to be his secondary wife.'

'His *second* wife, my dear; not secondary. If you play your part skilfully and with devotion, he will never spare Vashti another thought. But there is little reason for him to divorce her. It would only encourage more gossip; and the King is entitled to maintain as many wives as he wants. Besides, Vashti is easier to watch here in the harem than if she were let loose upon the world.'

'What *is* she like? Hegai said that her wickedness had destroyed her beauty, and you yourself warned me to be on my guard against her. Yet I've neither heard nor seen anything to suggest she has the slightest interest in me. If it wasn't for what people say, I wouldn't even know that she exists any more.'

'Oh, she exists all right, more's the pity. And if she has supplied you with no evidence of her interest in you, it's because she is biding her time until she finds out more about you, and where your weaknesses lie. She is passionate, wilful, spiteful, vengeful and brutal. But so far as it lies within my power, I shall ensure that she does you no harm.'

I shuddered. 'I wish Kshayarsha *would* divorce her. I don't like to think of her living here, with quarters under the same roof as mine.'

'She will be a closer neighbour still, once you move to the Queen's Apartment in the harem.'

'You mean, I shall have to live in *her* chambers, when they still smell of her perfume, and sleep in her bed, still warm with the heat of her body?'

'Not quite, Esther dear. She hasn't lived there since her disgrace, and the rooms have been stripped and refurbished thoroughly in the meantime.'

I was hardly comforted; but Hutaosa only smiled and said I should be grateful that Kshayarsha didn't keep the veritable bevy of wives to which he was entitled. She herself had been one of Darayavaush's four, and her own sister had been one of the other three. I decided that such a situation might have been preferable; at least then the rest of them could all have hated one another, and expended their energies bitching among themselves just as the Sisters did in the House of the Virgins. To share a husband with one dangerous woman who had no one to hate but me was not a prospect I relished.

It was only a day or two after we'd had this conversation that Farah brought me a message written on a thin wooden tablet, which had been pushed underneath my door. It purported to wish me good luck and fertility, but was phrased in such a manner that you could have taken it in any one of several ways, almost all of which implied the very opposite of what the message said on the surface; and the innuendo contained in the part about my fertility was frankly obscene. The seal on the tablet was Vashti's.

When I showed it to Hutaosa, she was infuriated. It was wholly unlike her to be so perturbed by anything, but I was meant to be in total seclusion, therefore no message whatever should have got past the army of eunuchs who surrounded my apartment. One of them at least must therefore be in Vashti's pay, and she was happy for us to know it; no doubt she derived some perverse pleasure from showing us that she could infiltrate any company she chose.

Another of her objectives had presumably been to set me shivering with fright; and in this too she had succeeded. I was so shaken that I began to mistrust everyone. So much for Hegai's admiration of my fearlessness! A hundred times a day my eyes strayed to the rug by the door, upon which the dreadful tablet had been found, and I would cut a piece from every individual morsel in a soup or sauce and give it to the young woman Hutaosa had provided to taste my food, before I would risk eating what was left.

I suffered little guilt over this, because the woman herself—once an assistant cook in the palace kitchens—had been found guilty of

poisoning a dish intended for the King's table. She'd done it acciden-
tally, having confused fresh ingredients with bad, but nevertheless
earned herself a death-sentence. This had been commuted to food-
tasting because she had a husband and three small children, and
because she made sheeps' eyes at her judge; but in reality there was
little to choose between the two punishments, as both tended to
amount to the same thing sooner or later.

Perhaps I'd overreacted to Vashti's communication, but Hutaosa
herself had every one of the eunuch guards put to death. She wanted to
make an example, she said, and when I protested that all but one of
them might have been innocent, she claimed that the rest must have
known that they had a traitor in their midst and ought to have handed
him over. We could take no chances where Vashti was concerned, she
reminded me. Vashti was practically unique, so it seemed, in her
ability to cast the kind of stones which would agitate the calm,
mirror-smooth surface of Hutaosa's soul.

Still, we heard nothing more from Vashti once the old guards had
been disposed of and new ones found; Hutaosa had conveyed a
message every bit as eloquent as Vashti's by responding so swiftly
and so decisively to her challenge. My ninety days of confinement
started to pass more quickly; spring arrived, with warmth and
flowers, New Year was almost upon us, and every night I dreamed
of Kshayarsha.

Most of these dreams were delightfully romantic, but others were
distressing. In these I saw Kshayarsha making love to someone else: to
Vashti, or to one of his countless concubines, or even to Ashpamithra.
For there is one law for Persian men and quite another for their
women, and there was no reason for the King to practise chastity
while I was being guarded like a convict. I found myself tasting
nostalgia for the Jewish ideal as Mordecai had expressed it: that one
man and one woman should love each other alone, and for life.

However, it was far too late now to have second thoughts about the
course I'd chosen for myself. The final few days of my incarceration
rushed upon one another like breakers made upon the shore by the
wake of a boat; they brought with them my seventeenth birthday and
the heat of a new summer, and then the news that the first tents had
already been pitched on the Shushan plain as the pilgrims arrived from
Parsa. The King and his vast retinue were once more in residence at
the palace, having seen in the New Year with appropriate pomp and

ceremony. Life became a bewildering swirl of mild panic as last-minute adjustments were made to my bridal garments, thousands upon thousands of summer blossoms were cut and woven into garlands and bouquets, and Hutaosa drilled me for the hundredth time concerning where I was to stand or sit or prostrate myself, and when. But I told her not to be anxious; I wouldn't be clumsy, and I would see to it that my conduct brought credit to myself and to her.

So she hugged me and kissed me and wept for my beauty as I donned my magenta robes shot through with gold and sewn with a thousand jewels, and she lowered the veil over my painted face and perfumed shoulders. As we began our progress towards the great Service Court in which the nuptials were due to be celebrated, it would have been so easy for fretfulness to get the better of me; after all, I hadn't even ventured from my own room for three months. But it didn't. Rather, I felt like a butterfly emerging from a ninety-day chrysalis; I felt lovely, iridescent, alive.

It appeared that every inch of space in the entire palace complex had been fought over by the teeming crowds who scattered flowers in my path. Everyone bowed low when I passed by, so that a wave ran along on either side of me, heads dipping and rising like a field of ripe corn in the wind. Just as every inch of ground was occupied, so every inch of wall was decorated, with billowing blue and purple awnings, and streamers and pennants; woven chains of Shushan lilies were wrapped around the columns, and their capitals were crowned with chaplets of gold.

In the Service Court a great dais had been erected, upon which stood a table and two golden thrones, and over the top of which an enormous canopy was spread, with fluttering tassels at each of its four corners. When the signal was given that I had arrived, Kshayarsha advanced towards the dais, accompanied by his advisers, his eunuchs and his page-boys; I could barely catch a glimpse of him, so closely did his attendants press about him, even though the milling guests had all sunk to their knees and faces in the prostration.

But the King alone ascended the dais; the presence of the canopy precluded the need even for the boy with the parasol. Once he was seated on the throne I could see him clearly, and my heart swelled and soared at the sight of him. He was clothed from head to foot in robes of brightest scarlet, but the fabric had been sewn with rosettes of gold and purple which looked to me like the eyes on the tails of his peacocks. He wore his tall ceremonial crown with its mitra of purple, and his luxuriant curled beard; his long shining hair had been curled to match the beard's curls exactly.

I was led up to join him by Memucan. The honour should have belonged to my father, but since I had none that could be found, it had devolved onto the President of His Majesty's Commissioners. After making my prostration I took my place on the second throne, exhilarated by the grandeur of my circumstances and by the roars of acclamation from the crowd. As I sat gazing out upon the sea of faces through a haze of tears, Kshayarsha took my hand; and when in surprise I turned towards him, he drew the veil from my face and the crowd gasped audibly. It wasn't so much my beauty which had confounded them, as the liberties the King was already taking with the established ritual; he ought not to have laid a finger on me as yet, nor exposed my face. But I didn't care. I positively enjoyed it, recalling how I'd always longed to trample Mordecai's stifling legalism into the dust.

After that, the rest of the ceremony became as much of a blur to me as the faces of the multitude. I know they drank toasts to the King, and special sweet cakes were tasted, and a portable fire-altar was brought in at some point, upon which a flame was kindled by a magus who'd borne a burning torch all the way from Ahura Mazda's holy fire on the Sacred Citadel. Then Kshayarsha and I had to pass our joined hands over the blaze, so that the heat of the god's breath might touch us and bless our union, and the ring which he'd put on my finger. There was an immense ritual feast, of which I was too excited to eat anything except my half of the nuptial loaf, cut into two by Kshayarsha himself with his ceremonial sword.

The proceedings culminated in the entry of a second magus who carried Vashti's jewelled tiara on a silken cushion, and placed it upon my head. Kshayarsha kissed me on each cheek, and then lightly on the lips; only for a second, but it was enough to bring the night that was coming into the realms of reality in my mind, instead of misty fantasy. Another toast was announced, this time for King *and* Queen, and then it was time for the wedding guests to offer us their gifts.

Not until this moment had it occurred to me as a possibility that the events of the day might indeed prove too much for me. But as the procession of aristocrats and government officials began to form up and to file past our twin thrones, each man prostrating himself and depositing his gift at our feet for Kshayarsha's attendants to take charge of and set aside, I was suddenly and dreadfully put in mind of the thirteenth day of Adar, nine years before. No longer did I see, even hazily, the faces of these pompous but deferential Persian strangers—now my own subjects—but those of my parents, and of Rachael, and most of all of Pithon.

Every kind of present was brought to us, from Libyan chariots and Arabian incense to Carian weaponry, Scythian jewellery, Sogdian axes, Indian spices and gold dust, and lionskin cloaks from Drangiana. But I saw only my father's silver charm in the shape of a trowel, my mother's earrings and necklace, Rachael's ring and Pithon's wooden doll. The tears which had started in my eyes now streamed down my cheeks despite all my efforts to hold them back.

But no one came to comfort me, for tradition made no allowances for the procession to be interrupted. Kshayarsha himself wouldn't have let that worry him, but he didn't even notice my distress. Thus something at the back of my mind started to question for the first time whether he was truly in love with me, or merely pleased to have found an acceptably decorative replacement for Vashti, who looked enough like her for him to be able to delude himself into believing that nothing had ever gone wrong for him, that none of the calamities which had befallen him during his reign had really happened at all. So I just sat there nodding and smiling at my subjects, who I suppose presumed I was crying because women always cry at weddings, sometimes even at their own.

The presentation of gifts went on till well after dark, but at last the final tribute had been offered, and the time was ripe for the royal bride and groom to leave the stage and retire to the King's private chambers whilst their guests feasted on into the night. Kshayarsha took my hand again, and now he did see that I'd been weeping, for my kohl must have run, and the powder on my face gone into streaks. I think he would have said something, but I smiled at him triumphantly, having now made up my mind that the past was the past, and this was my chance to kill it off for good. I was no longer Hadassah, Child of Abraham, Daughter of Zion. I was Esther, Queen of Persia and wife of Kshayarsha, King of Kings, and for better or for worse I would walk forward to meet my future with my head held high.

13

That first night with Kshayarsha was all that I had dreamt of, and more. Perhaps he *had* kept himself temporarily from other lovers, of his own volition, for his hunger was easily a match for mine. Ashpamithra was dismissed, as were Farah and her companions; only the services of Bigthana and Teresh—the King's eunuch door-keepers— were retained, and they were under strict orders to admit no one, for whatever reason, on pain of death.

Then Kshayarsha and I cast all convention and modesty to the winds, far too eager for one another to have time for Hegai's elaborate ritual disrobing. We were like a pair of adolescents who have run away into the woods together and are confident that no one can have followed them; as love takes its course they no longer care whether anyone has followed them or not. We had no more time for tenderness than we did for ritual; the prelude to our marriage's consummation was wild and tempestuous. The fire of my passion fanned his own, and when the deed was done, he took me again, and once again. For the first time in my life I was glad I'd been born female after all. I had attained the release which my heart and body ached for, but now I wanted more, and Kshayarsha was only too willing to give it.

It was wellnigh dawn when at length fatigue overcame us. Kshayarsha slept like a child, naked as the day Hutaosa gave him birth, and I decided that nowhere in the world was there anything so beautiful as his muscled torso, slick with oil and sweat, or his rampant curling hair—all dishevelled now and limp as he was in sleep—or his flushed, close-shaven face with its fine Persian features. I did reflect briefly that discounting his appearance and his virility I hardly knew him, but I cared little about that, either. He was the most powerful man alive, as well as the most handsome, and that was all that mattered.

When he awoke it was fully light, but he made no move to get up or to summon his attendants. He lounged on the bed beside me, his head propped on one elbow and his hair half over his face, and regarded me languidly, perusing every detail of my body, which was as naked as his own.

'You are a Semite, and no mistaking it,' he remarked, and it was virtually the first thing he'd said to me since leading me away from the bridal feast. 'A Babylonian, or an Edomite, or a bedouin. Well, so much the better, Queen Esther, for your swarthy nomadic mother bequeathed to you breasts as sweet and round as melons, hips curved like desert dunes, a mouth as full and wide and perfect as ever woman possessed, and made only to be kissed. How sick I am of taut-lipped Persian ladies with their high brows and narrow noses, their thin, unyielding bodies, and their hair-styles all stiff and severe and exactly alike. You are everything I ought to despise, and yet you excite me as no other woman has ever done since . . .'

'Since what?' I coaxed him, enjoying this flattery and wishing to hear more of it; but he took me in his arms and possessed me yet again, in broad daylight, before troubling himself to answer my question. Then he began to confess to me the fascination he'd always had for things which he ought not to want, and he threw back his head and laughed when compelled to admit that financial rewards were indeed offered to Persians who took pure Persian wives and bred pedigree Aryan children. I asked him if he didn't fear the anger of his beloved Ahura Mazda, the Aryan god.

'The Wise Lord said only that I must marry the loveliest girl in my Empire, and in this I have obeyed him; just as I obeyed him in removing your veil at our wedding. Don't you know that the blessed prophet Zarathustra did the very same, insisting on seeing *his* bride's face before they were married? He understood the importance of truth, and of openness. These are what matter, not convention or tradition; nor even race. Ahura Mazda is the god of all the universe. By heaven, how I hate duplicity and intrigue, and the fetters of custom that constrain me.' Then he lay back and stretched like a waking infant without a worry in the world. 'Still, nothing can constrain us today, my tigress. Ashpamithra is banished from my presence until I summon him, and my counsellors will attend to any business which cannot wait. But there should be little of it; the whole Empire is on holiday for seven days in our honour. Let us give our people good cause to celebrate.'

So saying, he embraced me once more, and I realized he'd no intention of rising and dressing until after the siesta at least. We did pause for breakfast—bread and fruit had been laid on in advance—for he said that if he didn't eat when he was supposed to, the stomach pains would come. He'd been careful lately, so concerned had he been that our wedding night shouldn't be marred. Here he was, the only man in Asia wealthy enough to eat caviar and peacock and spiced game at every meal, and saffron till it came out of his ears, but the inadequacy of his own digestion kept him often to bread and vegetables. He'd invaded Greece, but the forces of darkness had invaded his own body and he was powerless to expel them.

After we'd eaten, he went back to sleep; but I couldn't. There was a strange sensation of unease in the pit of my stomach, as though it were trying to feel what he so often felt, yet my own discomfort wasn't physical. It was more like the bad taste that is left in your mouth after uttering a filthy curse than that which comes of tasting rancid food. Then as I lay there beside him, watching the regular rising and falling of his chest, in a flash I knew where that uneasy feeling in my stomach had come from. Kshayarsha's mentioning of the dark powers must have unleashed their fury upon me, because the work of prayer which Mordecai had performed for me was suddenly subverted, and I remembered the fortune-teller's words.

You will be Queen of Persia, and you will cause the deaths of many thousands of people.

Suddenly nauseous, I could lie down no longer. I snatched up the first garment which came to hand and ran through into the reception room and out into the King's private courtyard, where I sat upon the rim of a fishpond and waited to be sick. But nothing came, and after a while I went back inside and found Kshayarsha awake, searching for his robe so that he might come after me; I realized that I was wearing it. He asked me what was wrong, but I didn't want to talk; thrusting the evil to the back of my mind I just said, 'Love me, Kshayarsha, I'm lonely,' and it was clear from the ardour of his response that he too was happier to seek refuge in our mutual passion than to have to speak to me of things which might stir up pain.

Thus a morning of ardour and sleep merged into a siesta of the same; but after this Kshayarsha announced that we must dress, for in the evening we were to attend a second banquet, and there would be a similar one each evening throughout the holiday period. I wished we could bathe and dress one another, just this once, without sending for our respective attendants; but we needed them to bring warm water, and milk, and fresh towels, and I needed Farah and her girls to bring me my oils and perfumes and cosmetics.

And so they came scurrying, and Farah stammered and curtsied continually as though called upon to serve a visiting goddess, knowing that I'd now been sown with royal seed and wondering, I suppose, if it had already taken root inside my womb. Ashpamithra was sullen and sulky, saying to me only what he had to, which was that I must confine myself to one of the dressing rooms until my toilette and that of His Majesty had been completed. I thought how ridiculous this was, when we'd seen all that there was to see of each other, and more than seen most of it. But I kept my thoughts to myself.

The banquet was held in the Service Court, just as our wedding had been; indeed it was in reality a continuation of the same, since most of the guests had stayed overnight and would continue to stay there all week, sleeping where they sat, whenever they needed it. But no one was overtly drunk, since it would have constituted the height of bad manners for a Persian nobleman to be thus incapacitated in the presence of the Great King and his bride. Such a clamour of approbation broke out upon our appearance—its volume swelling and its pitch rising exuberantly when Ashpamithra produced the bloodied wedding sheet—that I quickly ceased to resent having to share my new bridegroom with his people. To be the focus of attention was a delight to me, something which as a cosseted child I'd considered my birthright, along with so much else.

In this idyllic manner the first week of our marriage passed all too swiftly. Kshayarsha was as contented as I was; there was no shadow of sickness about him, either in body or in mind, and he told me himself that he hadn't felt so well in years. Our nights and mornings were consumed by passion; our afternoons were slept away in each other's arms; and our evenings were taken up with eating and drinking and admiring the antics of the jugglers, beast-handlers, snake-charmers, fire-eaters, tumblers and dancers from every corner of our realm who had flocked to the court to entertain us. Watching the dancers brought back to me the steps and routines I'd learnt and practised as a child in Jerusalem.

One night before we retired to bed I danced in private for Kshayarsha, and he was enraptured, for dancing is another thing which respectable Persian ladies of noble birth never indulge in. He called me his dusky bedouin temptress, and although the nomads had always been bitter enemies of my own people, I didn't care, because the notion made him greedier for me than ever. I understood perfectly why this was: nomads, like poisonous animals, should be anathema to the Sons of Light, according to the magi.

While the week-long nuptial feast went on inside the palace complex, there were parties outside too, in the streets as well as in the houses. Food and drink were provided at the King's expense, and gifts were liberally distributed in his name; the entire Empire was granted remission from taxes for a pre-ordained period.

But all good things must come to an end, as they say. It would not do at all for the King to go on living in idle dissipation with one woman, albeit his Queen, when there were affairs of state to be dealt with, and a harem of concubines to be kept sweet, some of whom were the daughters of satellite kings, or satraps or government ministers who must not be offended. I had to be installed in the Queen's apartment, and our wedding guests had to return to their everyday lives; it was with grave reluctance that I bade them farewell, for in future I should never again share the stage with Kshayarsha at a banquet, or bask in his glory. As Vashti had done, I should have to entertain the women, while my husband feasted the men. Only in private would we be able to share a table.

There was a route by which the King could walk from his own apartment to visit any one of his women, without being seen by anyone apart from the harem; no one else could use it unless sent for and escorted by His Majesty's attendants. I was conducted by this way to the chambers of the Queen, and in opulence found them second only to Kshayarsha's. They covered an area many times larger than that to which I'd been confined during my ninety days of betrothal: there were enough rooms and to spare for each of my women to have one of her own. A sizeable detachment of hefty eunuchs with spears guarded my threshold.

But exactly as I'd feared, I couldn't help recalling that Vashti herself had once been the occupant, and though all the decorations and furnishings were new and smelt of varnish and scented polish and freshly-dressed fabric, I somehow associated this heady cocktail of aromas with the woman I'd supplanted.

Still, I had little time at first to brood. Once again, all my things had to be taken out of the boxes in which they'd been shifted from my old quarters, and found new homes. Hutaosa came to see me almost as soon as I'd arrived; I hadn't seen her for a week except in passing, amid the bustle of the banqueting.

Now that we had a little privacy, she could ask me how things had gone between me and her son, and I told her better than I could ever have imagined; but now that I was alone once more, it felt like banishment.

'He will come to you tonight, or else he will send for you, never fear,' she assured me. 'He won't be able to stay away, if what you say is true. Oh my daughter, how I wish I could do more to thank you! But there is one small thing which I *have* achieved on your behalf...'

She snapped her fingers, and one of her two handmaids went to the door. In came a vision of courtly sophistication clothed all in magenta; he knelt at my feet and pressed my hand against his brow, and I was undone.

Hutaosa began to explain that she'd had it arranged for him to be transferred to my service; I should also benefit from the assiduous attention of another eunuch, one Hathach, who had automatically been assigned to me because it had always been his privilege to serve the reigning queen. He was duly brought in too: plump, middle-aged and shaven-headed, curiously mouselike in manner and exceedingly ob-sequious, he was the archetypal palace gelding. However, he had an endearingly benign and honest countenance, and I knew at first sight that I should come to like him and value him highly. Would that he had lived long enough for me to think to tell him so.

But Hegai... the briefest glance at his perfect face threw my emotions into ferment and I was speechless. He looked up at me and smiled his loveliest smile, and said, 'My lady, I hadn't seen such happiness in His Majesty's eyes for five years as I saw in them on your wedding day. Now I see the same happiness in the colour of *your* cheeks, and in the blossoming of your beauty. So I'm happy too, my lady. I'm happy for you both.'

This only made things worse, however, because I'd seldom seen him look less happy since I'd known him. I was utterly convinced that futile, hopeless jealousy was eating him up inside; if he'd been Ashpamithra he wouldn't have tried to hide it. I bade him rise, and held him in my arms, but it tore me apart to do so, because I already ached for Kshayarsha.

Presently Hutaosa took her leave, promising to come each day after siesta whenever it was possible. But Hegai and Hathach would have rooms within my suite, just like my seven girls; and so would Roxana, the woman who tasted my food. She still had a husband, who was a slave like herself; he now looked after their three children on his own. On a whim I asked her if she loved him, and she said yes. So I said that once a week I would let her go to him, knowing what it was like to pine. It was unlike me to be so considerate, but I was in love with love, in all its manifestations.

With such a crowd of companions, I ought not to have been lonely; yet I was, dreadfully. I spent most of the day drifting listlessly from room to room, exploring my domestic realm with little interest although it was fit to house an immortal. Its proportions were so elegant, its fluted columns with their lotus-bud capitals exquisite, and bright sunlight dappled through lattices of milky alabaster onto its glazed tile walls. On these were embossed wonderful pictures, idealized scenes from palace life as I'd once imagined it, and as it might once have been before Persia subsumed Babylon and its ways, with smiling young couples holding hands as they walked or sat among lilies. Cypress-wood clothes chests, already bulging with gifts to me from the King, stood open to welcome me in my dressing room. Like Kshayarsha I had a bathroom, and silver toilet-vessels inlaid with gold were arranged on enamel-topped tables.

But all I could feel was Vashti's aura, and disappointment because I didn't have my own courtyard, nor even a balcony as I'd had in the House of the Virgins. The apartment was on the ground floor, but gave access only to the main harem courtyard, my entrance to which was guarded by another detachment of armed eunuchs. Although I was informed by Hathach that the concubines and kinswomen of the King were required to quit it as soon as I appeared unless I granted them permission to remain, it was still as though my specialness were already being eroded; although I was Queen, I was only one woman among many.

It was Hathach who showed me around and answered my questions that afternoon, and attempted to lift my spirits with quirky little anecdotes and jokes about harem life, of which he had long years of experience. He was like I imagined someone's favourite uncle ought to be: affable, affectionate and indulgent, yet perhaps a little absent-minded, and nervous because he is only too aware of his own failings.

It seemed that Hathach was fully adjusted to his emasculation, however, and almost enjoyed his role as Queen's errand-boy and lap-dog despite his advancing years. He'd served Vashti, he told me, and Hutaosa herself when the great Darayavaush had been alive. Hutaosa was a gracious and generous lady, and always had been; Vashti, he said—venturing to wink at me as though he'd known me from a child—was a vixen.

Meanwhile Hegai kept his own counsel, standing apart, then seating himself on a couch when I invited him to do so, his posture poised and relaxed but belied by the storm in his smoky eyes. I couldn't imagine that he'd asked to come to me; more likely it had been a well-meant idea of Hutaosa's. All along he'd so much wanted to put the happiness of the two people he loved before his own; and while their union had remained in the future, he'd succeeded. Now that it was reality, he'd found he could master himself no longer, but had never wanted me to know. Presently he asked to be excused, and rushed out into the harem courtyard.

I couldn't do otherwise than follow him. A lifetime in service to royal women had taught Hathach discretion, and he didn't interfere. Hegai was sitting beneath an orange-tree heavy with blossom, taking great deep breaths to calm himself, his eyes closed and fingers kneading his brow. But nothing seemed to be working, nor had he found the solitude he sought, for everywhere groups of palace girls stood, or sat, and whispered, and stared. They began to melt away when they saw that I'd come outside too, but as slowly as they felt they could get away with it, and their faces wore the same ugly masks of resentment as those of the Virgin Sisters.

And so, although I'd gone out to try to bring some comfort to Hegai, I found myself sinking into melancholy also, wondering just how many people must hate me now. By this stage the Jewish community must surely be aware that Queen Esther was none other than Mordecai's cousin and adopted daughter Hadassah; might they too make trouble for me? Did Mordecai himself intend somehow to drive a wedge between me and my royal husband? How much would it matter if Kshayarsha himself found out that I was Jewish? Just how far did his fascination with exotic foreign beauties go, and what would happen when it came into conflict with his mission to exterminate the practitioners of heathen religions?

I was startled from my gloomy reverie by one of my slavegirls tugging urgently at my elbow. Forgetting Hegai entirely, I ran inside to see what was amiss; and Farah was standing by the door holding a small wooden tablet exactly like the other one, with a message written in the same hand. It welcomed me to the harem, hoped that I found my new apartment to my liking, and trusted that I and my gelded lover would enjoy the privacy it afforded.

I gave a half-stifled little scream, and showed the tablet to Hathach, instructing him to send for Hutaosa. Then I wheeled round, sensing someone's presence close behind me, and saw that Hegai had read the message over my shoulder.

He said, 'My lady, I shall get my things and go, and you'll never need to see me again. It's all wrong that I should be here; I knew I shouldn't have come.'

But I seized him by his upper arms and snapped, 'No, Hegai... Tammuz. I forbid it. We must not let her intimidate us. Hutaosa will find the traitor amongst the guards, or else she will despatch them all, like last time.' I guess I came across to him as confident, authoritative; in reality I was desperate, because I could read his own despair and feared he might go off and put an end to his torment. In spite of the distance which had come between us, I knew I couldn't have lived with his blood on my head.

Hutaosa came at once and wanted to know precisely what had happened: when and where had the tablet been found, and where had I been at the time? I said I'd been in the courtyard with Hegai; but the sight of us together couldn't possibly have prompted the spiteful gibe which formed the conclusion to Vashti's note, because by then it must already have been written and sent. Someone must have known in advance that Hegai had been appointed to my staff; and someone must once again have corrupted one of my guards to enable the message to get through to me.

I was beside myself with dread and fury, and despite Hutaosa's exhorting me to calm myself, I could not. It was as though Vashti were some disembodied spirit, capable of pervading the entire harem, capable of hiding behind sheer curtains and perforated lattices, capable of passing through walls unobserved, watching and listening, and invading the bodies of whomever she chose as her instruments. Just like any evil spirit, she had left me alone until such time as I'd become a threat to her. Now her presence would plague me like that of an uninvited guest who has grossly outstayed her welcome.

So Hutaosa left Hegai to minister to me while she went off to conduct her enquiries; but Hegai was little less distressed than I was, and it was Hathach who brought me poppy wine to smooth out my tangled nerves.

It was almost time for evening meal when Hutaosa returned, her lips tight as only a Persian lady's can be, and her face whiter than any ointment could have made it. She had only one of her elderly women in tow; having made me sit down, she braced herself to explain what had happened. None of the guards had been corrupted, so I need not concern myself about that. Rather, her own attendant—the one now absent—had been given the tablet and threatened with a fate worse than death if she failed to deliver it. She had left it with one of my girls, telling her to place it on the rug near the door, and the girl had obeyed, being too dim-witted to do otherwise. There was no need to punish this latter; she must simply be told that from now on she must obey *no* one's orders except my own. As for Hutaosa's maid, she no longer had to fear a fate worse than death, because death itself was what she'd already earned.

I said quietly, 'But she'd served you faithfully for years.'

'Yes.' Hutaosa swallowed very hard. 'It was a painful decision for me to take. You know that according to our laws a person is not as a rule to be executed for a single offence, but his crimes must be balanced against his deeds of goodness. Treason, however, can be treated as a special case.'

'I—didn't mean that. I didn't mean you should have shown her mercy. I meant: how could she do a thing like this when she's been with you so long, and knows what kind of mistress you are, and what kind of a demon Vashti is?'

Hutaosa forced a smile. 'My daughter, let us devote our minds to pleasanter subjects, shall we? If I'm not mistaken, His Majesty's Chamberlain will be appearing directly, to announce his master's intention to dine with both of us here, and then to spend the night with you. We must decide what you shall wear to receive him, and we must order his favourite delicacies to be served.'

In this Hutaosa was most certainly not mistaken, and for once, the sight of Ashpamithra's waspish face warmed my heart because I knew the joyous nature of his errand before he spoke. My hatred and fear of Vashti and my unease over Hegai were swallowed up in desire for my lord; after the meal Hutaosa left us, our attendants made themselves scarce, and Kshayarsha and I repaired to my bedchamber.

It was the custom of the harem that the King could visit any one of his women in their own quarters or on occasions summon them to his own, and the same was true of his dealings with the Queen herself. At first, everything was just as it had been when we'd come together in his great canopied bed: our mutual passion was all-consuming, and all the fiercer for our having been apart a whole day. Yet the longer we lay together, the more I started to think of the bed beneath us as being Vashti's rather than my own, and the more her presence seemed to fill the whole place, and her eyes to pry upon our pleasure. After a while my distraction became evident to Kshayarsha; with more irritation than concern for my feelings, he asked me what was the matter.

But there was no way I could tell him the truth. So I said I thought I'd eaten something which was disagreeing with me, and at once was pricked by guilt because I'd told another lie. Cursing Vashti's interference, I threw myself into things with renewed vigour, and soon my anxieties were once more engulfed in the tide of Kshayarsha's concupiscence and swamped in the deluge of his rampant black hair. Then he slept in my arms until daybreak, when he left with Ashpamithra and the rest. I invited Hegai to breakfast with me, but he declined.

So the pattern became established which persisted through the second and third weeks of my marriage. In the mornings I continued with my beauty routines; after noon I slept, then dressed and had myself got ready to receive Hutaosa; she would stay for the evening meal, to which Kshayarsha would come also, along with Ashpamithra, his pages, his own food-taster, and a couple of bodyguards. After we'd eaten, Hutaosa would leave Kshayarsha and me to spend the remainder of the night together; then at sunrise he and his retinue would depart also.

I have to say that in all that self-indulgent fortnight I never tired of taking my pleasure with Kshayarsha. But I became increasingly unable to cast other things out of my mind, even in our most intimate moments. There was my anxiety over Hegai, with whom relations were still strained, to put it mildly. Then there was the disconcerting realization that I knew Kshayarsha the man, as opposed merely to the lover, little better than I had as a nine-year-old girl watching him enter Shushan flushed with the glory of his coronation.

Worse than these, however, was the waking nightmare that recurred to me almost daily, in which I saw with hideous clarity the face of the fortune-teller from Arderikka, and heard her ominous words.

And worst of all was the haunting of my chambers, and of my very mind, by Vashti. Eventually I could hide this truth from Kshayarsha no longer.

'We shall have your apartment refurbished once again, completely, and this time to your own personal specifications,' he declared without hesitation. 'Every item of furniture will be replaced, as well as the carpets and the hangings. You have only to say what fittings or ornaments you would like to embellish it, and I shall have them brought from the outermost reaches of my domains, or specially manufactured by the finest of my craftsmen right here in the palace. You are the apple of my eye, Queen Esther; I worship you. Everything I have at my disposal is yours. You have only to whisper your wishes to the wind and they will be granted.'

I doubted very much whether the extravagance of his promises could be justified; but I agreed meekly to his proposal, and went with all my entourage to stay with Hutaosa for several days until the redecoration was completed. While I was with her, my monthly flow occurred; she raised her eyebrows a fraction, apparently somewhat put out because I wasn't already expecting. I thought nothing of it, having been taught by my mother that children are a gift from God and that he gives them when he wills; I was upset only because my week of uncleanness kept me apart from the King.

As soon as I was back in my own rooms I knew that their refurbishment had been to no avail; it takes more than a change of clothes to exorcize an evil spirit from someone possessed. Nevertheless, I determined that Vashti should *not* maintain her stranglehold upon my life. Instead, I would devote my attention to another of my problems: one I could more easily do something constructive about. I resolved to *talk* to Kshayarsha the next time we were alone, so that he would no longer be a stranger to me in any sense.

So that was what I did. When Farah and Ashpamithra and their respective colleagues had retired for the night, and I lay in lazy intimacy with the Great King of Persia upon my brand new bed with its virgin sheets and pillows, I entreated him: 'Tell me what you do with your days, my lord. I miss you in them, and should like to be able to picture you going about your daily round.'

He raised his brows, in exactly the way his mother had done on learning that I wasn't carrying his son; just for that moment he was very obviously hers. 'Most of what I am required to do is extremely tedious, my sweet child. Why should you want to hear about it?' He twisted a coil of my hair between his fingers. 'I live for the nights at present, as I'm sure you do.'

I was vaguely annoyed by his patronizing arrogance. But I'd wanted to talk, not to argue, so I said, 'Surely matters of policy and administration don't take up *all* of your daylight hours, my lord?'

'Well, no,' he admitted, smiling, and he took the coil of hair which was twisted around his finger and passed it suggestively between his pursed lips. 'I seek to confine business to the mornings only. At noon I mostly go up to the Holy Citadel to offer worship at the Wise Lord's altar. After my siesta I may play polo with my courtiers, or hunt lions and tigers with them in the Paradise Gardens.'

Then he must have seen some glimmer of anxiety in my eyes, and interpreted it as concern for his safety, for he assured me that these hunts weren't remotely dangerous, being staged artificially, and scrupulously managed by the royal gamekeepers. But I hadn't been thinking about him at all, except in so far as he'd suddenly become the object of my jealousy. Rather, I was beset when I least expected it by a rush of self-pity, because Kshayarsha could ride and sport and joke with his friends in the sunshine whilst I, though in theory the Queen, was in truth a prisoner no less than I'd been at Mordecai's. There was no law to say that His Majesty's consort could not walk abroad if she so chose, but in practice there would have been a national scandal had I left the harem without being instructed to do so by my husband.

Still, I reminded myself a second time that it was conversation and not confrontation which I was craving. So I made polite enquiries as to the names of the noblemen to whom he was closest; and what were they like, and were they all young and dashingly handsome, and to whom were they married?

But he took my keen interest the wrong way entirely; and now I saw for myself that Hutaosa had been guilty of no misrepresentation in telling me that her son wasn't the self-possessed sovereign he pretended to be. For all his arrogance and his flagrant displays of unorthodoxy, he was profoundly insecure underneath; and was quite as capable as Hegai was of using the formalized conduct expected of him as a shield behind which to hide. He said, 'So now I must inform you of my every movement, and catalogue for you the pedigree and reputation of every person with whom I have dealings, lest you disapprove? Next you will be asking me what I ate for breakfast, and whether my bowels have been performing adequately.'

'No, my lord...!' I began, but broke off, acknowledging to myself how intrusive my questions must have sounded. 'It's just that... I do get lonely without you, and I do wonder who you are with, and whether you're missing me too.' He relaxed a little at that, and tried to kiss me, but I put my finger to his lips. 'You know, when we spent our first night together we *talked* before we went to bed,' I reminded him. 'In fact I never came into your bed at all because of your sickness, yet from the words we exchanged you made up your mind to take me as your wife. We must have said more to each other that night than we have on all our nights since, taken together.'

'And we said enough for me to learn all that I wanted to know about you, except where you were born; and *that* you will not tell me.' His lips sought mine once more, and this time I deigned to kiss them; he said something about deeds speaking louder than words, and there being more than one way for the tongue to express love.

But as he rolled me onto my back, I found myself staring up at the ceiling and reflecting that I'd forgotten all about it when planning the alterations to my rooms; it still had the same plaster mouldings as it had had when I'd fancied that I was lying on Vashti's bed, and from between its repeating rosettes and stylized palm leaves her leering face seemed to mock me even now, saying: *I don't haunt only you, you know. I haunt him too. It is my interference in politics which makes him afraid lest you harbour similar interests; so you may be sure he'll always keep you in the dark, where you can do no harm. It's my possessiveness which causes him to want to keep secrets from you about his private life too. And it's my beauty he sees when he looks at you.*

Thus all the desire in me was quenched utterly, and I did something I'd never done before. I lay like a corpse, unmoving, unresponsive, and let him have his way with me to his own exclusive satisfaction. Then I said, 'I can't live in these rooms any more, Kshayarsha. I want to move out of them. Permanently.'

'By all the gods of Babylon, what has got into you tonight?' He turned over and lay away from me; I could see how taut his spine was. 'First you subject me to interrogation; now nothing that I give you is good enough! Do you know how much this furniture would cost a man to buy? Or these carpets and tapestries? The richest Pharaoh of Egypt could never have bought them.'

'My lord ... you don't understand. It's not that I want anything more expensive. It's nothing like that—'

'No, I'm sure it isn't. It never is. No husband *ever* understands, does he? At least in this I am no different from the lowliest of my subjects. Clearly I share the obtuseness and lack of sensitivity which every male is born with.'

'My lord, please ... it's just that this apartment still doesn't feel like mine. It never can. Can't another place be found for me, somewhere in this vast sprawling labyrinth of a palace? Can't—'

'Esther, the reason why this apartment doesn't feel like *yours* is that it is *not*. It is the *Queen's* apartment, and as such it is assigned to whoever holds that position, which for the present happens to be you. So long as you are my wife, you will live here whether you like it or not. It has housed two queens before you, and will house many more after, if Ahura Mazda is gracious and my dynasty survives.' Then all at once he swung himself off the bed and stood looking down at me, splendid in his angry nakedness. He said, 'I shall retire to my own rooms, Queen Esther, and we shall spend what remains of this night apart, since I believe we have spoilt it beyond redemption. Let us hope that tomorrow finds us both in better mood.' And before I could protest, he had swept out, taking his bewildered, sleep-fuddled attendants with him.

I lay on my bed and cried my heart out. In a while I felt a hand on my shoulder, and caught my breath in excitement, supposing that he'd relented and returned. But it was Hegai.

'Go away,' I wailed, burying my head in the pillows. 'Go to sleep. It's late.'

'And how am I to sleep, my lady, when you are so unhappy? Please ... tell me what happened.'

I contemplated insisting that he obey me as Queen, but when I glanced up at him he looked so distressed that the command died in my throat. Manifestly he feared that my rift with the King might be serious, perhaps unmendable; only then did I ask myself how far, or how little, I would need to stray from the path ordained for me before being put out of the Queen's apartment whether I desired it or not. I must have turned white.

He murmured, 'I'm sorry, my lady,' and lowered his eyes.

'*You're* sorry? What for?'

'For frightening you. You're pale as a wraith.' Then still with his eyes averted he added, 'And for so much else as well.'

251

He would have spelt it out to me, but I told him there was no need. At last our eyes met, and it struck me that never before had I seen him without make-up, his face all scrubbed and ready for sleep. It rendered him very defenceless somehow. I told him I was sorry too; then laid on him the burden of my misery, namely that Kshayarsha had promised me the earth but wouldn't even let me have one room I could call my own.

'But he cannot,' Hegai reasoned gently, as though explaining to a child why she must not play with fire. 'You are Queen, and he is King, and there are many tiresome things which both of you must therefore endure. Surely I made all this clear to you when you were in my charge?'

'If those who rule are not free to do as they wish, then who is?' I demanded, my voice wavering and all the tears rushing back. '*You* don't understand, either, do you? You always take his part. Anyone would think he was *your* lover still.'

This was hardly fair, since Hegai had never previously been called upon to side with either of us. I apologized at once, and tried to kiss him, as though I thought like Kshayarsha that a touch of the lips could make everything all right. But he squirmed away from me, still too confused about his own feelings, I presumed, to appreciate mine. I couldn't guess how deeply I'd hurt him.

He did go back to bed then, without even bidding me goodnight, and in spite of our apologies the tension between us remained.

The following morning I conceived a fanatical desire to see Iphigenia. I think it was because she was the only person left alive who I felt had ever loved me selflessly and with unmixed motives. All at once I was woefully remorseful that we'd parted on less than friendly terms, and that I'd spared scarcely a thought for her since. It seemed that my past was littered with the debris of unmended arguments and broken relationships. But it was fully a year since I'd seen her; in all likelihood she would assume that I'd forgotten about her entirely now that I was Queen.

Nevertheless, I sent for Hathach and had him take a message to Arderikka, summoning Iphigenia to appear before me. He returned at noon, alone, saying that he'd delivered the message to my friend's mother, for my friend herself was indisposed and begged leave to come as soon as she was well again.

I was angry, and took it out on Hathach, lashing him with the whip of my tongue. But he was well used to the tantrums of my predecessor, and let it all wash over him. Vashti had probably whipped him with more than words.

I had to wait a fortnight for Iphigenia to come. I sent Hathach twice during this time, but on both occasions he brought back the same reply.

Meanwhile, Kshayarsha returned to my apartment the night following our quarrel. He made no reference to it, and therefore neither did I, and we went through the motions of making love. When he left at dawn he told me that I could no longer expect to see him every night, because I was not the only woman for whose happiness he was responsible.

I wept again, inconsolably. Of course I'd known all along that such a point must come, and that just as there were other cares and recreations to fill the King's days, so his nights would not always belong to me alone. Yet I couldn't help thinking that if I hadn't displeased him, he would have kept himself to me for longer. Thenceforth, just as I spent my days wondering whom he spoke and sported with, so I passed many a sleepless night imagining him lying with some thin-lipped, pencil-browed Persian concubine, or perhaps even with Vashti herself.

And as if all this were not enough, I detected a change in Hutaosa's attitude towards me also. She didn't visit quite so frequently, and when she did, there was a faint but unmistakeable frostiness about her manner which I'd never seen before. Her serenity now seemed more that of a distant mountain, aloof and veiled in mist, than that of a beckoning pool. I didn't say anything to her about how things were between myself and Kshayarsha, but I think he must have done; and I began to grasp that Hutaosa's love for me was grounded entirely in that which she bore toward her son, and was dependent upon my continuing to bring him happiness. She did tell me one afternoon that I needn't worry my pretty head about whose bed he'd warmed the previous night, because he'd been confined to his own, with stomach pains.

Eventually, when I'd begun to fear that Iphigenia would have to be dragged to me on her sick-bed, she sent word that she was strong enough to leave the house and would walk to the palace if someone would escort her.

I despatched Hathach at once, with a curtained litter for my friend as well as one for himself, and teams of burly slaves to bear them; in addition I sent Farah and all six of her companions, and an escort of mounted guardsmen accompanied them. It was no concern for the delicate health of my guest that prompted me to lay on this extravagant service, but rather I was keen for the Arderikkans to note that a deputation from the Queen was no less impressive to look upon than the one from the King which had long ago borne me away to the House of His Majesty's Virgins.

All the same, I was eaten up with apprehension as I waited for the cavalcade to return. I didn't know how Iphigenia would respond to me, and I was acutely conscious that once again she was coming to visit when my circumstances were not as I would have wished them to be.

So far as Iphigenia's attitude to me was concerned, I needn't have worried. She seemed less in awe of me now that I was Queen than she'd been when I was but the elect of the Virgins. I think it was because she herself had grown up so much since our previous meeting; far from looking ill, she seemed to have entered into the full bloom of her womanhood. She'd put on weight, her cheeks glowed with a colour which hadn't come from any bottle. But she ran to me like the callow girl she no longer was, and spun round with me in her arms until I was breathless.

'Oh, Hadassah—I mean, Esther—you don't know how much I've missed you, and how happy I was to hear from you after so long! I couldn't believe you would still have time for me now that... now you're... I can't even say it, it sounds so strange! Oh Esther, it's so good to see you, and to know we can still be friends.'

I said, 'You look so well, Iphigenia. Hathach made out that you were almost at death's door.'

'Oh no,' she laughed, still hugging me. 'Nothing could be further from the truth. I'm expecting a baby, Esther! Oh, it's too early for the midwife to confirm it, but I know, because I've had the sickness exactly the same as with Philos. I still get it, but only in the mornings now. For the first few weeks it was all day, every day.'

'The—same as with Philos? You mean...?'

'Yes, Esther, I *do* mean what you're thinking! Nikias and I have our first child already: a son. We named him Philos after my father. He's *so* beautiful! I would have brought him with me to see you today, only he's cutting a tooth and cries all the time... Esther, what's wrong?'

'Nothing. Nothing is wrong.' I forced a bright smile, then offered her something to eat and drink; it was late morning and almost time for the lunch I took alone each day before my siesta.

She accepted the invitation to join me in refreshments, and deliberately declined to pursue her questioning of me as we waited for them
to appear, so determined was she that things should stay light and
merry between us. She chatted gaily about little Philos, and Nikias,
and her parents. But she knew well enough that all was not right with
me. It wasn't just my quarrel with Kshayarsha any more. It was that
Iphigenia must have conceived her first child more or less on her
wedding night, and her second within three months of his birth. This
was remarkable, I was certain, even if for some reason she wasn't
feeding him herself. Surely it was her fecundity that was unusual,
rather than my tardiness? But I wondered.

Presently our lunch arrived, and conversation turned upon the
exotic delicacies I'd ordered to delight her palate. When we'd eaten, it
was the hour for my siesta; I made Iphigenia lie on the bed beside me,
so it would be like the old days.

But in those old days we'd talked about anything and everything:
our private hopes and our fears, our innermost feelings. So, gradually,
in whispers, the truth began to find its way out. And when I put it into
words, it all seemed worse than ever, instead of being eased by the
sharing. By the end of it all, I couldn't have cared less about keeping up
appearances. It was enough that I could keep myself from tears.

'Poor Esther,' Iphigenia murmured, and I thought she might start
to reproach herself again for letting me come to the palace in her place.
But she'd grown beyond that now; I'd come of my own free will, and
there was no sense in pretending otherwise. I mumbled something
largely incoherent and frankly trite about how strange it was that she
had found contentment in her poverty whilst I who had everything I'd
ever dreamed of was miserable as sin, but she said, 'No, Esther. It's not
quite as simple as that. There has been sadness for me too, and anxiety.
And it isn't over yet.'

I blinked at her, uncomprehending. She had living parents and a
husband who loved her, and a healthy son, and another baby on the
way; what could she possibly have to be sad about? But she started to
tell me about various cousins and neighbours of hers who'd been
injured in the recent violence, and a family of Greeks who'd moved
from Arderikka into the city itself and had their house set on fire by
rioting thugs. She was all set to give further examples, when I asked in
perplexity, 'What recent violence? What thugs? What are you talking
about?'

It was her turn to be nonplussed. 'You mean, you don't *know*? But surely ... how can you *not* know? *Everyone* knows.'

'Everyone knows what, Iphigenia?'

'About the riots, and the victimization of Eretrians who work in Shushan. There has been talk of little else for months, except for your wedding, which did at least take people's minds off the troubles for a week or two. But there have been more incidents just in the last few days ... Surely Kshayarsha—I mean, His Majesty—must have told you?'

I set my jaw. 'Kshayarsha tells me *nothing* about politics.'

'Then your eunuch, the one who came to see me—'

'Hathach.'

'Yes, Hathach. He's been to Arderikka for himself. He must have sensed the atmosphere and heard the talk. He must have seen the gangs of youths on the corners of the streets plotting revenge; as if there is anything a handful of boys can do against terrorism condoned by the authorities.' Suddenly she tossed her head and gave an incongruous smile. 'I'm sorry, Esther. I didn't come here to talk about all this; nor do I mean to sound as though I'm blaming your husband. I don't suppose it's his fault. He probably knows no more about what really goes on in the streets of his capital than you do.'

I said nothing; there was nothing I felt I could say, but my mind was reeling. How could it be that I lived my life at the very core of the Empire, the hub of its great spinning wheel, and yet it appeared that I was more ignorant than I'd been when I'd lived as a child in Jerusalem, one little speck on its outermost rim? My anger at Kshayarsha was renewed, because he'd kept things from me; yet was it possible that things were kept from him too? I resolved to send Hathach into the city every day to report to me what he saw and heard; though life outside the palace already seemed unreal to me, like events in a dream. In an attempt to make it all more immediate, I demanded that Iphigenia tell me exactly what had caused these riots, and this whole outbreak of ill-feeling against her people.

'Oh, there is nothing new about the ill-feeling,' she answered me. 'The Persians have hated the people of Eretria and Athens since the time of Darayavaush, when they helped the Greeks of Ionia to rebel against his despotism, and he deported my family and so many others here to Shushan. True, it's been worse since Kshayarsha's expedition to Greece. So many mothers lost their sons, and children their fathers, and wives their husbands. But now they see Arderikkans beginning to prosper and put down roots here, just as your own folk the exiled Jews have done; and they resent it, especially the poor. They are treating us as—what is that word your people use?—as scapegoats for their own poverty, because so many of their families lost their breadwinners in the war and have no one to support them. So they attack us when we walk in the city, and they make trouble for Shushanites who employ Arderikkans in their workshops or offices. At least they've kept away from Arderikka itself until now, so I haven't had to worry for my own safety, or Nikias', or our little boy's. But for how long? The numbers of those who hate us are growing.'

I said quietly, 'I shall speak to Kshayarsha. This has to be stopped before it gets worse.'

'And affects the Jews as well, you mean.'

'Not just that, Iphigenia. I'm not entirely without compassion.'

For a moment after that, neither of us spoke. Then Iphigenia said, 'I really *didn't* come here to talk about this, Esther. I didn't see any point, for one thing. Your husband isn't going to do anything about it. Why on earth *should* he? He hates us as much as anyone does, and who can blame him? Don't say anything to him, I beg you. It will only make things worse for you, and maybe for us as well. And maybe for the Jews.'

I murmured, 'What *about* the Jews, Iphigenia? Have they escaped persecution entirely?'

'Would it please you if I said that they had?'

'Not if I thought you were lying.'

'Then no, they haven't.' She looked straight at me, with the same intense expression as the one she'd worn months before when she'd tried to convey to me how distressed Mordecai had been at my loss. She said, 'The Jews are prosperous too, Esther; much more so than the ablest man from Arderikka will ever be. It's true that the Jews can't be blamed for the destruction of a Persian army and navy the way the Greeks can. But prosperity alone breeds envy, even hatred. There have been attacks on Jewish property too, in particular their business premises. Hatred can be as fickle as love; who can say who its next chief object will be?'

I was too ill at ease to remain seated at the table. I got up, pushing away a half-eaten plateful of prawns, and went to the courtyard entrance to breathe some fresh air, hugging myself for comfort though the temperature was soaring. Without looking over my shoulder, I asked in a hoarse whisper, 'And what of Mordecai my cousin? Is he still working at the palace? I've heard nothing from him. Not a word.'

'I think you will, soon.'

'What do you mean?'

'I mean that he knows Hathach, and from the way that they talked, I should say that he has made your eunuch's acquaintance just in these past few days, and not by accident.'

'What are you saying, Iphigenia? By the Wise Lord's blazing altars, how do you know this?'

'Because when we were passing the Royal Treasury in our litters, your cousin made straight for him, since his curtains were all wide open and anyone could see who was inside. I think Mordecai is handling Hathach's investments, and seeking to make a good friend of him while he's about it.'

All at once it was coolness I craved, not warmth; I leaned my head against a lotus-capped pillar and took great deep breaths to slow my heart rate. Iphigenia came and put her arms around me, but she could do nothing to help me. No one could.

14

As soon as Iphigenia had gone I summoned Hathach, intending to rebuke him in no uncertain terms for consorting with scheming bureaucrats behind my back; didn't he know that as my servant it was incumbent upon him to refer *everything* to me, even his own financial arrangements, and that all bankers were robbers by another name, in particular the one he'd chosen to deal with?

But he took the wind from my sails before I could open my mouth. His podgy face wreathed in smiles, he exclaimed, 'Your Majesty, the most wonderful thing has happened. The gentleman from the Treasury who has taken over my account has turned out to be an old friend of your father's! He says he knew you when you were a little girl, and was *most* insistent that I pass on his very best wishes to you. Isn't that a remarkable coincidence? What a small world we do live in.'

It seems that *I* do, at any rate, I thought angrily. 'The man's name?' I demanded aloud, wanting to sound superior but coming over even to myself as shrewish instead.

'Mordecai. Mordecai ben Jair,' replied Hathach; so it was no longer possible for me to remain in any doubt. 'It's a Jewish name, I'm told. He was once a partner in a private banking firm; it was founded by Babylonians but there were several Jewish partners.'

'And what else did he tell you?'

'Nothing else, Your Majesty. Merely that he was an old family friend of yours and wished to be remembered to you. Do you have any message for me to pass on to him, next time we meet?'

'No,' I said stiffly, then dismissed the eunuch forthwith; I needed time to think. At least Mordecai had claimed only to be my father's friend, and not his kinsman. But it would arouse suspicion all the same if I forbade Hathach to see him, since in Persia even common slaves are permitted to earn and save money and invest it how they will.

Every so often during the next few days, I enquired casually of Hathach whether he had encountered Mordecai again. He said no, but

259

that he would ask to see him if I desired it. I told him I didn't, and decided to try and forget the whole episode.

In the meantime things between Kshayarsha and myself improved a little, because I made no further attempt to engage him in conversation. On the nights that he came to me, I concentrated my efforts upon making myself as alluring and seductive as I could, and this achieved the desired effect of enticing him back to my bed somewhat more often. Hutaosa warmed to me again also, but continued to express concern over her son's poor health.

It was true that his stomach was troubling him more frequently than it had in our first few weeks together; either he was taking less care over his diet, or the regime his doctors had prescribed for him was no longer of any avail. I saw evidence of his mental malaise returning too; more than once he woke me in the night crying out in a dream.

Sometimes when I shook him awake he *did* want to talk, so I made the most of it, holding him close and stroking his hair as he mourned the thousands of brave young Persians he'd sent to their deaths in Greece, and grieved to think how their widows must hate him— women who had swooned for his father Darayavaush, and thrown flowers for him, and keened at his funeral as though they'd all been his wives or daughters. Then there was the bitter loss of his cousin General Marduniya at the Battle of Plataea; he'd been a rash and ambitious daredevil if ever there was one. But Kshayarsha was bereft without his advice and encouragement; he'd been a close friend and confidant as well as a kinsman, a brave warrior and inspiring commander.

My sympathy for my husband was genuine enough, because I was only too keenly aware of what it was like to lose loved ones, and also to know oneself the object of anonymous and largely unexpressed hatred.

But he never once asked after *my* health or happiness, assuming, I suppose, that my irrational desire to change apartments had been but a passing phase such as women and children alike are prone to fall prey to.

As the summer progressed and the temperature climbed higher and higher, Kshayarsha's doctors advised him to move the court to Ecbatana, his mountain capital, but he ignored them, saying that he couldn't face the upheaval. I tried to persuade him, but he upbraided me for fussing over him like a mother hen, and then suggested that perhaps this was my senseless desire to quit the Queen's chambers rearing its ugly head in a different guise. So I didn't mention the subject again; and acknowledged to myself that what he said might be right.

Then Hathach brought me another message from Mordecai. This one was in writing, though its contents were studiedly unspecific and it carried no signature—perhaps he feared that it might be intercepted. It addressed me as Queen Esther of Persia, wished me good health, and urged me not to forget a loyal and humble friend of my dear late father. Its tone struck me as ingratiating, almost pathetic, not like Mordecai at all; but the handwriting was his, I could tell, even though the script was Aramaic, not Hebrew. So he still hadn't betrayed me.

Once again I told Hathach there was no reply, and I wandered out into the courtyard to look at the flowers and hear the birds' sweet singing. The girls who were there cast me sidelong glances and drifted away; I'd never yet given any of them leave to remain.

The following day I'd gone again into the courtyard and was sitting beneath the orange-tree playing a mindless board-game against myself. I chanced to look up toward the northern side of the yard, where only a portico and railings with one locked gate cut it off from the south-west corner of the palace gardens. Standing behind the railings was Mordecai.

I cried out, and dropped the game; its counters rolled away into the cracks of the pavement. I ran back inside, and a moment later Hegai was at my elbow, ready to lead me to the nearest couch, where I could sit down before I fell down. He grasped my hands and prevailed upon me to say what was wrong, and I was too shaken up to tell him anything but the truth.

He said, 'It *can't* have been your old guardian, my lady, even if he does now work at the palace. Access to the gardens is severely restricted; anyone lurking anywhere near the harem is at once moved on.'

'It *was* him, I tell you!' Seeing Hathach approach, I dropped my voice to a whisper. 'Tammuz, you mustn't tell *anyone* of this, Hathach least of all. You're the only one who knows the truth about me. If you say *anything*—'

'You don't need to threaten me, my lady.' Even in my distress I detected the indignant hurt in his voice; it was hardly surprising he no longer felt able to use my pet name the way I deliberately used his, nor would he even call me Esther. 'Come, stop fretting. I shall send Hathach away, and go into the courtyard myself to check that no one is there.'

I sat with my head on my knees until he returned. Then he ventured to place his hand upon it—something he would once have done so easily, yet now scarcely dared. I looked up, but not directly at him; I hadn't looked him in the eyes more than once since my wedding day. Sounding baffled and half amused he said: 'That is *only* the Clerk in Chief of His Majesty's Treasury, a politer and more inoffensive man than you could ever hope to meet. He walks in the gardens nearly every day; I've seen him often. No one would think to challenge *him*. It would be like questioning the morals of the Wise Lord himself.'

'But it *was* Mordecai, Tammuz, I swear it! Perhaps he *is* Kshayarsha's chief banker now, how should I know? He must be removed at once, and stopped from coming back. A proper wall must be built, instead of those railings. I can't think why there isn't one. As if my husband wanted all and sundry feasting their eyes on his women!'

'My lady, there is no wall because it is thought healthy that the Great King's women should be able to look upon trees and bushes and grass, just like lowlier mortals. I remember the days when you longed to see such things for yourself. And it is as I said: undesirable characters can quickly be moved on.'

'Then move *him* on, Tammuz, at once. I command you! Go and tell him that if I see him there again I'll have him impaled.'

Hegai wrung his hands, suddenly looking disconcertingly like Hathach. 'You expect me, a slave in the law's eyes, to give orders to a free man, and one of the most senior executives of the imperial court? On what grounds am I to threaten him with impalement?'

'I expect you to do as I tell you!' I yelled; and my chest was heaving and my hair flying, and both so wildly that he nodded and hurried to do my bidding, with me screeching after him that I was Queen and could do as I liked, and order *anyone* to do *anything* I liked, and remove *whomever* I chose from *wherever* I chose, and have scores of them impaled on any grounds or none. When my lungs were exhausted I flung myself on the couch face down, beating the cushions with my clenched fists.

Hegai returned a second time and said, patently much distressed, 'The poor fellow wept as soon as he saw me, my lady. He said he was the happiest man alive because he could now get a message straight to you, and have no fear of its interception.' He handed me a tablet, sealed with the seal of the Saulides.

I croaked, 'He wrote this in front of you? Just this very minute?'

'No, my lady. He must have been carrying it with him every day, in the hope of seeing you.'

'Open it, Tammuz,' I said. 'Read it out to me. The world has gone blurred.'

So he broke the seal and read; and everything which Mordecai had hinted at before was made specific, and lots more besides. The greater part of the letter comprised a chain of apologies for the way he had treated me as a child—apologies addressed not only to me but to Adonai, because he had been such a poor witness to me of the love of his Creator. He had sorely underestimated how badly the loss of my parents and my brother and sister must have affected me, and so he'd censured my disturbed behaviour instead of seeking to alleviate my grief. None of these powerful home-truths might have been revealed to him, had it not been for Ninlil's dying plea that he should strive to put things right between us. As soon as she was gone, he'd repented in sackcloth and ashes, and given up everything he had to take a post at the palace and get this message to me. Now he craved my forgiveness and urged me not to forsake my God or my own people.

I didn't know whether to laugh or cry. So Ninlil was dead; that was undeniably a sorrowful thing. But the loss of her had manifestly robbed Mordecai of his wits, and his belated penitence disgusted me. Hegai ventured, 'Shall I take him a reply?'

'Yes!' I shrieked. 'Tell him to be gone before I strangle him with my own bare hands! And you be gone too! Get out of my sight. I can't abide your snivelling servility a moment longer.'

He obeyed me, but this was by no means the end of the matter. Over the next few weeks Mordecai tried anything and everything to elicit a more favourable response from me, but all of it increased my determination to have nothing to do with him. I instructed Hegai to receive nothing from him whatever, so he went back to importuning Hathach. When I gave the latter the same instruction—much to his bewilderment—Mordecai's messages found their way somehow into the hands of Farah, and even Roxana. This compounded my fear that Vashti too would still be able to breach the bulwark of security which Kshayarsha and his mother had built around me, should she choose to.

Then I awoke one morning to find blood on my sheets; and Hutaosa tutted and shook her head when she came to visit. But I was glad, because it meant I could confine myself to my bed, entertain no one, and do nothing, if I so desired. Consequently, for the whole week of my uncleanness I saw no one but Farah who brought me my meals, and that suited me down to the ground.

As soon as I was up and about, I received a note from Iphigenia seeking permission to visit me again. I granted it, and she arrived that same afternoon. She told me that Mordecai had been to her house in Arderikka, begging her to intercede with me on his behalf. I could only groan.

'Esther, he is desperate to see you, or even to receive at second hand an assurance that you've forgiven him. Just one *word* from you would be enough, if it were a word of pardon. Surely you could spare him one word?'

But I shook my head, unable to say one word even to her. It was beyond credibility that Mordecai could have humbled himself sufficiently to enter Arderikka, a cesspit of paganism, of his own volition, and then to beg help from the very girl he'd once tried to forbid me to associate with.

Iphigenia said, 'He really loves you, Esther... Hadassah. He's making himself ill over you, just as poor Ninlil did. He says I am his last hope of getting through to you.'

'Then let him *be* without hope,' I spluttered between ground teeth, and turned away.

After she'd gone home I went back to bed again, telling Farah I was sick. But when she informed me a little later that Ashpamithra had come to escort me to His Majesty's chambers, I staged a miraculous recovery and had her get me ready. Not since our first week of marriage had Kshayarsha received me in his own rooms; that had to be better, and besides, no one else would be able to reach me there.

Indeed it *was* better. So airless and hot did it become in his bedroom that towards dawn we wandered out into his private courtyard among the lily ponds, and made a marriage-bed with our garments upon the marble pavement. The waking birds serenaded us from their cages, falling blossoms lighted on our faces like silent snow, and it was so wonderful to be outdoors without there being resentful eyes all about me. With my own eyes closed, I could imagine that we lay in wild grass and poppies on a hillside above Jerusalem, each of us free and unburdened by care. All at once I was reminded of the beautiful Song of Songs which is found among the writings of my own people; and its words were running through my head, the words which the girl sings to her royal lover. *Your lips cover me with kisses; your love is sweeter than wine. There is a fragrance about you; the sound of your name evokes it ... Take me with you, and we'll run away ... We'll be happy together, drink deep, and lose ourselves in love.*

'What?' murmured Kshayarsha into my hair.

I was taken aback; had I spoken the verses aloud?

'You sing more charmingly than the nightingales in my gardens,' he declared. 'Where does that lovely melody come from, and those words?'

I was embarrassed now, and didn't know what to say; I didn't dare admit that the song came from my homeland, or he might take note of it and set his scholars to find out where that was. So I answered, 'Oh Kshayarsha, they come from my heart. I wish we *could* run away, just you and I, and leave behind all our servants, and all your fawning courtiers, and the rituals and traditions that stifle us and encroach upon our joy.'

He chuckled under his breath, and smoothed the hair back from my face. 'Your bedouin blood is as thick as ever it was, then,' he said. 'And yet I seem to recall that on our first night together—the night you say you took so much pleasure in, when all we shared was words—you gave me the distinct impression that you had come to the *palace* in search of freedom, freedom from the obscurity in which you'd lived before.' He chuckled again, more patronizingly. 'It seems I was right, my sweet Esther. Some women are never satisfied. Do you think you could exist now without your baths and your perfumes and your manicures, and with no one to prepare your food or fashion your clothes? I must say I cannot see you milking goats, or chipping your fingernails scrubbing down tables and mending my sandals.'

I was annoyed, but strove not to show it. I said, 'It's just that there are too many people here spying on us, criticizing, trying to manipulate—'

'Well, they don't seem to be having much success, my darling. I don't see many people watching us now, for if they were they would *certainly* be critical. Since when has a Persian king lain with his bride in the open air like a peasant?'

But the sun was rising, and although in theory no one *was* able to see us, I suddenly felt exposed and vulnerable, and tried to squirm free of his embrace. He asked me what was the matter, but not as though he expected any answer, and by sheer physical strength kept me where I was. Then in a simpering, mocking tone he began complaining that I didn't love him any more, he wasn't enough of a man for me, I no longer found him exciting. In the end I could take no more of it and blurted out, 'If *you* really loved *me* you would send Vashti away from this place, *right* away, into the desert somewhere for the jackals to devour her!' I should have liked to say the same about Mordecai too, but how could I?

Yet my fury served only to inflame his lust. He purred, 'Can this truly be my sweet little Esther talking? How gorgeous you are when you're angry, how positively irresistible!'

With tears pouring down my face I fought him like a cat, but all the sport and staged hunts he indulged in had made him strong as a wrestler when he wasn't sick. So the more I fought him the more aroused he got, and calling me his tigress, his wild nomadic sorceress, he forced me, and then lay back panting like one of his hunting hounds.

In physical pain and mental anguish I wept and wept, and despaired of ever finding freedom, of ever resuming control of my own fate; if indeed I'd genuinely had any before. Briefly I wished once again that I were a man, and could stride through the world doing as I pleased, forcing whom I pleased, and taking violent revenge on all those who had wronged me. But Kshayarsha, confound him, imagined I was weeping from ecstasy, and when he had breath enough to speak he said, 'You see? There is no need for me to banish Vashti from the palace, my darling, when you have the power to banish all thought of her from my mind. There is no need for you to give way to ignoble feelings of jealousy. Even if I were to take another wife, she would be no rival to you in the sphere of love.'

Something in the way he said that set off warning signals in my brain. I whispered, 'Another wife? You're thinking of taking another wife?'

He raised his head and gazed down into my eyes; his pupils were so dilated that the irises themselves seemed black. He said, 'We *are* in a nervous condition today, are we not? Of course I'm not intending to take another wife; not for the present, at any rate. One day, of course, you may leave me no choice.'

'No choice? What are you saying?'

'Well...' he shrugged his broad shoulders, and answered as though explaining an obvious joke to a simpleton. 'I have to have worthy heirs, you will appreciate, and there must be several suitable candidates so that I can appoint the best man possible to be my successor. Vashti's boys show promise, I admit, but will they all survive to manhood? And how much will she have poisoned them against their father by the time they are of age? As for you . . . well, people talk, you know.'

'Talk? What do you mean, talk? Talk about what?'

He seemed incredulous that I could be so obtuse. 'My dear Esther, how many seeds must I have sown by now in your fine fallow soil? Yet not one of them, it seems, has put down roots. Perhaps you have not watered them well enough, my darling. Or you have allowed the Gulf winds to blow them away.'

It was only after this that I began to worry seriously about my failure so far to conceive. At first it was only one more worry to add to all the others, but before long it consumed them, because I heard no more from Mordecai, his last hope having failed, nor from Vashti. When my third period arrived with exasperating punctuality, I blocked Hutaosa's path as she prepared to leave my apartment, and exclaimed, 'Three months *isn't* a long time, is it? Say it isn't! My own older sister wasn't born for almost two *years* after my parents were married.'

Hutaosa smiled, with studied indulgence, and sat down on a couch, holding out one hand to me. 'Esther, my daughter, if we are going to discuss this matter, shall we not do so in a civilized fashion? Come, sit beside me, and don't glare at me like that. It doesn't become you.'

I sniffed a little, and acquiesced. Still holding my hand, as though reassuring a child she herself had scolded, she said, 'Now all soils are different, and some strains of seed are more fruitful than others. I cannot comment on your parents' case, since you won't even tell me who they were, but it may be that for some reason they didn't *want* a child too soon. Isn't that possible?'

I sniffed again, recognizing that it was. When I stopped to think, there were many Pioneer couples who had kept themselves apart for months at a time in order to dedicate themselves more fully to the work of reconstruction, and others who had limited the size of their families by various means known to wise women among the pagan Earth Folk still living in the land.

'But as for Kshayarsha,' Hutaosa continued, 'when he was with Vashti, she was pregnant with one of their children or another for almost the whole of the time. She used wet-nurses of course; there was no need for her to suckle the babies herself.'

'Then there is something wrong with me? You're saying—I'm barren?'

'No, my dear, of course not. It is far too early to be sure. For every woman who conceives within her first month of marriage there is one who takes six, or even a year, and a few take longer still. But we must do all that we can to hasten the process.'

'Like what?' I asked, suddenly apprehensive; I imagined myself being bustled away to some Mother Goddess's temple or high place at dead of night and compelled to take part in lascivious fertility rites. But this was Zoroastrian Persia, where the only permissible ritual was the Wise Lord's fire-worship. Hutaosa said, 'We must pray, and we must ensure that you eat plenty of fresh fruit. And you must not exercise too vigorously, lest any seed which germinates in you should be uprooted.'

So I did as she advised me. I abandoned my routine exercises altogether, and ate oranges, apples and pomegranates until their juice was practically running in my veins. I gave myself to Kshayarsha with a new urgency. But none of it did any good. Summer mellowed into autumn, and my periods came as regularly as ever. Kshayarsha took to asking me every other week whether I felt any spark of his life quickening within me, or whether I ever felt sick in the mornings. I could only shake my head miserably; so miserably in fact that I actually made him sorry for me more than once.

'I don't mean to upset you, my dearest,' he assured me, cradling my head against his chest. 'It's just that there is nothing that would bring me greater contentment than to father your son. He would be so beautiful, and so proud, were he to partake of all your best qualities and all of mine. He would bear perpetual witness to our love, and carry it forward into the future, when we are gone.'

Hegai had told me long ago that the King was obsessed with his own mortality, but never before had I had it from Kshayarsha's own mouth. Now, when I'd abandoned all hope of engaging him in any meaningful conversation, he chose to bare his soul. He said that the name of his illustrious father Darayavaush would be found on the lips of all generations to come, for he'd been a man of exceptional wisdom and strength of character, and a monarch without parallel. Kshayar-sha's own fame, however, would fade like unfixed dye, like that of the forgotten princes of ancient Elam who had reigned in Shushan in days gone by. In common with theirs, his name would mean no more to the men of the future than would the names of the thousands upon thousands who had marched with him to Greece in a vain quest for glory, and for whom he had wept as he watched them parade their colours before him, reflecting that within a hundred years every last one of them would be dead. As things had turned out, all too many had been dead within three.

I shuddered. 'I don't want to think about death, Kshayarsha. How can we kindle a spark of life in my womb when our minds are full of morbid things?'

'You speak like a fool, Queen Esther,' he said, solemn as a magus. 'Only those who are prepared for death can be fully alive. Don't you know that the prophet Zarathustra was told by the Wise Lord himself that death is merely a bridge, to a life infinitely richer than this one, a life that lasts for *ever*? But eternal life is only for those who meet the standards that Ahura Mazda requires of them: those who venerate his altars of fire, speak the truth, promote order rather than chaos, and keep themselves pure of pollution and idolatry.' He closed his eyes momentarily, and pressed his fingers against the lids as though his head ached. 'But I've made so many mistakes, Esther, and taken so many wrong turnings. If only a man could know before he died that in the judgment he would be accounted worthy. If only he could know he had passed the tests which God had set him.'

After this he sank into a meditative silence, and I found myself wishing that someone could promote order rather than chaos inside my own skull. Mordecai too had often spoken about the final judgment of Adonai, and the prospect of eternal life. Yet for him there had been no question of his being found unworthy. He had the assurance that his God would lovingly forgive the sins of *all* his people if their repentance was sincere and they offered the sacrifices required for their atonement. For Mordecai it was the nature of the afterlife which was much less certain. There were prophets among the Jews who had spoken of it, but not frequently, and not plainly. Mordecai had always said that there was much which Adonai hadn't yet revealed to us in full, because we were not ready to receive it.

So I was wretchedly confused; and when Kshayarsha suddenly asked me what *I* believed, I simply stared at him, because I was so unaccustomed to his seeking my view on anything at all.

'Come now,' he encouraged me, wearing a beatific smile which was no doubt intended to put me at my ease, but had the reverse effect. 'No man, woman or child has ever lived who didn't worship *something*, however bizarre. Even the philosophers of the Greeks who say that the moon is a stone and the soul nothing but a puff of wind have to admit that someone measured out the heavens, and divided the seas from the land, and fixed the seasons and the paths of the planets.'

I demanded, 'And what of your magi, then, Kshayarsha? What do *they* say about such matters?'

He didn't respond; but disarming him did nothing to make things clearer in my own mind, and I wondered if it could be true that I was the only person in the world who professed no religion. Perhaps this was why no god or goddess would grant me a child.

The following day I summoned Hegai to my bedside during siesta and instructed him to tell me of the gods of Babylon, and what he himself believed about them.

But although he'd once lain with his head in my lap and told me with limpid eyes the hauntingly beautiful story of Ishtar and Tammuz and of the new life she'd given him, it seemed that now he was no less confused than I was. He said, 'My parents brought me up to honour Baal-Marduk, and Shamash the sun-god, and Ishtar the goddess of love and war. But I don't know any more. Our gods couldn't save Babylon from destruction. Baal-Marduk couldn't save his own graven image from the metal-worker's forge. None of them saved me from the gelder's knife. And they didn't . . .'

'They didn't what, Tammuz?'

But my use of that name in such a context made him squirm; I suppose he wanted to say that they hadn't honoured his love for me. I'd been his friend; I'd restored him to life just as Ishtar had restored her own Tammuz, but then I'd kicked him back into hell. He cleared his throat and said instead, 'When I was with Kshayar-sha he taught me that the only true god was Shamash, whose glory is the sun, and that his real name wasn't Shamash at all, but Ahura Mazda. I didn't understand; I'd thought that the Persians had other gods and goddesses too. But he said that that was long ago, when his ancestors were ignorant.' Hegai shrugged, then looked at me suddenly; I wasn't quick enough to avoid meeting his gaze. He went on, 'If I were ever truly to worship a god again, my lady, it would have to be one whose power I could see for myself, and whose hand I could see in the history of all peoples.' And I thought: Mordecai would tell you that there *is* such a god, but I don't know, any more than you do.

I sent him away, vowing never to call him Tammuz again, and lay on my back staring up at Vashti's ceiling, struggling to remember the words of the Shema, the prayer so holy and so central to the faith of any Jew that I ought to have been able to chant it in my sleep. I abandoned the attempt, and strove to recall the Ten Commandments instead, but knowing I had broken the very first of them I couldn't get any further. I tried to picture the Holy City, Jerusalem, as I'd sought to fix it in my memory on the day that I'd left it, but failed. Here I was, a Daughter of Zion and a descendant of King Saul; and I was living in a foreign land, married to a Gentile king, and a queen myself only by virtue of this heathen despot's ring on my finger. And unless I bore him a son, I was unlikely to remain a queen for much longer.

In the weeks that ensued, Hutaosa cautioned me not to be anxious, for bad humours would infect my womb and make it unreceptive. But I couldn't stop myself. I grew irritable and fractious, and took out my frustrations on those around me, Hegai especially, because he was the easiest to hurt. Also, the very sight of him brought home to me my own inadequacy: it seemed that I was no more fully a woman than he was a man, though both of us were cruelly blessed with more than our fair share of sensual beauty.

Then just when I'd begun to forget about her, Vashti sent me a chilling reminder of her continued existence and malevolence. It was a gift, delivered late one afternoon by none other than Ashpamithra. It took the form of a magnificent robe, cut to follow the lines of one's figure exactly, and every seam was piped with gold. There was nothing even to say who it was from, so naturally enough I assumed its donor to be the King. Unsurprisingly, my guards had drawn the same conclusion, and this was the ruse by which she who was truly responsible had got it into my hands.

Ashpamithra said frigidly, 'With the compliments of Lady Vashti, Your Majesty. She says that it was made for her by her own personal seamstress whan she was Queen, but that she is no longer slim enough to wear it on account of all the children she has borne. She says that you should experience no such difficulty.' I could have sworn he was sneering as he bowed his way out.

I shrieked a curse, and tore the sheer fabric to shreds with my own fingernails, imagining that he'd left. But as I stood there wailing with the tattered remnants of the garment fluttering to the floor all around me like rose petals falling into a pool, Ashpamithra walked back in, cool as sherbet, and said, 'Oh, and Your Majesty, I almost forgot. The King invites your peerless self and his venerable lady mother to dine with him this evening in the formal dining room. There will be another guest in addition to the two of you: a gentleman marked out for singular honour, so I understand.' He bowed again, and was gone.

It wasn't the first time that I'd received such an invitation, though the occurrence was rare. The formal dining room was where Kshayarsha generally dined if he wasn't with me but chose not to eat alone. A select group of his courtiers might eat with him, or rather, near him; the custom was that the King should sit on one side of a curtain and his guests on the other, waited upon by different kitchen-slaves; Kshayarsha's wore muzzles lest their common breath pollute the royal platter.

If one of the guests was deemed worthy of special honour, however, he might be invited round to the King's side of the veil, and here on occasions Hutaosa and I might sit also, as women had sat with men in Persia's past. This was most likely to happen if Kshayarsha wished to solicit his mother's opinion on the personal qualities of some new minister or candidate for political promotion; knowing that she was a better judge of character than he was, he was often prepared to defer to her assessment. He seldom if ever consulted me; I was there to be admired, like the golden plates and goblets, and the cutlery with its carved ivory handles.

But how could I go with my eyes all red and puffy, and my fingers trembling like a crone's? I sank to my knees and crouched curled up with my head between them, while Farah cleared away the mess. Eventually Hegai coaxed me to my feet and gave me poppy wine, and I resolved that I *would* go to dinner with the King. Otherwise, Vashti would be sure to find out from Ashpamithra that her dreadful gift had brought me to tears, and the last thing I wanted was to afford her that satisfaction. Next time I was alone with Kshayarsha, I would enjoy informing him that she had corrupted his own Chamberlain.

The guest to whom Ashpamithra had referred was a lean, svelte, dapper man, perhaps forty years old. Although he wore the simple white robe into which a nobleman was required to change when dining for the first time in the presence of the King, he wore it as proudly as if it were dyed with sea-purple or saffron. His deep-set eyes were almost black, and disconcertingly wily in an unusually handsome face; his nose was aquiline and he sported a short black beard, fastidiously trimmed. Judging from his profile, and from the swarthiness of his complexion against the white robe, he was thoroughly Semitic, though the expensive rings and torques he wore represented the height of Persian fashion and of refined taste spiced up with a dash of flamboyance. So far as I was aware, I'd never seen him before, but when he was introduced I had a vague recollection of his name: Haman, son of Hammedatha.

Throughout the meal I was wholly unable to relax, and it wasn't merely because of the shock I'd experienced before it. Even when looking down at my plate I was conscious of this man Haman's guileful eyes trained upon me, and whenever I glanced up at him he made no attempt to look away. There was something distinctly intrusive, distinctly insolent, about his expression, almost as though he were mentally undressing me as I ate. Yet now and again I caught him gazing at Kshayarsha in just the same way; and there was no denying that for his age he was exceptionally good-looking, and in conversation witty, charming and impeccably courteous.

Discussion revolved around a new phase of construction which Kshayarsha was minded to implement at Parsa, his religious capital. This constituted his latest endeavour to attain some kind of immortality: if he couldn't be praised by posterity for his mighty conquests, he would be renowned for his outstanding contributions to the splendour of the Wise Lord's precincts. Thus he was most anxious to appoint the best possible architect to undertake the design of the new buildings, and of the extensions to those already existing. Of course, scores of brilliant architects were already in the royal employ, but he'd heard tell of a certain Babylonian who was also a mathematician and a philosopher, as well as being a fervent devotee of Ahura Mazda; did Haman by any chance know his name, and where he could be found, and any examples of his work?

It transpired that Haman didn't merely know these things; he knew the man himself, and could have him brought to the Apadana whenever the King wished it. In fact it seemed that Haman knew everyone worth knowing, and had contacts the length and breadth of the Empire, in any field you cared to mention. In addition, he came across as being uncommonly cultured and well-read, familiar with the ideas and beliefs of a wide range of ethnic groups living within the King's domains, though he was surprisingly superstitious himself, pointing out that care should be taken to ensure that the building work at Parsa was not begun on an inauspicious day.

His own claim to fame was that he had rendered exceptional service in the Imperial tax office, having collected the taxes of some notoriously difficult province more quickly than anyone had ever done before. This he had achieved by the application of his own somewhat unorthodox and elegantly ruthless methods. Even at the dinner table he chatted breezily about some tax-dodging tentmaker he'd once had hanged with one of the scoundrel's own guy-ropes as an example to any of his colleagues who might be similarly tempted to deprive the King of his rightful income.

I was distressed to observe Kshayarsha smiling and looking keenly impressed, as though Haman had told some subtle joke; Hutaosa by contrast shuddered, visibly and deliberately. Haman inclined his head and apologized most civilly, rebuking himself for failing to take account of the fact that there were ladies present. Kshayarsha smiled again, but Hutaosa remained impassive; Haman glanced sidelong at me, but I pretended not to notice.

When we'd finished eating and the wine was about to be served, the two men asked us to excuse them since they had further business to discuss; we yielded graciously to their request, and Hutaosa invited me back to her own apartment, where we might take wine together. Dismissing our respective attendants out of earshot, she began to criticize Haman quite frankly, and with considerable venom; I was stunned, for I'd rarely heard her speak so spitefully even about Vashti, and as a result I clean forgot to tell her about the horrendous experience I'd had that afternoon.

I did remember, though, that it was from Hutaosa that I'd heard Haman's name before. She'd singled him out as one of the few government officials she knew who might have the will and the ability to lead Kshayarsha seriously astray. In those days he'd had much ambition but little real influence, being a very junior minister. Now things were changing; already his name had been entered on the list of the King's Benefactors.

However, for all Hutaosa's vitriol, and for all her warnings about how dangerous Haman might prove to be politically, it was the unctuous way in which he'd looked at me and also at Kshayarsha that remained with me when I returned to my rooms. That was the way my mind always worked; from time to time I would be shaken into taking an interest in the world outside of my own narrow social circle, but I could never maintain that interest for long. What mattered to me was how I myself stood in the estimation of those around me, and whether I perceived any new threat to my own special place in the heart of the King.

On this latter score I grew more and more concerned over subsequent weeks, because Haman was bidden to Kshayarsha's table with increasing regularity. I watched him worm his way deeper and deeper into my husband's affections; it seemed that at last Kshayarsha had found a male confidant to take the place of his dearly-departed cousin Marduniya. Haman knew exactly how to treat the King, how to get around him by using a carefully measured mixture of encouragement, provocation and flattery in a way I secretly envied, and wished I myself could master. Kshayarsha for his part lavished countless extravagant gifts upon his new friend, and one evening over dessert actually kissed him more than briefly on the lips as he hung a heavy gold chain about Haman's neck. Scarlet fury rose up before my eyes, and in a half-strangulated growl I asked Kshayarsha's permission to see him alone in his apartment after the meal.

He granted my request, though it was a trifle irregular, and when we were alone I gave my wrath free rein; I hadn't lost control so completely since leaving Mordecai's. I didn't stop for a second to consider how foolishly I was behaving, and how much peril I might be placing myself in.

'Isn't it bad enough that I have to live with the thought of your visiting other women's chambers, and warming their beds, and opening their thighs? Isn't it bad enough that I have to watch you kissing Ashpamithra like that? Isn't it bad enough that I should have to live beneath the same roof as your first wife whom you will not even divorce, and her brats whom you will not disinherit? But no, all that means so little to you, it is all so natural, so *conventional* in your eyes that you must now take a *man* as your lover—a man who was born in the gutter and has dragged himself up through the ranks by grovelling to all the right people and probably by sleeping with half of them! A man whom your own mother despises!'

Kshayarsha leapt up and slapped me so hard across the face that I staggered and fell. At once he apologized, helped me to my feet, and clasped me close so that my anger dropped away and I broke down. He tried to comfort me, but what he said hurt so badly it would have been easier to take if he'd yelled it at me in temper. He said, 'I'm sorry, Esther. I'm sorry. I've loved you as much as I've ever loved anyone.

But lately . . . I haven't been sure that you truly love *me*, if indeed you ever did. You're cold with me, you don't respond to me the way you did at first. Sometimes you sulk, and there is a hardness behind your eyes when you look at me, just as there was behind *hers*. Nor have you yet brought forth for me the fruit which should rightly be produced when a man and a woman come together. So how can I fairly be blamed for looking elsewhere?'

What could I say? I don't know what I *did* say, except that his comparing me with Vashti suddenly reminded me of her gift, and I told him that Ashpamithra had fallen beneath her spell. I was assured that the errant Chamberlain would be punished, then I was requested to return to my own quarters.

For more than a week after that, I saw nothing of the King at all. I sent Hathach to fetch Iphigenia to see me, and poured out my burgeoning troubles to her; she patted my hand, and laid it on her swollen belly so I could feel the baby kicking, and said at least it was something that I'd made up my quarrel with Mordecai.

'What?' I stammered, and could barely manage that.

'I saw him today in the Court, and he was so much more cheerful. He said he'd found another eunuch prepared to bring you messages and ferry back your replies.'

I croaked, when able to summon sufficient voice: 'But I've sent no replies. He must be going mad. He must be imagining that the thing he's so desperate for has really happened. He's going senile, Iphigenia.'

Then out of the blue Kshayarsha summoned me to his chambers very late the following evening. His face wreathed in smiles, he exclaimed, 'Esther, my sweet, sweet Esther, how can I ever thank you? Alas, I have treated you harshly, but you have repaid me with abounding love! An acquaintance of yours has saved me from a plot on my life, and it's all because of you. Be assured I shall reward you richly; in fact, I have taken the first steps already. Come, Ashpamithra.'

While I stood speechless and confounded, the young Chamberlain stepped forward. His petulant face was white, and he looked faint. The King raised the eunuch's right hand, and I saw that his index finger had been severed at the root; it was bandaged neatly, but the dressing was wet and red. I heaved; Kshayarsha said, 'This is what comes to any of my boys who pollute their hands by bearing burdens not placed in them by their King. If his offence is repeated, the next cut will be made at his wrist. And also...'—Kshayarsha folded his arms and squared his shoulders—'Also, I am profoundly displeased that he failed to notice what your esteemed friend observed and brought to my attention in the nick of time, through your own loyal agency.'

Of course, I couldn't ask him what he meant; I dared not risk jeopardizing my apparent and mystifying restoration to his affections. So I had to pretend that I knew what he was talking about while he informed the trembling Ashpamithra that the two eunuchs who guarded the royal apartment, Bigthana and Teresh, had conspired together against the life of their lord, His Imperial Majesty Kshayarsha son of Darayavaush, King of Kings and ruler of half the world. One Mordecai ben Jair, Chief Clerk at the Treasury, had overheard them muttering together in the palace gardens when off duty and had conveyed this information to me, the Queen, with whose father he had once been acquainted, and I in turn, through the medium of servants, had alerted the King.

Kshayarsha then smiled at Ashpamithra, and without a hint of sarcasm exhorted him not to be afraid; on this occasion, because of his excellent record of service until now, he would be granted the benefit of the doubt. Neither his acting on Vashti's behalf nor his failure to uncover the conspiracy would be interpreted as treason, but rather as a lack of intelligence. This was just as well for him, since treason automatically carried the death-penalty; which Bigthana and Teresh had already paid.

Ashpamithra keeled over like a felled tree and had to be carried out; meanwhile Kshayarsha announced his intention to invite Mordecai to dinner that evening, along with myself and Haman.

'Oh no, my lord,' I protested. 'I—don't think that would be a good idea. You see ... he belongs to an obscure religious sect which enforces strict rules about what can and cannot be eaten. You would place him in an extremely embarrassing position, my lord.'

Kshayarsha raised his eyebrows. 'Very well, my dear, if that is your considered opinion. But I shall certainly inscribe his name on my List of Benefactors, and award him jewels and gold. Perhaps I shall even grant him a city from whose taxes he may supplement his meagre income from the Treasury.'

I managed to gasp that Mordecai would no doubt be superlatively grateful, before Kshayarsha took me in his arms and led me to his bed.

Next morning I hastened to Hutaosa's apartment and gave her the whole story, swearing that I barely knew this Mordecai and had had no contact with him whatever since coming to the palace. So who could possibly have acted on my behalf and passed his information to the King?

'The answer is simple,' Hutaosa said. 'It can only have been Vashti. Only she has the will and the acumen to interfere in your affairs in such a way.'

'Vashti? But why would she do something that resulted in my being reconciled to Kshayarsha? Surely that's the very opposite of what she wants.'

'Who can say,' responded Hutaosa drily. 'But she will have *some* ulterior motive, of that you can be certain. We must renew our vigilance, my daughter. Vashti is a clever woman. A very clever woman.'

I said wretchedly, 'Suppose Bigthana and Teresh had been successful? One of Vashti's sons would be sitting on his throne already. Do you suppose *they* were working for her as well?'

'Those two blundering fools? Not a chance. Kshayarsha was never in any real danger, my daughter, though he was no doubt right to make a show of gratitude to this family friend of yours. No, he has a hundred spies who would be aware well in advance if any serious plot on his life were to be hatched; neither he nor we would ever need to hear anything about it. But you may be confident that such a plot would never emanate from Vashti; I cannot see her taking refuge in blatant assassination. Besides, you forget: she loves Kshayarsha still.'

GIMEL

'Though I have scattered my people
among the nations,
In distant lands they will remember me.'

ZECHARIAH 10:9

15

It was almost noon, one morning in early summer; I was sitting alone beneath the orange-tree in the courtyard where it was far too hot to be good for my health or my complexion, but I didn't care. There was little I *did* care about any more.

I was twenty years old. Four whole years had gone by since my coming to the palace; in fact, today was the eve of my third wedding anniversary, and I wondered if Kshayarsha would remember. I doubted it. He'd forgotten my recent birthday until Hutaosa reminded him, and arrangements for a celebration had been thrown together at the last minute. Just before the party I'd found and pulled out my first grey hair, and lately when the light fell a certain way I could see fine lines at the corners of my eyes.

It was unspeakably depressing, for no matter how many hours I spent with my oils and my ointments, I knew that from now on I could no longer hope to look lovelier with each passing day. I'd begun to fight a losing battle against time itself; I was going to grow old, and meaningless day would continue to follow meaningless day, bath after bath, meal after meal, until the boredom and futility destroyed me. A hundred times a day I found my thoughts straying back to the years of my Pioneer childhood when life had had a purpose, even though it was a purpose I could no longer embrace. My parents had been so poor, we'd possessed little but dreams. Yet now all my dreams had come true, whilst inside I was poorer than I'd ever been.

I sighed, and leaned back against the trunk of the tree, gazing up at the patches of clear blue sky which showed between the heavy clusters of blossom. I wished there was someone I could talk to, but could think of no one who would understand. I hadn't seen Iphigenia in months; she had three children now—or was it four? Sometimes she'd brought them to visit me, and I'd cooed and fussed over them as I was expected to, but their mother and I no longer had anything in common. Then there was Hegai: although in body he was still my servant, and still as comely and courteous as he'd ever been, and as attentive to my needs, in mind he was far away, if indeed he remained alive there at all.

As regards Hutaosa: she was disappointed in me, and for all that she did her best not to show it, I knew, and that made real talking difficult. I'd failed to provide her with a grandchild, and it appeared that she'd resigned herself to the fact that I never would. I began to wonder whether the serenity I'd once admired in her hadn't been resignation all along, a passive willingness to bow before the will of fate. She'd never genuinely loved me; Kshayarsha and Persia were all that she cared about, and since I seemed incapable of doing good to either of them, it was possible that she was already on the lookout for another young woman who might. Perhaps she was right: perhaps there was no one on earth who could escape the fate the gods had decreed for him. There was nothing for me to do but wait for the rest of the Arderikkan seeress's dreadful words to come true.

I still heard on occasions from Vashti: the usual malicious little gibes, made just often enough for me to be unable to forget her. But of Mordecai I heard nothing more after his disclosure of the eunuchs' conspiracy; I didn't even know whether Kshayarsha had got around to rewarding him. According to Hathach, my father's friend was still at the Treasury, and from his countenance was apparently quite content with his lot. Perhaps he'd been given money or honour enough to divert his attention from me.

With Kshayarsha, things were at a lower ebb than they'd ever been, except that we didn't argue. There was nothing to argue about; the fire had gone out of our union, and we both knew it. It was scarcely surprising. When the initial inferno of lust had burnt itself out, we'd had nothing to put in its place, and he sought his satisfaction elsewhere. As Great King of Persia he was perfectly entitled to do so; if *I* had found an alternative outlet for my appetites, there would have been no more need for me to dread the future, for I wouldn't have had one.

My alienation from Kshayarsha caused me to recognize for the first time just how alien was the entire culture he represented, and in particular its religion, certain disturbing aspects of which were dominating him more and more. He'd taken to drinking the sacred haoma—almost daily, though in theory it was reserved for his consumption at the New Year festival only, and then in very small doses. But some magus had told him that the prophet Zarathustra had been granted 'ecstasy in the presence of Ahura Mazda by the spirit of wisdom' when he'd taken haoma at the inception of his ministry. I don't know whether it was the wisdom that Kshayarsha craved, or the ecstasy, or simply, as ever, immortality. But it sent him into trances and gave him hallucinations, and in time began to play havoc with his delicate constitution. Once he even tried to give judgments in the Apadana while under its influence, and had to be led away quietly and placed in the hands of the magi. I couldn't help thinking: Mordecai considered ecstasy attainable through his religion too, but he had no need of drugs.

The personal decline of a king cannot fail to carry with it evil consequences for his kingdom, though I knew less about these than I ought to have done. Hathach still went out for me into the streets of Shushan, but I showed so little interest in his reports that he seldom told me the half of what he saw or heard, especially if he feared it might distress me. I didn't know then that the League of Greeks was harassing the Persian mainland. Its fleet had actually captured some of our islands, and a city called Eion, the most important Persian stronghold west of the Hellespont.

So much for the invaluable political advice of the matchless Haman. For two years now he'd held the office of First Minister for Civil and Foreign Affairs—a previously non-existent post whose functions had traditionally formed a substantial part of the mandate of the Hazar-apatish. The latter was left only with his military responsibilities—he continued to captain the King's Own Regiment of Immortals—and his job as glorified doorkeeper at the entrance to the Apadana when the King sat upon his throne to receive official visitors. No doubt the fellow took a very dim view of Haman's being promoted above his head; so did the immediate subordinates of Bigthana and Teresh, who'd presumed they would inherit their late superiors' much-coveted, often lucrative duties as foremen of the team of eunuchs who guarded the door to the King's private chambers. These too had been usurped by Haman and his own underlings.

As far as I could see, Haman was respected by no one except himself and Kshayarsha. They had become thick as thieves, holding court together each morning, relaxing together at midday, walking together in the gardens after noon discussing Imperial policy and shaking out poppy seeds into one another's hands. Haman's spectacular rise to power was all the more perplexing when you reflected that he was a self-confessed pagan who didn't even pretend to revere Ahura Mazda.

But he was exceedingly competent at one highly significant thing: the subtle, and not so subtle, manipulative flattering of the King. Kshayarsha was desperate for reassurance on so many scores, and Haman could be relied upon to furnish it at every turn.

Concerning my own relations with Haman, his very presence sent shivers down my spine. Often at dinner he would cast me sidelong glances when Kshayarsha wasn't looking, and I didn't know whether to be disgusted or thrilled. He *was* good-looking, there was no getting away from it, and so starved was I of the love of a man that temporarily I nursed perverse fantasies of conducting an affair with him in order to get my own back on Kshayarsha, even telling myself that since I was barren, no one need ever find out. Yet when I was more myself, one glimpse of his unctuous face was enough to make my flesh crawl. Once I complained to Kshayarsha about the way his First Minister looked at me, but he said that Haman had a wife of his own to whom he could turn if he felt the need of a woman's ministrations. To be fair, Haman treated both Hutaosa and myself more civilly than either of us treated him. Hutaosa would no longer even eat at the same table.

But the major source of my deepening depression remained my inability to bear children. There could be little doubt now but that something was seriously wrong, and so distraught did this make me that I even sent for Anahita to examine me, but nothing was found to be amiss.

However, I reckoned it odd that throughout the time she'd been in my service, Roxana my food-taster had borne no children either. She still saw her husband regularly, and they'd been fecund as rabbits in the past. Yet when I mentioned this to Hutaosa, she was brusquely dismissive: what herbs or minerals did I imagine could be being fed to us which would cause infertility without harming our health in other ways? I was at liberty to change my food-taster if I wished to put my preposterous theory to the test, but I should be condemning Roxana to summary execution, for that was the sentence which still hung over her.

Still, I might have done it anyway, if I'd thought there was any chance of my being proved right. But I knew there wasn't. Even if some substance existed which was capable of doing what I was suggesting, then if Vashti was clever enough to have it introduced secretly into my diet she was also clever enough to escape detection and go on doing the same thing whoever I had to taste my food. I did raise the matter with Kshayarsha, but he reacted more contemptuously even than his mother.

All the same, in my heart of hearts I couldn't believe that Vashti *wasn't* casting some spell over me—perhaps literally. Why else should a healthy girl of twenty whose monthly courses ran as reliably as the imperial postal service be incapable of performing one of the basic functions for which she was made? Oh, I'd heard other reasons put forward: I knew there was a rumour going round that I was a Semite, and that Aryan and Semitic blood could never mix. It was like trying to mate a sheep with a goat; a certain magus had allegedly stated that when Kshayarsha had married me, it was like a *man* trying to mate with a goat. Of course, this was so much stuff and nonsense: Shushan was crawling with the offspring of mixed marriages, for the races had intermingled there since time immemorial. But it is amazing what people will believe when they have a reason for wanting to believe it.

Such were the thoughts which were churning round and round in my head as the sun rose to its zenith above my orange-tree; it was so hot now that I lacked the energy required to go indoors. I might have remained there all day and made myself thoroughly ill, if Farah hadn't appeared and told me that Ashpamithra had left a message from the King. I followed her inside, took the tablet and broke the seal. There was an invitation for me to dine with Kshayarsha alone, in his private quarters, the following evening; then we should spend the night there together, in honour of our anniversary.

I tried not to get excited, telling myself that no long-term improvement in my circumstances was necessarily implied; like as not Kshayarsha had decided to take pity on me just for our one special night of the year. But as soon as I arrived on his threshold with my entourage, I saw that this wasn't the case. There was no sign of Haman—a pair of eunuchs I didn't recognize stood guard at the door—and Kshayarsha was got up as though ready to play host to some mighty foreign potentate, except that he'd discarded the ceremonial beard. The spectacle of him clad from head to foot in scarlet, purple and gold, with his handsome, clean-shaven face powdered and pencilled and his scented black curls cloaking his shoulders began to melt the ice around my heart. Then when he folded me in his strong arms and murmured, 'My poor sweet Esther, how I've missed you,' it fell away like the clay mould from a statue cast in bronze.

Inside the room he had a whole coffer full of jewels, which he said were my anniversary gift. He picked out a delicate choker of gold and amethysts and lapis lazuli, and as he clasped it about my neck he whispered, 'Neither of us has been happy these past twelve months, my darling. Maybe even longer.' Only then did I notice how weary his eyes looked, and that his face-powder masked hollow rings beneath them. He continued, 'So many things have come between us: my resentment at your childlessness, your mistrust of Haman and your jealousy of Vashti. But our estrangement has done neither of us good. We need each other, and as of this very hour, none of those things will be mentioned again. We shall write down our differences on papyrus, then burn what we have written in the Wise Lord's fire. Thus we shall start afresh, if you are in agreement, and he will purge us of their very memory.'

So I agreed—how could I not?—and at the clap of the King's hands a black-garbed magus came in with a fire-stand, the contents of which he ignited with his sacred taper. Kshayarsha himself wrote the causes of our mutual discontent upon papyrus as he'd described, and we watched them eaten by the flames. Then he cupped my face between his hands and kissed me, his own face half flushed by the fire's heat and light, and half plunged in shifting shadow. After that I could think about nothing but how best I might please him, until dawn found us sleeping in each other's arms. When Kshayarsha awoke he said, 'Now we must be prepared to demonstrate to one another that our promises were sincerely made. We shall dine with Haman tonight; there will be just the three of us, and you will convince him that you accept and approve of him, and that he has nothing to fear from you.'

I smiled, and said, 'Very well,' though taken aback by the implication that Haman could ever have had grounds to fear me. I was no Vashti.

Dinner was served in the King's private chambers again, not in the formal dining-room—and Haman was late.

Evidently this caused Kshayarsha no little concern; his First Minister was accustomed to be as punctilious in his time-keeping as he was about his personal appearance. When he did arrive, he was as dapper and deferential as ever, and profuse in his apologies. But though his apparel and his carefully styled hair gave the impression that he was quite unruffled, his movements were rather too rapid, and his sharp little eyes flicked hither and thither like the tongue of a snake. Kshayarsha asked him outright what was troubling him.

It transpired that he'd fallen foul of the Hazarapatish, Artabanush, over some matter of policy for which each of them claimed responsibility. They had argued in front of their subordinates, and Artabanush had made 'slanderous personal accusations' against him in an attempt to undermine his dignity and authority.

'What manner of slanderous accusations?' Kshayarsha enquired, narrowing his eyes and leaning forward across the table.

Haman avoided his gaze. 'I shouldn't care to repeat them, my lord. Certainly not in the presence of your gentle lady wife.'

'I order you to repeat them!' Kshayarsha roared. 'Am I not King here, and is my wife not Queen? Do we not have a right to know what our own ministers are saying?'

'My lord ... he implied that my education had been neglected, that my mother had not been lawfully wed to my father ... and that I had only got where I am today by ... by assuming some of the more intimate duties of your Chamberlain, my lord.'

Once Kshayarsha had grasped his meaning, he was livid; thundering and cursing he threatened to have the Hazarapatish dragged before him in chains and made to restate his allegations before having his tongue torn from its roots. Haman hastened to placate him, making a great show of magnanimity towards his fellow public servant—no doubt Artabanush would have told the tale rather differently, had he been granted the opportunity—and said, 'My lord, it isn't vengeance I seek, but a little reverence. If my junior colleagues were only required to make some sign of submission when introduced to my presence, it might encourage them to think twice before slighting me.'

'And what—*sign* did you have in mind?'

'My lord; I feel it would be appropriate for them to do obeisance to me as they do to you, since everything I do is sanctioned directly by Your gracious Majesty, and I act solely on your immediate behalf. I feel that they should therefore make the prostration, my lord.' And when Kshayarsha's jaw dropped, Haman added hurriedly, 'Of course, it would be done differently. They would not bend quite so *low* before me, nor would they be expected to wait to be bidden, before arising.'

Kshayarsha was still dumbfounded, but I think that I was more horrified than he was. For a Persian to accept such obeisance, it means that he must regard himself as King's regent at very least, or King at most. But among the Semites, you only prostrate yourself before a god; and Haman was Semitic through and through.

Although I was unable to believe that the distress he'd exhibited earlier had all been an act, one look at the greed in his eyes now told me that he'd recovered himself thoroughly, and had—as always—turned things round to his own advantage. He loved Kshayarsha not a jot, and power completely, but he put his head in his hands and stammered with convincing contrition, 'I have upset you, my lord, and caused you grief. It was foolish of me to suggest such a thing, I see it now. But I wasn't myself; that miserably misguided creature's words cut me to the quick; and more than anything because they besmirched *your* immaculate name, my merciful lord—though I'm sure he cannot have meant them to.'

Kshayarsha seized Haman's wrists, and forced his hands away from his face. 'You have caused no one grief but yourself, my friend, and that most unjustly. What upsets me is that you, who have been made to feel insulted, punish yourself into the bargain while those who would decry your abilities hold their heads high. You shall have what you ask for, Haman son of Hammedatha, and gold and treasures and horses besides, to compensate you for the embarrassment which you have been caused. We shall have it decreed that from tomorrow every man, woman and child who is my subject, with the exception of the members of my own family, must kiss the ground at your feet whenever their paths cross yours. Artabanush will be the first to perform the obeisance, to set an example. Will this go some way at least towards restoring your self-esteem?'

'Most certainly it will, my lord. Your gracious Majesty is too kind.'

Cocooned in my private quarters, I was spared any personal experience of the consternation caused by the King's latest edict. My attendants were less fortunate; both Hegai and and Hathach were compelled to make the prostration in front of Haman several times each over the course of the following week or so, and then as if this were not bad enough, they began to be accosted in shadowy corners by various high-ranking palace officials begging them to use their influence with me to have Kshayarsha revoke his decision.

Hathach took it all in his stride, having long been familiar with the whims of the supremely powerful. In fact, he found the whole business mildly amusing, and chuckled impenitently to himself as he told me of the august bureaucrats and foppish courtiers who'd virtually prostrated themselves before *him*, a lowly eunuch who was technically a slave, in their indignation. We giggled together at the farcical notion that *I* had the power to do anything about their humiliating predicament. Even if I *had* exercised the requisite degree of influence over

Kshayarsha, and even if I could have got him to see the error of his judgment, this wouldn't have been the end of the matter. A royal decree is irrevocable in Persian law.

Hegai, however, was furious. Yes, he was as much my slave as Hathach was, in terms of legal status. But it was as I'd been told long ago: there are slaves and slaves in Shushan. And Hegai had been King's Chamberlain, which was unofficially acknowledged to be the highest position in the land after that of the Great King himself; a pretty, beguiling young Chamberlain, if he were clever enough, could wind the ruler of half the world around his little finger. Hegai stalked into my apartment with a countenance blacker than a thundercloud, and when he'd slammed the door, the storm broke; he tore off his turban and smashed his fists against the wall. I bade Hathach restrain him, which he did, but Hegai cried out, 'By all the gods of heaven and hell, my lady, we have to do something! *You* have to do something! Haman will destroy us all.'

I stared at him, astonished, because I wouldn't have suspected he had it in him; just enough of his spirit must have been left alive to make him want to fight a rearguard action against the ultimate threat to what little remained of his once-renowned pride. Finally I said, 'There's nothing I *can* do, Hegai. I swore an oath to Kshayarsha.'

'What is an oath, compared with the survival of his dynasty, his very Empire? There will be rebellion if he doesn't show Haman his rightful place! Freeborn Persians of ancient and noble families are forced to bow the knee to him; *I* am forced to bow to him, when my father was a master craftsman who built half this wretched palace, and *his* was an Amalekite slave, a descendant of nomads, who ate locusts and beetles and cooked his food with camel-dung!'

There was a long and dreadful silence. Then I whispered, 'An Amalekite? Did you say that Haman is an *Amalekite*?'

'Yes.' Hegai shrugged, glowering, irritated at my asking what he no doubt considered an irrelevant question. It wasn't irrelevant to me. Just about the only thing which my parents and Mordecai had had in common was their inveterate loathing of the Sons of Amalek, the most vicious and cowardly of all the ancestral enemies of the Jews, worse even than the Canaanite Soil People or the Samaritans. No other race but Amalek had ever been marked out by Adonai for total destruction because of its sin against God's People; yet that destruction had never quite been completed, and Mordecai himself had warned me that we hadn't heard the last of that accursed name. Was it possible that survivors of the purges had wound up in Shushan, and that the detestable Haman was one of them?

'Hegai, are you sure?' I expostulated. 'How do you know?'

'Because he calls himself an Agagite, and Agag was one of their so-called kings, was he not? Haman reckons he's descended from him, though why anyone in his right mind should want to claim kinship with a wilderness chieftain who was no better than a bandit—'

'He's descended from Agag himself?'

'Yes, but—'

'My God, Hegai.'

'What? What's the matter?'

I thought about sending everyone out except him, and telling him everything; he knew I was Jewish, so why shouldn't he know the rest? Why shouldn't he know that 'Amalekite' had been the foulest insult you could possibly throw at anyone, when I'd been a child in Jerusalem; that sparing Agag himself had cost my own forefather Saul his throne? Once upon a time, I *would* have told him, but now . . . I *had* sworn an oath to Kshayarsha, and the last thing I wanted was to imperil our fragile reconciliation. So I said, 'Nothing, Hegai. It's nothing.' And although he didn't believe me, he could tell from the tone of my voice that the casebook was closed.

Nevertheless, the next day it was thrown open again with a vengeance. For Hathach scuttled in, uncommonly excited, and announced that some senior executive had flatly refused to make the prostration in front of Haman, maintaining that it was an honour due to God and the Great King alone. I asked who would dare to defy a royal edict so flagrantly, but Hathach didn't know.

I very soon found out. I'd been invited to dine with Kshayarsha and his First Minister again that evening, and Haman arrived in a high temper. From the florid description he gave Kshayarsha, there was one man, and one man alone, to whom it could apply. However, when asked the renegade's name, Haman claimed that he didn't know it.

I didn't believe for a moment that he wouldn't have found it out; but then I realized he dared not repeat it because the King would recognize it as that of the man who'd once saved him from conspirators. I smothered a sigh of relief; but too soon. When Kshayarsha requested Haman's opinion as to why this solitary individual should have adopted such a refractory and perilous attitude, he answered, 'I think it's because of his religion, Your Majesty. I'm told that he belongs to a pernicious cult which practises the most primitive forms of sacrifice and believes that a great prophet will one day bring down your Empire and enthrone himself as King in your place.'

I caught my breath, my heart beating harder and faster as Haman went on, painting for Kshayarsha a hideous picture of my people which was concocted from a palette of truth and lies mixed together in equal measure. By the time he'd finished, you would have thought that the Jews burned children on their altars, lived on nothing but air because of their aberrant dietary restrictions, and were plotting some kind of conspiracy to murder Kshayarsha and every member of the royal family. Worst of all, perhaps, he made tham sound like some heretic sect of magi, who possessed arcane knowledge and dark powers and wouldn't hesitate to use them for the subverting of decent society and the annihilation of civilization itself.

But at no point did he call this group by its true name, for Kshayarsha knew very well who the Jews were, and that they'd done nothing remotely treasonable in the history of the Hakhamanish Empire—how could he *not* know, when the wisest of monarchs Kurash and Darayavaush had each given express permission for them to rebuild their Temple and their Holy City? Instead Haman called them Hebrews, a name which harked back to the time of the exodus from Egypt when our enmity with Amalek was born—a name of which the Great King had never heard—and reassured him that despite their dangerous beliefs, the group constituted no immediate political threat, owing to the paucity of their numbers.

Still, I don't know how Kshayarsha didn't detect the deep-seated bitterness that soured every word Haman spoke; he must have been brought up to hate us every bit as much as we'd been brought up to hate Amalek. But I watched my credulous husband swallowing Haman's every syllable, until at length he said, 'Haman, you must *make* this man submit to you, for he and his kind must be crushed at once before their noxious influence spreads. I give you leave to deal with him as you see fit.'

I noted that Kshayarsha didn't offer to see to the matter himself, and Haman didn't ask him to. No doubt he knew that the King had once spared two Spartans who wouldn't prostrate themselves even before *him* because it contravened the customs of their city.

That night I couldn't sleep. I'd returned to my own apartment after dinner, saying I felt sick; and indeed I did. There was a nagging, nauseating cramp in the pit of my stomach, and I thought I'd eaten something that didn't suit me. It was almost dawn when I accepted the truth: I was acutely anxious about Mordecai's fate.

I tried to cast the worry from my mind, scolding myself for becoming concerned over an iron-hearted prig of a man who'd shown nothing but contempt for me. Did he not deserve everything that was surely coming to him, the stubborn fool? With his excessive piety he must be courting martyrdom deliberately; in his own way he was as fanatical as the craziest of the Pioneers.

Having argued myself into exhaustion, I fell at last into an uneasy doze, and dreamed for the first time in years of the violent deaths of my own parents and my sister, and the disappearance of Pithon my beloved brother, of whom I'd never heard anything since.

When I awoke I got up at once, although it wasn't yet fully light, for I was afraid to dream the dream again. But at siesta time I could stay awake no longer, and the dream returned. It was followed by another, in which I glimpsed afresh the spark of love I'd once seen in Mordecai's eyes when he prayed for the remission of my summer fever.

So in the afternoon I ordered Hathach to go at once to the Treasury and check that my father's friend hadn't been harmed. It appeared that he was quite safe, and manifestly unconcerned about his own well-being, and I realized that Haman wouldn't dare to move openly against a man who was listed among the King's Benefactors.

When several days had passed and still nothing evil had befallen him, my fears began to subside. But again my relief was ephemeral. Utterly unexpectedly, Iphigenia arrived on my threshold, and in an advanced state of agitation informed me of a sudden escalation in atrocities against my people in the city. Two expensively-dressed Jewish youths had been attacked in the street at night on their way home from a party, and beaten up so severely that one of them later died. A well-known Jewish jeweller had been set upon and strangled in a tavern. A Jewish cloth-trader's stall had been turned upside down and his goods looted in broad daylight in the bazaar; he himself had been knifed in the gut and no one had lifted a finger to help him. A rich Jewish widow had had burning torches thrown over her forecourt wall after dark; they'd set fire to the awnings that hung from her poplar trees, and she'd perished in the flames along with her many possessions. All these incidents had taken place within the space of two days.

But it seemed that the crimes were unrelated; some young men *had* been arrested, and brought before Haman the First Minister, but he'd dismissed them with a caution, alleging that their conduct had been the result of juvenile high spirits and a surfeit of alcohol rather than malice.

The conclusion was inescapable. Haman wasn't only condoning anti-Jewish terrorism, but encouraging it; nay, probably sponsoring it. He couldn't punish my cousin directly so he would make his compatriots suffer on his behalf—a thing which would distress a man like Mordecai far more than his own personal suffering in any case. And much as the majority of folk at the palace hated Haman, most of those outside it had reason to hate the Jews far more. Jewish businesses thrived while native-born Persians struggled to make ends meet; compared with this, the issue of whom one ought to kiss the ground for seemed laughably irrelevant. The disaffected masses had merely been waiting for a catalyst to turn them into a yowling horde, and Haman would fill that role for them as willingly as he had filled Marduniya's for the King.

'And what of things in Arderikka?' I challenged her. 'Are *your* people still being victimized too?'

'Not so much as yours, Hadassah.' She wouldn't call me Esther however obviously I cringed. 'The Greek Expedition is a thing of the past; Jewish prosperity is paraded in front of every man's face every day. The mob has found a new target for its fury; except that it *isn't* so new, is it? For God's sake, you yourself were once attacked because you were Jewish, else we should never have met.'

Then she wrested her gaze from mine quite suddenly, as though startled and upset by her own words; perhaps she wondered if it might have been for the best if we'd never met at all. I muttered sullenly, 'Those were children who attacked me, probably beggars' children at that. Children always call names, they don't know any better.'

She made no attempt to contradict me, though both of us knew I was vainly searching for a reason not to believe what was irrefutable. I blethered on, 'And Mordecai always used to say that the Jews of Shushan lived in too much comfort and had grown too much at ease with Hakhamanish culture. Perhaps a little persecution will do them good.' Then I tossed back my head and declared, 'Anyway, I don't want to talk about this. We haven't seen each other for ages, and I seem to remember a time when *you* didn't want to spoil things by talking politics. Why haven't you brought little Philos to see me? He must be getting quite grown up by now.'

Iphigenia's prodigious patience had run out. She blurted, 'Hadassah, how can you be so *blind*? I'm not talking about *politics*! I'm talking about flagrant cruelty, cold-blooded murder!'

'Things can't be as bad as you say, or Hathach would have told me.'

'Would he? Has he *ever* told you what *really* goes on? Does he even know? Oh, Hadassah, he's like everyone else in this gilded cage of a palace—his life has been so sheltered he wouldn't recognize a murder for what it was if it were carried out before his very eyes.'

'Don't you believe it, Iphigenia. *You* know nothing of what goes on *here!* And stop calling me Hadassah. My enemies have ears everywhere.'

'You've changed, I swear it, along with your name. You used to think of yourself before anyone else; now you think *only* of yourself, and you're embittered and pitiless besides. You would sit here on your padded couch painting your nails and watch your entire race swept from the face of the earth.'

'And precisely what do you expect me to do to redeem them? Prostrate my*self* in front of Haman and beg for their lives? I don't recall *you* bowing to *me* when you came in here. I am Queen of Persia and you think you can rebuke me like some leper in the gutter. Get out of my sight, before I have you *compelled* to show me some respect.'

She did, without another word; I flung myself upon my bed and howled, but when Hegai tried to approach me I threw my slipper at him and struck him on the nose. It bled like a punctured pipe and he ran out to find a napkin. Hathach and Farah too I cursed out of my presence, then wailed all the louder because I had no one to confide in. I *was* selfish, I knew it—Hutaosa had thought I would grow out of it, but I'd known all along that I wouldn't—and I *was* bitter. But I wasn't pitiless. I just felt trapped and helpless; there was no way I could see of aiding my people without jeopardizing what little affection I'd regained from Kshayarsha, and Heaven alone knew what would become of me if Haman learned I was a Jew. My frustration found its outlet in anger: anger at Haman, at Kshayarsha, at Mordecai who was to blame for all this because of his petty refusal to observe what could be viewed as a simple, inconsequential formality.

Night came again, and I didn't sleep at all, nor take any breakfast next morning. Catching a glimpse of my hollow cheeks and black-bagged eyes, I hurled my mirror across the room and it gouged a chunk out of one of the lovely glazed tiles on my wall, ruining the peaceful scene depicted there. I was suddenly reminded of the bronze mirror I'd held up to admire myself the day I turned eight, and of the words my mother had spoken that afternoon: *You are a Shining One, after the pattern of Moses and Joshua, Saul and David. You are marked out by the radiance which comes of having met with Adonai; you have his spirit within you.* For the first time in many, many years I found myself trying to pray; but I might as well have talked to the lotus-topped columns or the mouldings round the ceiling, and I burst into tears again because I knew that what she'd said wasn't true, and it never had been. I'd never come any closer to Adonai than I had to the foot of a rainbow.

Now it was too late for me; I was too far gone along the road of uncleanness and greed. Adonai was simply one more of those I'd flung out of my way, whose wishes I'd trampled in the mire. He wasn't going to overlook all that and pay heed to me now.

As the days and weeks dragged by, I felt I could do nothing but wait and watch things get worse. I sent Hathach out daily, and made him swear to report to me *all* that he saw and heard, and soon it was like listening to a demon-possessed man relating his nightmares. Obscene anti-Jewish graffiti appeared on walls and no one washed it off. The isolated groups of youths who had first made attacks upon Jewish individuals were growing more numerous and more co-ordinated, and no longer kept their crimes secret; they even shouted their slogans in the streets. Jewish children were shunned by their Persian playmates; Jewish adults became afraid to venture outside their own quarter of the city, though they were scarcely any safer within it; Jewish businessmen lost much of their trade and many went bankrupt; employers found reason to dismiss their Jewish staff. Violence against Jews became commonplace: some were jumped by total strangers as I had once been, but not by children, whose tender age might have excused them. Others were murdered by those who had once been their friends or

lovers. It made no difference whether you were a devout follower of
Adonai, or so assimilated that your sons were uncircumcized and your
daughters wore trousers and your grandchildren thought themselves
Persians.

And all the time, Kshayarsha remained in blissful ignorance of what
was going on upon his very doorstep. Haman made sure of that, for he
was seldom out of the King's presence, and when he was, one of his
minions would be hovering in his stead. Thus a once-great people with
a glorious history, whom Kurash and Darayavaush had respected and
honoured, began to be ground down like grains in a quern. Every day
the grinding stone grew heavier, and the quern larger, for no longer
was the persecution confined to Shushan. I, who alone was in a
position to tell the King the truth, kept silent, because I fancied that
once again he loved me.

Kshayarsha *was* aware that *some* sort of persecution was going on, of
some esoteric minority within his domains, but Haman's financial
inducements to agents of his intelligence service ensured that the
identity of this minority was kept from him. Whenever the First
Minister dined with us, he would assure Kshayarsha that the measures he'd taken against the perfidious sect to which he'd often
referred were beginning to have an effect, though its membership was
larger than had at first been suspected.

'What exactly *do* these people believe?' the King enquired once,
when the subject came up. 'To what god do they make their vile
sacrifices? Is it one of whom we have heard before?'

'It's my opinion that they have no god at all, in any normal sense of
the word,' Haman answered smoothly. 'I cannot discover what he
looks like, or where he dwells, or over what aspects of nature he
claims dominion.'

'The same could be said of Ahura Mazda,' Kshayarsha pointed out,
and a suggestion of reproof sharpened his tone. 'He has no form like
that of mortal man or beast; he dwells everywhere and rules over
everything—'

'Ah, but the two deities could not be more unalike,' Haman rejoined
hastily. 'Ahura Mazda, as I'm given to understand him, represents
light, and goodness, and order. This being whom the Hebrews
venerate requires offerings of fresh blood, whilst forbidding his
people to taste it themselves in any form. The worship of fire or of
the sun is specifically proscribed among them, and they abide by

295

strange laws of their own, ignoring those of Your Majesty the King of Kings except when it suits them.'

'*Which* of my laws do they ignore? How dare they do such a thing? My requirements of my subjects are not harsh or unjust, and I permit all nations within my jurisdiction to enforce their own traditional laws in addition to mine, if they so desire, and provided that there is no conflict of interests.'

Haman only shrugged, for in truth the Jews have always obeyed *all* the laws of Persia, so far as I'm aware. But Kshayarsha, evidently much impressed with his own spontaneous eloquence, lost the thread of his initial question and asked instead, 'What part of the world do they hail from, anyway? Where is their ancestral home?'

'I'm not sure that they *have* a home, Your Majesty, any more than they have a god. The Hebrews are not so much a nation, as adherents to a set of subversive beliefs. I've heard that virtually anyone can join their sect and call himself by their name, so long as he agrees to live by their twisted and impious code of conduct. I've also heard that the sect has planted congregations all over the Empire—very small ones, you understand, yet potentially dangerous nonetheless.'

'But the steps you are taking to curb their influence are proving adequate, are they, Lord Haman? You are convinced of this?'

'For the present they are indeed, Your Majesty. But there is no need for you to trouble yourself about such trivialities; after all, that is why you have appointed me to my current post. It is my purpose and my pleasure to ensure that no frowns of anxiety impair the noble tranquillity of your royal countenance, and that no ill humours upset the balance of your sensitive constitution.'

'What would I do without you, Haman? You have lifted burdens from my shoulders the enormity of which no other man who is not a king has ever comprehended. You have made it possible for me to carry out the charge which the Wise Lord himself laid upon me: to eradicate the evils of paganism from my domains so that I may truly be called great. With your assistance I shall crush all who deny the supremacy of Ahura Mazda; I shall wipe them from the face of the earth, I shall drive them screaming into the abyss! Haman, in a thousand lifetimes I could never repay what I owe you!'

And in a thousand lifetimes the pair of you could never atone for all the blood which is upon both your heads, I thought, not for a moment pausing to acknowledge that it was upon mine also.

But if I wasn't prepared to fight for my people, there were those
who were. Hathach reported to me that the younger male Jews of
Shushan were organizing themselves into defensive brotherhoods, so
that the day-to-day assaults and muggings were turning more into
gang brawls, with casualties on both sides. Not that these youthful
Jewish warriors knew the first thing about combat skills; they possessed no weapons, and in any case it was illegal for them to carry any.
Their fathers and grandfathers had lived peacefully in Shushan all
their lives, and apparently persisted in advocating appeasement and
the use of reason; the more religious among them relied purely on a
passive trust in Adonai. Indeed, the influence of the religious was
waxing, along with that of the belligerent: according to Hathach there
was a resurgence of sabbath observance, and of compliance with the
dietary laws. I derived some perverse comfort from this; persecution
was doing the Jews good after all.

Unfortunately I wasn't the only one to draw this conclusion.
Haman viewed the rise of militant Jewry with some alarm, and
measures were duly passed forbidding 'Hebrews' to meet together in
groups larger than three, except with the members of their own
immediate families. Thus, overnight, Torah-schools such as the one
Mordecai had once held in our house became unlawful along with
councils of war; both found ways to go on with their work, but
underground. No Hebrew was to be appointed to a position at the
palace; those already employed there could remain in their posts for
the time being, but their work was to be regularly scrutinized for
evidence of dishonesty or incompetence.

Throughout that autumn and winter and into the following spring,
life for the Jews of Shushan continued to deteriorate, until most of
them had lost all their capital and any stable source of income.
Malnourished and ragged as many of them became, their reputation
as society's scum appeared to be well-deserved. According to Hathach,
the strain was telling on Mordecai; he still held on to his government
post, but seemed no better fed than his brethren who were unem-
ployed—perhaps he was giving away most of his wages to salve his
conscience. Nevertheless, he was no longer alone in refusing to bow
the knee to Haman. Other Jews were joining him in defiance of the
King's decree, and not only Jews, but Babylonians and Persians also.

Yet through all of this, I saw no evidence of his attempting to
contact me. Unlike Iphigenia, he didn't seem to reckon it worth

trying to persuade me to use my influence at court to end the torment. I put this down to his having seen sense at last, and recognized once and for all that I wanted nothing more to do with him. But I should have thought again.

At Passover, things seemed about to come to a head. When those Jews who dared to celebrate the festival openly went outside to paint the blood of the sacrificial lambs on their doorposts, they found blood already there: foul, evil-smelling pigs' blood, daubed on their thresholds and lintels and walls and doors, as well as on the doorposts themselves. Then when their less devout Jewish neighbours—even those who imagined they'd kept their ancestry a secret—went outside too, to see what had happened, they found that their own homes had been desecrated in exactly the same way. So did Jews who had moved right away from the Jewish quarter years before. Terror gripped every Jewish heart in Shushan from that instant, and suspicion blighted every relationship, as frightened folk tried to guess which of their kinsmen or acquaintances had betrayed them.

However, before anything could come of this, I suddenly lost all interest in the political situation, and couldn't have cared less if every Jew in Shushan had been massacred in a single day. For without warning, everything I'd rebuilt with Kshayarsha came crashing down about my ears, and I didn't know why. He simply stopped inviting me to dine or sleep with him, in fact for ten whole days I received no communication from him whatever. Then on the eleventh I was presented with a formal summons to appear before him in the Apadana.

I clung to Hegai, beside myself with dread, babbling, 'What can have happened? Do you think he has found out what I am?' But Hegai could offer me no consolation, and his face was grey as pumice; one glance at it told me that this was how it had happened for him when he'd been told of his dismissal from the rank of Chamberlain. I begged him to go with me, and together with my train of maids he and I set out with leaden hearts for the throneroom. At the entrance the Hazarapatish informed us that he was instructed to admit only me; my servants must wait outside, and Hegai must report to Shaashgaz for general harem duties, as must Hathach. Neither of them would be permitted to serve me until further notice.

More terrified than ever, I was led up the great stone staircase by the Hazarapatish Artabanush himself. Once, long ago, Hegai had admired me because I was scared of nothing; four years at the palace had so changed me that I was scared of everything. As I walked slowly forward alone towards the great golden throne, with the pungent smell of burning incense clogging my nostrils and its wafting smoke stinging the back of my throat, I saw that Kshayarsha had his seven advisers and Hutaosa at his side, in addition to Ashpamithra, his other eunuchs, his pages, and the ubiquitous Haman.

It was almost a relief to go down for the prostration, so that my legs would no longer need to bear my weight, nor my eyes to look into all those others, every pair fixed implacably upon me. But all too soon the sceptre was extended towards me; I rose, and beheld with abject misery the wrathful, maddened face of the man who had once been all I could have wished for in a bridegroom. How different he'd looked then, how different *everything* had looked, on the day I'd first stood in that awe-inspiring hall, arm in arm with the lovely Hegai, both of us decked out in magenta and riding on a wavecrest of hope. I closed my eyes, waiting for the inevitable torrent of abuse to assault me.

And so it did; but it bore no relation to what I was expecting. Haman began to recite the allegations being made against me, but because they were written in liturgical Old Persian, whose pronunciation was quite alien to him, he faltered several times. Kshayarsha, impatient and manifestly as agitated as I was, interrupted him and accused me outright, in blunt but slurred Aramaic, of committing adultery.

Bewildered, I stared at him speechless; beneath his ceremonial robes I could see that his chest was heaving, and above the artificial beard his cheeks were burning and his bloodshot eyes unfocussed. I was unsure whether he was ill, or drunk, or doped with haoma. Because I didn't speak, he began lambasting me again, his voice so slurred and so shrill by turns that it took me all my time to distinguish his words.

'Ten whole days I have waited before sending for you; ten whole days, hoping I was dreaming, hoping I might awake to find the millstone around my neck dissolved away! But it hasn't gone away; it *won't* go away, because that millstone is the truth, and truth can *never* be wished into untruth. God help me... when I think that on our anniversary you stood calmly by and let me resanctify our marriage over the Wise Lord's holy fire, while all along you were deliberately, shamelessly deceiving me, your tender flesh tainted by the touch of another man!' He broke off, his voice choked up with what had to be drug-bloated emotion; those around him looked away in embarrassment. Then Memucan, who had chosen me himself for the House of His Majesty's Virgins, stepped forward and demanded that I give a response.

Naturally, I said I had no idea what the King was talking about; I'd had no contact with any man whatever since coming to the palace.

'Then what is your explanation of these?' snarled Memucan, snapping his fingers; Ashpamithra came forward bearing a large tray, upon which was heaped a jumble of small wax tablets. I could only blink and ask what they were, which enraged Memucan more than ever.

'Is it not enough for you to have deceived your royal husband by your vile actions, without compounding your sin by lying to him with your lips? The angels of Ahura Mazda will see that you rot in hell for this, you Daughter of Evil!' So saying, he thrust several of the tablets into my hands seemingly at random. As soon as I saw the handwriting upon them, I understood everything and wished the ground would swallow me.

Your Gracious Majesty the Queen, read the first tablet, *you who have always been dearer to me than my own soul; I beg you not to harden your heart against me. You have to believe that I love you, though Heaven knows I have not expressed my feelings very clearly. Please, please send me an answer to this letter, saying that you forgive me.—M.*

And the next: *Your Beneficent, Bounteous Majesty: no language of men could express the joy that overwhelmed me when I received your courteous reply. To get word from you after so long, after sending so many letters and hearing nothing ... Yes, I understand that it would be much too dangerous for us to attempt to meet face to face at present, with things as they are, but you may be certain that it is enough for me to have your letter, which I cherish; and may it be but the first of many! One day we shall meet again in the flesh, of that I am now confident. May God, and the assurance of my love, keep you in perfect peace.—M.*

What was I to say? It was little wonder that my poor distracted husband and his counsellors had assumed these to be love-letters— what else could they be? Yet if I tried to explain to them now that 'M' was none other than the Chief Clerk at His Majesty's Treasury and that he was in fact my cousin and adoptive father, while Haman his sworn enemy was standing right there in front of me... I just gazed down at the marble floor and wrung my hands, too miserable and frightened to be angry, either with Vashti who alone could have wanted to intercept Mordecai's letters and forge replies, or with Kshayarsha who was entitled to seek love wherever in his harem it could be found, whilst I was expected to keep myself to him alone regardless of how he treated me.

'Well?' Memucan thundered, snatching back the tablets and brandishing them in front of my nose. 'Have you *nothing* to say in your own defence? Speak, woman, for your silence denotes only guilt.'

I mumbled, 'Lord Memucan, I don't know who this man is. Someone must be trying to discredit me. I never received a single one of those tablets. Certainly I never replied to them.'

'No? Then why does he say in one of his letters that he is confident you will one day both meet *again?* And how do you account for the presence of *this* tablet, which my own servants found in your chambers during the last night you spent there with the King?'

Ashpamithra stepped forward a second time, and handed Memucan another tablet which had been kept apart from all the rest. It was one which Farah had delivered to me before I instructed each of my attendants to accept nothing from anyone on my behalf; I thought I'd destroyed all such communications, but this one must somehow have been overlooked. It wasn't signed at all, but the handwriting was indisputably the same as that upon the others. I whispered, 'My lord, it's as this letter suggests: the man must be an old friend of my father's, but not of mine. I swear I don't know him.'

'You swear falsely! Your tears and your stammering and the pallor of your face condemn you for the liar that you are! Admit that you know this man, or we shall torture your eunuchs until they tell us who he is.'

'No! Oh no, my lord, I beg you ... Kshayarsha, Your Majesty ...' Without even thinking what I was doing, I fell to my knees before the throne, kissing Kshayarsha's feet and staining his kidskin slippers with my tears. But Haman took it upon himself to drag me away from him, and I found myself grovelling at the feet of Hutaosa. 'Please, Mother, please ... *you* know I've been faithful to your son. *You* know I've never loved another. *Please* speak for me, please don't let them touch Hegai, or Hathach.'

Hutaosa, however, merely shook her head, her own cheeks glistening with tears, and said softly, 'My daughter, it seems to me that you *do* care for your precious Hegai more than for your husband. What *can* I say, when I do not know who has written these letters any more than anyone else does?'

'All right,' I sobbed, still on my knees, but addressing Kshayarsha directly; he was clutching his stomach and scarcely seemed to see me. 'All right, I admit that I know the man. I *did* receive this message from him . . . but not all those others as well. I *didn't* reply to him; I wanted nothing to do with him. He *does* claim to love me—but not the way you're thinking.'

'What other way *is* there for a man to love a woman?' barked Memucan; but I knew this wasn't the question burning on the lips of his fellow inquisitors. Nor were they primarily interested in the identity of the man to whom I'd referred. Rather, they wanted to know how I'd dared to utter lies, which I'd now retracted, in the presence of the King himself. Some of them, I'm sure, would have had my tongue cut out on the spot.

But by some miracle I was saved from having to invent a plausible answer, for at that very moment the King gave a groan, then retched, then threw up all down his gorgeous robes and almost fell sideways from his throne. It was high-backed but had no arms, and only his mother's quick thinking preserved him from the ultimate indignity. She sprang to his aid, while his so-called friends were too fascinated by my dramatic discomfiture to have noticed that his stomach had been troubling him more and more as the interview progressed; his affliction always did get worse when he was unduly anxious or over-wrought. Now his unhealthily flushed cheeks had turned ash-grey, and the lines of tension and pain that scored his brow went slack as he passed out.

Momentarily I feared that Memucan was intending to continue my interrogation with the King slumped unconscious in his mother's arms, and so did she. 'Memucan!' she snapped, as though he were a schoolboy. 'Can you not see that His Majesty is ill? My son must not be subjected to any more of this, do you hear me? Have the Queen confined to her rooms until further enquiries can be made. We shall find this lover of hers without resorting to torture, I think. If her eunuchs are as concerned for her as she would have us believe she is for them, they will tell us his name of their own accord. It will be in their mistress's best interests.'

16

For two whole weeks I was held prisoner in my chambers without seeing anyone except my seven maidservants, Roxana, and the surly soldiers who guarded us but were forbidden to step across my threshold. They were men, not eunuchs; their presence constituted a precedent in the harem, but mine was a unique case, and perhaps eunuchs were considered too weak and soft-hearted—or corruptible—to keep me contained. Eunuchs would have done just as well, as things turned out.

Men or no men, I gave up bathing, and oiling my skin, styling my hair and painting my face and my nails. Farah brought my food: plain, unappetizing fare such as the lowliest palace employees got. I took this as a bad sign.

On the other hand, I was still in possession of the Queen's apartment, so perhaps my prospects weren't necessarily so grim after all? That's how it was with me throughout those fourteen dreadful days: I went over and over what had been said to me in the Apadana, and speculated endlessly about what the King and his agents might be saying or doing about me now, all the time looking for good or bad omens in everything.

I took comfort from the fact that Kshayarsha had seemed so distressed; surely that had to mean he still cared about me? Yet he'd been so ill, too . . . supposing this latest crisis had actually pushed him beyond the point from which recovery was possible? If the unthinkable happened, what would become of me, left at the mercy of the likes of Memucan, Haman and Vashti? I could no longer expect Hutaosa to take my part. And I was quite convinced now that the serenity of character I'd so much admired in her had been the result of fatalism rather than real inner peace. Her religion gave her nothing which Mordecai's hadn't given him.

But what *was* Kshayarsha doing? What was he thinking? If he was merely languishing on his sick-bed, incapable of speech or action, what had Memucan and his worthy colleagues decided to do about my case? It was just possible that they'd decided to do nothing at all, being content to keep me shut up in seclusion for ever with only seven stupid maids and a condemned criminal for company; the mere thought of that made my blood run cold.

In fact, when a week had gone by, I was left with only five of my slave-girls; two of them who were sisters had received word that their grandmother was dying, and begged me to let them go to her. The old woman was a slave too, but in the city somewhere. I gave them leave to join her, and never expected to see them again.

Still, I couldn't really believe that the King's counsellors weren't taking active steps against me. I had visions of their henchmen doing unspeakable things to poor, loyal Hegai and Hathach; yet I was hardly in a position to criticize, after the way I'd treated them myself. I knew I should never forgive myself if they ruined Hegai's beauty, but I was already responsible for breaking his heart, which I had to acknowledge was the viler offence.

Then there were Vashti's machinations to consider. Was it enough for her to have succeeded in destroying my relationship with her husband, or did she want to destroy me entirely? I was in no doubt but that it was she who had collected Mordecai's letters, and written him replies. This explained at least three things which had baffled me: why Mordecai had reputedly enjoyed a period of comparative content-ment at the palace, before he'd succeeded in offending the First Minister; why Iphigenia had been of the firm opinion that Mordecai and I were reconciled; and why Vashti hadn't appeared to be doing much to harm me in all the time I'd been married, beyond unnerving me with spiteful messages and malicious gifts.

Finally, much as I would rather have forgotten all about him, I couldn't do other than fret about Mordecai's fate as well as my own. What would become of him if Kshayarsha *did* identify him as the author of those letters? Was this what Vashti wanted, or not? Quite possibly it was; why else would she have seen to it that my name was connected with Mordecai's at the time of the conspiracy of Bigthana and Teresh? All at once her apparently benevolent interference on that occasion became explicable too.

But would things be any the worse for me if I were suspected of having a Jewish lover rather than one of unknown background? I couldn't imagine how anyone would think me capable of defiling myself with a man as aged and unattractive as His Majesty's Chief Clerk, but stranger things have happened in the harem, where the chance of contact with a fully-equipped male of any description is seized upon with alacrity. If we *were* assumed to be lovers, Haman would experience no difficulty in persuading Kshayarsha to have his mortal enemy executed, King's Benefactor or no.

It was all so ineffably depressing, and all my own fault. I'd made so many impulsive and selfish decisions in my life; I'd compromised every principle with which I'd been brought up, and yet, with cruel irony, I was almost certainly going to die for something of which I was innocent. And there was nothing at all I could do to prevent it. I did once try sending Farah with a message to the King begging him to take pity on me and let me speak with him alone, just once, but she got nowhere near him, and I was gripped by the same frustration which Mordecai must have felt when trying to make contact with me. It got to the stage where I began considering how I might take my own life, for whatever method I chose was sure to be quicker and less agonizing than the one in store for me.

Then on the fifteenth night of my imprisonment I was awoken by a sudden flare of torchlight immediately above me, and by its heat on my face. Dazzled, I gasped and shrank back, shielding my eyes. But when no gruff voice ordered me out of bed and no brutish hands seized hold of my shoulders or clamped themselves about my throat, I dared to look up, and there was Hegai bending over me.

Despite everything which had come between us I might have thrown my arms around him if his face hadn't been so pasty in the vacillating torchlight, and the bags beneath his frightened eyes hadn't been so big or so dark. He held a finger against my lips, but I demanded shrilly, 'Hegai, how did you get in here? You can't imagine how glad I am to see you!'

'Please, my lady, we must be quiet,' he hissed, and I realized that the finger at my lips was trembling. 'I disguised myself, and bribed the night-guards. It cost me dearly, and I must be gone before their shift changes.'

My eyes now being adjusted to the torchlight—he'd hung the brand on the lamp-bracket above my head and sat down on my bed beside me—I drew back and saw that he was dressed like one of my slave-girls, a woman's veil thrown across his tumbling hair. With his down-less cheeks and feminine good looks he carried the costume off well. I moaned, 'Oh God, Hegai, what are we going to do? They will kill me, I know it. I wish I'd never come to this evil city. I should have run away into the desert when they tried to bring me here... Why didn't you come to me earlier? I've been so afraid.'

My voice was rising; again he hushed me, then said, 'My lady, I'm sorry. I couldn't get away... where I've been working, no one trusted me out of their sight until these past few days...' He faltered, reflecting I suppose that they would never trust him again if he were found here, and the gods alone knew what would become of him. But I was too wrapped up in my own self-pity to offer him any consolation. He cleared his throat and said, 'Besides, I had no news to give you until now. But I've heard things, and I know they're *not* going to kill you; not yet, anyway. That's why I came: to allay your fears, my lady.'

'I don't understand. Has Kshayarsha found out that Mordecai was just my guardian? Does he believe I've been faithful to him after all?'

'He has no idea that Mordecai has anything to do with all this.'

'You mean he still doesn't know who wrote those letters? I don't believe it.'

'He hasn't found out because he doesn't want to. No one has so much as questioned me, or Hathach.'

'He's too ill to care. That's it, isn't it? I knew it. He's going to die.'

'He's kept to his bed these last fourteen days, my lady, it's true, but they say he's more depressed than sick. He's in despair at the thought that you could have betrayed him. His counsellors are at their wits' end with him, begging him either to execute you or to give permission for you to be formally tried. But he keeps telling them to wait until he is better, lest he make the wrong decision. And I think he is afraid of what a formal investigation may turn up.'

'Why should he be afraid? He's already convinced I'm an adulteress. Why should it be any worse for him to learn the name of my lover?'

'I don't think he *is* convinced any more, my lady. Your reaction to Memucan's accusations upset him badly. They say he fears that you may have been unjustly accused, but that an investigation may unearth some *other* dreadful secret about your past which he isn't ready to face. He's confused, and not well enough to sort things out in his mind. At least he *realizes* that; we ought to be grateful.'

I whispered, 'So what will happen? Will he keep me captive here for ever? Hegai, I couldn't abide it. I should go mad.'

'I don't know what will happen, my lady.'

'Can't *you* talk to him?'

'With Haman hovering around him like a bad smell all the time, and the pouting Ashpamithra? I might as well try to steal the crown jewels.'

'Then how have you found out so much about Kshayarsha's state of mind, if you haven't been able to go near him?'

'You forget; I have been working in the harem. Its walls have eyes and mouths as well as ears. You can learn anything from anyone at a price. And one thing I've learnt is that Haman has bewitched the King so completely now, he can make him do anything he wants.'

'But surely Haman is worried about Kshayarsha's condition? Doesn't *he* want the issue resolved? If anything happened to Kshayarsha, Haman wouldn't last two minutes.'

'Perhaps. But he's not so worried that he'd want you reclaiming your place at his dear lord's side, any more than he'd want Vashti reinstated there. And that's if he truly appreciates how important Kshayarsha is to him, and hasn't come to regard him simply as another obstacle to be overcome on his road to real power.'

'*What?* You think Haman desires to be King in Kshayarsha's place? Hegai, you must be as mad as I'm going to become. *No* one would back his claim. He isn't even a Persian, let alone of Hakhamanish blood.'

'True enough, but that won't be how he sees it. He's growing used to the sight of august courtiers grovelling on their pointed Persian noses in the dust whenever he walks past. No doubt he supposes they are starting to accord him the respect in their hearts which they indicate with their buckled knees and upturned backsides.'

Just then the torch he'd hung above my bed began to sputter, and made him jump. He said, 'I must go now, my lady. I came only to reassure you, and that I have done as best I can. It's not safe to stay any longer.'

'Hegai, don't leave me! I've been so lonely,' I implored him. And when he rose adamantly from the bed, and lifted the torch from its bracket, I added, 'I've missed you especially.'

It made him hesitate, but only for a moment, because he could see quite clearly that this was no more than a ruse to delay his departure, rather than a genuine attempt on my part to restore the warmth to our friendship. He said, 'Goodbye, my lady. I shall come again if I can.' And he was gone.

I lay on my back, peering blindly up into the darkness which gathered about me again once the light he'd brought with him had disappeared. My own tiny lamp was alight, yet so feeble was its flame that the night seemed to mock it. It occurred to me then that I didn't even know what Hegai was going back to; perhaps he had to peel vegetables all day long in the harem kitchens, or scour pans, or empty out latrines. I ought to have asked him about his circumstances, and I ought to have reimbursed him for what he'd spent on bribing my guards. I hadn't even thanked him for risking his life to come and see me. But I hadn't thought, and now it was too late.

I didn't expect to see Hegai again after that; at least, not for a very long while. In the event, he returned in broad daylight just before noon the following morning, with Hathach in tow.

The latter appeared prodigiously flustered. For some reason I couldn't at first make out, he was desperate to see me; by contrast, Hegai looked wan and haggard, and as though he heartily wished he could have stayed away. Both were dressed in the unpretentious garb of the ordinary harem eunuchs, having made no attempt to effect a disguise. Since they no longer possessed enough ready money between them to offer my guards an inducement worthy of consideration, they hadn't thought the measure worthwhile. All they'd been able to do was come openly and ask to see me, not expecting for a moment that they'd be allowed to. However, the captain of the morning shift had turned out to be a man who owed Hegai a substantial favour from the past.

I hustled the pair of them into my apartment, but strove to persuade them to leave at once before we all got into trouble; heartened by what Hegai had said to me the previous night, I now felt that once again I had something to lose. Hathach, however, fell to his knees at my feet and pressed my hand to his lips, babbling, 'Your Majesty, something terrible has happened, but I don't know what it is.'

'Come, come, Hathach, you will have to do better than that. You might at least talk sense.'

'Your Majesty—it's Mordecai ben Jair from the Treasury, your father's friend who used to want to speak to you all the time—'

'Well, what about him?' I interrupted, suddenly seized by foreboding. 'Hegai, do *you* know what all this is about?'

'Only what Hathach has told me, my lady. Mordecai is sitting outside the palace gates wailing like a demoniac, dressed in torn sackcloth and heaping dust on his head.'

'But why? What can it mean?' Alternatives were already chasing one another through my head, every one concerned with my own predicament and what the King might have learnt or decided concerning me. Neither Hegai nor Hathach knew the answer to my question; but according to Hathach, Mordecai had spent most of the morning going up and down the streets of Shushan crying woe after the fashion of some deranged prophet, and had now ensconced himself outside the gates because no one wearing sackcloth is allowed inside the palace complex unless a member of the royal family has died.

I said to Hathach, 'And what was the point of your coming here to tell me this if you haven't troubled yourself to discover the *cause* of the madman's behaviour? Go and find out; take him clean clothes so he can come inside the gates and stop making a scene, but don't tell him who sent them. See to it that you return here to me as soon as you've spoken to him.'

Hathach bobbed and bowed and scurried away, though the assignment I'd given him was fraught with difficulties, not the least of which would be regaining admission to my presence once the guards' shift had changed. But Hegai didn't go with him. As soon as Hathach was out of earshot he ran up and fell at my feet just as his companion had done. In all the time I'd been at the palace I couldn't recall him ever doing that.

'My lady, I didn't think I should say this while Hathach was here. I wasn't lying when I said I didn't know the cause of Mordecai's behaviour, because I couldn't see how he could have found out about this already. But I believe that Haman has made up his mind to destroy the Jewish people utterly.'

I threw back my head and laughed brittly. 'What? Throughout the city? He couldn't possibly do it. There are hundreds of them; maybe thousands.'

'Oh, my lady, I don't think it's only Shushan he's decided to purge. It's the whole Empire.'

The notion struck me as too preposterous even to be amusing. 'And how does he propose to do that, when there are Jewish communities in almost every province which the Persians took over from Babylon? Some of them have been established for a century at least. You *have* gone mad, Hegai, haven't you? Did you dream all this last night?'

'No, my lady. I didn't dream it. I was—drinking. With some of the other boys from the harem.' He and his kind always called themselves boys, never eunuchs, though some were old enough to be grandfathers.

I laughed again. 'So that explains the dark rings under your eyes. Two weeks away from me, and you have become a frothblower. And here I was, worrying that you might have been having a hard time of it . . .'

I left off then, chastened by the intensity of the anger and reproach in his eyes. I was still more abashed when he told me straight out that things *had* been hard; in his brief career at the palace he'd now been spectacularly demoted twice, and everybody knew it. Still, it meant that few people were jealous of him these days, and gradually his lowly new colleagues were accepting him; enough to share their wine with him when the day's chores were completed. Lingering over their cups they would chat about their lives and their loves; some had admirers among Kshayarsha's concubines, others among his male friends. And one or two who were comelier than the average had attracted the attention of Haman himself, and become closer to the King's First Minister than they ought to have been. They liked to flaunt this dubious symbol of status in front of their companions, and relished passing on snippets of classified information which they picked up at their lord's private dinner parties.

I whispered, 'And you were drinking with this crowd last night, after you left here? Whatever hour was it when you got to bed?'

'I went to bed as soon as I got back to the harem, my lady, but I couldn't sleep. There was too much noise. One of the boys had had a birthday and spent the evening with Haman and his cronies; he'd just got back and his friends were waiting up for him. I think they had one or two birthday surprises lined up. But he wasn't as surprised as they were when he told them what he'd overheard. Some of them are Jews, you see; or at least, they say they were until they came here. My lady, they are terrified.'

'Hegai, tell me what the boy said, the one who'd been with Haman. Tell me exactly.'

'I can't tell you exactly. He was drunk, and pretty frightened himself. But he said Haman had been almost too slewed to stand, and certainly too far gone to watch what he was saying. He'd climbed up on a table and was lurching and swaying, boasting that he could make Kshayarsha eat out of his hand like a horse. Someone put a chair on the table, just behind his knees—I think they were concerned he was going to fall—and he sat on it with a pomegranate in one hand and a staff in the other, pretending he was King with the lotus and sceptre. All his guests were prostrating themselves, and his ten sons were there shouting, "Hail, Haman, true ruler of Persia," and "The honour of Agag of Amalek is retored." It was when they said that, that Haman started boasting about how he was going to reverse all that the wicked King Saul of Israel had done; how he was going to wipe out the nation which had tried to destroy his own. He called upon everyone present to drink a toast to the extermination of the Jews, for he had that very afternoon prevailed upon Kshayarsha to agree to it.'

I felt faint. 'Kshayarsha would never agree to such a thing. He knows that the Jews are an influential and well-respected people. He knows that Kurash and Darayavaush deemed them worthy of special honour.'

'In truth, my lady, I'm not sure that Kshayarsha knew or cared what he was agreeing to. But resentment of the Jews is rife in Shushan according to those boys who have reliable contacts outside the palace; Haman has whipped it up himself. Mordecai is no madman, I fear, my lady. And he no doubt had friends at Haman's party, just as I did.'

There was nothing I could say. Nor was there anything I could do, save waiting for Hathach to reappear and confirm all that Hegai had said. This duly happened, towards sunset; the guards' shift had changed and changed again, and Hegai's ally was once more on duty. Hathach brought back the clothes I'd sent for Mordecai to put on, for they'd been rejected—an irony, when they constituted the only genuine and kindly gesture he'd had from me in all his time at the Treasury.

In short, all that Hegai had said appeared to be true, and more and worse besides. Kshayarsha, although apparently no longer confined to his bed, was showing less and less interest in affairs of state by the day, and Haman in the meantime was appropriating more and more of the Sovereign's responsibilities for himself. Allegedly he was now in possession of the King's own seal ring; Kshayarsha had given it to him so he could issue a public proclamation to the effect that on the thirteenth day of Adar, all members of the accursed Hebrew sect were to be put to death. Haman had drawn lots himself—over Passover, too, another irony—to determine the most auspicious date for the slaughter to take place. His loathsome gods had chosen my own birthday—of all ironies, surely the ultimate.

'Get me wine, Hegai,' I stammered; he'd been with me all day, for I'd been too distressed to want to be alone, or for him to feel he ought to allow it. It hadn't occurred to me to worry that he might be missed in the harem, and that his his new employer Shaashgaz might send someone to look for him. Turning to Hathach I asked weakly, 'Has the proclamation been made?'

'Yes, my lady. Notices have been posted in the market at Shushan already, and imperial couriers have taken copies to every satrap and governor and city council in the Empire. Translations are to be put up in public places. All Jews are to die: every man, woman and child, and all Aryans are expected to assist in the operation. Businessmen are to kill or hand over their partners; husbands or wives in mixed marriages are to hand over their spouses, and children their former playmates. Haman has guaranteed to pay ten thousand talents of silver into the Royal Treasury when the purging is accomplished, to the glory of Ahura Mazda. Ten thousand talents of *Jewish* silver, I don't doubt— the property of those he's doomed to destruction.' Hathach bowed his head, suddenly grief-stricken. 'A new Chief Clerk will have to weigh it in.'

'As if Kshayarsha needed silver,' I said, between clenched teeth.

'Oh but he does, my lady, desperately. He has won no foreign wars in the whole of his reign, and has added no new territory to his domains, from which booty could have been seized. In fact he has lost cities and islands which used to pay him tribute; they've seceded to the League of Greeks.'

While he was speaking I'd almost dropped the goblet of wine Hegai had brought to me. Hegai steadied my hands with his own, and I laced my fingers into his and wouldn't let go. Hathach discreetly begged leave to depart, saying he hadn't eaten all day. I waved him away, but made Hegai stay; he raised the cup to my lips, my own hands still entwined in his around it, and asked what I was going to do.

'Do?' I choked. 'What *can* I do? If I breathe a word to anyone, they'll find out I'm Jewish too. Oh Hegai, I thought I was ready to die, my life has become so hateful to me. But I'm not. Not like this. I cannot believe such a thing could happen.'

'Oh, it could, my lady. Something like it already *has* happened, when the magus Gaumata usurped the throne after the death of Kambujet. Gaumata was assassinated, and every Persian citizen was specially licensed by Darayavaush to take up weapons and slaughter any magus he could find before sunset. Only the fall of darkness prevented the entire caste from being wiped out.'

I said, 'Don't lecture me, Hegai. All this is bad enough already.'

'You should get some sleep, my lady. I should go.'

'No, please . . . They'll never let you in here again once you get out. You don't know who will be captain of the guard tomorrow.'

'You—want me to stay the night here? Shaashgaz—'

'I don't *want* it. I command it.'

He obeyed me—once I'd sworn my female attendants to secrecy on pain of death—and lay on a couch at the foot of my bed because I wouldn't let him out of my sight. It was as well that he did, because three times in the night he had to wake me from hideous dreams, and it was so much better somehow to be woken by him than by Farah.

Would that I could have stayed awake too. Then I shouldn't have had to endure the ordeal of my family being butchered all over again, this time with me standing there watching, even conniving at what was taking place.

In the morning Hathach got word to me that he'd seen Mordecai again, and the latter had pleaded passionately with him to use his influence with me so the dire proclamation might be rescinded.

Hathach couldn't bring me this message himself, for the guard was indeed captained by a stranger, and one who looked about as approachable as his ceramic counterparts on the glazed tile walls. But the two slave-girls I'd released to wait upon their dying grandmother returned unexpectedly, bearing a package from Hathach in which a tablet and a roll of papyrus were hidden beneath a tray of sweetmeats; and the girls said that all Shushan was in a state of shock. The proclamation about some group of dissidents known as the Hebrews had caused universal consternation, and Mordecai was not the only man who had taken to the streets, beating his breast and smearing ash upon his brow.

I said to Hegai, 'Read me what is written on the tablet, and the scroll. My eyes hurt, and the words would dance in front of them.'

He broke open the tablet and read: *Your Majesty Queen Esther, from Hathach your obedient servant; greetings. I was approached early this morning by an apprentice clerk from the Treasury, asking me to meet Mordecai ben Jair at the main gate. I went, Your Majesty, concluding that the instruction you gave me yesterday, to find out from him what I could, must supercede your previous directive that I should keep out of his way and receive nothing from him. So I hope I have done right in sending you the scroll which he gave me; if not, please forgive me. He says he cannot understand how his people's plight can have been worsening by the day when he has written to you so often concerning it, and you've sent him so many such positive replies, offering assurance that the persecutions would soon come to an end. He fears that it is in reality his very race which you want to see brought to an end. If you would be so generous as to send him a reply today, our captain is taking the afternoon shift; I shall come to you then. Farewell.*

'And the scroll? What does it say on the scroll?'

'I don't know, my lady.' Hegai shook his head and bit his lip as he pored over it; then he said, 'I think it's in Hebrew.'

I snatched it from him, pressing my fingers to my eyelids to ease the aching and make my eyes home in on the letters. It was so long since I'd read any Hebrew, at first I thought I should glean little more from it than Hegai had done. Then as the words came back to me, I realized it was nothing other than a translation of the imperial proclamation.

Kshayarsha the Great King, the King of Kings, Emperor of Persia and Media, Lord of Lands, to the satraps and governors of our provinces, from India to Cush, and to their subordinate functionaries:

Sovereign as we are over many nations and rightful master of all the world, it is our will—not in the arrogance of power, but because our rule is benign and just—to ensure for our subjects a life permanently free from disturbance, to pacify our Empire and render it safe to travel to its uttermost limits, and to safeguard the peace that all good men cherish. We asked our noble counsellors how this objective might best be achieved, and received a persuasive response from Haman son of Hammadatha. Haman is eminent among us for sound judgment, one whose worthiness is proven by his constant goodwill and unflinching loyalty, and who has by his own merit attained the honour of second place at court.

He represented to us that scattered among all the many races of our Empire is a disaffected faction, whose laws and values are diametrically opposed to those of any other nation and cause its members continually to disregard our royal ordinances, so that our superlative plans for the unified administration of our Empire cannot be made fully effective. We understand that this faction stands alone in its antagonism towards all other men, that it denigrates our laws by its bizarre manner of life, and in

its recalcitrant attitude toward our government commits heinous offences,
thus undermining the security of our domains.

We therefore order that those who are identified as members of this sect
in the indictments drawn up by Haman our viceregent shall all, together
with their wives and children, be eliminated by the swords of their enemies,
without mercy or pity, on the thirteenth day of Adar, the twelfth month of
the present year. Those persons who have long been seditious shall meet a
violent end on a single day, so that our government may henceforth be
stable and equitable.

I let the scroll drop from my hands; it rolled itself up on the floor at
my feet. The tranquil, dispassionate polish of the diplomatic language
made the systematic destruction of the Jewish people into something
horribly possible rather than frankly inconceivable; though despite
what Hathach had said earlier, the proclamation still didn't mention
Jewry by name. It didn't need to; everyone would know who its target
was—everyone excepting, apparently, Kshayarsha. By now he and
Haman would be celebrating together, with the gullible King happy
to think he was doing the best for Persia, for Ahura Mazda, and for the
eternal glory of his own name.

Looking neither at the scroll nor at Hegai, I said in a small, distant
voice, 'Mordecai *never* wrote to me concerning the plight of his people.
I never responded positively; I never responded at all, and offered him
no assurances. There was nothing about such things, even in the letters
which Vashti passed on to Memucan.'

'Then she must still have them, my lady. Perhaps she intends to
produce them at a later date and render your situation worse than it is
now. If Kshayarsha is not prepared to have you impaled on grounds of
adultery alone, Vashti will make sure that he learns of your involve-
ment with the Hebrews whom he is sworn to destroy; she may even
have proof that you are one of them. But she is not the kind to display
all her gemstones in one exhibition.'

I said, 'I'll have to tell Mordecai the truth. When Hathach comes
here this afternoon ... I'll have to send him to tell my cousin I received
none of his letters, and that because of his persistence in trying to reach
me I'm in disgrace with the King. *All* of this is Mordecai's fault, not
mine.'

So I tried; Hathach appeared just before sunset, and I tried to make
him return to Mordecai at once and inform him that this was the first
genuine contact there had been between us since my coming to the

palace, and that it would most certainly be the last. But Hathach bowed low before me again, and implored me, 'Don't tell him that, Your Majesty, I beg of you. He must be relying on you to save his people. He can have no other hope.'

'How many times must I say this? There is *nothing* I can do. *Nothing!*' I swept up the scroll, which had still been lying on the floor, and brandished it in front of Hathach's face. 'This is an Imperial proclamation! It is irrevocable! Not even Kshayarsha himself can retract what has been published in his name. Hathach: you *must* tell Mordecai that I am out of favour with the King and if there is any hope of redemption for his people, it does not lie with me. I cannot leave my own rooms; I cannot even send Kshayarsha a message. And even if I *could* leave here, I should have no right to appear before him in the Apadana without being invited. Only as his principal wife could I do that without risking death; I'm not sure that I rank as his wife at all any more, since it is almost a month since he sent for me. He would *never* raise the sceptre for me, after what he thinks I've done. And Artabanush would be putting his *own* life at risk if he agreed to admit to the King's presence a woman who had expressly been banished from it. Hathach, you *have* to make Mordecai understand that things are not as he imagines they are.'

'Your Majesty, he will not take it well. He's an old man; his suffering has *made* him old. Even his eyesight is failing him. I have seen—'

'Hathach, by *God* I'll have you flayed alive if you dare to argue with me again! Do as I tell you! Do it *now!*'

'Very well, Your Majesty. If that is your wish.'

'It most certainly *is*!'

Hathach gulped, nodded, bowed, and ran to do my bidding. I rounded on Hegai, and shouting 'What are *you* staring at?' I stormed into my bedroom and threw myself on the bed.

No one came near me until after dark, when Farah, Hathach and Hegai approached me all together. Farah said that the captain of the guard had been to the door and instructed her to tell me that some boys had come from Shaashgaz, seeking Hegai; our captain had assured them that he hadn't been here, but thought he should warn me that they might return sooner or later with a warrant to search my quarters.

I winced, understanding full well what the captain was risking for us, and that we'd no means of knowing how deeply his allegiance towards us ran, or at what point he would deem his debt to Hegai repaid in full. I tried to catch Hegai's eye, but he looked away, as though by denying the existence of the threat he might rob it of its power. And as for Hathach, it was another thing entirely which had caused him to risk visiting me yet again. He ventured timidly, 'Your Majesty, my lady... I went to Mordecai and spoke to him as you commanded. But he gave me something else to pass on to you.'

'I want to hear *nothing* more from that man! By my own mother's sacred memory, Hathach... will he never give up? Will *you* never give up?'

'My lady, it isn't a letter; at least, it's not *only* a letter. It's a gift of some sort. Look.' And when like Hegai I attempted to turn away in denial, Hathach added, 'He has promised it is the last thing he will ever send you, unless you yourself permit him to do otherwise.'

Exceedingly irritated, and yet intrigued in spite of myself, I turned over again to look at him. In the soft lamplight the two eunuchs' anxious faces each seemed more feminine than masculine, like the faces of midwives around their mistress's childbed. Hathach had a parcel in his arms, just about the size of a newborn baby; he bent down and laid it beside me.

For a while I did nothing but gaze at it, wanting and yet not wanting to know what was inside. Then I gave in to my curiosity, sitting up and loosening the tapes that bound it. The cloth wrappings fell away to reveal a plain wooden box, with an open tablet fixed to its lid.

The tablet read in Hebrew: *Hadassah. Don't imagine that you are safer than any other Jew simply because you are a member of the royal household. If you remain silent at this critical hour, you may be assured that the Lord your God will find a means of preserving a remnant of his holy nation without your assistance. Saul was Adonai's anointed servant, yet when he turned his back on the God who chose him, Israel survived, and went on to prosper against all odds. But Saul himself died in anguish, and thus you will die, rejected by your Creator just as Saul was, if you choose to reject your own people. Not only that, but if you die now without issue, Saul's line will thereby be cut off for ever. Condoning a crime is no better than committing it, my daughter, and unless you act now, you will be the cause of the deaths of many thousands of people. It may be that God had a purpose in making you Queen of Persia after all.—Mordecai.*

'What does he say?' Hegai asked eagerly, then seeing the horror on my face he whispered, 'Is he threatening to denounce you?'

Perhaps he was; but that wasn't what I found so appallingly shocking. Nor was it his bald manner of address, with no greeting nor any valediction, nor even his blatant use of my Hebrew name. No; it was his quoting of the prophecy of the old Arderikkan soothsayer, word for word, when I had never so much as hinted at that aspect of it on the day he'd prayed for me; at least, I hadn't done so when conscious.

Hathach prompted me gently, 'What about the box, Your Majesty? Don't forget about that. Shall I help you undo it?'

But I simply shook my head slowly as though in a trance, and my fingers began to loosen the hasp as though they didn't belong to me. All at once I knew what was inside before I got it open, for I realized I'd seen the box before: it was Saul's old knife with its tarnished blade, and empty sockets where jewels should have been.

However, there was something else in the box along with it, wrapped up separately from the knife. I tore away the coverings, and it was the necklace my mother had given me, repaired as good as new, all polished and shining.

If I'd seemed entranced before, I was utterly paralyzed now. Somewhere a long way off Hathach was asking me whether he should go to Mordecai again, and what he should say; I heard Hegai tell him to leave us, and a decision would be made in due course. Someone else was babbling incoherently about prophecies and predictions, loyalty and betrayal, birthdays and deathdays, hopelessness and faith; it was a long while before I grasped that the someone else was me.

Then there were other voices in the background: other women's voices, shrill and frightened like my own, wanting to know what was the matter with the Queen; was she sick? Hegai said, 'Farah, go away, and take the others with you. Please.' His voice was no longer in the distance, but close, almost as though it came from inside my own head, and I realized he was supporting me in his arms, for I felt as weak as a cobweb. I mumbled, 'Hegai, you go away too. There's nothing you can do. I know what I have to do, and I'll do it alone. Pass me the knife; I know why Mordecai sent it.'

Naturally he refused; although he had no idea what Mordecai had written to me, he said he was quite sure my cousin didn't mean me to use the knife on myself. He had his hand so tight around the hilt that I couldn't prize any one of his long thin fingers away from it. I shrieked, '*Give* me the knife, Hegai; *give* it to me, that's an *order!*' and I beat against his chest with my fists, but to no avail. He clamped his free hand over half my face so I couldn't scream, then hurled away the knife so as to be better able to restrain me. Even so, there were scratches all down his cheeks and arms before I exhausted myself and slumped against him, crying silent tears of desperation into his neck.

I'm still not sure what it was that began from there to turn everything inside out in my soul. Perhaps it was the thought of Saul's rusty knife lying discarded and probably broken in a corner, the only thing left to remind me I'd once been a daughter of that ancient, briefly glorious dynasty. Perhaps it was my mother's necklace, which, despite the firm tone of the letter accompanying it, was surely sent as a symbol of Mordecai's repentance, an acknowledgement that he'd been wrong to seek to deprive me of my parents' memory, and to impose his rigid asceticism on a grieving and sensitive child. Perhaps it was Hegai's disconcerting loyalty, his willingness to risk what little he still had on my behalf, when for years I'd treated him like dirt. Perhaps it was nothing more nor less than the spirit of Adonai, which had lain dormant within me since childhood, quenched by my rebellious pride yet now set free because I'd journeyed to the end of myself and found nothing but despair.

But whatever was the cause of it, something began to well up inside me like the first bubbles rising when milk is boiled; I wept, 'I'm sorry, Hegai . . . Tammuz. I'm sorry for everything,' and it was so long since I'd called him by his pet name that he fell to weeping too. Our tears began to wash away all the tension between us just as the first rains clear the summer dust from trees and grasses. It was like the time when we had stood on my balcony in the House of the Virgins, laughing like lovers in the downpour, before I'd been married and so much had come between us.

As I sobbed against his neck, Hegai was trying to say how sorry he was, too, for shutting me out of his heart when the time had come for me to be taken from him and presented to Kshayarsha; Hegai had loved me so wildly, so futilely, he'd known no other way to protect himself. I said, 'It doesn't matter any more. None of that matters,' and he said indeed that was true; it was too late to worry about anything, for all my people were going to die, and so, most probably, were both of us.

'No, Tammuz. You don't understand. This isn't the end. Everything is coming clear to me now; I feel as though a storm has blown up,
and cleared all the haze and heaviness from the air. Something is just
beginning, being born right down inside me. Adonai has come.'

Hegai stared at me, nonplussed, but what was happening to me was
too strange, too miraculous for me to explain in a way he could have
understood. Though I wasn't conscious of having got up out of bed, or
of having moved at all, I found myself kneeling on the floor with my
forehead pressed on the tiles and arms outstretched as though
Kshayarsha himself stood before me, but it was no mortal king for
whom I was making my prostration.

And as I knelt, it was as though all my selfishness, all my rebellion, all
my anger began to flow out of me, and a love so enveloping, so
overwhelming fell upon me in its place that I seemed to be pinned to
the ground. I became oblivious of everything around me, yet acutely
aware of myself in a way I'd never known before. It was as though I were
looking at myself through the very eyes of Adonai; I saw that all my
loathing of Mordecai had sprung from my resentment toward the God
who had allowed my family to be destroyed. Although I no more knew
now than I had then why such a desperate tragedy should have befallen
my loved ones rather than anyone else's, I did know with awesome
certainty that Adonai was King of the Universe, and that in struggling
against him I'd denied myself access to a father far stronger, wiser and
kinder than the one I'd lost. I'd scoffed at the Laws of Moses, poured
ridicule on the traditions of my own people, hurt everyone I'd ever had
dealings with; but in all of it, the person I'd hurt most was myself. I'd
been a spoilt, self-seeking child who'd grown up into a spoilt, self-
seeking woman, and none of the things I'd wanted and procured for
myself had brought me any real happiness.

Yet even as I recognized myself for what I was, I knew that it was all
changing. The evil which had insinuated itself so early into my soul
was withering up and falling away. Its root had been severed, and free
of its crippling stranglehold, my spirit was coming alive. I discovered
that I was laughing now more than I was crying, and though I was
lying almost prone on the hard marble floor, I felt for all the world as
though I lay on a finely woven carpet, whose weft was the love of
Adonai, and whose warp was the endless thread of prayer which
Mordecai had offered up for so many years on my behalf. Yes, he'd
had his faults, just as my parents and their Pioneer friends had had

theirs. Yet Mordecai *had* somehow loved me, just as they had, and his faith in Adonai was equally real, and much more powerful, because it was grounded in a genuine personal experience of the divine. Now I was experiencing that very same thing myself, and all because Mordecai had steadfastly refused to give up on me; I knew that it wasn't so much for our people's sake that he'd pursued me, as for mine.

Momentarily I was assailed by guilt, and by a sense of shame so oppressive I feared its burden would crush me. But then the guilt and shame too were washed away on the tide of love which buoyed me up and rolled me in its foaming surf; I lay on my back floating in the joy of Adonai's presence, never wanting to get up, because, in comparison with this, the ecstasy I'd known in bodily union with Kshayarsha was like the pale luminescence of the moon which is rendered invisible by the coming of the dawn.

I've no idea how long the experience lasted, nor what brought it to an end. But presently I grew aware once again of the ornately moulded ceiling above me, the lamplight and the shadows, the hardness of the floor; and Hegai's face staring down at me, his eyes liquid with wonder, terror and perplexity. He saw that I'd returned, and he seemed desperate to speak, to ask me what had happened and whether I was all right. Yet he couldn't bring himself to shatter the sacred silence, and though his lips were parted no words came from them until I said, 'Don't be frightened, Tammuz. But I'm the one who should be called by that name now. It's I who have been reborn.'

He whispered, 'Esther, your face... I've never seen you look so beautiful.'

'So the story is true.'

'What story?'

'That when Moses came down from Mount Sinai where he met with God, his face was so radiant the people couldn't bear to look at him. That's why he was known as a Shining One: he, and Saul, and David, and Solomon; all those who have met with Adonai. And to think I once fancied I belonged to their number already because my parents were of the Remnant.'

Hegai had little but the dimmest notion of what I was talking about. He'd known that Adonai was regarded somehow differently from the gods of pagan nations and even from Ahura Mazda, but like so many people he imagined that religion had to do with temples and priests and rituals, and that union with God was not something which could be attained in the privacy of one's own bedroom. I said, 'I have to pray now, Tammuz. I have to find out what Adonai wants me to do to help my people.'

'But it must be past midnight; you need to sleep. There's nothing you can do before morning.' He caught his breath, meaning: there's nothing you can do at all, surely. Nothing has changed.

I said softly, '*Everything* has changed, Tammuz. I can do whatever is required of me. And it's *you* who need to sleep. Those rings around your eyes weren't put there with a kohl-brush.' I got up from the floor and smoothed out the covers on the great high bed which Kshayarsha had had made specially for me. 'You can sleep here till daybreak; I'll see that no one finds you. I shan't be needing to lie down.'

He tried to protest, but was all but asleep on his feet already; a mixture of anxiety and a fortnight's hard work of a kind he wasn't used to had worn him out, and now the fatigue had caught up with him. I helped him take off his turban, and when his glorious mane of hair fell free I combed it out for him the way he'd been used to combing mine. He closed his eyes while I worked, and although his head drooped from exhaustion, his eyelids quivered for quite another reason. I hugged him, wishing there was some way I could share with him what I'd found, but convinced it was impossible because a gelding could have no place in the Kingdom of God. I comforted myself with the knowledge that the rekindling of our friendship had given him peace enough to sleep, if nothing else; for even as I held him his head nodded forward onto my shoulder and I didn't have to struggle to get him to bed.

Then I knelt on the floor nearby, my own eyes closed and my palms upturned in my lap, and gave myself once more to communion with Adonai. Only this time I didn't weep or laugh; I prayed aloud, sometimes in the Aramaic I spoke every day, sometimes in the Hebrew I'd grown up with, and sometimes in words I didn't even know, which were torn from the secret depths of my spirit whose sighs and groans no human language can express. It all seemed so simple, so natural, like flying in a dream, when you find yourself wondering why you have never accomplished such an easy and exhilarating feat before. I think perhaps it is always like this for those who are newly reborn; it is later that the struggling comes.

The longer I stayed there, the stronger I felt, and the more certain that everything *had* changed. For although I was still a prisoner of my apartment, in all likelihood about to be sentenced to death if I hadn't been already, I felt freer and more in control of my own destiny than I ever had in the past. When I'd left Jerusalem as an orphaned child in the care of Sarah and Judah, Judah had said I'd been spared for a purpose; now I was about to fulfil it.

Presently there was light beyond my closed eyelids, and this was no inner vision, but the rising of the next day's sun. I blinked and struggled to my feet, only now discovering that my knees ached like fury and my feet and ankles were numb. Hegai still slept, but he moaned a little with every breath and there was the hint of a frown about the bridge of his nose. I laid a hand on his brow and stroked back his hair; he woke at once.

I said, 'Tammuz, we must find out who is on guard this morning, and if it's safe you must go back to the harem at once. It's not right for me to keep you here. I *do* know what I have to do now, and you needn't be afraid for me. It doesn't involve Saul's knife.'

But he made no move to rise. He didn't even ask what my decision involved, nor how I'd reached it. I told him anyway.

'I must pray and fast for three days, and instruct Mordecai to gather the Jews of Shushan together and do the same. After that, I shall walk out of here straight past the guards and defy them to lay a finger on me. I shall go to the Apadana when Kshayarsha and his court are in session, and tell him everything; everything I've kept from him since we were married. Then he will understand, and he'll believe me when I tell him that the people Haman is resolved to destroy have done the House of Hakhamanish no harm.'

No doubt my new-found faith came across as naivety; but I *did* think Kshayarsha would believe me. Hegai didn't, however. He just lay there and looked at me, but as the drowsiness left him and he perceived the intensity of my expression, he sat up, seized my hands and blurted, 'Oh Esther, no!' All the misery and fear bottled up inside him gushed out in a torrent, the pitch of his unbroken treble voice rising higher and higher as he forgot to control it. Most of what he said was barely coherent, but what he meant was clear enough. For so long, our friendship had been like the smoking cinders left behind when a fire has gone out; but last night we'd fanned the dying embers and once again he'd begun to hope I truly cared for him.

'I *do* care,' I protested. 'That's why I must send you back. I've kept you here because I was lonely; it was wrong of me. You must take gold in return for the bribe you paid the guards, and go back to Shaashgaz.'

But Hegai wailed all the louder, maintaining that he'd be punished dreadfully if he reappeared now; I implored him to consider what might happen if he didn't. He said, 'The captain of the guard won't betray me, Esther, I know it. If he did, they would only ask him how he came to let me get in here in the first place. The only hope for him *or* me is to keep our secret. And the only hope for *you* is to wait and see if Kshayarsha decides to pardon you; if he does, you can plead for your people then. Please, Little Star, please don't try to go to him. You'll be arrested as soon as you step outside your door, and you'll be killed.'

He let go my hands, and buried his face in his own; at such moments it was all too evident that his emotions were more like those of a woman than a man, just as his voice was. But there was enough of the man in him to be vainly in love with me still.

I said softly, 'And just how *long* would you have me wait here and hope? Until all my people are dead? I thought you and Hathach and Iphigenia all *wanted* me to do something? Tammuz, if you love me you must not stand in my way now.'

'Mordecai told you that your Adonai could save his people whether you got involved or not! And don't pretend he didn't. I heard too many of your prayers last night; they kept waking me. I heard what you said.'

'Adonai will always find a way to preserve a remnant of his people, that's true. But why should thousands of innocent individuals die in the process? That's what will happen if I don't obey him, and I couldn't live with that. When I was a child, a Greek soothsayer told me I should one day cause the deaths of thousands, and I can't let it happen. Not after last night.'

As long as I had been weak and afraid, Hegai had had to be strong for both of us, but now that I'd discovered a fresh source of strength within myself, he was going to pieces. He sobbed, 'Why should you pay any heed to the ravings of a pagan witchwoman? I thought the heathen gods were idols to you, no more than faggots of firewood or lumps of quernstone.'

'So they are, Tammuz, so they are. But behind their lifeless images evil forces are at work, evil powers who *do* sometimes know the future because they have stolen that knowledge from God himself. It isn't *right* for us to know our own futures, except in so far as Adonai wishes to reveal them to us. We should place ourselves in God's hands, and if he chooses us as his vessels we should be thankful.'

'Let Adonai choose someone else. You've suffered enough already.'

'And if his second choice fails him, and his third? It won't be thousands that die then, it may be tens or hundreds of thousands! Suppose Moses had rejected God's call, or insisted that he choose someone else? The Jews might still be slaving away making bricks for the Pharaohs! Moses was the only man who could have achieved what he achieved, because he was the only Hebrew who'd held high rank at the Pharaoh's court. And I'm the only Hebrew who can get near to Kshayarsha.'

'But *you* won't achieve *anything*, can't you see? If you *do* get to speak to Kshayarsha, as soon as you admit you've been deceiving him left, right and centre ever since he laid eyes on you he'll hate you worse than ever. He's a devotee of Ahura Mazda; a wife who lies to him is no better than one who defiles herself with lovers.'

'I haven't deceived him, Tammuz. Not really. He knows full well that I'm not who it says I am on Memucan's records. And if he's a true Son of the Light, why doesn't he do something about the evils of his own court; his own government? It's my duty to see to it that he *isn't* deceived, by Haman. Oh Tammuz, I used to think that life at the palace must be like heaven on earth until *I* came to live here! All the gold and jewels, the marble and the porphyry, the sparkling fountains, the shaded courtyards, the handsome noblemen and ladies walking together in the rose-gardens whispering sweet nothings in one another's ears... But it's a wicked place, and you and I have been as guilty of its sins as anyone else here! Tammuz, don't you realize that outside these walls honest folk are starving, whole families are being murdered, an entire race lies under threat of destruction? And it isn't only Jews who are suffering. What about the Persians and Babylonians and Greeks and God knows who else, whose daughters were stolen and debauched while Memucan and Shaashgaz sought a wife for Kshayarsha? And what about the boys who have been unmanned, boys like *you*, for heaven's sake? It cannot go on. It *will* not. One day this whole corrupt empire will crumble away like a rotten tooth, just like Nineveh did. Just like Babylon.'

I had to pause for breath; my chest was heaving, and Hegai was staring at me as though he suddenly found himself being harangued by a total stranger. But my remark about the making of eunuchs had stung him hard; I'd meant it to. I went on, 'Kshayarsha and the fools like him imagine that they are free, because they have cast off the shackles of the old traditions. But they have thrown away love and trust along with them. So now they are trapped, just like the lions and tigers brought here to be hunted in the Paradise Gardens. Their keepers release them into the royal park and they suppose that they *are* free, until Kshayarsha and his cronies shoot them down. That's what will happen to Kshayarsha himself, Tammuz, Kshayarsha and all his proud dynasty.'

Still Hegai regaded me fearfully, as though he didn't know who I was; and indeed, I hardly knew myself, for the words which had poured forth from my lips weren't my words, and the delivering of them had left me strangely enfeebled yet aroused. Hegai so much wanted to understand, yet it was as clear to him as it was to me that I'd forged ahead along a path he could not tread, and he was afraid he'd lost me again already.

I murmured, 'I wish I *could* be like your Ishtar; I wish I *could* help you be reborn. But I can be an Iphigenia for my people. I can offer myself as a sacrifice for them, if a sacrifice is what is needed. I can release the stream of living water which Mordecai once saw when he dreamed of what was to come. I can be the myrtle tree of Zechariah's prophecy, the symbol of life, the meaning of the name my parents gave me.'

He said, 'So it's Hadassah who has been reborn. Not my Esther. My Esther is dead.'

'Tammuz, *please* don't ruin everything now. You've been so patient with me, so loyal, for so long, when all the time I was using you and everyone else as stepping stones across my own river. Don't give up on me now, when I've come to see what a bitch I've been. I love you; I'll always love you. That hasn't changed.' I kissed him gently on the brow. 'In a perfect world we might have married and I might have borne your sons. But we have to live in the world as we find it, and do what it requires us to do.'

'But I haven't been loyal,' he muttered. 'Not really. I didn't want to serve you any more after you married Kshayarsha. I only followed you here from the House of the Virgins because I was made to.'

'No one made you follow me here two nights ago. You risked your life to do it.'

'My life is worthless. I risked nothing.' Then as I clenched my fists in exasperation, something I'd said struck home with him and he whispered, 'Esther, did you mean that? Did you mean that if things had been different for both of us, you might have married me?'

I lowered my eyes. 'You know I would. Or have you already forgotten the day we walked in the palace gardens; the day I kissed you, and—?'

'Of course I haven't forgotten. I could never forget.' Suddenly he closed his eyes and said, 'Esther, kiss me again, like you did that day. Just once, so I know you aren't mocking me.'

I opened my mouth to protest, to assure him that I had never mocked him, even in my most selfish moments. But his parted lips were already trembling, his eyes still closed in expectation, the long, tear-dewed lashes brushing his cheeks, and his strong Semitic hair rampant over my pillows. So I slid my hand around his back as I'd done so long ago, and did as he'd bidden me. After a moment I drew back, knowing that it would be unfair of either of us to continue; and perilous too, for my heart and soul were so much in ferment with divine effervescence that I feared my fledgling desire for God would all too soon become entangled with desire of an altogether different kind. We *didn't* live in a perfect world, neither of *us* was perfect; Hegai could never know the joys of marriage and family, and I was wed to Kshayarsha for better or for worse.

To my great relief, he didn't attempt to prolong things either; he uttered a great sigh, knowing as well as I did that nothing but frustration lay in wait for him along that road. He turned his head away, out of my reach.

But I gave up on the idea of sending him back to Shaashgaz. I called Farah and told her to fetch me a tablet and stylus, for I wished to send a message to Hathach. By the time she'd brought them Hegai was asleep again, and I let him be, knowing it was what he needed. I sat on the bed beside him and wrote: *Please go to our friend at once and command him to gather our people in Shushan together. All of them must pray and fast for three days and nights, beginning now; my attendants and I shall do the same. I wish also to study the Torah, if he will send me some of his scrolls. After three days I shall go to the King, and if I die, so be it.*

17

Neither food nor drink passed my lips for three whole days and nights. Farah and her companions fasted with me, as did Hegai and Hathach, all in full knowledge of what they were doing and why, because I took care to explain it to them in such a way that none of them could fail to comprehend. Hegai alone had previously known that I was Jewish. Now *all* of them knew, and I told them that before the week was out Kshayarsha would know it too.

The time I would have spent eating, I spent at prayer; and the hungrier and thirstier I grew, the more sharply focussed did my mind become, and the more intense my devotions. In the mornings I recommenced my beauty routines, knowing I must make myself as desirable to Kshayarsha as it was possible for me to be. The remainder of my time I made use of to prepare myself in other ways for the confrontation ahead of me.

Mordecai was only too happy to comply with my instructions, and sent me copies of all five of the books of Moses. Smuggling them into my apartment entailed prodigious risks. But if I was to identify fully with my Jewish heritage and be its champion, I had to understand it; and now that my spirit had been quickened, the ancient stories and baffling genealogies and endless lists of rules and regulations seemed to spring to life also.

I spent hour upon hour poring over the sacred texts, until Hegai became so intrigued by my absorption that he sidled up and sat beside me at my table, frowning at the words, which were so like Aramaic and yet so different. After a while he mustered enough courage to ask me questions about what I was reading, and was profoundly impressed when I told him about the exodus of the slaves from Egypt, and the conquest of Canaan by Joshua and his armies which came later. He could see quite clearly that Adonai was a god who had always taken an active part in his people's history, intervening to save them from crisis after crisis, forgiving their waywardness and gradually teaching them more about himself, and about their own selves too. In contrast, the gods of Hegai's native Babylon had never ventured outside the fairy-tale world of mythology, and as for Ahura Mazda, he was so highly exalted above the everyday lives of his worshippers, so transcendent, so abstract, as to be scarcely approachable or relevant at all.

But on the third day of our fast I came to the passage I'd once read with Mordecai which stated in so many words that no one who has been gelded can be included among the community of the godly. For the first time since the wellspring of Adonai's spirit had gushed forth into my soul, I sensed something deep within me interfering with its flow. Hegai heard me catch my breath, and demanded to know what was wrong; I couldn't bring myself to lie to him. I told him the meaning of the words, straight out, and that I was sorry, but I hadn't written them, and God's ways are not our ways. Hegai said, 'So that is why the Jewish boys in the harem say they are Jews no longer. And that's why you were so upset to think that the same fate might have befallen your brother.'

I caught my breath a second time; outrage at the injustice of it all exploded inside me, its debris briefly damming the tide of Adonai's love altogether. I expostulated, 'Yes, and I *know* it isn't fair! Did Pithon ask to be cut? Did *you*, or your friends in the harem? Yet you've all been robbed of the love of God as well as that of a wife and children.' Then the blockage dissolved somewhat, and I mumbled, 'I'm sorry. I shouldn't have shouted like that. I don't know what came over me.' Perhaps I'd begun to imagine that Adonai had changed me so much, I should never sin again.

In a confusion of mortification, remorse, returning doubt and subdued anger I continued, 'But there are so many things I don't understand yet. Like the Restoration: were my parents right to return to Israel and seek to rebuild our nation? Were they right to use violence to drive out the Earth Folk who'd settled on our lands while we were captives in Babylon, and exiles in Persia? Yes, Joshua was told to evict and destroy them, but is something which was once the will of God automatically right for all time to come? I wish my faith was stronger. I wish I could understand why Adonai gives us laws which seem so unfair and so unfathomable. Mordecai always said there was a good reason behind every word in the Torah, if we took the time and trouble to meditate upon it. Yet this...' I gestured helplessly towards the offending passage on the scroll.

'You mean—if I were whole, I could have received Adonai's spirit inside myself? Me, a Babylonian?'

I sighed resignedly. 'You could have converted to the Jewish faith, yes. Whether you could have become a Shining One... that I don't know. Only Adonai can fill us with his spirit, and it is for him to distribute it as he sees fit.'

The following morning I rose early and broke my fast. I drank only water, however, and ate only bread. Then I had Hegai dress me and make up my face so that I looked exactly as I'd done when Kshayarsha had first set eyes on me some five years earlier, whilst in my mind I ran over and over what I was going to say.

Never since arriving at the palace had I ventured forth from the women's quarters except when sent for by Kshayarsha and escorted by Ashpamithra; indeed, I'd rarely wandered abroad within the harem itself. Even if I hadn't been under orders to remain in my apartment, the sight of my stalking the palace corridors with no one but my personal attendants for company would have caused something of a stir.

Before setting out I donned a heavy veil, something I'd had little cause to do since leaving Mordecai's. It wasn't merely custom or embarrassment that made me do it, though I was quite aware that everyone we encountered would stare at me. No; for the first time in my life I saw the value of modesty.

Hegai for his part had fashioned his turban in such a way that the merest slit was left for his eyes to look out of, but there was precious little chance of his going unrecognized. He alone of the harem eunuchs carried himself like a prince; having been a professional escort long before I'd been Queen, he'd been so thoroughly trained that when the occasion demanded it he could clothe himself with sophistication just as easily as he could change his apparel. Had this not been the case, I don't think he could have found the courage to take my hand and lead me calmly over the threshold of my apartment. Once that first step had been taken, there could be no going back.

The guard that morning was captained by a man whom neither of us recognized. However, a substantial inducement from Her Majesty's coffers achieved the desired effect, assisted no doubt by the poor fellow's unwillingness to restrain the Queen of Persia physically, along with her proud eunuch chaperon and her formidable retinue of slave-girls.

Never had the palace seemed so large, or the way to the Apadana so convoluted and crowded with people. The harem itself had become a vast sprawling labyrinth, whose very walls had malevolently staring eyes; I'd never before appreciated how gloomy and oppressive it was, how dark in comparison with the House of the Virgins. The musty rooms were tiny and windowless, and so many of them were inhabited not by glamorous foreign princesses, but by forgotten, toothless crones who had been there since the time of Darayavaush and before, or by scrawny half-mad bawds who still had their baths in milk and put on make-up every day, despite not having had a night with the King in a decade. There were the plain ones, the ugly ones, and the vacant ones with empty eyes, whose mothers had been concubines before them, and who had never known any other home. There were the Sisters whom the King's Commissioners had dragged from their mothers' arms; among them would be the three who had reclined catlike on couches and poured scorn upon my head when I'd come to the palace in my commoner's clothes, and the Median girl who had offered me friendship of a kind I preferred to be without. Somewhere, of course, would be Vashti.

As I moved among them, trying not to see them, trying only to focus my thoughts upon my husband, I couldn't help but reflect that he had slept with all of them too; that night after night they would still be bickering over which of them he'd liked best, how frequently each had been summoned, or whether one or more might even now be carrying his child. Every girl there lived for nothing but the one night in a hundred, or a thousand, when he might summon her again, and oh, the agony she would go through if it chanced to be her time of the month, or if she were ill, or tired, or had overeaten in her boredom and grown fat. How the others would laugh at her then . . .

No wonder that Hegai had sought to shield me from all this. Whatever happens, I thought, I must not end my days here. *Please, Adonai, spare me only that.*

Once we reached the Apadana our progress was abruptly halted. There was nothing inconsistent about the vigilance of the imperial guardsmen; nor about the conscientiousness of Artabanush the Hazar-apatish, and he at least was sufficiently well paid as to be incorruptible. I asked him outright to have me announced to my lord, but he refused, stating as tactfully as he could that I had no appointment.

I declared, 'I am Esther, Queen of Persia, principal wife of His Majesty Kshayarsha, King of Kings. I need no appointment.'

My words, my tone and my bearing had him intimidated, as I'd intended; he folded and unfolded his hands, and moistened his lips with his tongue before responding: 'I'm sorry, my lady—Your Majesty—Haman the First Minister has given orders that the King is not to be disturbed.' Clearly he didn't consider it his place to remind me of the edict confining me to my quarters, carrying with it the implication that I was entitled to my unique privileges no longer.

I said, 'I don't care what orders the First Minister has given you. I am Queen, and my orders countermand them.'

He looked frankly panic-stricken now; I wondered if this was a scenario he had dreaded, or one worse than he could ever have envisaged. I suspected that he feared Haman more than he feared Kshayarsha himself.

'Is the King conversing with anyone other than Haman and his advisers?' I asked. 'There are no visiting ambassadors or satraps with him in conference?'

'No, Your Majesty.'

'Then I shall approach him unannounced. It is my prerogative. Hegai, wait here with my handmaids.'

Artabanush was all but frantic; Hegai grasped me by the elbow and hissed into my ear, 'At least let me come with you.' But I shook my head; he'd risked his life once too often for me already. When he tried to insist, I rebuked him as sharply as I could without raising my voice; I pointed out that if he disobeyed me, he'd be saying that I was no longer Queen in *his* eyes either.

Slowly, regally, nauseous with fright, I ascended the great stone steps to the hall where the Great King of Persia sat enthroned. With my own two hands I parted the heavy curtains which ought to have been drawn deferentially back for me, and then I stood motionless, head demurely bowed, but not so low that I couldn't look down the length of the hall to the dais upon which the King and his entourage were assembled. The court had been in session since soon after dawn; my toilette had taken such a time that it was now almost noon, so the air was thick with the smoke and scent of incense. It stung my throat but I dared not cough, because the casual conversation of the courtiers which echoed among the soaring pillars died into silence as they became aware of my presence.

For a long, long time, no one moved and no one spoke. Perhaps no one knew whose place it was to do so, in a situation for which there may well have been no precedent in the whole history of the Hakhamanish dynasty. Then Kshayarsha stood up, and beckoned me to approach him.

A rumble of shock and disapproval stirred among the courtiers; this must have been the last thing they expected him to do. It wasn't done for His Majesty to rise in order to greet anyone, even a visiting potentate, and no one quite knew how Kshayarsha meant his unorthodox gesture to be taken. Hesitantly I walked forward, with every step seeking afresh to interpret the strange expression on his face. Was he brimming with joy, or with wrath? Was he experiencing a renewal of his love for me, or of his hate? Was he high on haoma, or was he sick?

Unable to proceed any further, I fell to the ground where I was, pressing my veiled face to the floor, wanting only to feel the cold marble against my brow and to get my head lower than the rest of me lest I faint. Then with a start, I realized that Kshayarsha had stepped down from the platform and was standing right in front of me. With his sceptre's tip he caught hold of my veil, spread out like blood on the pavement, and lifted it back to reveal my face as he'd done on our wedding day. He motioned for me to get up, and as our eyes connected, I knew at last what I was seeing in his. He *was* sick—with desire.

I hadn't thought to seduce him so easily, but I suppose there was nothing unduly surprising about his reaction. He'd loved Vashti, and Hegai, and me; but the only available outlets he'd had for his passions in recent weeks were the depraved Haman, the frosty, frigid Ashpamithra, and his jealous, spiteful, carping concubines. If he ever had believed me guilty of adultery, he no longer believed it now. It was the pious and implacable anger of Memucan and his colleagues which had kept me a prisoner for so many days, rather than that of Kshayarsha, but as he too often did, the King had let his counsellors have their way. He'd no more wanted to banish me permanently from his presence than he'd wanted to do so to Vashti, yet had found himself constrained to do so. Now Ahura Mazda in his benevolence had granted him the perfect opportunity to reassert his own authority.

All this I could now read quite clearly in his dilated pupils, his reddening lips and his over-flushed cheeks. As he looked into my eyes, and read in their unblinking candour the incontrovertible evidence of my fidelity, the whole glorious mélange of his emotions fermented in my favour. Tossing his lotus and sceptre to whoever stood closest, he cupped my chin in his hands and drawled, 'Queen Esther, star of my night and solace of my soul: tell me what it is that you desire, and you shall have it, even up to the half of my Empire.'

The hum of disapproval at his back grew louder, but he didn't care; I suspect that he relished it. Although he was probably wanting me to say that I desired only him, I wasn't going to speak of such things in public. Nor was I going to admit in public that I was Jewish, nor reveal to him that the Jews and the detestable, doomed Hebrews were one and the same. So I said, as I'd planned to say all along: 'If it please Your Majesty, I should like you and His Excellency Lord Haman to be my guests tonight at a banquet I am preparing in your honour.'

His eyebrows rose, but I don't doubt that my pupils were as wide as his own, and that my cheeks and lips were redder than Hegai's artistry had made them. I hadn't anticipated that my own passion for my royal husband would flare up so fiercely when so much was at stake. Because he could discern the need in me just as I could sense the same in him, he said simply, 'Yes, Queen Esther. We shall come.' But his eyes, his moistened lips, and the dew of sweat which glowed on his skin said very much more.

For the whole of the rest of the day, I was like a child on the eve of a festival, unable to relax or sit still for a moment. I couldn't have been higher if I'd quaffed a whole pitcher of haoma, and I drove Hegai to the end of his tether.

'What did he *say*, for the gods' sake?' he kept demanding. 'What did Kshayarsha *say* to you?'

'He said yes,' I beamed, gliding past him like a bright summer cloud playing hide and seek with the sun. And Hegai wailed: yes he'll forgive you, or yes he'll set your people free? 'Yes, he'll come to my party,' I answered blithely over my shoulder, and Hegai was left snorting with exasperation: what party?—whatever did you tell him?—didn't you mention the Jews at all?

I suppose he feared I'd thrown all my noble intentions out of the window, having effected some kind of reconciliation with the King. Knowing me as he did, such conduct on my part would have been perfectly well within the bounds of possibility.

Yet nothing could have been further from the truth. Although I was indeed on fire with passion for Kshayarsha, I was also inflamed with the white heat of Adonai's spirit, and the two fires leapt up together, their tongues entwined. For how else could Adonai use my marriage-bond with the King to redeem his people, unless that bond was strong?

Meanwhile, the banquet had to be organized. I took delight in informing the veteran guards at my door that their services were no longer required; they sent to the King for clarification and were told that this was indeed the case, at least for the present. Thenceforth Hegai and Hathach were not to be denied access to me; and Farah and her companions could come and go unimpeded. So I had them go to the kitchens and order Kshayarsha's favourite dishes to be prepared—oyster and crab in particular. I took steps to enquire what Haman most liked to eat, and discovered that he shared Kshayarsha's predilection for poppy seeds to whet the appetite.

Hegai helped me ready my apartment for the occasion; we had new curtains, tapestries and carpets, screens, awnings and cushions brought in, and scented oil for the lamps, and sprays of roses and oleander and Shushan lilies. Hegai threw himself into the work with frenetic enthusiasm; I sat him down forcefully when he rearranged the cushions for the twentieth time.

In the middle of the afternoon Hathach came to congratulate me, having been apprised of the favourable outcome of my appearance in the Apadana. At sunset I despatched him to escort my two guests to my apartment; he took with him a young eunuch friend he'd made in the harem, Harbonah by name, since I'd released Hegai for the evening and he'd gone to spend it with his new friends in the harem. It seemed wise not to complicate matters for Kshayarsha by having his former boy-favourite around to confuse his feelings for me.

The party was to be a cosy affair altogether, with no one else present but Roxana, my women, and whichever personal attendants the King and First Minister chose to bring with them. These turned out to be Ashpamithra and a couple of pretty pages, and a eunuch slave of Haman's. They'd come the private way, directly from Kshayarsha's chambers, because it would have been most improper for Haman to be granted passage through the harem.

My two guests had done me the honour of dressing in their finest. They handed their stiff brocade coats to their attendants, and the latter made themselves part of the background as was fitting, except that Ashpamithra pouted and glowered even more than usual, and the very air around him seemed charged with animosity towards everyone and everything.

In contrast, Haman was manifestly in the best of spirits. He bowed to me flamboyantly and kissed my hand, and I bestowed upon him a disarming smile. He was elated by a sense of his own importance, knowing full well that he was the only man who had ever accompanied the King to my quarters—and this was the mood in which I wanted him to stay. He'd taken his invitation as evidence of his unique relationship to Kshayarsha, and of my own acknowledgment of his entitlement to it. I was happy for him to think this, too, but I was also keen to exploit his improper interest in me as a woman, which I'd detected on numerous occasions in the past.

So whenever Haman glanced my way I would check that my husband wasn't looking, and then smile again, or flutter my lashes, or pretend to avert my eyes in beguiling bashfulness. I think my conduct surprised him at first, but not for long. He was as vain as he was handsome, and naturally considered himself irresistible.

In one sense my willing acceptance of Haman must have delighted Kshayarsha, for it symbolized my faithfulness to the vows we'd made when rededicating our marriage in the sight of the Wise Lord. But in another sense he was clearly wishing Haman out of the way, so we could cement our reconciliation in the only way that seriously mattered to him.

So throughout the evening I led them both a merry dance: making eyes at Kshayarsha blatantly and at Haman furtively; tossing back my head to laugh at their respective attempts at wit in such a way that the full length of my smooth white neck was shown to its best effect; licking at my sherbet as provocatively as I knew how. Then I would let my eyes linger upon Kshayarsha's broad oiled chest where it showed at the loosely laced neckline of his tunic, or upon a curled lock of hair that strayed across his forehead, or upon his strong square chin, which he still kept closely shaven according to the exotic fashion he favoured.

Finally, I would let my gaze connect with my husband's and purr, 'You will never know how much I have missed you, my lord, how sorely I have longed for you in the tedium of my days and the loneliness of my nights,' or, 'It almost broke my heart to think I could have caused you to doubt me. I've never loved *any* man but you,' or, 'I'm so sorry I couldn't speak freely in the throneroom, and crave your pardon. But there are some things which can only be said ... in *private*, my lord.' And I ran my perfectly manicured fingers around the rim of my plate, then licked them, my lips pursed, then parted, until Kshayarsha's tongue all but hung out of his head, and Haman said, 'Your benevolent Majesties, I do thank you both for so generously including your humble servant in on this auspicious occasion, but perhaps you would welcome the opportunity now to attend to your personal affairs.'

Kshayarsha was all set to say yes, but I pressed Haman's hand between my own two and said, 'Nonsense, my lord Haman! It would be the height of impoliteness on my part as your hostess if I let you leave before the King. I invited both of you here as my guests, because it was with both of you that I wanted to share my table—and my company.'

Haman withdrew his hand hurriedly, not knowing what he ought to think; Kshayarsha smiled with teeth clenched, unable to fault my exemplary etiquette.

Over the wine, his own manners deteriorated however. He hadn't had much, but perhaps it reacted badly with the haoma already in his system. He said, 'Kiss me, Lady Esther, just once, as a token of things to come. I'm sure that Lord Haman will not begrudge a single kiss between a husband and wife who have been parted for so long.'

'Very well then,' I consented, and instead of kissing him briefly on the lips, I went to sit on his knee, wound my arms about his muscled torso, and pushed my tongue into his mouth. Kshayarsha responded like a starveling to an offer of food, but before he had even begun to sate himself I opened my mouth still wider in an exaggerated yawn, then took my lips away from his.

'I'm sorry, my lord,' I murmured, putting my head on his shoulder. 'Today has been so exhausting. You cannot imagine how much it took out of me, summoning up enough courage to come before you in the Apadana when I knew my very life might be at stake. But I couldn't bear to wait any longer for you to send for me. Every hour that I was apart from you, fearing that you no longer trusted me, was like a thousand years. After noon I had to direct my maids to get everything ready to receive you; and now it is so late I can barely keep awake. It is so long since I've had cause to want to stay up past a child's bedtime.' I lifted my head from his shoulder and blinked sleepily into his eyes; he declared that I was the most exasperating, infuriating, gorgeous creature he'd ever seen, and swore again that I could have anything I wanted from him, even up to half the Empire.

I replied, 'I want only one thing, my lord, and that is for you and Haman to come to *another* banquet here tomorrow evening, when I shall be refreshed and more able to—entertain you appropriately. I do apologize for this, but I'm so very tired.' Then I slid lightly from Kshayarsha's lap and called for Farah, who draped my arm across her shoulder and prepared to lead me away, apparently asleep on my feet.

My guests took the hint and departed; through not-quite-closed eyelids I watched Kshayarsha looking back at me all the way in thwarted longing, unable to believe he hadn't accomplished what he'd set out to do, yet already looking forward avidly to doing so on the morrow. *I* had achieved my initial objective in full: to rekindle my husband's passion for me sufficiently to put all anger, doubt and suspicion out of his mind.

That night I slept like the dead, for what I'd told my guests in order to hasten their departure hadn't been so far from the truth. Some time late the next morning I was awoken by Hegai hissing in my ear that Hathach was anxious to see me; a bizarre incident had taken place which might threaten our entire enterprise.

Still euphoric over the way the previous evening had gone, I was half-convinced that one or both of them must be contriving to make a mountain out of some molehill. Nevertheless, I made myself vaguely presentable and went out into my living room, shooing away Farah and her companions who clustered about me with trays of creams and liniments; they'd decided that since I was indisputably Queen again, the correct morning rituals had to be strictly observed.

Once I'd got Hathach calmed down, he explained to me that he'd been out and about in the city shortly after dawn, as was his wont, and had come upon a large crowd gathered in the main public square. Shoving his way to the front, he'd been confronted by the spectacle of an elderly man being led back and forth, with much pomp and ceremony, astride a magnificent white horse. The horse was splendidly adorned with trappings in imperial colours, and its mane was twisted forward into the top-knot which only the King's horses are permitted to wear; the old man too wore kingly robes of purple and scarlet. Then Hathach had realized, with horror, that the man guiding the horse was none other than Haman, son of Hammedatha, and that its rider was one Mordecai ben Jair. Haman was declaiming at regular intervals, 'Witness how the Great King of Persia rewards a man whom he wishes to honour,' but his countenance was black as thunder, while Mordecai's was alabaster white.

Mine must have been whiter still by the time Hathach reached the end of his somewhat garbled explanation, and my euphoria had been consumed like camel-tracks by a sandstorm. 'What can it mean?' I entreated him. 'Was it some kind of punishment?'

'Punishment, my lady? To be escorted through the streets of Shushan wearing royal attire, riding His Majesty's own horse, and being squired by the most prominent of all noblemen? It is just about the highest honour which can be conferred on any Persian subject, and is scarcely ever awarded. It wouldn't surprise me if this were the first time since Kshayarsha was crowned.'

'But for *Haman* to act as escort for *Mordecai?* It must have been some sort of elaborate mockery, Hathach. They must be going to have my cousin stoned, or impaled, or . . . oh, by all the stars of heaven, this is dreadful. Were people cheering? Or were they throwing things?'

'Neither, my lady. There was silence. They know who Haman is, and Mordecai too. But they didn't know what was going on any more than I did, and most were so astonished they clean forgot about making the prostration. I don't think Lord Haman even noticed.'

'Dear God,' I whispered, recognizing that Hegai was right; this wasn't at all what we needed when my plan for the Jews' salvation had only just begun to be put into effect. I said, 'Where are they now, Hathach? Are they still in the square or have they returned to the palace?'

'I don't know, my lady, but they were still in the square when I left it.'

'I shall have to see Mordecai. I have to find out what is going on. Hathach, go back and find them, then follow them. When they come back, you must arrange for Mordecai to be taken to an audience chamber and I shall meet him there, openly. A secret rendezvous will only play into Vashti's hands.'

Hegai sought to dissuade me, maintaining that *any* meeting with Mordecai could be misconstrued. But I couldn't see that I had an alternative. There was no way I could receive Kshayarsha and Haman again that evening and make the best use of it, if the political situation had altered without my knowledge.

So I had myself dressed as for an official state occasion; but while my face was being painted, my hair crimped and curled, and my nails shaped and polished, I found I was getting more and more nervous at the prospect of seeing my former guardian and adoptive father after so many years of guilt-ridden separation. Of course, the moment had to come, but I'd somehow assumed I would have time to prepare for it, and that it would arrive when I'd already secured the future of our people.

Hegai and my women accompanied me to the chamber I'd had Hathach reserve for us; and it was like going to the Apadana all over again, but worse, because the encounter I'd had with Adonai was no longer so fresh in my mind, and there were now too many questions crowding in upon it and distracting me from turning to prayer.

I'd arrived before Mordecai, which pleased me because I should have more time to settle myself. In the event, I had too much; then when I'd begun to fear that he wasn't coming at all because he'd been stoned or impaled already, he entered leaning on Hathach's shoulder, with a boy of his own—either servant or pupil—holding his other hand.

Sure enough, my cousin was arrayed from purple mitra to saffron slippers just like the King himself. But the royal robes swamped him; he'd lost so much weight he looked like a sparrow cloaked in the feathers of one of Kshayarsha's peacocks. Beneath the heavy cape his back was stiff and stooping, and his limbs were frail; his face was as grey as his hair, and as deeply lined as the mud on the plain of Shushan in the summer, when there has been no rain for months.

I ordered a high-backed chair to be brought for him to sit on, and wine to restore his strength and his spirit; he seated himself carefully, painfully, and sipped at the wine, holding the cup between quaking fingers. It wasn't until I knelt down before him and spoke his name clearly, several times, that he realized who I was; I saw with a shock that his eyes were cloudy and pale and he was almost blind.

It was some while before either of us could compose ourselves sufficiently to speak of what Hathach had witnessed. There was much confession to be got through first, on both our parts, and very much weeping; and we both knew that this was only the beginning, for half a lifetime of resentment and misunderstanding cannot be washed away by a single flood of tears. But eventually I managed to glean that his exhibition by Haman in the public square had been no mockery, or at

least, it hadn't been intended as such. It was to show him the honour
due to him for saving the life of the King from the conspirators
Bigthana and Teresh.

'Bigthana and Teresh?' I repeated blankly. 'Not those pathetic old
eunuchs who used to stand guard at his private chambers? That was
years ago. Why should Kshayarsha choose to make a big issue of it
now?'

Mordecai shrugged his shoulders helplessly; the gesture was only
just visible beneath the stiffened yoke of his cape. He said, 'I was
summoned to the Apadana this morning at first light. I thought it
was because of my refusal to do obeisance to Lord Haman, though I
was was at a loss as to why *that* had not happened earlier, too. It was
only when His Majesty began to praise me for my loyalty, and to
apologize to me for not having taken the trouble earlier to accord me
appropriate honour for what I'd done to protect him, that I realized
he didn't *know* I was the man who had refused to bow the knee to
Haman, and that he didn't know because Haman didn't *want* him to
know, lest he be found seeking to punish a Royal Benefactor. It is
little different from his determination that the King shall not discover the Hebrews and the Jews to be one and the same people, until
it is too late.'

Overcome by the poignancy of his own words, he broke off, and it
was some while before he could compose himself again sufficiently to
go on: 'The King told me that he was unable to sleep last night. He said
he'd summoned a scribe to read him extracts from the royal records,
and the conspiracy had been one of the events to which reference was
made. He'd asked the scribe if he could recall how the discoverer of the
plot had been rewarded, and the man could not; no one could, because
nothing had been done. His Majesty said he was perplexed as to how
such a monstrous omission could have been made, so he determined to
set things to rights straight away.'

I thought, I know very well why nothing was done; it was because I
diverted Kshayarsha's mind from the matter deliberately.

But I didn't interrupt, so Mordecai continued: 'He asked the scribe
whether any of his ministers was up and about yet, for by then it was
almost dawn. The scribe had seen no one, so the King sent his
Chamberlain to look, and he came across Lord Haman waiting on the
very threshold of His Majesty's private quarters.'

'Before dawn? What was he doing there?'

'I don't know. But he was brought inside, and asked for his opinion on the question of how a uniquely illustrious citizen for whom the King had the highest possible regard might be publicly honoured, when this man was renowned for the simplicity of his lifestyle in spite of his wealth, and was thus likely to despise any financial reward or else squander it upon the poor. So Haman said, "Dress the man in your robes and seat him on your horse, and have him led through the city by a nobleman announcing that this is what the King will do for those whom he wishes to exalt above all others." And Kshayarsha said, "The Royal Progress, of course! It was a practice much favoured by my excellent father Darayavaush. What a genius you are, Lord Haman." So that is what they did to me, Hadassah. I would rather they had killed me. And Haman was appointed as my escort.'

If circumstances had been different I might have laughed. I was sure that Haman must have thought the King was referring to *him*, Haman himself; after all, in his own eyes, he alone in the entire Empire could be described as uniquely illustrious, held in the highest regard by Kshayarsha, and he was one of the wealthiest men in Persia. His lifestyle was scarcely a simple one, but no doubt he himself regarded it as tastefully unostentatious, and certainly he could afford to be generous to the poor; gold ran through his gem-encrusted fingers like water. I could vividly picture his unctuous face falling as he was made aware of his error; God moves in mysterious ways indeed, and some of them are most amusing.

So I asked, 'Why are you so distressed, my—cousin?' (I'd suddenly wanted very much to say 'my father,' yet found I couldn't bring myself to do so.) 'Surely you must discern Adonai's hand in all this. Kshayarsha knows that you are Jewish. When I tell him that he has unwittingly condemned the Jews to destruction, he will surely be much more inclined to find a way of granting us a reprieve if a Jew's loyal service is fresh in his mind.'

Mordecai gazed at me, his complexion greyer than ever, his clouded eyes scanning my face as though by sheer determination they might make it and everything else come clear. He murmured, 'You still haven't told him? You have said *nothing*?'

I answered hastily, 'Don't be alarmed, Cousin. There is no need to fear on that account. I had to be reconciled with him first as my husband, and that, I believe, I have accomplished.'

But then, observing him struggling with his doubt, and with his longstanding mistrust of me—which I'd fed every day that I'd spent beneath his roof—I was engulfed in a tide of guilt and pity. I found myself blurting apologies all over again, and soon we fell once more to weeping, then to embracing—a thing I could never previously have imagined happening if both of us had lived as long as Methuselah. Then he was confessing more of his own guilt too; how in truth he *did* know that Adonai had had a hand in the morning's events, just as he'd had a hand in my coming to the palace. He'd used this morning to teach Mordecai that abstemiousness and asceticism did *not* necessarily glorify God, and that if Mordecai had not been so irrationally fearful of wealth and its trappings, he would have been able to derive pleasure and not pain from his triumphal tour of Shushan. It was a lesson he'd needed to learn all his life, and if only he'd learnt it earlier, how different our relationship would have been. 'I love you, Hadassah,' he concluded. 'I always have. You were the daughter I never had; at least, you could have been.'

'I love you too, Cousin Mordecai.' I still couldn't quite call him 'Father'. 'You gave me a home when I had nothing and no one else in the world, and when I was as spoilt as an Egyptian cat. I loved Ninlil too, but it's too late to let her know it.'

Then he began to tell me all about Elizabeth, the wife he had lost to the summer fever so many years before I was born. Although he'd prayed for her, and laid hands upon her for her healing, Adonai had taken her, and the baby she was carrying too. From that day on, Mordecai had hardened himself against the world and taken no pleasure from the beauty to be found in it.

He explained, 'When I heard that you were coming to Shushan, it was like a miracle. Those who knew me said it was the first time I had taken an interest in anything but the Torah since my Elizabeth was buried. Yet Leah, the woman who kept house for me, saw things more clearly than I did. She saw that neither of us was used to children, and that we were quite unprepared for what we were taking on. So I mistook your grieving over your parents for sulky insolence, your love of beautiful things for frivolity, your impetuosity for obstinacy, and your friendliness towards the boys in my class for brazen wantonness. I threw Adonai's gift back in his face, Hadassah, and he took it. He took you away. And at once I knew I'd wronged you. In fact I'd known it all along, if truth be told. I knew it on the day when we quarrelled and I broke your mother's necklace. I spent all that night on my knees—collecting every bead.'

I admitted, 'The fault was not all yours. I *was* stubborn, and selfish. Even if I hadn't come to the palace, I would have dragged your name through the dirt in some other way.'

'But it was cruel of me to take away what your mother had given you. You see—I wanted you to forget her, to forget both your parents, and the Pioneers, and Jerusalem. I'd never agreed with the Pioneer dream. I didn't think it was Adonai's way.'

'Do you think so now?'

'I think that Adonai has many ways, Hadassah, many channels, many vessels. He will see his purposes achieved by whatever means he chooses, and we are fools if we suppose we can think his thoughts for him. He calls each of us to do what we can do best, with the gifts he has given us and the strength he can bestow upon us if we trust him.'

I said quietly, 'What about a eunuch. What can a *eunuch* be called to do.'

He was taken aback; blind as he was, he probably wasn't even aware that I hadn't come to him alone. But holding him in my arms and bringing him comfort had reminded me so powerfully of Hegai, I could scarcely concentrate on anything else. I beckoned Hegai forward; he approached with reluctance, not sure that he ought to intrude on such an intimate and significant moment of my life. Yet I could think of no one with whom I should ever want to be more intimate than with Hegai, in mind and heart if not in body. I prized myself from my cousin's embrace, raising the latter's hand by the wrist and guiding it towards Hegai's face. I drew apart the folds of his turban and said, 'May I introduce Master Hegai, sometime Chamberlain to His Majesty the King, and now chief personal attendant to the Queen; the best friend I ever had.'

I watched Mordecai explore by touch the flawless forehead and the long aquiline nose, the perfect cheekbones, the generous mouth and girl-smooth chin; I seemed to see Hegai with new eyes myself, and to reflect for the first time in years upon how impossibly beautiful he was. I said, almost defiantly, 'He has risked his life for me more times than enough; he has studied the Torah with me, and he fasted with me for three whole days and nights, for the sake of a people who are not his own, and who will never accept him, whatever he does for them.'

But Mordecai turned again to me, and said, 'Times have changed, Hadassah. Although Adonai remains the same for ever, the revelations he divulges to us of himself and of his laws grow more complete with each passing generation. If God himself can accept a eunuch, then so must we.'

'I—don't understand. Are you saying we can rewrite Moses' laws? We can adapt them to what we see around us?'

'No, my daughter. That is very far from what I am saying: as far as Heaven is above the earth. To adapt the laws of God to the fickle opinions of mortals is compromise, and compromise is sin and will plunge us all into the pit of destruction because it is born from a wayward desire to become like the nations and reject the unique identity Adonai has given to the Jewish people.'

'Then what *are* you saying?' I demanded, too sharply, because I was listening to Mordecai's words and trying to hear them as Hegai must be hearing them.

'I am saying that in confusing a gradual revelation of the truth with lies and compromise many well-meaning people have foundered, Hadassah. But Adonai can only teach us the lessons we are ready to learn. What good would it do for a teacher to expect his pupil to read aloud from the Torah when the child does not yet know the shapes of the letters?' I smiled, for once upon a time Mordecai had expected that very thing of me. 'There is much he hasn't yet revealed to us: the nature of the life beyond death, the mysterious workings of atonement and forgiveness, the signs which will accompany the coming of the Messiah and herald the time of judgment. But that time is fast approaching; the age of fulfilment is well nigh upon us, and fresh revelations are received almost daily by those to whom Adonai vouchsafes them. Thus Isaiah and his disciples have prophesied that *all* who once stood barred from God's kingdom will one day be able to enter it; when the Messiah appears, Gentiles will flood into his kingdom so fast that an army of demons wouldn't be able to keep them out. In our day we are seeing the harbingers enter it already.'

'Even eunuchs will enter? When it says in the Torah that they may not?'

'It says in the Torah that no Moabite may enter, either; yet was there not a daughter of Moab named Ruth, who became the wife of Boaz of Bethlehem, and the mother of King David's own line? And it says that no bastard may enter, yet wasn't Jephthah, one of the greatest of all our national heroes, the son of a harlot? Wasn't Saul's blood-brother Eliphaz an *Amalekite*, of all people? His entire race was accursed by God, yet he alone was redeemed because as a boy Saul loved him, before he was old enough to hold a sword, let alone be commanded to annihilate a nation. Saul had him circumcized so he belonged to Amalek no longer.'

I said, 'But was that fair? Was Eliphaz the *only* son of Amalek who deserved to be loved? I'm not sure any more that a whole race ought to be accursed because of something its ancestors did long ago.'

'Hadassah, it isn't for us to judge whether Adonai's ordinances are right or not. We must not water down his words to make them acceptable to ourselves or to others. If Adonai told Moses, then Joshua, then Saul, to wipe every Amalekite from the face of the earth, it isn't for us to question him or accuse him of cruelty. Consider the countless generations who have suffered unspeakably because Joshua failed also to eradicate the Canaanites from Israelite territory. The repercussions of his failure are still being felt in our own day, and will go on being felt for all time to come. No; God's word must never be diluted. But it must be understood. We have to search humbly and honestly behind the letters of our laws to discern their spirit, and only when the spirit of wisdom—the spirit of Adonai himself—resides within us can we hope to do that rightly. It is a desperately difficult thing to do, and one which we get wrong at our extreme peril. But the meaning of the law excluding eunuchs from the people of God is relatively clear. Adonai wants no man to take a knife to his own flesh and geld himself as an act of religious devotion, as the pagans do.'

'So... Hegai *can* be converted to our faith? He can become as though he'd been born a Jew?' I darted a rapid glance at the one of whom I spoke; his eyes were glued to my cousin's and he seemed entranced, overcome.

'If he so desires, and subject to ratification by the elders of the Jewish community in Shushan. Membership of the *true* Remnant, the *true* Israel, is not an accident of birth, Hadassah. Nor has it anything to do with whether one's parents were exiled to Babylon, or of whether one gives up one's home and moves one's family back to Jerusalem. These are Isaiah's words: "A man who has been castrated should never think that because he cannot have children, he can never be one of God's people. The Lord says to such a man: 'If you honour me, and keep my covenant faithfully, your name will be remembered longer than if you had sons and daughters. You will never be forgotten.' " It is by keeping God's commandments and by living all our days in fellowship with him that we demonstrate our belonging to the Remnant. Is this what your friend Hegai here wants for himself?'

The words of the prophecy were so beautiful that I barely heard the question, let alone felt able to answer it. However, Hegai didn't need me to answer for him. It was for him to decide what he wanted, and for him to speak his decision aloud. He took hold of my hand, but it was to Mordecai that he addressed himself, and he did so with neither embarrassment nor fear. He said, 'Sir, if it truly is possible, I *should* like to be part of what you and my lady Hadassah are part of. I want the trials that lie ahead to be my trials too, and the triumph my triumph. I want to be part of a family again. I want to put the past behind me; after today I don't even want to think any more about what has been done to me. I want peace in my heart, peace like Hadassah felt when your God came into her. I want to know Adonai.'

Mordecai lost little through being unable to see Hegai's earnest face; he knew without a shadow of a doubt that this eunuch son of Babylon was utterly sincere in what he said. He asked me to send my other attendants outside, Hathach included, and his own page-boy too; I couldn't see why it should be necessary, but soon found out. Then he bade Hegai and me kneel down on the floor, where he insisted on kneeling with us. He laid his hands on Hegai's head, and I did the same, knowing instinctively that this was what I should do. And as the old man started to pray out loud, his thin voice husky and cracked as a damaged flute's yet laden with spiritual power, the miracle happened for Hegai as it had happened for me.

But the way in which it happened couldn't have been more different, at least at first. So much misery, confusion and terror had been locked up inside him for so long, hidden away behind his studied sophistication, it was little wonder that the sudden release of it now should be frightening, awesome, and not something to be witnessed by those who don't understand.

Even I, who had pierced his veneer before and glimpsed the bitter anguish that lay behind it, couldn't have predicted what would happen when it came crashing down once and for all. His face contorted by the spiritual battle that raged within him, he wailed, he howled, he lashed out with his fists so I had to restrain him lest he do himself or his frail intercessor some grievous damage. But all his own, inner damage had

347

to be undone, all the sin dealt with, all the confusion and agony and torment done to death before the gentle spirit of Adonai could come in its place.

But once it was gone, it would be gone for ever. Though the painful memories would remain, they would have no power over him unless he allowed them to. When at last he lay shattered, his head in my lap and his energy spent, the spirit of Adonai settled upon him like a dove upon an olive bough, or a gentle fall of snow upon a windless mountain. His lovely features were no longer contorted, the tears dried on his cheeks, and the battle was over. The peace he'd searched for was his; he'd been made alive in a way Ishtar could never have done for her Tammuz. Mordecai left off praying, knowing there was no more need; he too was exhausted. So I said to him, 'Thank you, Father,' and kissed him as a daughter would do, for Hegai was free.

18

As a child in Mordecai's house, I'd made up my mind more than once to start over again with him, putting quarrels behind us. But only now did I possess the means to achieve it; only now did I fully understand what the prophets such as Joel and Zechariah had meant by new life, and the pouring out of God's spirit upon his people.

When Hegai had regained his senses and collected himself enough to face walking back to my apartment, it was high time for our meeting with Mordecai to be brought to an end. Everything had to appear normal, in readiness for my second banquet.

I had my quarters entirely refitted all over again: I commissioned awnings and wall-hangings of magenta and gold, which were run up in a day by an army of stitchers; luxuriant garlands of lilies, oleander and cultivated roses of every hue hung between the polished marble pillars. I procured a brand new dinner service, with bowls, plates and jugs of the finest silver inlaid with figures of gryphons and serpents cast in gold, and horn-shaped silver goblets to match, with golden gryphon heads for stands. Musky perfumes were applied to the furnishings and fabrics, and burned slowly in elegant crucibles on tall, delicate tripods made of solid gold.

For the meal I ordered crab and oysters, shrimps and prawns, in garlic and sesame oil; smoked fish of every kind, with rich vegetable sauces; veal and venison, horse and peacock, pheasant and quail; pastries filled with poppy seeds, and sweet honey-glazed cakes; candied apricots, citron sorbet; and the most expensive Syrian wine. Hegai laughed at the blatant extravagance, and said we should never consume the half of it; I said that the pair of *us* wouldn't, it was true, for the greater part was by no means kosher. But I knew it wouldn't go to waste; palace fare never does. Food from the King's own table is given to his courtiers if he doesn't require it for himself, and may be passed on by them to the free employees, and by them to the slaves.

349

When all was ready, I bade Hegai adjust my apparel and repaint my face, then sent him to bed in his room; he was out like a torch plunged into water. I styled my hair myself, and when I was quite satisfied with my own appearance I had Hathach and his young friend Harbonah go once again to fetch my guests.

But they were away so long, I began to grow fretful. I tried to pray, yet couldn't settle to it; I paced about rearranging flowers and plumping up cushions and repositioning the gathers in the awnings, until presently there were clipped voices outside as the King's personal guard took up its station about my threshold; a moment later Kshayarsha and his entourage swept in.

Kshayarsha looked as handsome as I'd ever seen him. He was bareheaded but for a band of plaited gold, and his loose black hair swung about his shoulders like a second cape. His true cape was cut to a fishtail at the back, and trailed across the floor behind him; in place of his customary saffron slippers he wore studded leather boots with pointed toes, and above them tight Median leggings belted by a broad sash that showed as he walked, for his gold-bordered robe swirled open at the front.

But despite the splendid appearance of the King, it was upon Haman that my gaze lingered. He didn't look like himself at all: the pleats in his garments were uneven, as though he'd dressed in a hurry, and his hair was neither oiled nor curled. He started to apologize for having caused their late arrival, alleging that he hadn't felt well earlier in the afternoon, and had feared he might be unable to come at all. He did seem a little grey about the jowls, whilst his cheeks were decidedly florid; and the divisions between his words were disconcertingly blurred. Hathach drew me to one side as the party occupied itself with disrobing and sampling trays of hors d'oevres, and whispered that if Haman had indeed felt ill, he'd brought it upon himself.

'When Harbonah and I arrived at the King's chambers, Haman was nowhere to be found, my lady. We had to go to his own house in the city; we didn't even know where it was, so Ashpamithra had to guide us. Haman was there with his wife and sons and friends, all of them drunk as—well, drunk as Amalekites; I think they'd set out to help him drown the sorrows brought on by what happened to him this morning.' Hathach lowered his voice again, and led me a little further away, seeing that the King was still being distracted by some arcane ministrations of his Chamberlain. 'My lady, Haman was boasting flagrantly

350

about how important he is, how rich he is, how many fine sons he has bred to carry the glorious name of Agag on into the future; about how he's the only man apart from the King ever to have been invited to dine with the Queen in the whole of Hakhamanish history, and how he's universally recognized to be the second most powerful man in the world! But he said that the sweetness of his success was so much soured by Mordecai's ubiquitous presence, none of this meant anything to him at all. And everyone was sympathizing with him, and saying he must dispose of Mordecai swiftly, lest this scurvy Jew worm himself any further into His Majesty's affections, discredit Haman himself, and undo the work which all of them had put in to foment hatred against the Jewish race.'

'And *has* he done anything about it?' I hissed fearfully.

'Not irrevocably; he hasn't had the time, being more interested in dissipating his own evil humours first of all.' Haman was certainly no Persian, with their abhorrence of overt inebriation. 'But Harbonah did a little—research, shall we say; he looks so young and innocent, no one ever thinks to challenge him. He managed to get out into the courtyard while Ashpamithra and I were encouraging Haman to hurry lest he risk displeasing the King, because we'd overheard someone suggesting he make haste to complete the gallows he's been building in his garden. It's true, my lady. He's erecting a gibbet on his own premises,which must be nigh on fifty cubits high already. He means to hang Mordecai there in secret.'

'Fifty cubits?' I mouthed, incredulous. 'That's some secret gibbet, Hathach. It must be visible from half the city; and probably from the palace walls too. Has he gone mad?'

'Quite probably, my lady; but the gibbet *isn't* visible from outside. He has poplar and cypress trees around his walls, higher still.'

Then noticing that Kshayarsha was no longer being distracted by Ashpamithra I turned to Haman, smiled benevolently, and assured him that there was absolutely no need for him to apologize for his condition, since no offence had been meant, and none taken.

He muttered his thanks; in spite of his intoxication, he hadn't failed to notice my tête-à-tête with Hathach, even if Kshayarsha had; and he must surely have been worried about what we were saying. I didn't mind; it only got him more flustered than ever, and put him at more of a disadvantage. I said, 'I'm *so* sorry you've been unwell, my lord Haman. Summer is on its way; perhaps you have a touch of the fever.

Farah? Bring Lord Haman some chilled wine. It may cool his tongue, and settle his stomach before we eat. I should be *so* upset if all our elaborate preparations went to waste. We have sour cream pudding with honey and cinnamon among the desserts—your favourite, Lord Haman, or so I believe?'

Haman sought ineffectually to disguise a retch, and his jowls turned from grey to a delicate shade of green. Unwisely, he accepted the chilled wine, and I said, 'There, you are looking better already. You ought not to work yourself too hard, you know. The pressures of high office are many and heavy; to carry such a load without respite isn't good for body or soul. And as for you: your burden of responsibility is *so* great, it would be a wonder if any mere mortal could bear it without collapsing under its weight. You must be a truly remarkable man.'

'Haman is unique!' declared Kshayarsha, so delighted by the apparent goodwill which persisted between his Queen and his First Minister that he failed entirely to appreciate my sarcasm. For once I was grateful that he lacked the perspicacity of his illustrious forefathers; as for Haman, he was too fuddled to attempt to work out what I was up to; all he could do was goggle at me blear-eyed over his wine-cup, while I smiled back at him knowingly, as though his intoxication were a guilty secret between the two of us.

By the time the savoury dishes had been served, even Kshayarsha was aware that all was not as it seemed, but he wasn't quite sure *how* he knew, so there was nothing he could say. Haman picked at his food, hoping, I suppose, that no one would remark upon his poor appetite. I didn't. I was too busy harping on his greatness, cataloguing his accomplishments and avowing that not a day went past without my eunuchs bringing me word of another worthy cause he had espoused, or another noble goal he had achieved. Why, only the other morning I'd heard of his monumental scheme for the eradication of that layer of human scum from the dregs of society which went by the accursed name of Hebrew; and then *this* morning, he had excelled himself by honouring a man whose name I was sure had been associated with that very sect.

Haman's eyes bulged wider, and he began twisting and shifting on his couch as though there were ants' nests all over it. I merely smiled all the more sweetly and said that without a doubt this was evidence of the First Minister's high-mindedness; he was refreshingly willing to forgive, to let bygones be bygones, and to give credit where it was due regardless of a man's colour or creed, and with no thought for his own advancement. The reputation of such a paragon of virtue would unquestionably live for ever.

'But then again,' I continued—as the sweets were brought round and I reserved an enormous portion of sour cream pudding especially for Haman—'Then again, you are the product of an ancient and noble house, are you not? I am told that the tribe of Amalek is one of the oldest on earth, and that you yourself can trace back your ancestry to a king who lived almost half a millenium ago?'

Haman nodded slightly, and muttered something noncommittal, whilst staring dismally at the sour cream pudding; Kshayarsha exhorted him, 'Well, answer the Queen, Lord Haman. She speaks truly, after all, for would I entrust so much royal business to a man who was not of royal blood himself? Would that that blood were Aryan; yet Ahura Mazda in his wisdom has fashioned *every* race of men, both lesser and greater.'

I turned to Kshayarsha, granting him a sidelong smile which meant, 'Later...' But aloud I said, 'My gracious lord and husband, I pray you, do not seek to embarrass the gentle lord Haman. He is much too modest to boast about his own credentials. However, I have taken the trouble to learn something of the history of his excellent tribe, and most fascinating it is too. For example, my lord, did you know that, although his ancestors had a land of their own, and even a great capital city at one time, the vast majority of them elected to travel about from place to place, wherever the fancy took them—or should I say, wherever the pasture took their goats and camels? How romantic it must be, to live a life so free from constraints, not tied to one place as we are compelled to be.'

Although I'd avoided the word 'nomad' on purpose, the thrust of my meaning was lost on neither of my guests. Kshayarsha squirmed, and coughed to hide the offence to his Zoroastrian scruples; Haman interjected, 'Your Majesty Queen Esther, I am sure that the King does not wish to be bored with tales of my humble origins. *All* of our forefathers were wandering herdsmen once.'

'Quite so, quite so,' I asserted blithely. 'But some of your fellow-tribesmen in Amalek's dim and distant past were much more interesting than others, wouldn't you say? And some found themselves living settled lives much earlier than others. Take the one called Eliphaz, for example, Eliphaz son of Korah, of whom I'm sure you have heard, being an erudite scholar yourself. He was sold into slavery by his own father, and went on to become friend and confidant of a foreign king. His story has a little in common with your own, I think you would agree. To rise so spectacularly from obscurity to power; this must surely be an indication of the extraordinary capability of so many men of your tribe. Now let me see... I'm sure I used to know the nationality of the king Eliphaz befriended, too. Of course, he wasn't the ruler of a mighty empire like Persia, in fact he was merely a petty tribal chieftain if truth be told. Can *you* remember his tribe's name, Lord Haman?'

Haman shrugged his shoulders, but knew he wasn't going to get away with saying nothing, or with lying. I reminded him once again about his own reputation for erudition, until he was forced to mumble, 'The king was a Jew.'

'Yes, of *course!*' I agreed, laughing. 'How silly of me to forget. I kept thinking of the word 'Hebrew' instead. It's *so* tiresome when a wrong idea takes root in your mind and leaves no room for the right one; though I'm sure you never experience such a problem, being so much more learned than I am, and with my being a mere woman.'

Haman looked as though he might be sick at any moment, though he hadn't touched the cream pudding. Kshayarsha glanced from one of us to the other and back again, his brows knit together, more confused than before. I made no comment, wanting to give him time to begin putting two and two together, and to give Haman time to suffer. But the latter started prattling into the silence, no doubt wanting to distract the King from making the vital equation. 'Eliphaz was a traitor to his people. He could and *should* have *poisoned* Saul and his entire family, before the wretched upstart was even *given* a throne, before he wiped our city and most of our population from the face of the earth. Eliphaz should have stood by his own people, instead of sucking up to a weak-minded foreign princeling who ate bloodless meat, and whose own blood was fetid, and whose beliefs were like the fantasies of children.'

I affected astonishment at his outburst; indeed I *was* somewhat astonished that he should have been so eager to run into the trap I was setting for him. But not only was he drunk; also his hatred of Jews was so deeply ingrained in him, and so infused with the anger of generations that he could barely keep a lid on it at the best of times. Kshayarsha was patently astonished also; Haman growled an apology and sat glowering into his wine, knowing full well that he'd made a spectacle of himself, if not something worse. After all, *he* had done plenty of sucking up to a king who had no more regard for the gods of Amalek than Saul had had.

But by the time the desserts had been cleared away—with Haman's dollop of sour cream pudding still untouched—and Farah had poured each of us wine, I had steered the conversation back round to things Jewish frequently enough for Haman to begin to guess at the truth. His face was no longer florid, nor grey, nor green, but chalky-white, and I was happy for it to remain that way while I turned my charms upon Kshayarsha. I began to flirt with him, subtly at first, then blatantly, until Haman was virtually swooning from the agony of his suspense and from the embarrassment of the intrusion which his presence constituted into the tempestuous royal marriage.

Presently I slipped from my own couch onto the King's, and he rolled over on his back to draw me down beside him. With his arms about my hips, his lips nuzzling my hair, his heart pounding like a galleymaster's hammer against my breast, and every muscle in his body taut with desire, he murmured, 'Queen Esther, my loveliest, cruellest, Queen Esther, why must you lead me on like a hound on a leash when you know I would follow you to the very Gates of the Underworld of my own free will? Please, please tell me what it is that you want, and you shall have it, up to half of my Empire; indeed, you might persuade me to give you the whole of it, in return for one night of the pleasure we once shared.'

The moment had come, I knew; Kshayarsha was sick with lust, and Haman with apprehension. So I said, 'Very well, my dearest lord. You shall have your night with me, and I shall tell you what I want, and why I have invited you here with the noble Lord Haman two nights together. I crave no empire; I have riches already more than I know what to do with, and never in my life have I longed for any power save that which I might gain over the heart of the only man I have ever loved.' I kissed him long and lingeringly, twirling coils of his hair between my fingers, my eyes speaking devotion and utter fidelity into his own. 'My request is a humble one, my lord, if you would be so gracious as to grant it. I ask that I and my kinsfolk may be permitted to live.'

I waited deliberately for him to ask me what I meant, and made use of the pregnant pause to trail my long-nailed fingers around his neck and draw his head onto my shoulder so that I could look at Haman beyond it. The proud son of Amalek's kings was shivering like corn in a storm-wind, knowing his worst suspicions confirmed. Kshayarsha posed the question I was awaiting, pulling away from me a little so as to study my face. Looking directly at him, I responded: 'My lord, there is a plot against my life and against that of my brothers and sisters. We have been sold, like common slaves or chattels, but not to merchants or market-stall keepers. We have been sold to butchers.'

Predictably, Kshayarsha was nonplussed. He must have clean forgotten about the edict which Haman had had him issue against the Hebrews, since it never had been of much interest to him personally. 'A plot, against the life of my Queen? Are you saying that you have uncovered evidence of *treason*, my sweetest Esther? From what quarter? What man would *dare* to threaten you?'

I whispered, 'Yes, my lord. It *is* treason of which I speak. And, my lord . . .' I extracted myself from his embrace and sat upright on the couch beside him, clutching at its edge as though in fear of him. 'My lord, I was in disgrace. Everyone knew it. I suppose the conspirators imagined you didn't love me any more, and would not defend me. I even imagined the same thing myself, in my darkest hours, though in all my life I have loved no man but you.' And I put my face in my hands.

Kshayarsha's hackles were rising; he sat up too, and hugged me fiercely, swearing that he loved me as he loved his own body, and that even if this were not so, he would tear limb from limb any man who dared to draw his own conclusions about the private thoughts and feelings of his King. He asked me once again whose was the wicked mind behind this abominable scheme, but I wanted him angrier still before I told him. So I feigned a fit of weeping, and said that the thing was worse even than I'd made out, for it wasn't any literal brothers and sisters of mine who were under threat, but my entire nation. 'Oh, my lord,' I sobbed, 'We have been sold for slaughter, every one of us. If it were merely enslavement which we faced, I might have kept quiet. I know how little time for leisure Your Majesty has, and how many cares and anxieties. I should never want to distract you with meaningless trivialities. But it is destruction which we face, my lord. Extermination.'

My words and my manifest anguish achieved the desired effect. Kshayarsha railed and fumed, incensed and alarmed at the outrageous notion that a conspiracy could be hatched against an entire race within his domains, without his knowing anything about it. He'd been told many preposterous things in his time as King, but this capped all of them; how was he to know that I hadn't been deceived, or worked myself up into making something out of nothing?

'You don't believe me,' I wailed. 'Oh my lord, Kshayarsha, my husband . . . do you think I would have risked my life to come before you in the Apadana, for nothing? I have evidence to prove that what I'm saying is true. And I know the name of the chief conspirator.'

'Then who is he, for the Wise Lord's sake? *Where* is he? What race does he seek to destroy? Why wouldn't you tell me the name of your people when you came here, so that I could guarantee their protection from the beginning?'

There was scarcely any need for me to answer the first two of these questions, because Haman's teeth were chattering so violently that his terror was audible. So I began by confessing that I was Jewish, but had always been afraid to say so because I'd known how unpopular Jews were in some quarters of the palace; I'd loved Kshayarsha since the first time I'd seen him, when I was nothing but a child and he'd ridden into Shushan to assume his throne, and so desperate had I been to become his bride that I hadn't dared let my ancestry stand in my way. Even after our marriage I'd been terrified he would renounce me if he found out the truth; but now I *had* to confess it, I'd been given no choice. For his own Benefactor, Mordecai ben Jair, was my cousin; he had once been my guardian, too, but was now my legal father—and he was the 'Hebrew' who had refused to bow the knee to Haman. The Jews and the Hebrews were one and the same; and Haman had tricked his King into annihilating one of the most loyal and law-abiding peoples under his dominion, a people who worshipped no idols and contributed more per head to His Majesty's coffers than any other race, by dint of their hard work and honesty.

No doubt there was some slight exaggeration in my claims, but the point went home. I'd never seen Kshayarsha so enraged, though it wasn't hard to guess why. He'd been used once again, and once too often. In the past he'd been manoeuvred into mounting an insane expedition against Greece, and into casting off one after another the three people he'd loved most, and now, just when he imagined that he'd reasserted his own authority, he had discovered he'd been duped all over again. His own First Minister, his friend and more, to whom he'd given his own signet ring, the token of regency, and whom he would have trusted with his own life, had turned out to be a despicable schemer; there was no need for any further evidence to be brought, Kshayarsha roared, for Haman's guilt was already clear enough.

So saying, the King leapt to his feet and strode outside into the courtyard, lest he strangle Haman on the spot with his own bare hands.

Ashpamithra and his pages scuttled after him like so many shadows, as they were expected to; it would have been better for Haman perhaps if he had done the same. But the last place Haman wanted to be just then was anywhere near the King, and he proceeded to make things worse still, if that were possible. Snivelling and gibbering like the coward he was, he threw himself upon my couch, seizing hold of my hands and kissing them, and begging me to intercede for him.

And so this was the scene which confronted Kshayarsha when he'd calmed himself sufficiently to come back inside; and it was the final straw for him. Misconstruing things at a glance, and probably recalling the complaints I'd once made to him about Haman's own lascivious glances, he thundered: 'Is my Queen now to be raped right here in front of me, inside my own palace? Does my regent consider himself entitled to take *everything* that belongs to me, even my own wife? Will this man stop at nothing?'

Just then Hathach and Harbonah returned from the kitchens, and into the awful silence which descended after the King was through with his shouting, young Harbonah ventured, 'Please, my lord, Your Majesty... Lord Haman has built a gallows on which he means to hang Mordecai your Benefactor, Queen Esther's cousin. I saw it with my own eyes. It's fifty cubits high.'

'Well?' raged Kshayarsha, rounding afresh upon Haman, who grovelled on the floor at his feet. 'Have you nothing to say for yourself, you miserable worm? Is this true too? You meant to *hang* a citizen of Shushan, a respected palace official, and a Royal Benefactor? On your own authority, and without so much as the semblance of a trial?'

Haman could barely reply for stuttering. I think he was trying to claim that this was why he'd been skulking about outside His Majesty's private chambers at dawn; he'd intended to seek the King's approval for his plan.

'And you think I would have given it?' roared Kshayarsha. 'You think I would have let you hang a man who had saved my life, however grossly he'd offended you? You would have tricked me, just as you tricked me by using your own obscure name for the Jews. I trusted you, Haman; I trusted you more than I have trusted any other man in my life, and you betrayed me.'

Haman was still pawing at the King's studded boots; Kshayarsha kicked him aside like a dog and sat upon a couch clamping handfuls of his hair between his fists. With his eyes closed so he wouldn't have to look at Haman's face, he said, 'All of you here are witnesses to this man's guilt, and he deserves no other jury. Mordecai would have died without trial; now this man will die the same way. Take him away. Hang him on his own gibbet.'

I'm not quite sure at whom Kshayarsha's order was directed; I don't think he knew himself, or cared, so long as it was obeyed. It was Ashpamithra who obliged him, and the task gave him evident pleasure. He threw a cloak over Haman's head—a sign among the Persians that a convict is doomed to die—and sent Harbonah to summon the guards who stood outside the door. I never set eyes upon Haman's obnoxious face again, and the last thing I heard from him was a muffled whining as Ashpamithra and Hathach handed him over. I think it was the first time I ever saw Ashpamithra's eyes smile.

Predictably, Kshayarsha was in no mood to reconsummate our beleaguered marriage after that. Wan and distracted, he was coaxed back to his quarters by Ashpamithra, and neither of them spared a word for me. Hathach sought to reassure me in his own obsequious manner, patting my hand nervously and saying he was certain that everything would work out; Kshayarsha would return the next day having made sure that Haman was dead and that the Jews' safety was secured.

But it was Hegai I wanted to see; only with him could I be myself. I slipped silently into his room, though I didn't believe he could have slept through Kshayarsha's fulminations. Indeed he hadn't; he'd been listening at his door, still deeming it wisest to keep out of His Majesty's way. Aware all at once of how much the evening had drained me, I embraced him, releasing my pent-up emotion in a garbled account of what had taken place. Most of it he'd probably overheard already, but he was happy to let me run on; and I basked in his easy affection, wishing I could be so relaxed and so open with Kshayarsha who was supposed to be my husband, and wondering whether I ever would be.

After that I slept all night, without stirring or dreaming. In the morning Ashpamithra came with a message from the King: His Majesty would visit me in person at noon, and in the meantime thought I would be gratified to know that Haman had already been hanged—the responsibility for this had fallen upon the Hazarapatish, who I'm quite sure had found the duty far from onerous. Nonetheless, the post of First Minister for Civil and Foreign Affairs was to be retained; and it had been granted to Mordecai ben Jair, in recognition of his singular integrity, and in sincere appreciation of his services rendered to the Empire.

At last allowing myself to believe that my troubles and those of my people were over, I prepared myself delightedly for my husband's return. I had some real misgivings as to how Haman's death might have affected him, but wouldn't let myself dwell on them. Indeed, I bandied jokes with Hegai whilst taking my exercises, and sang old Pioneer songs which my mother had taught me, and whose words I thought I'd forgotten years before. Hegai laughed and tried to sing them with me, struggling to get his tongue around the Hebrew sounds. I laughed too, to hear a Babylonian singing songs of Zion, a city which his forebears had plundered, and which he himself had never seen.

When the King's arrival was announced, Hegai made himself scarce again, going off to visit his harem friends. Then the royal party entered: Kshayarsha himself, with Ashpamithra and his pages. All but Kshayarsha withdrew at once into the courtyard, having been told I suppose that this meeting was a private one between the King and his consort; and hopefully not merely private, but intimate.

Farah and her companions also retired to their rooms after bringing our lunch, over which Kshayarsha spoke of matters practical and safe. Mordecai had been confirmed in the office of First Minister, and would receive the King's signet ring, wrenched from Haman's finger. All of Haman's property and assets—which were considerable—were to be confiscated from his widow Zeresh and his sons, and bestowed upon me.

But when such practicalities had been discussed, conversation faltered, and somehow conjugal desire couldn't take its place. I think Kshayarsha realized now as never before that he'd no real idea of who I was, and that the more he found out, the more alien I might seem. I started to tell him nevertheless, to fill up the gulf between us. I told him everything: I painted him a rose-tinted picture of my idyllic childhood in Jerusalem, and divulged my Hebrew name and its prophetic meaning. I explained the Pioneer vision which my parents had passed on to me, and how it had been shattered, its broken pieces being buried for me in my loved ones' sealed-up tombs. I described my journey to Shushan, and my life in Mordecai's house, and how I'd failed to understand either him or the faith he'd sought to inspire in me. Now I *did* understand, and I mourned the lost years, the wasted love, the many hurtful words said in anger. But through it all, Adonai had had his hand upon my life, and had brought me to the palace for the salvation of my people.

Kshayarsha listened attentively, yet made no comment whatever about the Jews in general, or about their fate. He'd said nothing about them over lunch either. He merely rebuked me quietly: 'You should have told me all this earlier, my sweet one. You have made yourself a stranger to me.'

'My lord...' I rose from my couch and knelt beside his, gently prizing a silver goblet from his hands and placing my own hands between them. 'My lord, I was foolish, and I was wrong. I know I should have told you. But I *was* frightened; I didn't know what you would say.' And when he made no response, other than a faint nodding of the head and a blinking of his lonely eyes, I asked, 'What *would* you have said?'

But he didn't seem to know; my talk of Adonai had confused him. Ahura Mazda ruled Kshayarsha's universe, and all other gods were as nothing. Surely I must know that in my heart, he argued, or I wouldn't have turned my back on Mordecai's god when I was a child?

I replied, 'Of Ahura Mazda I know little, my lord. But Adonai lives; that I do know, because he has preserved his Chosen People through a thousand years of famine and war, and exile, when our very land was lost to us. And I know because he has forgiven me, and I have felt his peace within me.'

Kshayarsha shook his head in perplexity. 'No, that cannot be. No mortal man—or woman—may know that God has forgiven him. Our souls must be judged, and weighed in the Wise Lord's balance when we die. We can only hope, we can never know.'

'Then your god is very cruel, Kshayarsha. He would have you live your life in fear, never knowing which way that balance is tilting.'

I expected him to rebuke me again for saying such a thing, but he only murmured distantly, 'Perhaps.' Then he bowed his head, until his brow touched his hands which were still clasped between mine, and said, 'I went to your native land once, did you know that? It was when I had just become king, and I had to travel to Egypt in person to quell the rebellion. I passed by Jerusalem, and thought it one of the loveliest places on earth, with the kindest inhabitants.' He cleared his throat with a bitter cough. 'They turned out of the city gates to welcome me, laying palm fronds at my feet and praising the House of Hakhamanish because its kings had honoured Adonai in their edicts, giving permission for their fathers to return from exile and rebuild their Temple.'

Only now did he raise his head once more, and his eyes were red where they should have been white. 'I didn't know what to say. I believed that King Kurash had been wrong to allow it; he'd been lax in his duty to Ahura Mazda, and muddled in his thinking because half the time he seemed to fancy that the gods of the nations had real power, and that he should pay respect to those of whichever land he chanced to visit. I resolved to have Adonai's Temple levelled when the right time came. Yet later, when I could have done it, I recalled the Jews' smiling faces, and the noise of their cheering, and the gifts they brought me, and the babies they held out for me to bless; and I couldn't give the order. So how could I have allowed Haman to trick me into issuing a warrant for the destruction of the very race itself? How could I have let him convince me that your people were worse than pagans? I've been a fool once again, my sweet Esther. I shall never be my father's son. With so many deaths upon my conscience, I suppose I *do* know which way my balance is tilting.'

I'd already withdrawn my hands from his, and laid his head against my breast to bring him solace. Then all at once I grasped what he was saying. He must have felt all my muscles go stiff, because he began to assure me that I myself would be safe, as would my kinsman Mordecai, so there was no need for me to be afraid. But I blurted, 'My lord, do you think that's what I care about? What value will *my* life have, with all my people dead? How could I go on living, with their ghosts constantly reproaching me? Haman is dead, Kshayarsha; the edict must be rescinded.'

He sighed, a great heavy sigh that reached right down to his bowels. 'You must know that it isn't so simple, my darling. An official decree from the Great King of Persia cannot be revoked for any reason. That is the law.'

I tore myself from him, regarding him in outraged disbelief, sensing the spark of my fledgling faith sputtering inside me. I said, 'But you are the King of Kings, the most powerful man alive. Surely you can do something.'

'I may be the most powerful, but I am also perhaps the least free. Would my subjects take my words seriously, if they knew that these could be spoken with one breath and unsaid with the next? And Haman's execution, though it may satisfy the demands of justice, will not change the minds of those whom his propaganda has indoctrinated. If anything, it will make them more hostile to the Jews than ever, because they will proclaim him the first martyr for their cause.'

My incredulity was subsiding as despair took its place, mingled with contempt. 'You are frightened!' I expostulated, too devastated to bridle my tongue. 'You're afraid that if you revoke the decree, your subjects will defy you, and rise up to massacre us regardless of your disapproval! You're terrified that your own personal authority will be undermined.' And at the same time I was thinking: I don't want to be saying all this. I wish I didn't have to. It was with Haman that I was at loggerheads, not with Kshayarsha; I don't *want* to fight my own husband. I want us to have the kind of marriage which every woman dreams of.

But his own eyes had begun to blaze, as mine must have been doing; their fire matched that of the plaited gold band in his hair. 'You consider it reprehensible that I should take thought for my own supremacy?' he retaliated. 'What do you suppose would happen if I did not? Do you *want* to see this Empire torn apart and plunged into anarchy? *Millions* would die then.'

'You would make my people into sacrifices so that Persian lives— Aryan lives—might be spared! That's what you mean, isn't it? I thought you and your precious Ahura Mazda had no use for sacrifice! Yet you will allow genocide to be perpetrated in the name of the Wise Lord and the King who serves him! You most certainly are *not* your father's son, Kshayarsha. Darayavaush would never have done such an evil thing. Nor would Kurash. They *helped* my people; they honoured Adonai with their actions, and with their lips! But *you* . . .'

I couldn't go on; and there was no need to. I had wounded Kshayarsha in his most vulnerable place already; he struck me with all his strength across the face. I cried out in pain and fear, for the first time believing that he *did* have it in him to raze cities and pagan temples, and reduce entire populations to cringing subservience as he'd done in Egypt, and in Babylon. I cowered on the floor clutching my stinging cheek, while he stormed about my room sweeping gold and silver utensils onto the floor, hurling scent jars against the walls, smashing glass ornaments, upturning tripods and bowls of flowers, tearing the garlands and the brand-new hangings from their rails, and ripping the plush upholstery with the knife he carried for ceremony. My heart sent up a silent cry for his attendants or mine to come and restrain him, but only Hegai might have had the courage, and he'd quitted the apartment altogether.

When eventually the King had exhausted himself, and collapsed spent on a ruined couch grasping at his stomach, I crawled wretchedly to his side and sought to melt him with my tears. I repeated over and over that I was sorry, I'd meant nothing of what I'd said, but please, please, would he consult his advisers and see if there wasn't some way of saving my people without either breaking the law or putting the security of Persia itself in jeopardy.

At length he apologized too, head between his knees, one hand clamped behind his neck and the other still kneading his belly, saying he couldn't think what had come over him. For my sake he would see his experts in the law, though the discussion would be futile; then he summoned his attendants and left.

I went to my bedroom and lay on the bed in abject despondency. I tried to pray but no words would come; I called for Hathach and sent him in search of Hegai. By and by the latter appeared; I didn't even need to tell him what had happened, for he'd lived among Persians and been familiar with their laws much longer than I had. But he said, 'Don't give up hope, Little Star. Surely Adonai hasn't brought us so far, to abandon us now?' His great dark eyes were questioning, misty with the first hazing of doubt. I felt so guilty then that I let him coax me up, and for the first time we prayed aloud together; once again I was contrasting our closeness and intuitive understanding with the distance between myself and Kshayarsha.

Nevertheless, I'm not sure that either Hegai or I would have had the faith to go on hoping, had not Mordecai come to see us just after the siesta. Dressed in opulent robes of blue and white, a purple cloak and a turban as grand as any, I hardly recognized him. He kissed us both, reminding me—not without a pinch of sarcasm—that where Adonai is at work, there is always scope for change; and he showed us the royal seal-ring which he'd inherited from Haman. Then he said, 'You have done well, my daughter. You have brought about the demise of our enemy, and enabled me to rise to a position of influence above Memucan and his youthful colleagues, above Hutaosa, perhaps even above Ashpamithra. I have permission to enter the presence of the King without being summoned, just as you have once more; and I have been granted special dispensation to enter the harem to visit you whenever I so choose, provided that I have an escort, since it is I who must administer Haman's confiscated property on your behalf. Now we can truly begin to work for our people's redemption, you and I.'

'No, Father.' I shook my head unhappily, knowing that if Mordecai's faith wasn't strong enough to bear the full weight of my unbelief, then no man's could be. 'Haman is gone, but *nothing* has changed.'

'Oh, but it has. You and Hegai have changed; and I have changed. I may be almost blind, Hadassah, but I see things now more clearly than I ever have before. I have found the intimacy with Adonai which I always craved, yet could never quite attain when you and I were fighting like cat and dog, and when I took the worries of the world upon myself. A change of the heart accomplishes more than all the political proclamations ever made, Hadassah, and prayer is stronger than armies. You will see, I promise. Kshayarsha is in session with his legal counsellors already.'

19

But days went by, and we heard nothing concerning the outcome of these deliberations. Nor did I see Kshayarsha even once, though I got word from Ashpamithra that his master was ill with his stomach again, and wanted me to know this lest I be afraid that our quarrel over the Jews had imperilled our reconciliation.

This only made me more afraid than ever, for to put something dreadful into words, even for the purpose of denying it, can give it power. The faith which had sprung up so readily within me seemed to be withering as the shallow-rooted grass does when the summer sun scorches the Shushan plain.

Things weren't helped by the fact that I'd seen nothing of Hutaosa either. Surely if I'd been confirmed once again as Kshayarsha's principal wife, his mother would have been to offer me her congratulations? She had been so kind, so welcoming, once upon a time ... but that was when she'd been anticipating the arrival of a grandchild with none of Vashti's corrosive blood. And what of Vashti herself? If *she* had reason to believe I was reconciled to the King, surely she would soon be doing something about it?

A week or so later, Hathach discovered that Kshayarsha had indeed had several conferences with his legal advisers and with his seven chief counsellors—conferences from which Mordecai was excluded because of their subject-matter and his own vested interest in it. However, it had been decided that other opinions should be sought, namely the opinions of satraps and governors throughout the Empire as to the feeling within their respective provinces regarding the Jewish populations who lived in colonies there. I'd been correct in my assumption that the King feared large-scale rebellion if he attempted to oppose the prejudices of significant numbers of his subjects. But this meant we might have to wait two—or even three—months for the provincial representatives to arrive and for a conclusion to be reached.

'Two *months?*' I wailed. 'I cannot bear it, Hathach. And am I not to see Kshayarsha in all that time, either? I shall be unable to eat or sleep. I shall die, either from starvation or from exhaustion.'

Hathach began exhorting me and chiding me in his own inimitably nervous but well-meaning fashion, pointing out that the King was no doubt unwilling for me to see him indisposed; I retorted that he'd been indisposed the first day we met, but that hadn't done any harm. I begged him to go to Kshayarsha's quarters and ask permission for me to visit him there, if the King was too weak to come to me.

Hathach returned with the message that I could visit that very evening if I so desired, but that I must not expect an elaborate meal such as *I* had laid on for *him*, because at present His Majesty couldn't abide the sight of food after sunset.

I didn't care; I could barely abide the sight of food at all.

I'd expected to find him mildly under the weather, possibly languishing on a couch, but not confined to bed, which was where he was. He bade me approach him, but leave my attendants outside the bedroom along with his own, so we were quite alone. I said, 'My lord, I'm sorry. I shouldn't have come. I didn't realize...'

He smiled a watery smile, like pale winter sunshine. 'Don't be dispirited, my sweet Esther,' he said. 'I'm not as bad as I look. I wanted an excuse to do away with formalities and have you to myself straight away. Come.' And he turned back the bedclothes to receive me.

I bit my lip in confusion, not feeling ready. I faltered, 'My lord... you ought not to overtax yourself. I *know* that you've been very sick again. Please... can we not talk first?'

'Talk? My dear Esther, it is talk I am sick of! Besides, whenever we talk we quarrel, and I don't want that. My days are bedevilled by quarrelling ministers and minions; I don't want my nights bedevilled too.'

So, reluctantly, I began to shed my clothing, fumbling awkwardly with brooches and buckles because it was so long since I'd unfastened them for myself, and because there was no escaping the disquieting notion that I was undressing for a total stranger. All at once it was like being back in Iphigenia's cottage, being inspected by Memucan and Shaashgaz, and I wished I could have gone behind a screen to prepare myself, as a respectable Persian lady would have done. But Kshayarsha had never wanted me respectable; both of us had prided ourselves on our indifference to tradition, and now I was paying the penalty.

'You are as lovely as you were on our wedding day,' he remarked, when I stood quite naked before him in the lamplight, hiding my face and my breasts with my loosened hair and wishing it were long enough to hide the rest of me. 'Come,' he said again, 'You have been starved of love just as I have. It is not good for a man or a woman to sleep alone. You need me as much as I need you.'

Do I? I thought, as I crept miserably between the covers and felt his arms go around me. He started to kiss me, to devour me, but there was a strange desperation in his hunger, as though he needed to prove something, or even as though he felt he must make the most of limited time.

I tried to respond, to bring him satisfaction, but had to force myself, and was sure he'd be able to tell. I rebuked myself for being so foolish: all week I'd been looking forward to this moment—fearing it might never come—and in fact for months before that as well. But now we were together, I couldn't help but picture him with Vashti, or Hegai— or worst of all, Haman. What was I doing, defiling myself with a sinner who had consorted with the bitterest enemy of my people, and who was himself their enemy now? The awesome horror of what must shortly overtake the Jewish race came home to me afresh; it was as though the palace walls were suddenly made of Egyptian glass, and at last I could see through them clearly to the world outside, with all its violence and terror, prejudice, and sordid, meaningless suffering. I was in bed with my lawful wedded husband who was Great King of Persia, but I felt like a prostitute lying with a murderer.

At length he entered me; soon it was over; he slid away from me, panting and soaked in sweat, though the thing hadn't been roughly done, for him, and I knew then that he was indeed iller than he wanted me to believe. Presently, when I thought he'd fallen asleep, he pulled me towards him and said, 'Esther, tell me you love me. It is so long since I heard those words from anyone, except in my dreams.'

What was I to say? He was looking right at me, his face a patchwork of shadows, the new hollowness in his cheeks stressed by the low light from the lamps, with its unforgiving angles. I stammered, then managed: 'My lord, please forgive me. I'm so anxious about my people. How can I say I love you when you hold the key to their fate but will not turn it?' It was the most tactful reply I could think of.

'Oh, Esther,' he said, sighing up my name from the depths of his being. 'I hoped that for just one night we might forget all that. I'm doing all I can, believe me. You must be patient.'

'I'm sorry, my lord. But it is not so easy. If I hadn't come to the palace, neither would Mordecai have done so. Then he would never have come into contact with Haman or been ordered to bow the knee to him, and the Jews would never have been threatened. The guilt is hard to bear, and impossible to cast aside.'

'You are lying to me again, Queen Esther.'

'I—'

'You said that your god had forgiven all your sins. That must include your sin in coming here—if sin it was. The reason why you cannot say you love me is that you don't know whether you do. You don't know what love is, any more than I do.'

Again there was nothing I could say. I stretched out one hand and tentatively stroked his beardless cheek; he closed his eyes, and laid a hand over mine lest I withdraw my small comfort. He must have shaved especially for my visit, because his cheek was smooth as a boy's and reminded me of Hegai's; there was a voice in my head saying: you *do* know what love is; and the voice was Hegai's.

So disconcerting was this that it was some while before I became aware that Kshayarsha was still talking.

'I used to think I knew. When I married Vashti, and she was so beautiful, so full of life ... my subjects loved her too, and showered us with gifts, and sang in the streets for our happiness. But I wouldn't have cared if I'd been the meanest beggar in Shushan, so long as I had her. How did I let it go wrong? How did I let one drunken mistake ruin my life?'

I said, 'There was Hegai. You made her jealous of him, long before the night of the party when she defied you. Things must have been wrong for many months.'

'Hegai...' He repeated the name so softly, so wistfully, that a great lump rose in my throat and I had to choke it down. 'With Hegai it was different altogether; surely she must have been able to see that? He was just a child; lonely, homesick, and so eager to please. I was all that he had.'

'You were all that he had, because you had destroyed *his* people too. And a woman's love is as jealous as it is powerful, Kshayarsha.'

'I know; I know that all too well. But why was she so stubborn, Esther? Why didn't she come to me when I summoned her, however improperly it was done? She could have rebuked me afterwards, in private. But she drove me away ... she drove me to look for love in

places where it could never be found. There was Marduniya who only
loved me because he was greedy for power; he led my armies to
destruction because he wouldn't give up on Greece, of which he was
determined to be satrap. So now the Greeks are *still* harassing our
islands and our shores. Then there was the wife of my own brother, in
Sardis; oh God, what a mess that was! And there was Haman, may the
Wise Lord's angels torment his soul . . .'

'And there was me.'

'You? I—I don't know what you're saying.'

'Yes, you do, Kshayarsha. You chose me because I reminded you of
Vashti. It's Vashti you love still, if *you* are truly honest with yourself
and with me. And you would reinstate her tomorrow, if Persian law
were different. But she is the victim of another of your edicts which
cannot be revoked.'

Now it was he who was lost for what to say. His beliefs wouldn't let
him lie; and something else inside him was unwilling to hurt my
feelings by his honesty. I'd never known such a thing worry him
before, and because of that, for that one moment at least, I *did* love
him. I put my fingers to his lips so he would know that I understood,
and he sighed a great sigh of relief, and of unspeakable heaviness, both
together. Then feeling for one another a little more than we'd ever
done before, we came together for the second time that night. Perhaps
it was the closest we'd ever come to making love.

Two months later to the day, I learned that all the representatives
who were intending to be present for the conference concerning the
Jews had now arrived in Shushan. In the meantime, I'd seen Kshayarsha several times each week, Hutaosa more than once, and Mordecai
whenever I sent for him to remind me that all would be well. I was
ashamed of the erratic nature of my faith, which flared up strongly one
day, and was feebly sputtering the next; once the initial blaze of
euphoria had died down, Hegai too had his moments of despondency.
But Mordecai simply smiled, and blessed us, and sometimes prayed
over us with his blue-veined hands laid lightly upon our bowed heads;
our inconstancy was natural, he said, for each of us had known Adonai
for such a little time. Only with years of experience and a regular
fuelling of answered prayers would the flame of our faith burn
consistently bright.

The conference was to last a full day. Mordecai would be allowed to attend its afternoon session, and when it ended, I should be summoned to the Apadana and the council's findings would be announced. Kshayarsha warned me in advance not to set my hopes too high; for all that we knew, anti-Jewish feeling might be stronger elsewhere in the Empire even than it was in Shushan.

That day was the worst in all my life since the day I lost my parents, Rachael and Pithon. I tried to eat, but brought everything back up again. I tried to sleep, but whenever my eyes were closed I saw sharpened swords clashing, bright as bolts of lightning against a background of smoke and fire and devastation. I tried to pray, but instead of joy I found hysteria, and instead of peace, the silence of death. Hegai was with me throughout, and Mordecai too in the morning, but I hardly knew they were there.

The sun had long set and the lamps were lit along the walls when my summons came. On such a momentous occasion, and in the presence of so many such august dignitaries, everything had to be done with exact and stifling formality. Ashpamithra came to escort me; he was wearing full ceremonial apparel, as I too had to do, though Vashti's royal tiara which kept my veil in place seemed to burn into my brow like something caustic.

With Ashpamithra leading, Hegai walking beside me and my seven maids behind, I proceeded to the Apadana like a condemned criminal going off to execution. I hadn't thought to have to go there again so soon after the day I'd gone trembling to invite the King and his First Minister to my banquet. At least this time I was expected, so my own life was in no danger. But that of thousands of men, women and children who shared my own flesh and blood depended on the words which would be said to me.

Ashpamithra announced me to Artabanush the Hazarapatish, in the Old Persian formula which was obligatory on solemn state occasions. Artabanush mounted the great stone staircase and passed within the curtains, which parted to receive me. I undertook my ascent with all my entourage in tow, and stood at the top of the steps looking down the length of the hall towards the throne. Beside it on the dais, illumined by a myriad candles, stood the faraway figures of Mordecai, the seven personal advisers of the King, and his eunuchs and pretty page-boys. From such a way off I couldn't recognize the men by their faces, and they all wore too much stiffened brocade for me to tell them apart even by the breadth of their shoulders or thickness of their girths. Only the black-hooded magus, still as a statue and holding aloof from the others, was distinguishable on sight. I thought of the hideous pagan practices of his not-so-distant ancestors, and shuddered. How much influence might he have exercised over what had been discussed?

Lining the central aisle for almost the whole of its length sat the satraps, cross-legged, on silken cushions, with their multifarious attendants on hand behind them. There were bearded bodyguards, eunuchs and boys; sallow faces, white faces, faces black as charcoal. I had my veil right over my face and was thankful that through its filmy texture I could see them all far more clearly than they could see me.

By virtue of his office it ought to have fallen to Mordecai to say what had to be said. But because of its nature, the speech was delivered by Memucan; in Persian, which had to be translated line by line into the Aramaic of everyday speech. It began with a bombastic preamble, as such things are wont to do, and all the while I gazed into the face of my adoptive father and sought to discern from it the answer to the question that burned in my heart. Only when Memucan spoke it out did I understand the reason for the phlegmatic expression which Mordecai was wearing. The answer was no answer at all.

The Great King had issued an official decree, Memucan declared, and consequently his words could not be revoked. However, this decree had not made specific the identity of the agents to be employed in the Jews' elimination. The Jews were to be killed by 'their enemies', it had stated, but no indication had been given as to who these enemies were. Therefore the King and the Court of Satraps and Governors had agreed that no Imperial troops would be deployed for this purpose, neither the Immortals, nor the regiments which went to make up the regular army, nor the garrisons of cities with Jewish inhabitants, nor the governors' own security forces. Each Persian subject must decide for himself whether to join in the assault upon his Jewish neighbours on the thirteenth day of Adar, or not; and the authorities would not censure him for his decision. Also, the decree had stipulated one day only as the period during which the annihilation was to be carried out, and the King in his wisdom had defined a day for this purpose to be the space between sunrise and sunset. Anyone found guilty of violence against the Jews, or against any individual Jew, before or after that day, would be treated exactly as the perpetrator of any other violent crime could expect to be treated. The King had spoken; long live the King.

So saying, Memucan rolled up the scroll from which he had read, and both he and his translator stepped back to stand once more behind Kshayarsha, who sat rigid and impassive as an idol. His illness had relaxed its grip on him gradually once more over the past two months, but having gone so many hours without the food he needed to absorb the ill humours in his gut, he would be in some small pain by now.

Then quite unexpectedly, Kshayarsha addressed me himself. He announced that Mordecai and I might write letters to the Jewish communities throughout his domains to whatever effect we wished, and might stamp them with the royal seal.

There was a murmur of surprise from those grouped about him; Mordecai too was clearly taken aback. For myself, I was at a loss as to how to interpret what I'd heard, and stood looking quizzically at the newly invested First Minister, who was utterly unable to see me, while Memucan proclaimed that the audience was at an end, as indeed was the session of the Court. Hegai touched my elbow and I let him escort me from the hall, my eyes smarting from the smoke of the burning incense, my thoughts and emotions in turmoil.

Shortly afterward, Mordecai visited me in my apartment. Without even thinking to greet him correctly or offer him refreshment, I blurted: 'I don't understand what has happened. Are our people to die after all? What can we write which could make things any better, if that is how they are?'

But the maturing of his lifelong faith had bestowed upon him clarity of mind as well as calmness of spirit, in contrast to my youthful excitability. While I had been panicking, he'd been thinking, and he'd spoken privately to Kshayarsha to ensure that his thoughts were running in the right direction. What he'd concluded was that Kshayarsha meant us to see that our people were equipped and trained to attack their attackers.

'He said so, in so many words?' I exclaimed.

'Of course he did not, my sweet daughter. How could he? Do you expect him to give express permission for a sizeable minority of his subjects to oppose the realization of a royal decree? But he left me in no doubt as to his meaning; and as to what he hoped the eventual outcome would be. We have as long to prepare ourselves as it takes for a baby to grow in a woman's womb; and any mother will tell you that it feels like forever. We have little to fear now, but a great deal to do.'

'I still don't understand. Kshayarsha has sanctioned what must become a hideous civil war, within his own Empire. There will be a bloodbath, Father. It will be appalling.'

'I do not think so. At least, any blood that *is* shed is as likely to be Gentile as Jewish; probably *more* likely. It took our Amalekite friend little enough time to stir up hatred against us among folk who barely knew who we were; in nine months I am sure we shall lay most of it to rest.'

'Oh, Father, how I wish you were right! But hatred is so much easier to fuel than love, or respect! I have lived in Jerusalem; I have seen what blind hatred is like when once it darkens men's eyes. I've seen them murder total strangers in cold blood because of their race; I've seen children scarcely old enough to talk, throwing stones at their parents' enemies, and then being beaten by full-grown men. I've seen...' But I couldn't go on, because what I was seeing even as I spoke was the funeral of those I had loved, and the shrill keening of the mourners rang once again in my ears.

Mordecai folded me in his arms and hushed me, saying nothing until I had gathered myself together. When I was still, he said, 'Hadassah, the number of those who truly hate us is very small. That is what His Majesty your husband was careful to ascertain from the delegates at the conference before making any decision. The further from Shushan one travels, the less the general population holds against us. Haman's influence was pernicious, and a great deal of noise has been made about it; but it was confined to a limited area nonetheless. Once the story spreads that the new First Minister is a Jew, as is Kshayarsha's Queen herself, it will be a reckless and foolish man who pits himself against us.'

Subdued but not yet convinced, I muttered, 'The world is too full of reckless and foolish men. Some of them will look for *any* excuse to resort to violence.'

'But many will think twice if they fear reprisals.'

'Reprisals? From whom? It is as you said—the authorities won't be able to help us, even afterwards.'

'Our enemies have but a single day on which they will be permitted to carry weapons and do us harm, Hadassah. Any violence perpetrated against us after that will be severely punished. Yet nothing has been said about punishing those who find ways of taking their revenge upon our attackers once the fateful day's sun has set. And until it does, Jews will be licensed to bear arms also. It is our duty to point this out to those for whom we care.'

The following morning, we settled upon the wording of the letter which was to be published under our auspices. Mordecai had been pondering over it most of the night, and the ideas he presented to me for my approval were already well worked out. All that remained to be done was the polishing of isolated phrases and the welding of the separate sentences together. Copies were to be sent by imperial post to the councils of elders of each Jewish community of the Empire.

On the twenty-third day of the month of Sivan, the letter was dictated by Mordecai to the royal secretaries and translators, and despatched to every province, from India to Sudan. Versions were rendered in every conceivable language and system of writing, and stamped with the King's seal. In every city, Jews were authorized to organize themselves for self-defence; if armed men of any nationality whatever were to attack Jewish men, women or children, the Jews could retaliate, taking the lives of those who had sought theirs. Indeed, the aggressors were to be slaughtered to the very last man, and their possessions were to be confiscated, but not one innocent person must be harmed in Adonai's name.

Despite this final note of restraint, I had my reservations about what we'd written. I wasn't sure that the actual slaughter of our opponents was strictly necessary, nor the confiscation of their property; wouldn't it be enough to drive them off and frighten them, to deter them from attacking us again?

But Mordecai was adamant. It was essential for us to complete the task which our predecessors had left unfinished, thereby subjecting us to generation upon generation of suffering and persecution. Joshua had failed to wipe out the Canaanites; Moses, Joshua and Saul in turn had left the Amalekites to lick their wounds and rise again. We must not fail as they had failed. The destruction of our enemies was the will of Adonai, and we must not shrink from it because of misdirected clemency or plain squeamishness. In the future there would come a time when Gentiles might enter God's kingdom in their millions and be forgiven all their trespasses against us; swords would be beaten into ploughshares, and all peoples would dwell together in harmony as the prophets had forseen. But that time had not yet come, and it never would if we imagined in our human arrogance that we knew better than God and could do the Messiah's work for him.

Rejoicing erupted in the streets of Shushan as soon as our letter was published. It was as though the thirteenth of Adar had already come and gone, and the battle been won. In the Jewish quarter there was dancing in the streets; girls tossed flowers, boys linked arms and chanted songs of Zion, tempting fate perhaps, but no one touched them because most of the Gentiles were nearly as relieved as we were. Haman was gone, and everyone knew why; most folk of moderate opinions were happy to lay his dogma to rest along with his bones, and pretend that they'd been perfectly well disposed to their Jewish neighbours all along. There were even those who took it into their heads to convert and become Jews themselves, having admired the courage of their victimized friends and colleagues, and having now been presented with incontrovertible evidence of the power of the God about whom they had heard. So Hegai became the first of many, though how many of them experienced the outpouring of Adonai's spirit in the way that he had done, I couldn't say.

Still, there is a time for celebration and a time for working, just as there is a time for everything under God's sun. The time had now come for working extremely hard, because not all the raised voices which rang along the city's alleyways were employed in the singing of joyous songs, and not all the stomping feet belonged to jubilant dancers. In the silences between the euphoric Hebrew refrains, disaffected Shushanite thugs and extremists could still be heard muttering against us, relentlessly sharpening their blades, and gnashing their teeth in their impatience to slit our Semitic throats.

None of the Jewish exiles had any experience of battle. They and their forefathers had lived in peace since the mighty Kurash had declared himself their friend, and even during Haman's ascendancy the older folk at least had been reluctant to use their fists to defend themselves, or else they hadn't been granted the opportunity.

So Mordecai sent to Jerusalem, for men to come and share with us the benefit of their experience with the Samaritans. Few could be spared because the Jews of Israel were under threat just like their brethren scattered elsewhere. But those who came were seasoned warriors, brave as lions and strong as bears, with the old Pioneer zeal glinting in their hard-bitten eyes. Some took up residence in Shushan, others in other cities of Persia which had prominent Jewish communities; and the young Jewish men flocked about them, fiercely eager to learn and to excel.

By contrast, many of their fathers and uncles still held back, refusing to believe that anything so dreadful could really happen to them when they had committed no offence—regardless of the evidence which had accumulated before their very eyes.

Mordecai strove to collect as much equipment for our ardent vigilantes as he could. He bought—or was lent, or given—swords, daggers, spears, bows and arrows, slings; I myself contributed enormous quantities of gold and saleable jewels, since I'd been unspeakably enriched by Kshayarsha even before acquiring all that had once belonged to Haman. Our resources might well have stretched to employing whole regiments of hardened Greek mercenaries, but against this a line had been firmly drawn. Imperial troops were already stationed at the gates of every city where Jews lived, strictly vetting all newcomers so that there should be no influx of bellicose hirelings on either side. Nevertheless, a comprehensive network of communication lines was established between our communities, along which information could be carried and kit distributed.

Gradually, therefore, structure emerged out of raw enthusiasm. The most promising of the recruits were rewarded with official rank and status, and each was made responsible for the instruction of the youngsters in his charge. The nature of the coming engagement had to be made perfectly clear to everyone: it was a holy war like that fought by our forefather Joshua to reclaim the Promised Land, and thus there was to be no looting of Gentile property, nor stripping of their corpses.

As the newly-appointed captains of our own Shushanite defence-force grew more confident in their abilities and more trusting of one another, and as they met regularly with Mordecai to discuss their progress, I did begin to wonder whether the old men might not be proved right after all. What mob would dare lift a finger against this expertly trained, determined, dauntless team of fighters, each of whom had a multitude of well-drilled youths under his command? But Mordecai warned me sternly against complacency. There were still plenty of debtors and landless, hopeless, unemployable wasters who attributed their own poverty to Jewish prosperity, even though much of that prosperity had been eroded under Haman's regime. Nor could we discount the possibility that whole tribes or nations with a traditional antipathy towards us—such as the Samaritans, the Ammonites or even the Philistines, all of whose territories were now included within the Empire—might seize the opportunity to move against us.

This was a contingency I hadn't considered. Mordecai exhorted me not to fear unduly; there was little chance of an initiative on this kind of scale achieving anything significant on a single day. Certainly the King would display no hesitation in ordering his generals to contain anything of this sort, for it could escalate rapidly into a serious threat to imperial security. But the possibility was still there, and had to be taken into consideration.

I did consider it, at great length. Indeed, once Mordecai had mentioned it, I couldn't put it from my mind. I had already begun to see the impending struggle as the culmination of the Saulides' conflict with Amalek; now all at once it was more than that. It was also the outworking of my own personal hatred for the murderers of my parents, my sister and my best friend, and the abduction of my brother. I wished I might wield a sword myself; as the days and weeks went by, I had moods when I would have had no qualms at all about using one. For things had moved on; the reins had been taken out of my hands, and cooped up in my chambers I grew increasingly frustrated because there was nothing for me to do but pray. Of course, part of me knew that prayer was the strongest weapon we possessed, but I had to remind myself of that a hundred times a day.

If anything, those weeks and months were worse for Hegai than they were for me. I was a woman, and I was Queen, and there could never have been any question of my being allowed within sight of a battleground, let alone joining in the fighting myself. But Hegai had been born and raised every inch as male as our neophyte captains, with most of whom he was of an age; yet whatever happened, he would *never* be able to fight alongside those he'd chosen as his brothers, for no commander worth his salt will welcome a eunuch into his ranks. Geldings are assumed to have lost their masculine courage and aggressive instincts along with everything else that goes to make a man. More than once during the weeks and months of waiting I came upon Hegai sitting alone beneath the orange-tree in the courtyard, with his ornamental dagger unsheathed and his fingers lightly running along the polished blade.

As the thirteenth of Adar came closer and tension rose in the city along with spring temperatures, Hathach still went out faithfully each day and reported to me what he saw and heard. But he brought back no evidence to suggest that our enemies were organizing themselves in the sort of way that we had taken pains to do. Possibly they didn't believe the tales they must have been hearing, about the co-ordination of Jewish resistance, or else they regarded us all as pious pen-pushers who would be too feckless or squeamish to use whatever arms we procured. Then again, most of those who meant us harm weren't the type of men who are capable of getting themselves organized with the best will in the world. Any direction they had, had come from Haman; now that he was gone, their so-called leaders squabbled amongst themselves, and were as likely to set upon one another with malicious intent, as upon us. Several of Haman's former associates were found one by one slumped in dusty gutters, with clumsy knife wounds in their backs.

Then at the beginning of the month of Adar, in the heart of the Jewish quarter of Shushan, a Jewish businessman's home was surrounded by ruffians illegally armed, and they set it on fire. The owner was esteemed and adored by all who knew him; something of a scholar as well as a bureaucrat, he was referred to affectionately as 'rabbi' by his friends and associates. As Mordecai had once been accustomed to do, he held Torah classes in his house, and informal gatherings for worship, and he'd carried on doing so in defiance of Haman's restrictions on Jews' rights of assembly. The attack upon him came on a sabbath morning when his home was thronged with the faithful, who had congregated in ever larger numbers as their day of doom approached. Men who hadn't thought about God in years and who had almost forgotten their Hebrew were resolutely chanting the ancient prayers like the priests and prophets of old.

Their host was strangled with his own prayer-shawl; none of the worshippers was seen alive again.

Neither were most of their murderers; incensed and grieving Jewish youths fell upon them in a frenzy, wrestling them to the ground and disposing of them with the weapons snatched from their scrabbling fingers.

But after that, no one could go on imagining that Haman's day of reckoning might pass without serious incident. The final battle had already begun.

20

The day dawned bright and cloudless, just like the one before it, and
the one before that. Each had been slightly but unmistakably hotter
than the last; spring had come to the plain of Shushan, and overhead
the sky was so thickly blue it was as hard to believe in rain as in the
senseless violence which must shortly break out all across the
Empire.

I rose as soon as I woke, and dressed in the plainest garb I could
find. It seemed inappropriate to wear anything else, or to make up my
face or varnish my nails. Hegai likewise donned a simple white robe,
bound back his hair in an austere twist, and left his face unadorned.

To Hathach I'd assigned duties which kept him mostly out of my
presence; Roxana and my seven maids I dismissed until sundown, for I
found that I wanted no one near me who didn't belong to my own
threatened people. Today I didn't want to be Queen of Persia, but a
Jew like other Jews, with whose suffering I wanted to identify. I ate no
breakfast and took no bath, and felt ashamed because it was a real
hardship for me to go for one day with my flesh unwashed and
unscented, when many of my brothers and sisters who lived beyond
the protection of the palace walls had lost everything except their lives,
and all too soon might forfeit these also.

Nevertheless, if I'd expected any visitors I might have taken more
care over my appearance. I'd thought to see no one but Hegai, and
occasionally Hathach, who was under orders to keep me informed of
developments in the city. He wasn't to go there himself; it was much
too dangerous now. Instead, he was to spend the day dancing atten-
dance upon Mordecai, who in turn must be all day at Kshayarsha's
beck and call lest any unforseen crisis should arise; Kshayarsha's spies
would tell Mordecai all that he and Hathach needed to know.

My own place was to keep out of the men's way, and to pray.
Although in my head I was convinced that I should accomplish far
more by doing this than by futilely seeking to involve myself physically

in what lay ahead, yet my heart wouldn't be told, and I couldn't even think straight, let alone prepare myself to approach Adonai.

Things got worse as hours dragged by and we heard nothing.

'Why doesn't Hathach come?' I demanded of Hegai, as if he had any more idea than I had. 'It's so quiet. Too quiet.' I got up and went out into the courtyard, then came back in; and went out a second time. 'Why can't I hear any birds singing? Why is there no one about?'

Hegai smiled resignedly. 'Little Star, you can hear no birds singing because you will not be silent long enough to listen. And I thought there was no one you wanted to see?'

'There wasn't. There isn't.' I'd flung myself on a couch but now stood up again in irritation because my skin itched where the cushions pressed upon it, and my teeth were on edge from nothing; my whole being was on edge.

Then about mid-morning there came someone at the door; I ran there myself, thinking it was Hathach at last. But it was his young friend Harbonah, and he hadn't brought news, but a gift swathed in linen wrappings.

My jaw must have dropped; I'd completely forgotten that today was my birthday. I asked him how he'd found out, but he said, 'Oh, Your Majesty, my lady, I'm sorry; this isn't from me. A friend of mine asked me to pass it on to you; he's an apprentice to one of the court tutors and could get no leave from his duties.'

I knew at once then who had sent it. I'm not sure *how* I knew, because the court tutors have always taught the sons of prominent noblemen as well as the young princes. But none of the other pupils' mothers was likely to have sent me a gift unless a birthday banquet had been arranged.

I said, 'Harbonah, take it back. Return it to your friend; I don't want it.'

Poor naive Harbonah did nothing but gape at me in shock. It is one thing to decline a gift politely when you are face to face with the giver, and plead your unworthiness to receive by trotting out the conventional phrases. Rejecting a gift which is delivered by proxy is something else altogether; especially since Harbonah could see I had no intention of relenting after the customary two refusals.

Then Hegai intervened. 'Hadassah, you must accept it. You must not risk offending her today. Surely we have enough to worry about already.'

'It will be a poisoned cake, and Roxana isn't here to taste it,' I retorted hoarsely. 'Or a cloak soaked in acid; or a venomous snake in a basket.'

'If it's a cake we need not eat it, and if it's a cloak you need not wear it,' Hegai pointed out, having thanked Harbonah in his most complaisant courtly voice, and then dismissed him. 'And if it's a snake, we shall find a charmer to make it dance.'

I managed a wan smile, but my insides had begun to cramp up as though I'd been poisoned already. Yet I couldn't do other than watch as Hegai unfolded the linen wrappings from Vashti's gift and stood it carefully on the table.

It was a silver menorah almost a cubit high—a copy of the seven-branched candelabrum which is one of the holiest artefacts in the Jerusalem Temple. In itself it was lovely, and had it come from any other source I would have been moved. Coming as it did from Vashti, I knew that it was meant as a symbol of my inferiority, a reminder that I was an outsider with foreign blood, and could never be anything else. This was obvious to me even before Hegai discovered that the gift had a note attached.

My dearest Esther—or may I call you Hadassah?—Allow me to take this opportunity to wish you the happiest of birthdays. I do hope you will like this little present; I was so pleased when I came across it again among my treasures, because it is so singularly appropriate for you, as well as being so exquisitely fashioned. Of course, had I known, I could have given it to you last year or the year before, but I have only recently become aware of your connections with the fascinating and—how shall I put this?—piquantly tragic tribe of the Jews. It is such a shame that their rich culture with all its charming customs and quaint beliefs will soon have no existence outside of the imperial archives. Still, civilizations become so much more interesting as objects of study when they belong to the dim and distant past, don't you agree? Time spins such an exotic web of enchantment about them! Sumer, Knossos, Nineveh, the lost continent of Atlantis... What wonderfully romantic images these place-names conjure up in our minds! And all because their cities and inhabitants are gone, and we are free to imagine them as we ourselves would like them to have been. Perhaps when you are gone this pretty little candlestick will find its way into the museum of some future King of Persia, perhaps a son or grandson of one of my own dear children. You might like to compose a paragraph or two to be displayed alongside it, so that visitors who are taken to see it will know what it was for? It is a pity that you won't have time to go into any great detail; but I don't suppose most of the Great King's guests could spare the time to read it if you did. Enjoy what remains of your birthday, Hadassah darling, because nothing good can last for ever.

I tried to take some deep breaths to calm myself, but nearly choked. I gasped, 'She's going to kill me; I've known it all along. And she's going to do it today, because only today will no one have the right to stop her.'

'Hadassah, don't be so silly. How do you know she doesn't feel sorry for you? Perhaps she wants to be reconciled to you at last.'

'Of course she doesn't; are you blind? She's been seeing Kshayarsha! She *must* have been, or she wouldn't know my Hebrew name! Oh, God, Tammuz, she will have been turning him against me all over again; and it's my own fault. Why did I have to say to him that Vashti was the only person he's ever really loved? Why did I have to set him thinking that way? She is so clever, and I'm so *stupid*; he's probably thought about little else ever since I put the notion into his head, and now he's been telling her all my secrets. She'll use her knowledge against me, Tammuz, I know she will. She says I won't have time to write more than a few paragraphs about the menorah; and she tells me to enjoy what *remains* of my birthday—'

'That could mean anything. It's getting on for noon now. Your birthday is half over.'

'I must go and see Kshayarsha. I must go at once. I have to find out for sure whether he's been talking to Vashti, and what he has said, and what it all means. And I have to insist that he protects me from her, today of all days.'

'Don't, Little Star. Please. Stay here. You'll only make things worse.'

But I didn't waste any words arguing back. I swept past him, and would have marched on out of the door except that right on my very threshold I came face to face with Hutaosa.

As usual, she was accompanied by her elderly handmaid, but she also had two eunuchs in tow, which was unheard of for her. Nor were they any ordinary palace geldings. They were two of the burliest fellows I'd ever seen, and each of them carried a dagger much too fearsome to be intended for ceremonial usage only.

But I was too overcome with shame at my own appearance to pay that of Hutaosa's formidable escort any further thought just then. I'd scarcely seen the Queen Mother to speak to for months, and here I was with my face unpainted and my hair as straight and flat and dull as a peasant-woman's. I made as if to apologize, but she kissed me and waved my half-spoken words aside, saying she understood that today was not like other days for me.

In spite of her superficial sympathy, however, I sensed distinctly that she *didn't* understand; if the entire Empire had been collapsing about her ears, they would have had diamond rings in them and she wouldn't have neglected her toilette. I was still more convinced that she hadn't the faintest inkling of what I was going through when she said brightly, 'I know we have had our differences, Esther dear, but it is you that Persia has to thank for the demise of the execrable Agagite, and I didn't think I should let your birthday pass without trying to make amends between us.'

Then Hutaosa beckoned her maid, who brought out a bouquet of lilies and roses from behind her back.

'Oh, you shouldn't have,' I mumbled, twice, as custom demanded; when she deposited the flowers in my arms I promised to have them put in water. But observing that my maidservants were nowhere to be seen, Hutaosa set her own to the task, greeting Hegai in passing, and inclining her head gracefully when he bent and silently kissed her hand. Then she devoted herself to engaging me in trivial conversation.

'You know, I shall be heartily relieved when today is over and done with,' she declared, after repeating the same piece of futile gossip to me for the third time and not eliciting the desired response. 'Kshayarsha is almost as distracted with it as you are. Oh, don't look so downcast, my dear. I'm sure the whole unfortunate business will work out for the best. And at least you shouldn't have anything to fear on your *own* account, from folk outside the palace or folk within.'

She looked at me oddly as she said that, but I didn't have time to reflect upon her words just then because she scolded herself for being so abrupt with me, and asserted once again that she appreciated how I must be feeling; but how pleasant it was just to see me and to talk to me, after so long!

Her words were sweet and her smile warm, yet whenever our eyes chanced to meet I couldn't help but discern from hers that she now regarded me as a stranger with an alien background and freakish beliefs. I felt more embarrassed and ashamed than ever, because for years I'd kept the truth about myself from her as well as from her son.

When eventually she left, I was no longer ready to face Kshayarsha. Not only did I feel ugly and unkempt, but confused and thick-headed as well.

'Why did she come here, Tammuz?' I beseeched Hegai, who took me in his arms and strove to calm me. I didn't resist him. Then as the fog in my mind began to clear, I added, 'And why did she bring those two enormous eunuchs? They were *armed*, Tammuz. Would *she* have sought to kill me, too, if I'd said the wrong thing?'

'Hadassah, Hadassah,' he whispered, stroking my straggled hair and easing my head forward onto his shoulder, 'Don't do this to yourself. Surely Adonai will protect us, if we place our lives in his hands? Come... let's kneel and pray together, just as we do when Mordecai is with us. Mordecai may not be here, but surely Adonai is not too preoccupied to listen.'

I swallowed hard, and nodded, and might have agreed to do as he asked, except that just then yet another visitor appeared at my door.

It was Ashpamithra, dressed up and made up to the nines, bearing a purple cushion upon which gold and jewels glinted. He walked stiffly towards us and set his burden down on the table, next to the menorah. Nestled among the folds of purple silk, weighting them down, was a heavy choker necklace with gem-encrusted pendants suspended from it all the way around. It had been laid out with the pendants spread like rays of the sun, and with the jewels being emeralds and rubies, the combined effect of colour and form made the whole thing look like the disc of Ahura Mazda. I questioned Ashpamithra with my eyes, and he said without engaging them, 'Your birthday gift from His Majesty King Kshayarsha, my lady. May you both live for ever.' And he bowed his way out.

Hegai said, 'You see, the King *does* care about you. It is a charming gift, Little Star. Let me help you put it on.'

But I shook my head wildly, almost dashing the choker to the ground when Hegai stretched out his fingers to touch it. 'How can he think I would want anything to do with tawdry baubles on a day such as this? And look at the colours of the stones, and the shape of the pendants. Kshayarsha mocks me!'

'I don't understand. In what way does he mock you? These jewels are worthy of a goddess, let alone a queen.'

385

'Worthy of a *god*, you mean! Just look at them! The whole thing is a token of Ahura Mazda, the cruel god who weighs the deeds of his disciples on his scales and makes them guess which way they are tilted! I shall *not* put it on. I shall *never* put it on. I shall take it back to Kshayarsha and throw it in his face! He hates me, Tammuz, just as Vashti does. And Hutaosa. They all hate me, for their own bigoted reasons.' Then I dissolved into tears, because I suddenly saw myself as though from outside, and realized what rabid nonsense I was uttering, and how there was no need for it because I could lay all my concerns and confusions at Adonai's feet, and ought to have done so already.

Hegai enfolded me in his arms once again, and I murmured into his hair, 'I'm sorry, Tammuz. I'm sorry. But I can't help it. I *am* afraid. I'm afraid to remain in this apartment, where Vashti could trap me and have me strangled or stabbed or suffocated, and no one would be permitted to lift a finger against her. And I'm afraid for my people; why have we still heard nothing? Why has Hathach not come to us? Mordecai ought to have sent him by now. Please, Tammuz... come with me to see Kshayarsha.'

He renewed his efforts to dissuade me, but then recognized the mask into which my features invariably set when my mind was not to be changed. I threw a heavy veil over my uncoiffed tresses, and made for the door.

We went directly to the Apadana, and Artabanush admitted us, though not without tacit reluctance. I all but ran the length of the hall and threw myself to the ground in the prostration, but with my head half raised because I was afraid to be unable to see what was going on around me. Kshayarsha was there enthroned, with his counsellors grouped about him, Mordecai among them. Even as I watched, a messenger scurried up to the dais whilst another was on his way out, but the newcomer didn't get to pass on his information for some time, because Kshayarsha saw me.

He was annoyed, that much was clear; I could tell that even Mordecai sensed it, though his eyes were too dim to make out why, until he heard my voice. As soon as I was directed to rise, I blurted, 'Oh Your Majesty, my lord Kshayarsha... please, my lord, I am frightened! No one has been to tell me what is happening, and—I'm frightened for my own life, my lord.'

Kshayarsha looked from one to another of his advisers; they merely upturned their palms in a communal gesture of perplexity. So he challenged me tetchily: 'What is this foolishness? How can your life be in any danger when you are locked inside the palace walls? Return to your chambers immediately, Esther. A council of war is no place for a woman, even for the Queen.'

'My lord, please, for once, just listen to what I have to say!' Although I'd got up from the prostration, I threw myself at his feet once more. 'I received a gift, and a letter, from Vashti. She—'

'Really, Esther! This is too much! How am I to take thought for the wellbeing of your people if you plague me with this sort of inanity? I thought we had solemnly agreed that you would make no more allegations of this nature, when you have no evidence whatsoever to support them? Are you surprised she should have sent you a gift? It is your birthday, for heaven's sake, or is the marking of such occasions another of life's harmless little pleasures which are censured as crimes among the Jews? Aren't you even going to thank me for *my* gift? I see you aren't wearing it. Perhaps it is indeed a surprise that Vashti should want to send a gift to someone so ungrateful.'

I didn't know where to put myself. Although in theory the King may address his wife or any one of his subjects as contemptuously as he chooses, in practice such rudeness is universally regarded as unbecoming to his exalted position. To take the heat from the moment, Mordecai asked the petrified messenger to tell His Majesty what news he had brought, and the poor fellow, with his nose still glued to the floor, stammered, 'No news, my lord. Your Majesty's security forces are still stationed around the perimeter of the Jewish quarter. But they have seen no action, nor any threat of it.'

'There you have it,' Kshayarsha rejoined triumphantly, addressing me. 'You have heard nothing because there is nothing to hear. Or would you like me to send you an errand boy on the hour, every hour, to tell you that I have nothing to tell you?'

I made a silent but desperate appeal with my eyes to Mordecai; an instinctive but entirely futile thing to do because he wasn't capable of discerning it. Might Kshayarsha have forbidden him to contact me, alleging that there were more important things to be done?

Then while I continued to kneel before Kshayarsha's throne, another messenger entered the Apadana at a run. He prostrated himself breathlessly and gabbled, 'Your Majesty, it has begun. Several companies of youths, armed like soldiers and hundreds strong, are converging on the Jewish sector of Shushan. They are chanting slogans, Your Majesty, and beating on shields or pans or anything they can get their hands on. Some of them have burning torches as well as clubs and swords. I saw one such company with my own eyes.'

'The Wise Lord preserve us,' breathed Kshayarsha. I realized then that he'd been angry with me because he too was afraid; afraid that in spite of the vast resources at his disposal, he might prove incapable of containing the violence which was shortly to be unleashed. The hours of waiting since daybreak had unnerved him, and had no doubt unnerved the Jewish defence corps too, which was precisely what our opponents intended. They must have possessed a greater capacity for co-ordinated action than we had given them credit for.

I could take no more. I heard myself wailing hysterically, and the King instructing Hegai to take me out; the latter bent down beside me and attempted to lift me to my feet, but I wailed all the louder, begging Kshayarsha not to banish me to my rooms where Vashti would be able to find me and kill me. Unsurprisingly the King paid no attention, deducing that the pressure of everything had driven me mad. I was dragged forcibly back to my apartment, and no more guards were assigned to protect me than were stationed there as a general rule; but these were given strict orders that on no account must I be permitted to go out again before twilight.

I tore off my veil in despair and retreated to my bedroom, where I threw myself on my bed and refused to leave it. Enraged, terrified and mortified by turns, I spent the afternoon bewailing my lot at one moment and grovelling in abject apology to Hegai the next. 'I *hate* being a woman!' I howled, sweeping a tray of bracelets and earrings off my bedside cabinet onto the floor. 'I've *always* hated being a woman. If I were a man, I would be out there today, fighting for the survival of my race! All my *life* I've been ordered about, ever since I left Jerusalem; why can a woman never do what *she* wants and go where *she* wants to go? I hate this place, I hate everything about it! I hate myself!'

Then remorse came over me, and I sobbed, 'Oh Tammuz, I'm sorry. I don't know what has got into me. I loved Kshayarsha from the moment I saw him, but our marriage will *never* work out, I know it won't. We are too different. Our blood is different, our beliefs are different. I'll only ever be second best, because the woman he truly loves is one of his own kind. I ought never to have stolen him from her.'

'You didn't steal him, Little Star. He put her away from him *years* before he met you. Please ... let me pray for you.'

'It won't do any good. I'm all worked up inside,' I protested, but he kept at me until I acquiesced, sitting up and allowing him to place his hands upon my head. Yet although I had yielded in body to his request, my mind would not submit, and I sat with open eyes studying his face as he tried to pray, his lips moving and eyelids fluttering in his intensity. All I could think about was how beautiful he was, and how even when he wore no make-up at all his fervency rendered him lovelier than poor, lost, empty Ashpamithra would ever be.

Soon he must have sensed my staring at him, because he opened his own eyes and smiled sadly, and told me not to be ashamed; Adonai would surely pardon my anxiety and see through my agitation to the faith deep down inside me.

I said, 'Oh Tammuz, you're so patient, so sweet. You always have been. It was only ever you who made my life here remotely worth living.'

'Don't say that, Hadassah. You have *everything* to live for here.'

'No, I haven't, Tammuz. Not any more. I was so happy when I first got to know you, before you told me ... I mean, before I found out ...'

'Hadassah, please. Stop it.'

'But I want you to know. I want you to know, that if things had been different—'

'I do know. You have told me before. But it doesn't matter any more. I've found the only kind of happiness I can ever know, and shall ever need. All I want now is to see you and Kshayarsha find happiness together.'

'You don't mean that, Tammuz. I know you don't. You do love me for myself, don't you? Even now.'

I continued to stare into his eyes, and watched them grow dark and liquid as half-submerged emotions began to rise to the surface. He tried to pull away from me, but I persisted, 'Please say you love me. I need to hear you say it.'

His patience had run out, and not before time. He thumped his fist down on the bed and shouted, 'Oh, *God*, Hadassah! Of course I still love you; do you imagine Adonai has given me a stone in place of a broken heart? But what is the use of saying it? You only make things worse for me! Because of you and your cousin, I had started to feel whole and acceptable for the first time in all the years I can remember;

389

why are you trying to destroy what you yourself began to build? I was happy, Little Star, and so were you, because for the first time in your life you'd stopped being so stubborn about grasping its reins for yourself! *No* one controls his own life, not even a man; not even a king! Are the Jewish men of Shushan free to make a choice about how they should spend this very afternoon? They either spend it fighting, or they die! Only when Adonai holds the reins of our lives are we truly free, whether man or woman—or eunuch.'

That was when I knew that he was in deadly earnest; never before had he been able to bring himself to use the word 'eunuch' instead of 'boy' when referring to himself. Yet so animated, so ardent did his uncharacteristic anger render him, that momentarily he was more like a man than he'd ever been, and I found myself loving him hopelessly.

Then simultaneously, both of us came to ourselves with a start. A figure had appeared without warning in the doorway to the bedroom; I looked up and saw that it was Hathach at last. In mingled relief and apprehension I snapped at him for entering uninvited.

'I beg your pardon, my lady, but I knocked at the door and there was no reply. I was concerned, and thought I should check that all was well. If I am intruding—'

'No, no, Hathach. You acted rightly.' I pressed my palms against my eyelids, then blinked my eyes until I could look at Hathach's face without seeing Hegai's. I bade him give us whatever news he had brought, but still found difficulty concentrating on what he was saying.

As far as I could make out, the chanting gangs of Gentile youths had converged at the very centre of the Jewish quarter—and found themselves trapped there. The Imperial troops surrounding the area had no intention of allowing them to leave it until the issue had been decided, and the Jewish defence forces had appeared as if from nowhere, driving the gangs before them until they came together in a great shouting, seething mass.

Archers up on the rooftops had then begun picking them off, but had been compelled to retreat as the torches were thrown and flames engulfed the very buildings on which they were standing. However, by this time the Gentiles had begun trampling one another in their efforts to evade the snipers, and were fighting savagely amongst themselves; it seemed likely that these valiant young warriors, being uncouth commoners by and large rather than members of the sober Persian aristocracy, had tanked themselves up in advance to bolster their courage, but the aggression which the drink had stirred within them was largely indiscriminate. In addition, they were at much at risk from the fires they'd kindled as their enemies were.

'You can see the smoke from the palace roof,' Hathach finished up. 'But no one can tell what the outcome of the fighting has been. It won't be known until the sun sets, and the troops can go in to break everything up and assess the damage and casualties. Please forgive me for not coming to see you earlier, my lady, but I didn't like to upset you with talk of bloodshed. It was Mordecai who said I should come, and that you would rather know the truth than be left in ignorance.'

I was about to tell him that Mordecai was right, when suddenly Hegai's eyes went wide with horror. Gripping the side of my bed with knotted white knuckles he yelled, 'Hathach, look out!'

But the warning had come too late. Rigid with shock, I watched helplessly as Hathach pitched forward towards me, his bland features contorted with fear and surprise. As he went down, his bald head struck hard against the foot of my bed, abruptly cutting off his involuntary cry of pain. He lay quite still, the knife which had felled him still protruding from between his shoulder-blades. The blood seeped only slowly through his clothing, but a thin trickle also issued from one of his ears.

His assailant stood in the doorway, where Hathach himself had so recently stood: a slender, veiled individual no taller than Hegai or myself, and dressed as one of Kshayarsha's lesser concubines.

She hovered there for a moment, looking from Hathach, to me, to Hegai, and back to Hathach again, because with her knife lodged in her victim's back she was defenceless. When she made a lunge to retrieve it, Hegai was aroused from his own shocked inertia. He leapt from the bed and shoved the intruder back through the doorway out into my living room, causing her to stumble and fall. Nauseous with dread, I dragged myself up from the bed and sagged feebly against the doorframe, watching the two of them wrestling together on the ground.

Hegai had ripped off his opponent's veil, and I saw that this was no woman, but a young eunuch like himself. Nevertheless, the lad fought like a woman, scratching, biting, kicking, and pulling Hegai's hair so it all came loose and got in his eyes. Neither combatant had any more training or experience of fighting than the other; they grappled desperately but without doing one another serious damage, until both of them were panting with exhaustion. Just when I thought that Hegai might be getting the upper hand, the intruder called for help and I realized that he was not alone.

His companion had hung back until now, immobilized by fear as I was myself; manifestly our attackers hadn't expected violent opposition. But seeing his friend in trouble, he spurred himself into action and ran forward with his dagger poised. Hegai and his opponent rolled over and over, locked in a furious embrace, nails gouging and hair flying, and the second intruder stood uncertainly over them, afraid to use his blade in haste lest he transfix the wrong spine.

Yet he wouldn't wait for ever; sooner or later the wrestlers' exhaustion would overcome them, and then Hegai would be lost. Wishing I still had the presence of mind which my father had instilled in me as a child but which palace life had sucked from me, I somehow summoned enough courage to walk shakily to the place where Hathach still lay motionless on my floor, and to grasp hold of the hilt of the protruding knife.

But I couldn't bring myself to extract it. There still didn't seem to be very much blood, yet if I pulled on the knife I was sure it would all come flooding out; we needed a physician to remove it safely and bandage the wound. Sick at heart, I moved back to the doorway. Hegai was pinned to the ground near the table, with his opponent on top of him; the second intruder still hesitated, unable to reach his target.

Just then, Hegai succeeded in freeing one hand, fumbling inside his clothing—and producing his own ceremonial dagger. I hadn't known that he had it on him; neither had his assailant. With a sharp little cry he let Hegai go; Hegai heaved him aside and onto his back, where he lay twitching and jerking with Hegai's knife in his chest, and his blood all down Hegai's white robe. Hegai knelt with his head on his knees, weeping with relief. He still imagined that the eunuch he'd defeated had been alone.

There was no reason now why the dying boy's companion should not go in for the kill, yet he continued to hold back. Finally he rammed his knife back into its sheath; the swift metallic sound made Hegai look up, and just as he did so, the eunuch seized hold of Vashti's silver menorah and brought it crashing down against Hegai's skull.

My hand went to my mouth, and I bit into the skin hard enough to draw blood. Hegai lay sprawled at the aggressor's feet, and my first thought was to run to him, regardless of the danger to myself. But the eunuch leapt over Hegai's twisted body and advanced towards me, his hand once more moving over the knife at his belt. Aghast, I retreated before him, knowing that I was cornering myself in the bedroom, from which there was no way of escape. He kept on coming, stalking me like a cat, until there was nowhere left for me to go but onto my own bed. When it wasn't quite too late I remembered Saul's knife, which I kept stowed in its box in the cabinet by the bedhead. I threw open the door, shook the box upside down on to the bed and gripped the knife's hilt with trembling fingers.

The eunuch hesitated again, but only momentarily. Next he sprang forward, wild-eyed, and with his own weapon he slashed at mine, trying to knock it from my grasp. Instead, the blade came clean off; the rivets had rusted through long ago. I crouched on the bed with my eyes screwed shut, thinking: if this is how it must end, then so be it. I have given myself to Adonai to use as he wills, and if I am to die, I shall do it well. Hegai is dead, so I do not want to live on in any case.

But rather than feeling the eunuch's blade against my skin, I felt the weight of his body topple onto the bed in front of me, as he collapsed grunting with a knife in his back.

Unlike Hathach, he hadn't been stabbed. The dagger had been thrown from a distance; when I dared to open my eyes I saw one of Hutaosa's burly escorts standing there grimly admiring his own marksmanship. Then Hutaosa herself glided past him and proceeded to clasp my hands in hers.

'You're safe, the Wise Lord be praised,' she murmured, then caught sight of Hathach lying prone on the floor beside the bed. She snapped her fingers for her eunuchs to examine him; while they were doing so, I fled to the living room and gathered Hegai up in my arms.

His grey face was covered in scratches and blood, and his limbs hung as limp as his blood-sodden robe. I pressed my lips against his, which were so slack and cold that I drew back again with a shudder and began keening for him instead.

But then he stirred and moaned, and my keening was abruptly transformed into a paean of praise to Adonai. I held Hegai close, and would have wept for joy if Hutaosa hadn't come out to us and informed me that Hathach was dead.

Still hugging Hegai fiercely to my breast I stammered, 'But... there was so little blood. I thought...'

'His skull is broken, Esther. That is what killed him. We can only be grateful that his end was swift.' Hutaosa spoke so steadily, but her eyes were brimming.

'I ... he ...' I began. But no more words would come, for in my heart I was thanking God that Hegai hadn't been struck harder, and then I felt horribly ashamed because I was glad it wasn't Hathach who had lived while Hegai died. Hegai moaned again, and struggled to sit up. After a few moments he managed to ask what had become of the second intruder, and was assured that he was dead.

'I knew him,' he croaked, then winced and put his hand to his temple as he realized how badly his head hurt. 'That's—why he didn't knife me. He didn't want me dead. Just out of the way.'

'You *knew* him?' I whispered. 'But—who was he?'

'A boyfriend of Haman's. The boy whose birthday it was the day Haman made Kshayarsha agree to destroy the Jewish people.'

'So—Vashti had nothing to do with this? Those two wretches made up their *own* minds to be rid of me, because I discredited their lover?'

'That will be what Vashti wants us to think,' Hutaosa interjected. 'As usual she has ensured that her criminal behaviour cannot be traced to its true source, and has employed willing volunteers rather than pay professional assassins. I am only sorry that I didn't get here a little sooner. I was misinformed; I expected the attempt to be made this morning. When it was not, I supposed that it had been abandoned. Fortunately for you, my spies react quickly.' She glanced briefly at Hathach, then away again. 'Would that they had been quicker still.'

Distressed because I'd thought ill of her intentions earlier that day, I muttered that there was no need for recriminations; she had saved my life, and would have saved Hathach's had it been possible. I was already weeping for my poor faithful servant and friend, who had risked his life for me in the past just as Hegai had done, and who had now lost it so suddenly, so brutally. Also I was weeping for myself, because I had been so miserably faithless at the last, but Adonai had protected me all the same.

Hutaosa and her two eunuchs-at-arms remained with us until sunset, for not until then could we be reasonably sure that Vashti wouldn't attempt to finish what had been begun. Hutaosa had Hathach's body carried away, and warm water and ointments brought so that I could attend to Hegai's cuts and bruises. I wanted to give him poppy wine to dull the pain in his head and the grief in his heart for Hathach, one of the few palace staff who had never been unkind to him. But Hutaosa said that the pain must be borne without drugs, lest he fall asleep and never wake; as for the grief, only the passage of time would alleviate that.

At dusk, Mordecai came in person to report on the day's events. He'd been told of my ordeal but said only that he had been quite confident that Adonai would protect me all along, for the Creator and Sustainer of the Universe is *never* misinformed. Then he launched into his own account.

Five hundred people had lost their lives in Shushan that day, hardly any of them Jews. Most of the dead were so horrifically burnt, it was impossible to tell whether they'd died in the fires or been fatally wounded already when the flames swept over them. The gruesome task of identifying the bodies had barely got under way, but Haman's ten sons were known to be among them.

I sighed, 'Then it's over. At last it's all over.' And I put my head against Mordecai's neck.

'No, it is not, I am sad to say,' responded Mordecai gravely. 'When the sun went down there were still some of our enemies left at large. In fact there were more packs of Gentile youths on the rampage than there had been earlier.'

'I don't understand; it doesn't make sense.'

'Regrettably it does. Most of those who wish us harm are cowardly bullies who only dare attack us when we cannot fight back. As sunset approached, they assumed that the Imperial troops would disarm our men while turning a blind eye to last-minute assaults made by their own kind, and so newcomers arrived to swell the Gentile ranks. And I should imagine there were others who initially had no intention of becoming embroiled in the conflict, but who entered the area later, to rescue their brothers or friends; or to avenge their deaths.'

'And these latecomers were left alive? How come they weren't shot down?'

'Because once the sun had set and the battle was declared over, our forces had to let them go. The Imperial troops took down the barricades we'd set up and allowed the survivors to disperse. But already they are regrouping, and marching through the streets jeering and bawling.'

'Through *Jewish* streets?'

'No; Kshayarsha's men are keeping them out of our quarter—or what is left of it. But they can't cordon it off for ever, nor can its inhabitants go on living there, not until their homes are rebuilt. Unless the King acts at once, things will be worse for us in the future than they have been in the past. The Jew-haters must be eradicated now, before their numbers multiply out of control. There may even be kinsmen of Haman still left alive to brandish the abominable banners of Amalek.'

'Father, what are you saying?'

'I'm saying that we need another day like today, when we, the Jews of Shushan, are permitted to arm ourselves and show these cowards what we are made of.'

I objected, 'But surely, a second day of slaughter will prove nothing; it can't achieve anything of lasting value. Another five hundred Gentiles may die, but each dead man will have had a father or a son, or brothers or uncles or cousins determined to avenge him. The whole thing will expand out of all proportion.'

'No, Hadassah. Something extremely important will have been proved. Our enemies will see that even if the King's decree against us cannot be rescinded, it can be supplemented as often as is necessary now that the Imperial administration is on our side.'

'And has this second day of fighting been officially approved?'

Mordecai took a long slow breath, and exhaled it heavily. 'No, Hadassah. Not yet. I suggested it to His Majesty, but he reacted as you did. With respect, your husband's understanding of politics is frequently flawed, because he has a warped perception of human nature—scarcely surprising, when one considers the bizarre life that he leads. You must make him see things as they are.'

'*I*? He would pay less attention if it came from me than he would to anyone else.'

'I doubt that somehow. He knows you, Hadassah. He knows what kind of person you are; he knows you wouldn't make such a request to slake a thirst for Aryan blood.'

'Is that what he thought about *you* when you spoke to him?'

'Something like that, yes. I think he did. He has only known me for a matter of months; he is afraid of trusting me the way he trusted Haman. You he has known and loved for years.'

I laughed bitterly. 'I know now that he has never loved anyone but Vashti. And he would tell you himself that he doesn't know me at all.'

'Come, my daughter, this is no time for spitefulness. We must make out a case for you to put to him. You must point out that there is nothing we desire more than to be able to live at peace with the King and Government and People of Persia, whose protection and favour we have long enjoyed. But sometimes lasting peace can only be procured by resorting to violence in the short term. We need ask only that Jews be allowed to carry arms in Shushan itself; there is no need to pursue the strife beyond the walls of the city. Elsewhere the Jews have slaughtered tens of thousands already, if the reports filtering in are correct, and the opposition to us has been entirely crushed. Some of the satraps and administrators of cities even allowed their own troops to fight on our side in spite of the original edict, knowing that Kshayarsha would make no effort to investigate such actions now that his First Minister is himself a Jew. Outside of Shushan it *is* all over. Only in the capital must we fight on, where Haman's influence was strongest, and where Kshayarsha cannot pretend not to notice if his own men intervene in our favour.'

By the time I set out to see him, it was late evening. I went alone; the King would have retired to his private chambers and I wanted our meeting to be as intimate and unthreatening as possible.

Before I left, Mordecai had blessed me in Adonai's name, and Hegai had felt well enough to come and pray for me also, as he'd wished to do earlier but never had done. As he knelt with his hands on my head, Adonai's spirit had fallen powerfully upon him, and not only had he found himself praying in a tongue he'd never learnt, as Adonai's spirit within him expressed on his behalf the prayers for which he could find no words of his own, but he'd been prophesying too. He'd said that he was seeing a vision in his mind which was evolving even as he spoke: there were dragons breathing fire, and mighty archers, their bows nocked with flaming arrows. But then there was a stream of living water bubbling up from the dry ground, and it quenched the fire of the dragons and that of the arrows.

I was awestruck, for the vision was the very same as the one Mordecai had seen when I was a child and had awoken in the night to hear him screaming; even the words Hegai had used to describe it were the same. But then Hegai had blinked his eyes as though waking himself from a trance, and said, 'You are that spring, Hadassah. You must not be afraid to go before Kshayarsha once more. He will grant your request.'

And so I'd got myself ready, and set out, and now arrived upon the threshold of the King's apartment. Ashpamithra seemed not in the least surprised to see me, and showed me in without troubling to consult his royal master. Kshayarsha himself came forward to greet me, dressed in his night robe and with his feet bare, but he wasn't surprised to see me either. He said, 'So, my lovely Hebrew bride, the sun has set and your people are saved. Have you come to ask me to share in your triumph? I thought you might.'

The tone of his voice was odd; I wasn't sure how I was meant to take him. I don't think he was sure either; perhaps the words had come out more sharply than he'd intended. So I simply averted my eyes and waited.

He clapped his hands at Ashpamithra, bidding him fetch two goblets of his best Syrian wine. When it was poured, he held his own cup to my lips and guided mine to his, and we sipped uncertainly, searching one another's eyes. Then he said, 'Will you not drink more deeply? I presume you must be pleased with the way things have gone. All Haman's sons dead, and five hundred of their drunken cronies here in Shushan, and the Wise Lord alone knows how many thousands out in the rest of the country and in the provinces, with a goodly number of worthy if misguided Persian noblemen among them, I shouldn't wonder. Are you not satisfied now, or do you come to ask something more of me?' He laughed, and threw back his head, and drawled in embarrassing self-mockery, 'Queen Esther, star of my night and solace of my soul, tell me what it is that you desire, and you shall have it, even up to the half of my own fishpond!'

I realized then that his jug of Syrian wine must have been half-empty when I arrived. It wasn't like him to over-indulge in private any more than it would have been acceptable for him to do so in public; yet he'd seemed to know I would be coming. Was this the only state in which he felt able to face me? Were we so much strangers to each other now that we couldn't even meet in private without first either drinking or having hands laid upon us?

So before things could get any worse, I presented my petition; and without even asking for a reason he waved one hand and answered, 'Consider it done. Ashpamithra? Fetch a scribe. I wish to issue a proclamation.'

Ashpamithra hesitated; I suppose it was highly irregular for the King to do such a thing without his advisers or magi being consulted. But he was perfectly entitled to do it, and I was relieved that I should have his promise in writing before he changed his mind—or before anyone changed it for him. The scribe arrived, and the edict was written, incorporating a clause stating that the bodies of Haman's sons should be hung from the city walls, as the bodies of Saul and his sons had once been nailed to the walls of Bethshan by the Philistines. I began to thank Kshayarsha for his kindness to me, and to praise him for his wisdom, but he said, 'Come to bed with me, Esther. I don't want to talk.' What he meant was, I don't want to argue.

Even as we came together on his great canopied bed, I think we both knew that it would be for the last time. There was a tenderness and a poignancy about it such as there had never been in the past, nor could there be again. I said nothing to him about Vashti's abortive attempt on my life, yet I somehow suspected that he knew, and that he would never do anything about it because he loved her with all of his being, and wished that it was she who lay with him; perhaps he even pretended that it was.

Once upon a time a crabbed old woman from Arderikka had said I should cause the deaths of thousands, and so I had, but not in the way that the dark powers which she served would have had it. She'd said I would be Queen of Persia, and so I was, but even that could change, for Adonai controlled my life now, and his power was stronger than that of any Greek soothsayer, Babylonian caster of horoscopes, or Persian magus, put together.

So when I said, 'Kshayarsha . . . after tomorrow, I don't want to stay here. I want to go back home, and help my people rebuild their homes and their lives in Shushan,' he said, 'I know.' Presently I said, 'I'm sorry, Kshayarsha. So sorry. I wanted to love you. I thought I *did* love you,' and he said, 'I know. I wanted to love you too.'

Then understanding one another as we never had before, we wept, and made what we could of our last night as man and wife, while all across the Empire my brothers and sisters feasted and danced and festooned the streets with pennants and banners in my honour. For in our own era, as in the glorious days of Moses and Joshua and David, the low-born had brought down the proud, good had triumphed over evil, and the power of Adonai had once more been seen among his people.

EPILOGUE

It's five years now since I took off Kshayarsha's ring and left his palace for the first and last time. Never before had I set foot outside its gates since being taken there from Arderikka as a wide-eyed innocent, preening myself in my curtained litter, believing that I was in love, and that I had secured my own eternal happiness.

It's five whole years since I turned my back on the life I'd once dreamed of, yet it feels like fifteen at least, for so much has happened in between, and I myself have changed so much too.

I suppose I've changed as much in appearance as in anything else. I haven't had one milk bath or one massage since I kissed my seven slave-girls goodbye, I can eat honeyed pastries and sweetmeats whenever I want to, and I wear precious little make-up. Yet Hegai swears that I'm more beautiful than I ever was, and when I chance to glimpse my reflection in a polished tile or a tranquil garden pool, I have to confess he is right. There's a quality of peace about my eyes and a vitality about my expression and my movements which I never saw there when my days were empty of everything but ritual and my nights were filled with passion but devoid of love. I seldom look in a mirror any more, though; I'm happy to be as I am, as Adonai made me to be. If others don't like what they see, it doesn't concern me, so long as Hegai isn't among them.

Of course, it wasn't possible for me simply to walk out through the palace gates the moment that Kshayarsha and I acknowledged our marriage to be over. There were a hundred and one formalities to be gone through, and before any of them could be looked into, there was the second day of armed conflict in Shushan to be prepared for and managed.

I say armed conflict; but this gives the wrong impression. For on that second day, only one of the two parties was permitted to carry offensive weapons, and this altered the complexion of things entirely. Under Persian law no civilian may go about armed unless granted special dispensation; this dispensation had been granted to the Jews and to their enemies for the duration of the thirteenth of Adar only. On the morning of the fourteenth a new edict went out allowing the Jews of Shushan to be armed for one more day—but not those gangs of jeering Gentiles who still jostled and shoved around the boundaries of the Jewish quarter, having been kept at bay all night by the King's troops.

When the sun rose, these troops once more let them pass, but they searched every man and disarmed him in the process. Most of them turned tail and ran when they saw what the situation was, but some had been knocking back cheap palm wine by the pitcherfull, and imagined themselves invincible. They staggered and lurched through the streets chanting their vulgar slogans, and fell one by one into the gutters. According to eyewitnesses, it was impossible to tell which of them had been brought down by snipers and which had simply collapsed in a drunken stupor. There they lay: Persians in the main, but there were not a few Amalekites, Samaritans, Babylonians, Egyptians, Greeks and the like among them. Some of these represented peoples who were bitter ancestral enemies of the Jews; others were members of despised minorities who were only too glad that some other ethnic group had been singled out for destruction rather than their own. Whoever they were, our vigilantes slit their throats without discrimination as they lay slewed and snoring or crouched blear-eyed and vomiting. Only a handful of them mounted any serious resistance: those who weren't drunk, but who had entered the battleground crazed with guilt or despair or a hunger for revenge, because someone they loved had been cut down the previous day.

In all, three hundred Gentiles were slaughtered in Shushan on the fourteenth of Adar, and not one Jew. At sunset the celebrations began, but there was no looting of Gentile property or violation of their dead. I was much impressed, because many of the young toughs who had fought on our side were no holier in their general pattern of life than the average Persian was. Yet something had restrained them; something had made them appreciate the fact that they were taking part in a holy war, victory in which must not be diluted by human greed or bestial brutality. I like to think that this something was the spirit of Adonai.

And many of my fellow Jews thought the same. Hundreds who had forsaken the traditions of their ancestors now returned joyously to their roots because of what they had seen, suffered and survived. Some even sold all that they possessed and prepared to go back to Israel to join the Pioneers in the rebuilding of Jerusalem. I'm still not sure whether such people have interpreted Adonai's will correctly, though for a while I did think I might go with them. But by the time Kshayarsha had had documents drawn up to divorce me, and to restore to me the kind of dowry which a woman who has once been Queen of Persia ought to have, I was quite convinced that there was more important work for me to do in Shushan.

Not that I was able to achieve anything very much until the scandal surrounding me had died down. It wasn't unknown for a Persian king to divorce his queen, but it was certainly rare; more usual practice would have been for him to take another wife in addition to the one who had fallen out of favour. Yet I should rather have died than end my days hopeless and helpless in the bowels of the harem somewhere, pitied for a while and then forgotten.

Instead, I became a target for all manner of abuse, and the subject of a thousand rumours. I heard folk say that Kshayarsha was divorcing me because I'd been unfaithful with a Phrygian pipe-player, or an Egyptian snake-charmer, or even with Memucan; or because I'd called Kshayarsha a toad in front of his mother, or because I was barren, or frigid, or Jewish. Jewish women who owed me their very lives would neither visit me nor invite me to visit them, and once I'd plucked up the courage to go to the bazaar from time to time like the ordinary woman I now was, they would shun me in the streets for a very long while. It was only when they saw me take in and look after children who had been orphaned in the persecutions and the fighting, and when they realized I wasn't pregnant by some travelling entertainer or palace lackey, that they began to relent and accept me as one of themselves. For myself, I wasn't bitter about any of this, because I'd expected it. I was happy to wait for them to come around.

I took up residence once more at the house I'd shared with Mordecai and Ninlil as a child; although he'd lived at the palace since Ninlil's death, Mordecai had never sold the place or let it out. It was all locked up and shrouded in sandy dust when I went back there, but I hired servants and we soon had it habitable. I hadn't scrubbed a floor or washed down a wall in years; and I enjoyed it. The novelty rapidly wore off, however, and the domestic servants were kept on. I sent for Roxana to assist them, because unless she remains in my service, her children will be orphans too.

Mordecai himself still lives and works at the palace, though he visits every Shabbat and brings presents for my orphans, who call him Grandfather. Sometimes Iphigenia visits at the same time, and her little ones play and giggle and squabble with mine. She and I never quarrel any more, except when she insists on reminding me how proud she is of me and of what I did for my people. I don't see myself as a heroine, and it embarrasses me when others do. I only did what I had to do, and I should have done it much sooner.

Farah and her companions continue to serve in the harem, for they could cope with no other life. I don't miss having them around to wait upon me. It's Hathach I miss, desperately. I do hope he knew how much I valued his loyalty and his gentle unobtrusive friendship.

As for Hegai, he came to join me as soon as his manumission papers were in order; and his acceptance into the Jewish community has been ratified by our Council of Elders in Shushan. His assimilation into my small household caused quite a stir—until it became generally known who and what he was. Besides, most folk were more interested by then in talking about Kshayarsha and Vashti than in spreading gossip about me.

It was no more straightforward for Kshayarsha to reinstate Vashti as his Queen than it had been for him to redeem the lives of the Jews. An official decree had been given out to the effect that she must never again appear before the King, and that decree could no more be rescinded than could the one which had sentenced my people to death. However, a convenient loophole was found by one of Kshayarsha's legal advisers. It was announced that the wording of the decree had echoed that of the legislation governing who and who was not entitled to seek audience in the Apadana uninvited. Thus Vashti by her insolence had forfeited her right as principal wife to appear before His Majesty whenever he was seated on his throne, but in all other respects she could be restored to her former position as Queen of Persia. The royal marriage was resanctified by the magi, I happily returned Vashti's tiara to her, and her sons were confirmed as being sole and rightful claimants to the throne. I don't yet know which of them Kshayarsha favours as his successor, but whichever emerges, Hutaosa will be disappointed. As for me, I just wish the royal couple every happiness, and pray that their mutual love will gradually soften Vashti's callous heart, since there is no need any longer for her to be jealous of anyone.

I don't suppose that *I* shall ever marry again, or have my own children. Most of the men I meet these days are in awe of me; the rest, I suppose, despise me as second-hand goods. I can't say that this really bothers me any more, as far as the living of my own life is concerned. It only saddens me when I reflect that I'm the last surviving Saulide, so far as I know, and that if I remain unmarried, that noble line will end with me. Adonai alone knows who will treasure what is left of Saul's battered old knife when I am gone.

Yet there are better ways of influencing the course of the future than by filling it with your progeny, who may not share your ideals even though they share your blood. I dare say that Adonai has no particular desire to see Saul's line continued, and I no longer believe that a Saulide will ever be permitted to occupy the throne of Israel even if our monarchy is one day restored. As for my ideals, I pass them on to my orphans, and they embrace them only too willingly because they know that as a child I suffered exactly what they have suffered. Also, I run a Torah class just as Mordecai did, except that mine is for girls; why should they be less well versed in their own scriptures than their brothers are?

Then of course there is Hegai to consider. Whereas I may never find out whether I can bear my own children or not, he knows all too well that no baby can be begotten from his mutilated loins. Yet he is a better father than most, and is utterly devoted to the children, for whom he has chosen to be jointly responsible. Sometimes I listen to him telling them stories, or I watch him playing knucklebones with them on his hands and knees in the dusty yard, or showing them how to tend Mordecai's little garden. Then I pretend for a fleeting moment that he is my husband, and that they are our sons and daughters. A futile fantasy perhaps, but in many ways not so far removed from reality.

Certainly he means so very much more to me than a friend or even a brother ever could. I still haven't found my beloved Pithon, and have heard not a whisper about him, but I haven't given up hope entirely, because without hope in our lives we die inside. During so much of my time at the palace I had no hope of anything, nor any purpose or meaning, and I *was* dying, little by little, with each empty day that slipped by. Now, my days are so full I could wish for more hours in them. I wish there was more time for visiting Mordecai's kinsfolk—my kinsfolk too—and showing them that I'm no longer the selfish brat who was the death of their poor Ninlil. I wish I could see Iphigenia more often too.

404

Still, soon I *shall* have more hours in each day, for the writing of this account is almost complete. Many people ask me why I have gone to the trouble of setting everything down in so much detail, when Mordecai has already circulated his version of events around the Jewish communities of the Empire. Part of the answer must be that I have done it for myself, to help me come to terms with the many strange twists which the path of my life has taken, and to enable me to find out who I am once again, now that the life I tried to make for myself with Kshayarsha has acquired some of the aspects of a dream.

But also, there is so much which Mordecai left out. He didn't say how wilful or quarrelsome I was as a child; merely that I obeyed him in everything, which is true, but only because he gave me no choice. He didn't say that it was my own fault that I was taken to the House of the Virgins, or that my marriage to the King was a disaster. He's made me out to be a heroine, unless you read his words very carefully, and sometimes you have to read between the lines as well. He's perhaps been a little too kind to Kshayarsha also, and laid all the blame for our people's suffering squarely on the late Lord Haman's shoulders. He has done this because he loves me, and because he's come to care for Kshayarsha too in the time he has served him.

Nor did he make any explicit reference to Adonai in his account. He's explained to me his reason for this: he wants those Jews—or Gentiles—who have no time for religion to read his account as an adventure, and to discern for themselves the hand of God at work without being told where to look for it. He believes the facts will speak for themselves: that it is impossible to draw any other conclusion from this story than that the Jewish God is very much alive, and concerned about his people wherever they may be, in the land of Israel or elsewhere. But it's my experience that so many people will look and look but never see; they'll listen and listen but never hear, unless things are made clear to them.

Since Mordecai became First Minister, many other Jews have been appointed to prominent government posts. Kshayarsha has recognized our talents, and has even admitted privately to Mordecai that many of us are more worthy to be called Sons of the Light than some who profess to be disciples of Zarathustra. Though neither of them would admit it, I get the distinct impression that the King and his new First Minister are each coming to the opinion that they worship the same God after all, in different ways and by different names. Adonai has chosen the Jews as the special channel through which his love may ultimately flow to all of mankind; but who is to say that he has not prepared the hearts ·of Gentiles to receive this love, by speaking through their pagan prophets? Adonai has worked in *our* history; yet through *their* prophets and philosophers he has begun to reveal the secrets of life beyond death. The time of fulfilment is fast approaching: the time when the Gentiles will flock to Zion and find their own salvation.

In the meantime, until that great day dawns, we his Chosen People shall celebrate each year the festival which Mordecai introduced to commemorate our deliverance from Haman the Agagite. I myself sent out a circular endorsing it with my full authority as Queen, wishing all Jews everywhere peace and prosperity, and exhorting them to keep holy the fourteenth and fifteenth of Adar. We celebrate the fourteenth because on that day the slaughter was over throughout the rest of Persia and the provinces; and the fifteenth because by then it was over in Shushan too. It is not the slaughter which we want to remember, but the peace that came after it.

Folk are calling the festival Purim, or Lots, because of the lots which Haman drew in order to determine the most auspicious day for our destruction. So much for his superstition and his trust in good luck; he didn't even live to see the light of that special day for himself. But though the mediums and the oracles and the horoscope-pedlars claim to know what lies ahead, and sometimes are right, it is not in such as they that we should put our trust or seek to find strength for facing our futures. When we place our lives at Adonai's disposal, it is he who assumes control. Only in surrendering myself fully to him have I at last found the freedom I craved.

HISTORICAL NOTE

The Book of Esther, short though it is, has given rise to almost as much controversy as any other single book in the Bible.

It is set firmly in the fascinating period of the Achaemenid (Hakhamanish) Empire of Persia, about which a great deal has been written by historians.

Unfortunately, however, little is known about the Jewish communities which existed under Persian rule in the territory which had once belonged to Babylon. (The Babylonians had deported a large number of Jews from Judah—the southern part of what had once been the united kingdom of Israel—to Babylon in the sixth century BC.) Even what we think we know about the Persian Empire itself comes chiefly from Greek sources, not from Persian ones. The Greeks and Persians were generally speaking mutually hostile, and scholars' opinions differ as to whether the ancient Greek writers can be regarded as reliable when discussing Persian history and culture. Pioneering archaeological work on the Achaemenid sites is still being undertaken.

Our chief source for Persian history up until the fifth century BC is Herodotus, a famous Greek historian who was in many ways more of a travel-writer and collector of bizarre tales than a historian in the modern sense. He did travel extensively in the areas about which he wrote, and was contemporary with many of the events he described. We also have an abstract of the twenty-three-volume *History of Persia* written by Ctesias, a Greek physician who lived rather later, but who himself spent some time at the Persian court. There is in addition a play by Aeschylus, another Greek, entitled *The Persians* (*Persae*) and concerned with the disastrous expedition of Xerxes (Kshayarsha) against Greece.

In contrast, although the Persians themselves seem to have kept some kind of official annals (see Esther 10:2) we don't know that they wrote any history books as such.

Many 'liberal' Biblical critics have cast even graver doubts over the historicity of the Book of Esther than their Classical counterparts have cast over Herodotus, choosing to see it as a 'historical novel' with no basis in fact whatsoever. They claim that Esther herself is nowhere mentioned in other sources; that the story contains too many incredible coincidences and fairy-tale elements (such as the 'beauty contest' held to find a replacement for Vashti as Queen); and that the Achaemenid Emperors were permissive in their attitudes to the beliefs and cultural heritages of their subjects, therefore Xerxes would never have issued an edict designed to stamp out foreign religious practices. One critic, Kaiser, has even maintained that the book could not have been written any earlier than 300BC because of the wording of its concluding formula in the Greek translation.

Certainly the Book of Esther was given a rough ride by the Jewish scholars in early times who were resposible for determining the canon of the Hebrew scriptures. Some early Christian councils were also unsure about whether to include it in their Bible. (As late as the sixteenth century AD, Martin Luther said he wished that the book had never been written!)

It was viewed with suspicion for a number of reasons. Firstly, it nowhere mentions God! Secondly, it was produced by Jews still living in exile after the Persian Emperor Cyrus (Kurash) had granted them permission to return to their homeland and reconstruct Jerusalem, which the Babylonians had destroyed. The Jews who *had* returned regarded those still in exile as worldly and godless, unwilling to give up security and wealth in order to rebuild the City of David and the Temple of Adonai. Ironically, some Christians have claimed that the book is 'too Jewish', of interest only because it purports to explain the origins of the Jewish festival of Purim. Not one Christian commentary on Esther was produced in the first seven hundred years AD!

However, many of these arguments betray a lack of understanding of Persian history or of the aims and themes of the Book of Esther itself. (It is significant that authorities on Persian history, as opposed to Biblical critics, are often happy to cite verses from Esther as evidence for certain Persian customs.) Luther's comments about it are blatantly anti-Semitic—as is much of what he wrote.

The book touches upon many themes of vital importance to all Jews and Christians: the dangers of assimilation as well as of persecution when living among people with different beliefs and attitudes; the power of prayer, and fasting; the recognition that God intervenes in human affairs when his people trust him, and that evidence for this intervention can be seen quite plainly by those whose spiritual eyes have been opened. Finally, and probably most importantly, the story of Esther shows that it is God who is ultimately in control of the universe, not 'fate'.

Moreover, there are some very cogent arguments in favour of accepting Esther as a historical account, as well as a valuable source of spiritual enlightenment.

Linguistically the book seems to belong to the fifth century BC, or to the fourth at the latest, as regards the style and characteristics of the Hebrew and Aramaic used by its author. Kaiser's argument about its concluding formula holds very little water because the Greek version is markedly different in content from the Hebrew/ Aramaic and may well be much later. (Some of its additional material is extremely sentimental; though other passages are admittedly rather good, such as Mordecai's dream—Greek Esther 11:5–9—and I have made use of them in my novel. Elsewhere its subject-matter actually contradicts the Hebrew/Aramaic, such as in the names of the months in which events took place, and even the identification of the Persian king with Artaxerxes rather than Xerxes seems to have been made erroneously by the Greek editor. The Greek version is not generally accepted as canonical, and is to be found only in the Apocrypha.)

Also, the canonical (Hebrew/Aramaic) Book of Esther is extremely rich in historical and cultural detail—about Persia as well as about Judaism. There are elaborate descriptions of the palace at Susa (Shushan), and of state functions held there. We are told of a remission of taxes and the declaration of a public holiday upon the succession of a new Queen; of the King distributing gifts; of protocol to be observed in the Apadana . . . all of these details are corroborated by other ancient sources. Haman is said to have accused the Jews not only of obeying their *own* laws, but of disobeying those of Persia; it was most important for the author to have had him make this latter point, because subject peoples were permitted to enforce their own laws so long as those of Persia were also kept. Clearly the author understood the Persian government and legal structure very well.

Nor was the decree condemning the Jews without precedent in Persian history. Xerxes' predecessor Darius (a Latinized form of the Greek Darios, in Persian Darayavaush) once ordered all the magi to be wiped out.

Furthermore, the events described in the Book of Esther fit well into the picture of Xerxes' reign which can be put together from other sources. For example, three years seem to have elapsed between the discrediting of Vashti and the choosing of a new bride for the King—and Xerxes' Greek expedition is known to have taken three years to prepare and carry out.

It *is* odd that God is not specifically mentioned in Esther, but the real reason for this is probably not unlike the suggestion I have made in the Epilogue of this novel. It may be that the book was actually written in deliberate imitation of Persian literary style, to make it accessible to Persians and to Persianized Jews who would not read a theological tome or religious tract.

Indeed, it could be argued that attempts to cast doubt upon the historicity of Esther have disturbing parallels with the attempts of certain neo-Fascist groups to dispute the historicity of the Holocaust. It seems inconceivable that the authenticity of such a significant episode in modern history could possibly be disputed, when our archives contain miles of newsreel and mountains of newspapers describing its horrors, and showing photographs of the emaciated victims' corpses being bulldozed into mass graves. Yet some Jews today fear that when the last of the Holocaust survivors is dead, the human race will begin to think that such an appalling thing could never truly have happened in the twentieth century, and that the press accounts must therefore have been exaggerated, or fabricated, and the photographs perhaps depict one isolated atrocity. People will disbelieve anything, however overwhelming the evidence supporting it, if their motivation is strong enough.

For the purpose of my novel I have taken the Biblical book of Esther to be identical with the account of Mordecai referred to in Esther 9:20ff. (This is the traditional Orthodox Jewish view.) The names I have used for the characters are those of their own people: Jewish names are given in Anglicized Hebrew form, Persian in Persian, and Greek in Greek. Some of the Persian characters may be more familiar under their Greek (or Latinized Greek) names (for example Xerxes, Darius), but I thought it would be strange to have a Jewish woman writing about Persians in Greek! A list of Persian/ Greek equivalents (and Hebrew where appropriate) can be found in the *Dramatis Personae* at the end of the novel. It is interesting that in an undated Persian text which may well belong to Esther's period, a certain 'Mardukiya' is named as an accountant who served on a tour of inspection launched from Susa!

Regarding the names of places, in particular those of nations, I have tended to adhere to the usual Anglicized forms which are used in English translations of the Bible and which will be familiar to many readers. For example, I have used 'Persia' (not 'Parsa' or 'Paras'), 'Babylon', 'Egypt', 'Greece' and 'India'. I have adopted this policy so as not to introduce unnecessary confusion!

The Persian king to which the Book of Esther refers is normally transliterated from Hebrew as 'Ahasuerus'. The Greek translator took this to be Artaxerxes, probably because the two names at first sight seem very similar. In fact, the King concerned was almost certainly Xerxes, because ʾaḥašwērōš is the Hebrew equivalent of the Persian Kshayarsha. (The basic consonants in the name are Kshyrsh—Xerxes.) A Babylonian version of Xerxes' name on an inscription at Behistun is very close to the Hebrew.

Xerxes' character comes across very differently in each of the ancient sources! He is variously depicted as a devout Zoroastrian; a barbaric despot; an ambitious and reckless warmonger; a capricious vacillator easily swayed by his counsellors; a good man eager to do the right thing but guilty of the grossest miscalculations; a pathetic failure; and a melancholy depressive obsessed with his own mortality. I see no reason why these apparently contradictory traits in his personality could not have co-existed, and I have attempted to account for them in the course of my novel. We do know that Xerxes was much less tolerant of foreign religious practices than Cyrus or Darius, and his barbaric treatment of Egypt and Babylon is historical.

Regarding the identity of Xerxes' wife, Herodotus calls her Amestris. Although again the name sounds similar to that of Esther, the two cannot have been the same person because Amestris' third son by Xerxes, Artaxerxes I, was born in 483BC, before Esther was married. Amestris is much more likely to have been the Biblical Vashti, because the Persian name Vashti includes two consonants ('v' and 'sh') which do not occur in Greek and could easily have been corrupted to 'm' and 's'.

Herodotus does not mention any other wife besides Amestris. But in Aeschylus' *Persae*, set at the time of the Greek invasion, Xerxes seems to have no wife in whom to confide. He turns instead to Atossa (Hutaosa), his mother, whereas Aeschylus has a great deal to say about the wives of other Persian participants in the war. This is peculiar, because Herodotus says that Xerxes was married to Amestris *before* this; and she appears again in his account, still married to Xerxes, many years *later*. I have attempted to reconcile these facts by tying them in with the Biblical account of the Queen's discrediting.

There is no proof that Esther came from the same family as Saul, but we do know from Esther 2:5ff that she and Mordecai were Benjamites (Benjamin was Saul's tribe), with a Kish and a Shimei (both unequivocally Saulide names) among their ancestors. It is unlikely that Esther could claim *direct* descent from Saul, however, for if this were the case it would seem strange for the Biblical text not to say so. Then again, many family records were lost by the Jews at the time of the Babylonian exile, and if you wished to claim ancestry from a certain historical figure, you had to be able to prove it.

The relationship I have described as developing between Esther and Hegai is largely fictional, though built up from the text which tells us that Hegai became particularly fond of Esther when she was entrusted to his care, and gave her preferential treatment (Esther 2:9).

There is no record of Esther ever having had any children, either by Xerxes or by anyone else. It certainly wasn't beyond Amestris to have made sure of this, when we read about some of her other 'achievements' (see below).

The latter part of Xerxes' reign was characterized by harem intrigue and by various political and military disasters. He lost significant territories to the Delian League (the 'League of Greeks', an Athenian-led federation of Greek city-states and islands). Pausanias the Spartan captured Sestos in 477BC; in 476 the Athenian Cimon took Eion on the Strymon; Skyros was snatched in 474/3 and the coastal towns of Caria in 468. By this time the Athenian federation now controlled all of Southern Asia Minor from Caria to Pamphylia.

Meanwhile Xerxes sought refuge in the undertaking of ambitious building programmes in order to ensure that he was respected by posterity for his architectural accomplishments if not for glorious conquests. He was ultimately assassinated in 465BC (three years after I have imagined Esther completing her account) by three courtiers including the Hazarapatish Artabanus (Artabanush). Aspamitres (Ashpamithra) the Eunuch of the Bedchamber let the assassins into the King's room, to murder him in his sleep.

Artabanus then persuaded Artaxerxes (Artakshathra), one of Amestris' younger sons, to murder Darius his elder brother, claiming that it was Darius who had been responsible for the murder of Xerxes; Artaxerxes became King. He and his successors gradually watered down their Zoroastrian beliefs, and pagan ideas began to infiltrate the religion. From this amalgam grew cults such as Mithraism, which was the chief rival to early Christianity throughout the Roman Empire, especially among soldiers in the Roman army.

It was during Artaxerxes' reign that the new walls of Jerusalem were completed. (The restored Temple was already complete by

Xerxes' time.) Amestris remained an influential figure throughout
this period, now being Queen Mother. She had quite possibly
connived at Xerxes' murder—which constitutes extra-Biblical
evidence for their relationship not having been all that it should be!
She emerged as a veritable dragon, demanding that Artaxerxes
ruthlessly punish anyone to whom she took a dislike. When she
grew older, she is supposed to have buried alive fourteen boys from
distinguished Persian families as a gift to the gods of the Underworld; she hoped that the Dark Powers would accept the lives of the
boys in return for her own!

The land of Israel remained in Jewish hands but subject to
successive foreign superpowers, until Jerusalem fell to the Romans
in 70AD. Only in 1948 was it restored to the Jews once again, amid
violent Arab opposition. The rights and wrongs of Zionism are still
hotly debated, not only by Christians, and by politicians the world
over, but by the Jews themselves. The current situation is strikingly
similar to that which must have existed in Esther's day. Modern
Israelis often despise those of their fellow Jews who have chosen to
remain in the West, particularly in America where they can lead
wealthy and comfortable lives, whilst at the same time expecting
America to champion the Zionist cause. Other Jews, as religious as
the Zionists, believe that the land of Israel should not have been
reclaimed until the appearance of the Messiah, whose task it will be
to reclaim it himself.

Persia—known today as Iran—although predominantly Muslim
rather than Zoroastrian, still retains many of its ancient characteristics. Periods of liberation and tolerance (or decadence and
corruption?) have alternated with periods when religious funda-
mentalism has gained ascendancy, and dissident groups have been
suppressed.

But what of Esther herself? *Was* she a heroine through and
through, as Jewish tradition has come to revere her? Or was she
saved by the skin of her teeth from complete assimilation into
Persian culture? In the Apocryphal, Greek version of the Book of
Esther, she is depicted as a pious, resolute woman who scorns the
luxury and immorality of the Imperial court from day one.

However, a careful reading of the Biblical book leads us to the
opposite conclusion. She keeps her religion secret (2:10), therefore
presumably eats non-kosher food and neglects the observance of
sabbaths and Jewish festivals. When each of Xerxes' virgins is first
presented to the King, she is allowed to wear whatever kind of
costume she is most comfortable in, but Esther wears what Hegai

tells her to (2:15). When Haman issues his edict against the Jews, and Mordecai puts on sackcloth, Esther tries to prevent him from drawing attention to himself and his cause (4:4). When Mordecai wants her to appeal to her royal husband on the Jews' behalf, she raises objections (4:11), and eventually Mordecai has to send her a very threatening letter (4:12–14) before she will lift a finger to assist her doomed people. It seems to me that Esther, in common with most of the Biblical 'heroes' and 'heroines' was no stained-glass saint, but a complex, flawed human being with whom the least heroic of us can identify.

DRAMATIS PERSONAE:
IN ORDER OF APPEARANCE

HADASSAH	The narrator. Born in Jerusalem, she is eight years old when her story begins.
RACHAEL*	Hadassah's older sister.
PITHON*	Hadassah's older brother.
ABIHAIL	Hadassah's father. He and his wife are 'Pioneers' who have returned from exile in Babylon to assist in the rebuilding of Jerusalem.
URIAH* & RUTH*	Pioneer friends of Hadassah's parents.
DEBORAH*	Daughter of Uriah and Ruth, childhood friend of Hadassah.
GEDALIAH*	Architect, Pioneer colleague of Hadassah's parents.
SARAH* & JUDAH*	Pioneer couple with whom Hadassah travels to Shushan.
MORDECAI (Greek: Mardochaios)	Hadassah's second cousin; resident in Shushan (Greek: Susa), capital of the Persian Empire.
LEAH*	Mordecai's housekeeper.
NINLIL*	Mordecai's sister.
IPHIGENIA*	Greek girl living in Arderikka, a village of Eretrian deportees just outside Shushan.
HELENA*	Iphigenia's mother.
PHILOS*	Iphigenia's father.
KSHAYARSHA (Greek: Xerxes, Anglicized Hebrew: Ahasuerus)	Crown Prince of Persia, and later her King, and Master of her Empire. Scion of the House of Hakhamanish (Achaemenid Dynasty).
VASHTI (Greek: Amestris)	Wife of Kshayarsha; Queen of Persia.

415

REUBEN*	Partner in Mordecai's banking company.
HUTAOSA *(Greek: Atossa)*	Queen Mother, widow of Darayavaush *(Greek: Darios, Latin: Darius)* and mother of Kshayarsha.
MEMUCAN	King's Privy Counsellor, and President of His Majesty's Commissioners; chief of his seven advisers.
SHAASHGAZ	Warden of the King's Harem.
HEGAI	Keeper of the King's Virgins.
FARAH*	Chief of the maids appointed to attend Hadassah at the palace.
ANAHITA*	Erstwhile senior concubine of Darayavaush; now in charge of the concubines of Kshayarsha; and their midwife.
ASHPAMITHRA *(Greek: Aspamitres)*	Chamberlain of Kshayarsha.
ARTABANUSH *(Greek: Artabanus)*	The Hazarapatish, Chief Minister of the King, with both civil and military responsibilities— arranges audiences with the King, and serves as Captain of the King's Own Regiment of Immortals.
BIGTHANA/TERESH	Eunuchs responsible for guarding the King's private rooms.
HATHACH	Eunuch attendant of the Persian Queen.
ROXANA*	Hadassah's food-taster.
HAMAN	A junior minister in Kshayarsha's Government; later its First Minister for Civil and Foreign Affairs.
HARBONAH	A young eunuch friend of Hathach.

* Fictional characters